Shadowed Souls

DIANA CASTILLEJA

PURPLE SWORD PUBLICATIONS
Romantic speculative fiction.
www.purplesword.com
Tucson, Arizona

HIS REDEEMER'S KISS

ISBN: 978-1-936165-45-2
ISBN 10: 1-936165-45-7
Cover Art Designed by Anastasia Rabiyah
Photographs Copyright Jimmy Thomas at RomanceNovelCovers.com and Gregg Williams, Dreamstime.com.
Edited by Brieanna Robertson and Traci Markou

Published by Purple Sword Publications, LLC
Tucson, Arizona, USA
www.PurpleSword.com

Shadowed Souls

chapter one

JOAQUIN made his decision.

He crouched in the thickening darkness like a silent wraith, unmoving beneath the extended arms of the shadow-laden trees, listening to the mockery of life all around him. His lip lifted with a derisive snarl as the single word knifed through him. *Life.* He had none. His had ceased to have meaning more than three hundred years ago. At this point, he didn't even know why he was still paying his penance. After three centuries, he was sure God, himself, would forgive him.

There was no joy on his features, no anticipation, not even the etched sadness he'd worn for decades. Now, there was nothing. Nothing in his heart. He was cold; existing, but not living.

He watched with unblinking attention from the shifting shadows as the young couple disembarked the horse-drawn carriage in the verdant public park. The man held his date tightly in the cooling night air, their heads together in quiet, tender conversation as they strolled the cobbled walkways arm in arm. The gesture meant nothing to Joaquin. Ironwork lampposts created a romantic ambiance, showering golden light onto the flowered trails, the perfect setting for a couple in love. Unfortunately, there were no feelings filling the frozen abyss in his heart as he watched the couple walk through the pools of light. To him, they were his subsistence, nothing more. Tonight, they would be his last.

With the ease of those endless centuries empowering him, he beckoned the couple from the path and into the tree line of the park with a simple command. The closer they came, the more the scent of hot blood raked his senses, and his hungers blazed to match it. Joaquin knew that same fire would shine in his eyes. It was part of his curse, a part of him. Yet, in all of his lonely, silent years stalking the night, he had never taken a life. He'd never cursed another with the cruel and cold creature consuming his soul one endless night at a time. Now, when he'd made his decision to accept whatever judgment waited for him on the other side of the sunrise, he was careful to keep a firm hand on those driving and demanding hungers. He knew if he failed to win the battle tonight, all the years of brutal penance, all the years of his own living hell, would be for nothing.

A firm mental push sent the couple safely on their way after sating his bitter appetite. Neither would ever know the travesty performed on their unsuspecting bodies, or how close to death they had stood.

With a leap, he shot into the night sky, changing his shape to fit into the nighttime world as easily as nature itself, unseen yet in plain sight. The trees of the park melted away as he rose above the earth, slipping through the breezes to leave it all behind. All he had to do was wait for the rising sun. He had no one to tell. There was no one left who knew he even existed. He guessed there should be sadness in that knowledge somewhere, but if there was, Joaquin couldn't find it.

He had no reason to continue this imitation of living any longer and hadn't for decades, but he had held out hope that God, someone, would show him why this abysmal hell had been laid at his door. Eventually, even hope dies. Coldness seeped into his skin the further he flew. It forced his concentration to his surroundings where he could easily push away the evening chill with a dismissive thought, recreating the blanket of warmth that would protect him in any form. The northern wilderness cooled faster once the sun had gone down, but he hated staying within the cities. It invariably caused him trouble.

Woods sprawled like a green jeweled sea beneath the beat of his long wings, with some glittering, faceless city left behind. He was sure another city lay somewhere ahead. Was this all there was giving him hope? The knowledge that another warm body could keep him alive for one more night? That some city's deep streets or the wide open countryside would offer up some treasure, a wisdom he had never been lucky enough to find? A peace of mind that had eluded him for these many centuries? Was this why he'd risen night after endless night? These eternal ages of silence weren't how he'd wanted to spend his lifetime. More than one lifetime. He released a rare, deep sigh into the silent chill.

This was why Joaquin knew it was time. There wasn't anything living left inside of him. His heart beat because he made it. He breathed because he could. He didn't have to do either if he didn't want to. He had become an emotionless void, no joy in life, nothing to inspire him to *feel,* to live as the man he had once been. This was not living. This was where he believed he should care, but he couldn't. Not even a trickled sense of resignation as he searched one last time and found no argument to negate his final decision. He would die in the morning.

"Stop!"

The sudden mental bark knocked him from the sky with the force of flying full speed into a brick wall. For the first time in at least a century, Joaquin lost his shape in mid-flight.

Tumbling, he caught his balance before impaling himself on one of the large trees beneath him. He floated downward, agape with stunned shock. His feet reached the leaf-marbled ground, instantly wary of the voice and of the power it held. Surprise widened his eyes when he realized she wasn't finished with him, either.

"Would you stop? I'm almost in tears over your self-pity. You have emotions. Good God! They're so strong, I can't stand to listen anymore. You've been at it for three nights. Just stop!"

He traced the path to the sender, completely shaken by the strength she wielded, and by the sheer power of her voice. *Her voice.* A woman. He stood in bewildered silence for several seconds, blocking out everything else around him.

Joaquin stared daggers in the direction her rich voice came from in the next instant as shock morphed into anger, not only for the invasion of his inner thoughts, but at the direct command in her voice. *"You've been listening to me?"* he demanded, outraged at the invasion of his privacy. His thoughts whirled with the implications that she could hear him, had been listening and could apparently touch his mind with hers, rather easily at that—without any bonding between them. The realization tore through him, shaking him to his core. Only a few had broken his mental silence over the centuries, and none had been human, or female.

Who was this person who arrived at his darkest hour? How could he hear her when he hadn't heard another who wasn't like him since his conversion?

"You haven't exactly been quiet about it," she informed him with a tart rebuke, breaking his dissection of their mental path into mere wisps of puzzlement to concentrate on later.

He shook his head at the curtness of her response. *"How can you hear me? I haven't spoken to anyone in years." Understatement of the century,* he thought to himself with a grim frown.

"That I don't know, but you're very disruptive. I'm trying to read and then I pick you up like a radio talk show." He knew he heard a sigh of frustration. *"You've made it rather difficult to concentrate."*

This didn't make any sense. *"Who are you?"* Silence met his question. Joaquin waited, and with a touch of fear that she had disappeared, demanded her attention. He whipped an energy pulse through the air.

"Hey! Don't do that. I'm here."

"Why didn't you answer me?" Something was happening inside of him. He didn't want to lose the unique connection with her. Over only minutes, it had become imperative. He wasn't sure why, wasn't sure of anything, only that he needed to hear more of her voice.

"Maybe I have my reasons."

Joaquin launched into the sky with a powerful rush of energy. He had to know who this woman was. No reason anywhere could remove the burning necessity to know who she was, where she was, or how she could touch his mind. He discovered the wood-framed cabin nestled in the abundant artwork of trees and nature a few miles away from where she'd knocked him to the ground, out in the wilderness, but nearly imperceptible to a wandering eye. His heart beat like a wild horse on the run as rare anticipation flooded his body.

To mortal eyes, the wooden shape would have been invisible. Even for him, had he not been openly searching for it, he could have overlooked the seemingly natural structure easily. It blended with the surroundings, the wildness of the landscape, as if it had been chiseled from the trees and nature itself. A muted light detectable through a few tinted windows was all there was to hint to those living within its walls. Dark shadows and creative camouflage literally buried the cabin into the landscape.

He settled into the trees a distance from the home, cautious and confused. There was something about this house that didn't fit. Becoming more comfortable in his spot, he took a moment to study the home and the surrounding protective walls of forest. There was a scent... Shock ripped through him when he took a deeper breath. *Brethren*. Several, if he hadn't lost his senses. And as many humans. He shook his head. This picture made absolutely no sense whatsoever.

He scanned the home and found several sleeping bodies in the rooms of the house, and... He froze, narrowing his gaze, silencing everything about himself. He was getting careless in his curiosity. There was someone inside, not Brethren—he wasn't sure what he was, but he was awake and aware. A guard? It was too hard to tell for certain as far as he was from the structure to make out all the details. He only knew this was not a normal home, and one of the males inside was not Brethren or human.

Shaking his head in deepening confusion, he remained a safe distance away, pondering the significance of this situation.

The tale of the house itself was difficult to unravel. With another sweeping search, he located a hollowed chamber in the soil beneath it and knew his first assumption had been right. There were Brethren living in this home. The woman he had discovered created a larger mystery. He sensed she wasn't bound, but resting. She was cared for, not wasting away as he had first assumed knowing Brethren were keeping humans in the house, but her pain was unmistakable. Even in the few traded words, the discordant tones had hummed on his nerves along with her voice.

Humans living with Brethren? The discovery left him puzzled, edgy and very cautious. He focused his attention to remain as unseen as possible.

Joaquin phrased his next question with a calm tone, not wanting to alarm her. If the answer wasn't what he wanted to hear, he'd steal her away without a single regret because he knew what he feared was totally possible. "*Are the people there hurting you?*"

The sharp tone of indignation was as easy to hear as her flung answer. "*No one here would hurt me. I am very safe here. I am protected here.*"

He fought against his reawakening male instincts to rush in and pull her out of there. He could clearly see how she may be in danger and not even know it. Mind manipulation, memory control; he knew those ways and more. He didn't know enough right at that minute to do exactly what he wanted—steal her away and keep this woman safe. Caution and patience weren't stopping him by much. "*Protecting you from what?*"

"*Why do you want to know?*" she shot back. "*I don't even know why you're talking to me.*"

"*Because you invaded my privacy!*"

"*Don't even try to pin that on me. You broadcast louder than a water buffalo.*"

He sagged against the nearest tree limb in astounded silence. How had she heard him, more than once? This had never happened to him. He hadn't been trying to find someone. The effort to remotely try had left him so long ago. He'd been traveling his dark world for centuries alone, and now, without any warning, here was *someone*.

Joaquin relaxed, making himself comfortable once more, projecting an apologetic smile into his next words. "*I'm sorry. This is new to me.*" He gentled his voice more, desperate she not sever the connection. Desperate in ways he couldn't name to learn about her, to hear her. "*What have you heard?*"

There was a short hesitation while she considered her answer. He found he was getting better at finding her through the distance, a heartbeat between them, the single sound a beacon making her real. She hadn't left him. He realized how hard his heart was beating to hear her unique voice in his void of quiet and calmed himself, unused to the infrequent reaction.

"You're lonely. You feel you have nothing left to live for. You've been thinking suicide all night, which I might add, only weak men contemplate."

Joaquin glared in her direction. "*Weak men? I assure you, I am not weak.*"

"And I'm sure you have a fantabulous excuse for wanting to slit your wrists, then, don't you? Sorry, but being lonely doesn't impress me."

He had no trouble hearing the absolute disdain in her words. "*Rather presumptuous, aren't you? You don't know me. I've lived a very long life, years of pain and silence.*" He released a hissed snarl out to the darkened woods. How dare she judge him?

"I'll trade you scar for scar," came the immediate retort. *"Look, if you want to kill yourself, fine, but can you turn down the volume when you do it? I can't read on my shift if I'm talking to you."*

He considered his options. He didn't want to leave her, and for the moment, he didn't want to 'slit his wrists' either. There were so many things puzzling him about this, and about her. He tried to go for the least intrusive to feed his desire to learn more, and to hear her voice. "*What are you reading?*"

"Just poetry for now. Are we trading questions?" she asked suspiciously.

Trading was exactly what he wanted to do, yet something made her very careful in her answers. "*If you'd like,*" he offered easily, hearing a deep mistrust in her words. He wondered about the echoes of pain laced through the words between them, but knew it would take more than casual conversation for her to divulge anything about that, and the cause. He had to find out more about her. He wanted her to relax so she would tell him what he wanted to know. "*Ask me anything you'd like to know.*"

"Where are you?"

He glanced around, taking in his surroundings for the first time. "*I'm sitting in a tree where the leaves are changing colors. Green fading to golden orange and shades of red.*" He surprised himself with the colorful description. When was the last time he'd noticed anything as common as when the seasons changed? When had he grown indifferent to the beauty of an elm tree or the color of a leaf as it faded from summer? None of it affected him. He didn't live his life by the seasons the way he once had. There were no foals to care for, no crops to tend, all of which had passed a long time ago into his history. He simply left one place until he found something to interest him if he didn't want to be where he was at any given moment.

"I've always loved the fall colors. So vibrant," she replied, her answer much more mellow to his ears.

On a whim, he sent her a visual of his surroundings with all the luxuriant beauty of the changing colors, adding the sheer shimmer of the pale moonlight shining against the lightly twisting leaves.

"That's beautiful." It was a whispered sound of awe, and it caused tingles from his chest to his toes. "*How did you do that? How gifted are you?*"

He shook his head, gathering his scattered senses. "*I am far from gifted. I am cursed.*"

"*Is that why you feel so lonely? You're not the only one out there with parapsychology gifts.*" The sudden shock was impossible to miss when she sliced off her thoughts with a flare of anger aimed at herself.

"*No! Don't. Please stay with me a little while longer.*" He threw his weight behind the words, and pulled her mind to his. It wasn't a hard battle. Surprisingly, wary and cautious, she wasn't fighting his strength.

"*I shouldn't. I don't know you.*"

"*I am Joaquin,*" he offered without hesitation. "*Now you know me.*"

Sparks shot up his spine at the sound of her laughter. Something bloomed inside of his chest, something bright and new. The animated sound was as intense as the brightest sun, sending light and energy rippling throughout his body. He gasped at the sensations, feeling all of them, feeling everything as if he could feel her touch on his skin, the gentle drag of fingers against his flesh. Electric, and so very rare.

"*Please, tell me your name.*" The freshness of her voice, of talking to someone, left him fighting for air when he didn't even have to breathe. He couldn't stop himself from leaning forward, wanting to hear her answer.

After several moments, he realized something was wrong. There was definite hesitation in her answer this time, but he knew she was still with him. He scanned the woods for the other Brethren he knew had to be near, but found he was alone.

His throat tightened even as he asked her, "*Do I frighten you?*" He discovered he didn't like the idea he may scare her at all. He never wanted to cause this person, or any, fear. He forced himself to relax, aware he may be projecting something she could find in the air or feel the same way he sensed her underlying pain.

"I...I have listened to you and know I shouldn't, but... It's hard to explain."

Something in her answer sounded wounded. He could almost picture her dropping her lashes, trying to hide thoughts he couldn't quite find this far from her. She had surpassed intriguing him.

"Do the ones you stay with control you? Do they monitor you?"

Her reply was again a snapped negative. "*No! They are caring for us, protecting us.*" She sighed, an underlying frustration in the quiet hum, and she wrapped him up in the sound. "*It's very hard to explain. This is unusual for me. I didn't expect for you to hear me.*" It sounded very much like a quiet admission to him.

The next thought occurred to him with no trouble and he found he hated it. "*You don't trust me.*" His frown reappeared. *Why should she?* he wondered. Even though he wanted her trust, it wasn't realistic to expect it blindly, or considering their circumstances. Voices from some dark corner of the night. Hers, offering a comfort he couldn't remember, it had been so long since he'd experienced it. His, hopefully offering something she needed in return.

The sadness coloring her thoughts told him his answer before she ever spoke, but the knowledge he was right didn't ease the ache her answer created. He wanted her trust.

"No, I don't."

"Tell me what they are protecting you from." Why would Brethren care for, much less protect, humans? The one who was neither Brethren nor human was still in the house, but his presence only made Joaquin more alert.

He could almost feel her indecision as he waited.

An uncomfortable ripple raked over his senses bare seconds before a shape loomed up from out of the darkness not five feet before him. He didn't flinch, and he didn't run.

Cold, silver-white eyes stared at him from an expressionless face, judging him. This male was easily inches taller than Joaquin, and by the energy crackling about him on the air, much more powerful than any Joaquin could remember meeting. He accepted running would have gained him nothing but his death. As it was, it surprised him Joaquin hadn't been attacked as soon as he'd been discovered. Brethren were not social creatures.

"I greet thee, Brethren," Joaquin offered in the formal manner of their kind. He waited, holding himself still to not provoke the man who hung effortlessly in the air before him.

"If I had wanted to kill you," he said in a low-rumbled, disinterested voice, "you would already be dead."

Joaquin's eyes dropped to slits at the ease his thoughts were violated. If there was a leader to the scene he'd been trying to decipher, then this was him.

"Why are you keeping humans?"

The one hovering before Joaquin barely arched a brow at the question. "Why does it concern you? If you think the one you have spoken with will come and save you from your own folly, you are wrong. She does not care that you have decided to destroy yourself, nor does she care why you have spoken with her. You have disturbed her nights, and she only wished for you to cease."

Joaquin was informed of all of this with hardly a molecule of compassion. He wasn't willing to let it go so easily. "Why are you protecting her?"

Fires danced in the silvery eyes, a warning. "That is less than you need to know."

"Why? You are holding her. Is she your prisoner?"

"You are asking questions I have no care to answer. Leave. You are not welcome." Those chilling eyes narrowed at him. "I do not want to kill you, but I can."

Joaquin stifled the glare daring to appear at the threat. After centuries of his own living hell, he was not going to be shoved to the side that apathetically. He may not be the warrior this one was, but he did have a few tricks he'd learned over the endlessness of his life. "*Do you welcome me?*" He pinpointed his thoughts to ensure there were no eavesdroppers this time.

Shocked awareness erupted on his senses as the feminine purity of her voice filled his mind once more. "*I thought you were gone! Diego had said he would find you and make you leave.*"

"He is trying. I have offered my name and promise you no harm. Do you welcome me?" he asked again. Silently, he prayed she didn't deny him this, a single touch of humanity he hadn't felt since Angelica's death.

"They are warning me not to talk to you anymore."

Anger made his blood boil, but he showed nothing of it on his face, knowing he was borrowing time to connect with her. "*So they are your keepers then, where you can't think for yourself, where they guard you as a prisoner.*" It was what he feared. She was being controlled, and the woman behind that lovely voice didn't even know of the deception being played against her.

"That isn't fair! You don't know what's going on here."

"I want to," he told her, his voice soft and pouring out with compassion. What wasn't in his voice was the knowledge he would find a way to rescue her from her prison, the sooner the better for

the both of them. *"I want to know the lady who has warmed me with nothing more than her voice. Am I a bad man for wanting to merely talk to you?"* He didn't try to hide the ache of his loneliness from her. He knew on some level they were the same. Her pain had not diminished any either. It bothered him as much as her 'protector' staring deadly daggers before him did.

Precious seconds dragged by, but he refused to drop his gaze or attention from Diego. He purposely remained motionless to not miss a single sensation, waiting for her answer.

"No."

The whispered word drifted like a seductive caress into his thoughts, and he swallowed at the aching sound. With his gaze never leaving the vampire in front of him, Joaquin knew his time had run out. He would have to leave or be blown into little vampire bits. *"I will do as your guard asks, and I will leave. For tonight."* He bowed his head in defeat to Diego, and shifted into a familiar owl to fly away on the night breeze. No sense in letting the powerful man feel Joaquin was more of a threat than he was. It may be his only advantage.

He was positive Diego followed, so he didn't try to circle around. He would find a place to rest nearby, though. He needed to know more about this woman who could reach him, who could speak to him. He wouldn't be able to do what he felt compelled to do tonight. Tomorrow, he would get closer to study the home and do as his instincts demanded—remove her from the threats surrounding her. There had never been any of the Brethren he could trust. The long line of mistrust had catapulted from his creator, and he'd learned that lesson all too well.

"Joaquin?"

His eyes eased closed in joy at her tentative contact a few moments later. She was reaching for him. It was all that mattered in the darkness surrounding him. "*I am here.*"

"You're not still thinking of, you know, killing yourself, are you?"

A knowing smile broke over his lips as he reformed to his natural shape, sliding through the air to fold himself into the V of a branch. Diego had lied, and the truth warmed him as much as her voice did. "*No. I believe I have found a reason to continue, if only for one more night. I will look for you tomorrow, when the sun has set. Will you welcome me?*"

"I shouldn't go against Diego, Joaquin. He's a good friend, and he is protecting us."

"I'm aware of what he is," he offered, wanting to soothe her. Silently, though, he believed she didn't know half the truth about the man she called friend. "*I'm only asking for your conversation, nothing more. And know this, I would never, could not, harm you. I know you are scared. I don't want you to be scared of me.*"

Several minutes lingered between them when he heard her voice once more. "*You're pretty mysterious, you know that? I think I can hear an accent, but it's hard to tell this way. And you're talking to me from who knows where."*

Her silent laughter floated between them. It felt to him as if the entire world had changed on its axis. Everything he knew and had accepted had been, in an instant, changed forever. For the moment, he was very willing to see where the next night would take him.

She fell silent as she thought it over. "*I guess this is all right, to talk to you like this.*"

"I look forward to tomorrow evening then," he whispered to her, feeling a relieved warmth in the pit of his stomach. "*It would be easier to speak with you if I knew your name.*" He prodded her gently, not wanting her to be nervous with the admission. Knowing her name would make it easier to find her voice in the mental openness they seemed to share. The sooner he could pinpoint her in the house hidden in the trees, the sooner she would be out from under the Brethren's controlling deceit.

There was only a slight hesitant pause, a quiet catch in her voice as she offered her name to him, and then like a light snuffed out, he knew she had closed herself off from his searching thoughts.

chapter two

LILY held the poetry book in her hands, waiting, but knew without trying too hard to find him again, that he was gone. She didn't feel any resistance or pressure when she raised her mental barriers as a test.

"He didn't frighten you, did he?" Tani asked, checking the monitors attached like long-limbed beings to the unconscious Tabitha, lying unaware on the bed.

Lily bit back the smile where she sat in the rocking chair, the book she'd been reading when she'd been interrupted by Joaquin's misery held on her lap. Tani didn't do unconcerned very well. She fiddled with the lines stretching from several monitors to the woman on the bed, checking Tabitha's signs and pulse while trying not to pounce on Lily with questions. Lily could spot each one of those worried questions lined up in her watchful blue eyes when she looked over her shoulder, ready to be ticked off by the mother hen whose chick had been bothered.

Lily shook her head, answering honestly, “When I first heard his pain a few nights ago, he really took me by surprise. I wasn’t expecting to hear someone like that, and when it continued... I just couldn’t take three nights of it. I wanted to smack him.”

Tani made a chuckling sound in her chest, repositioning Tabitha’s arm on the bed with a tender comfort. The myriad of monitor lines and feeding tubes draped all over from above the bed, but she moved around them effortlessly. “You’re healing, growing stronger every day, Lily. I’m very glad to hear you say that.” Joy glowed in her eyes now when she looked at her.

Lily blinked. Tani was right. Right after their rescue, she would have hidden, a shriveled body blind to the pain emanating from Joaquin. She had been helping care for Tabitha with the others, but feeling a stranger’s pain and wanting to help, it was definitely an incredible improvement for her. After three nights, she hadn’t been able to take any more of his debating.

So much had happened since the rescue from Albert Tenorio’s testing facility. All four girls and David had arrived at the unassuming cabin with the others from Tani’s band, a surreal situation that was still taking some time for them to understand. None of the rescued five could remember the details of their flight from the compound, only that they had all arrived here, completely hidden and safe in the deep woods of Oregon with Diego, Titania, Houston, and Laney to care for them all.

Lily refused to let the lack of memory bother her, considering where they were now compared to the conditions they had been taken from. She wished she could forget so many other long days and the horrors of those longer nights behind so easily. So she couldn't remember how they'd gotten out of California. Worse things could have happened than a rescue from their previous circumstances.

In the time since that fateful nighttime escape, they'd prepared to move everyone to a cavernous house hidden in the wilderness near the Canadian border in Montana. The outfitted bus was already outside, ready to transport them and to care for Tabitha in luxury on the way. Houston and Laney had taken a lot of pictures to show the girls where they would be going, detailed pictures of their new home from any angle they could reach, including a vivid layout of the surrounding wild nothingness encapsulating the large, mansion-styled home. The cabin was too small for the four rescued girls, Nathan, David, Houston and Laney, and Diego and Titania. Crowded was the only way to describe it, but they'd made do until the right house and location had been found. Titania and Diego had gone out of their way to ensure they'd found the best possible location and style of home to continue their recuperation.

The new house was wide open all over with large sprawling rooms and full, wall sized windows on every floor. It had apparently been some actor's secret getaway who had willingly sold it to Houston. The details weren't really important with so much of the process done while Lily and the others were still adjusting to not being behind bars. Considering Titania's notoriety, it wasn't hard to figure out her name had been used to sway the deal. Houston and Laney had taken special care with picking the house, to give the inhabitants the knowledge that they weren't caged any longer. The views were breathtaking. Deep woods and craggy mountains not too far in the distance. And it was nearly impossible to reach by anything. They would all be leaving soon for the new house, where all that room would be put to good use, and they would all have space and time to heal. Every day, Lily felt a little safer, a little stronger, and knew Tani was right.

Everyone had seen that all possible care was taken with Tabitha's condition from the moment they'd been found. Lily wanted to believe the reading was helping her friend to focus on the outside world, to bring her back from the unconscious state she was in. It helped Lily, gave her something to put her energy into, because she wasn't confident she could do or handle much more yet. It would happen. For the first time in years, she had faith in something.

Each day brought a new sign the trauma was really over. No more guards, no cameras, no tests, needles, or guns. Those facts above all else helped to convince Lily, Kathy, and Amy they had really found freedom with their benefactors. It was just hard for her to think about what that freedom meant, and now that she had it, what she would do with it. Everything had changed. She still had nightmares, and feared when she woke up, everything here would be gone and she'd find herself once more in that cold and demoralizing steel cage with cameras watching her every breath.

Lily gazed at Tabitha on the bed, the only of them who didn't know the truth about their freedom. She had fallen into a coma almost immediately after the rescue. Lily wanted to believe reading to her helped, but there wasn't very much any of them could do for her other than see she was cared for and comfortable. She understood hiring professional medical help or trying to get her attention at a hospital was out of the question. It was one of those facts about their circumstances she wished wasn't real. It made finding them through the normal channels far too easy, and being captured again was not something any of them wanted to do. Tabitha wasn't lacking for care, though. None of them were. She wished the woman who lay so unaware would wake up. Lily knew she had been almost broken more than once, and feared the last round of tortures and tests had finally destroyed what was left of the smiling woman inside.

A hand on her shoulder brought Lily's attention to the bedroom. She still clutched the poetry book, looking up from where she sat with wide eyes to the understanding blue of Titania's gaze.

"She will survive. When she is ready, she will awaken. Time is all she needs, and she has as much as she wants or needs here."

At Tani's words, Lily glanced at the woman in question, then rose to the woman at her side, still working through her own bevy of emotions that swam and rolled through her mind without any kind of regularity on a daily basis. "I know."

Tani crouched down by the rocking chair Lily sat in, brushing a wave of red hair from her face. Warmth and compassion radiated from Titania, and Lily basked in it, knowing it was meant in the strongest sense of compassion and friendship.

Now she trusted those feelings. At first, Tani's gifts had confused and scared Lily. People with gifts were the hunted, but not here. No one here was a prisoner, and many of them were gifted. It was the exact opposite of what she had been living with, of the way she had been living period.

"Diego assures me the one you spoke with isn't from Tenorio's compound."

Lily nodded. "I had guessed he wasn't after the first night. He hates what he is," she said, remembering his self-loathing, knowing exactly how he felt because she'd felt the same way for a very long time. She realized those feelings were partly why she was able to reach out to him. There was a strong sense of acceptance between them. Both of them had suffered. Both of them knew pain.

"I know how he feels. It surprised me more than anything to be able to hear him so easily, and to have him answer. Except for you, that hasn't happened very often." She tucked her chin into her chest with a guilty apology in her voice. "I shouldn't have said anything to him, though. It was unthinkable. What if he had been trying to trick me? To give away where we are?"

An understanding smile hovered on Tani's features, framed by the length of midnight black hair cascading around her. "That, I can guarantee, wasn't the case. Diego would have never let him near enough to harm anyone, or to let someone discover where you are. If it had been a trick, Diego would have done more than ask him to leave the area."

Lily's eyes widened. "Diego would kill him?" Lily knew she didn't want anyone killed, not just for talking to her.

"If that is what it takes." She said this without a trace of remorse, and Lily couldn't doubt her. Diego was taking every precaution at all hours to ensure they remained hidden and undisturbed. His vigilance amazed Lily every night. "No one here will be harmed or found again. Albert will eventually be stopped, but right now, the people in this house are the important people. That means you and Tabitha too."

Lily placed the book of poetry on the stand by the bed, noting the near silent hum of the monitor closest to her. "I don't know how she managed to survive as long as she did," Lily continued in a torn whisper, the terror of their time flooding her mind. It was nearly impossible to avoid the memories entirely, and tonight, it seemed they were right on the surface. The unintentional scare Joaquin's voice had caused had probably prompted their insidious return.

"Don't think about it," Tani said, offering a touch of comfort again, pulling her away from the sucking strength of the never ending replay of her tortures. "You know it will always be there. You need to be stronger to face them, to put them behind you enough where they can't hurt you anymore. All of you do, or the memories will trap you in their control and destroy you all over again."

"I know." Her voice sounded brittle as she fought the tears and the memories.

Soothingly, her voice floated over Lily, calming her before it all got out of hand. "One day at a time. You will get better. All of you will." The constant flow of comfort and understanding helped Lily to distance herself from the pain of her imprisonment. She knew Tani was right. It would take time to move beyond it enough to function normally again. For whatever normal was.

Tani stood from beside Lily and, with a final assessing look at the monitors, disappeared through the doorway. She'd been spending time with all of them to help them find a stability to begin to heal and over the last several months, all of the girls had made some incredible discoveries about their own resilience. No one made any cynical remarks or belittled them for their fears. It was constant support, around the clock. A moment later, laughter and the sound of chaos in the kitchen reached her from down the hall. Only one person made that much racket in the kitchen. Houston would be cooking again, but she'd be the last to complain about real food. He obviously loved being able to do it too, as much as he made for them all.

Lily sighed and stretched, rubbing the back of her neck with steady fingers. It felt so decadent to simply *move*. After three years as a *guest* of Albert Tenorio, she had forgotten how it felt to be able to breathe, eat, talk....everything, without being watched like a bug under a microscope, knowing it and unable to avoid it. To simply be relaxed enough *to do* those things naturally.

Every minute detail was watched and catalogued day and night, from when they went to the bathroom to how they ate their meals. Lab rats were treated better. They were at least left alone once they were in their cage. All Lily and the others had had were their cages. She and the others were never alone, always watched, either by the many cameras or by the guards.

She had lost count of the beatings, of the needle injections and tests, wanting nothing more than to never remember them at all, but they haunted her. Blood had stained her skin from their malicious methods, night and day. So much time stolen from her, her life, her family. Lily had no idea if anyone knew she'd disappeared, if they'd tried to find her, of anything. She'd only discovered when she'd been rescued that she'd been a prisoner for three years,

Tabitha for almost seven, and still alive, somehow. Whether Lily's family had looked for her or not, she didn't know. Her school, her dorm room, her *life*, all gone.

Without Tani there to distract her, the images and remembered agonies fell on her like a frozen wall of stone, suffocating and paralyzing in its weight.

Silent sobs racked her body as each memory clawed her from the inside out with a vengeance. Her arms wrapped around her middle as she fought to keep them inside, fought to restrain the gruesome scenes from detection from those in the cabin. Even if those flashes of pain strangled her for the effort. She was stronger. She refused to let them win, to continue to wound her.

Her head dropped to her hands and she rubbed her temples, gulping air in harsh swallows to push away the pressure of the memories, of the unforgettable pain, while she slowly won the battle to keep her sanity. The memories came and went, and often in ruthless doses, but each blow by blow replay of her history brought her closer to moving past it. She knew she would.

Oxygen filled her lungs, and she blew it out along with the anguish and pain. Time. All she needed was time. She was strong, and getting stronger. She *was* healing, at least physically. *Breathe in.* She had another chance. *Breathe out.* She would survive. She would live again.

"Lily? Are you all right?"

She gasped, taken by surprise, and snapped her head up to search the room, but it was empty beyond Tabitha's bed. She was unsure if she should expect him there or not. He sounded so clear, so close. She trembled at the worried masculine voice whispering into her mind.

It was a shock every time she heard him. She was telepathic, Tani was too, yet Joaquin's voice from out of the blue, reaching out to her so easily, unsettled her. "*I didn't think I'd hear from you until tomorrow,*" she answered him, twisting her fingers together to stop their shaking. She breathed deeply, forcefully slowing her beating heart when she realized she was alone, and he was only talking to her. She was still safe.

"That was my intention, but you're hurting." His voice was like a velvet caress, warm and cocooning in its low timbre. It washed over her and she immediately felt better, immediately felt herself falling into the wonderful tone of his voice, into the calming cradle of his words. "*I have to help the one who has helped me. It is only right.*"

An almost imperceptible quiver of her lip brought it up at the corner. She was surprised and wondering at his concern. "*I'm fine.*" She wasn't ready to discuss her past with anyone, much less a disembodied voice, no matter how comforting it was to hear. "*How did you know?*"

"It seems I can find you the same way you found me. Your...distress couldn't be ignored."

She shook her head, rubbing fingertips over her eyes to remove the signs of her pain. "*How is this happening? I've never met anyone who could talk to me so easily.*" Aside from Titania, her experience with other telepaths was very limited. Tabitha was able, but it wasn't her strongest talent, and Diego never spoke to her so intimately, though she knew he could. She sensed Joaquin was thinking about his answer when he didn't reply right away.

His voice hummed in her mind. She realized he was making an effort to not frighten her more, keeping his voice low and sedate. "*Honestly, I don't know. I can't remember the last time I felt another person's pain, or was able to hear their thoughts.*" He seemed as confused by their connected ability as she was. She thought she heard a low rumble of laughter when he added, "*You knocked the wind from beneath me. At a moment in time when I needed to know I wasn't alone, you shouted at me.*"

She felt the burgeoning grin and dipped her chin, hearing the rich sound of his voice. Her hands folded in on her lap. "*I am sorry for startling you.*"

"*Never apologize for saving me.*" It flowed over her like the gentle admonishment it was, firm, but at the same time, he would never accept any apology for it. "*You don't know the truth about me, and someday I may tell you, but you have given me something I had forgotten existed.*"

"*What?*" she asked, perplexed.

"*Compassion. I can sense your suffering. It hovers in your mind. Maybe someday you will tell me what happened that makes you cry on the inside. Yet, when I was at my worst, you helped me when I needed it. It is only right I repay your kindness."*

Unease flitted across her mind. At a distance, she felt almost secure in her private conversation, but the idea of meeting him face to face made her shake. She didn't know Joaquin, if he was really a threat to her, to any of them, or if he was hunting for them. If he was trying to trick her into exposing their hiding place. The fear of those unknowns almost made her nauseous, but she quickly swallowed it down. She could barely stay in the same room alone with any of the other men in the house, and she knew none of them would dare hurt her. Yet, here she was, talking, even if it was over a distance, to a complete stranger. No one but Titania dared to physically touch her. Would she be able to talk to him if he stood right in front of her, to look at him? She trembled in the chair where she sat at the idea of it.

"Repay? How? Why would you want to repay something so small?" she asked, hiding the shake in her body from her thoughts. *"I shouted at you,"* she reminded him.

"I will find a way. You have given me a reprieve from my own loneliness, Lily. I am indebted to you for that." She shook her head at the mild arrogance in his voice, a man who would do as he says and no less. *"You need to go eat with the others. They are worried about you."*

"How do you know?" she immediately demanded. She searched, listening to the chaos of voices in the cabin, but found it was only her in the bedroom watching over her friend. She was taking longer than usual to join them, but he couldn't have known that!

"Because Diego knows I am talking with you and has made his displeasure known to me."

She felt herself wanting to smile at the thinly veiled disgust in his response. *"How does he know?"* She tilted her head, listening to him, and to the noises of those in the house. While no one was rushing to tell her it wasn't safe to be talking to him, or that Joaquin was a danger to her as Tani had said he wasn't, she was just as glad he was *out there* and the people *in here* knew it. She wasn't exactly sure if she should take it as a good sign or not, especially if he was telling her the truth and Diego did know he had reached out to her again.

"I didn't hide it from him," Joaquin explained. *"He doesn't trust me with cause. Our natures make us solitary men. The connection I have formed with you disturbs him. I am doing as he has asked. I am far away to not frighten you. Though should you ever have need of me, I will only be a whisper away. You are safe with me, Lily. I promise you."*

She didn't understand. What did he mean that they had formed a connection? How much could he read from her? Could he do more than hear what she physically directed toward him? Could he read her mind, sense her agitation, her pain, or the cause?

How far was 'far away'? Was it far enough? Was she putting the whole household in danger by talking to him? The possibilities gave her a chill, and she rubbed her palms down her legs to chase the shivers away. "*Diego can talk to you too?*"

She knew she heard an annoyed growl come from him. "*Yes, he's been listening to every word.*"

She stifled the gasp. "*How gifted are you? How close are you?*" Real fear that she'd led him—anyone—right to them made her quake where she sat.

"*That is something that will be answered in time, and I am far away. You have no need to fear me because I can talk to you. I know you are scared of this, and of me, for more reasons than I know right now. I don't want you to fear me. Ever. Take a deep breath. That's it. Are you feeling better now?*" he asked her, warm concern in his tone again. "*Well enough to go eat? Diego's female is coming for you. I have outstayed my welcome, it seems.*"

Not two seconds later, Tani popped around the doorframe again. "Houston almost has dinner ready."

"I'm coming."

"*I have to go, Joaquin.*" She stood from the chair, making sure the book was marked for the next reader. Tani made a quick check on Tabitha and then turned, catching Lily's gaze before heading out to the hall.

"*Just tell me you are feeling better so I can rest in peace tonight.*"

She trailed behind Tani, toasted herb and pasta aromas floating on the air, making her mouth water. "*Yes, Joaquin, I'm feeling much better.*" Lily's steps dragged a pace when she realized she did feel better after talking to him. His interruption had dispelled the anguish of her previous memories completely. She wasn't a hundred percent comfortable with the discussions happening between them, but she didn't feel threatened by him either. Then again, having him somewhere far away may have had a lot to do with her level of ease in her ability to talk to him. She prayed he was telling her the truth, and he wasn't as close as his voice sounded. That he was only talking to her out of concern, and maybe a sense of duty. There was no way to determine how close he could be, but she knew Diego wouldn't let him near the house regardless, no matter who he was, or what his intentions were. She didn't want to think of why he may have connected to her, other than she'd had enough of his whining. "*You have been very kind to me tonight, Joaquin. Thank you.*"

"*I always will be. That is my promise to you. Goodnight.*"

As the first conversation had floated into silence, he was gone again.

"YOU ARE challenging my patience," Diego warned, appearing only a few yards from where Joaquin rested in the V of the large tree branch several miles from the petite cabin. One foot dangled, swinging with ease as Lily's flowing voice faded out of his ears, but with Diego popping up in front of him, his foot stopped. He wasn't surprised at Diego's arrival, only that it had taken him so long to come and do something about Joaquin's conversation with Lily. When he hadn't left at Diego's menacing orders, which only Joaquin had heard while he'd spoken with Lily, he'd come himself to make sure Joaquin abided by his command. Joaquin knew better than to think they were simply requests to vacate the area.

"You were asked to leave. You have not." Silvery eyes flashed as anger lit their depths.

"Why should I go anywhere when she is in pain and you're doing nothing to help her?" he demanded. The immensity of what he'd felt when he'd reached out for her again had been staggering. "If she is under your protection, then you are failing." He sneered. "She's in incredible pain. She's hiding it to not alarm those around her." He crossed his arms and leaned against the trunk. Joaquin wasn't convinced the vampire before him wasn't the cause behind her pain, especially as closely as she was being watched by everyone inside. The fear of what could be happening behind those walls prompted his worst nightmares. Joaquin wasn't close enough to Lily to find those secrets imbedded in her memory. Diego's insistence to leave wasn't encouraging him that he'd find out, either.

"What is it she fears, that she won't discuss? Are you controlling her? What are you doing to her?"

Anger rose within Joaquin, sliding under his skin like a current, but he managed to keep his feigned relaxed position sitting on the branch, barely. Hopefully, he'd find out something, but he wasn't expecting it. Given a chance to get closer to the house hidden in the crisscrossed canopy of trees, he would be able to find out more on his own, but getting closer almost guaranteed retribution from Diego. For the moment, he could wait. But not for much longer. He was growing more adamant in finding a way to remove Lily from her close-knit watchers.

Joaquin straightened until he was standing before Diego. An unmoving silence was the only answer he received to his questions. Something was different about Diego compared to his other run-ins with the Brethren, but Joaquin's growing fascination for Lily was making it difficult to pinpoint what those differences may be, or to care enough to make them priorities. Deception was often the game played between the Brethren. He was waiting to see what Diego had planned. Just because he didn't appear ready to filet him where Joaquin stood didn't mean he wouldn't try. He felt Diego's eyes on his every move. Caution was the word of the moment.

Diego frowned, his irritation with Joaquin's persistence apparent in the growing glare of his gaze. "Leave. Leave here, forget her. She is cared for. That is more than you need to know."

Joaquin shook his head. "I can't."

Sparks began to radiate from around Diego's fingers, brilliant blue and white pulses flickering into the night like fleeing insects. "You have one chance left." His fingers flexed, and Joaquin felt the energy he mastered building around them, buffeting him like a searing desert wind. It was hot while the dropped coldness of Diego's voice chilled him, making him feel weakened and defeated.

He shook his head, dispelling the weighty sensations. Mind tricks were a child's game he was able to dismiss with little effort, but it still aggravated him that Diego would try. He bared his teeth in a tight snarl, more than willing to take the challenge from Diego. He wasn't a fighter. He wasn't near to being the warrior Diego appeared to be. Only a few hours ago Joaquin had decided he was ready to end the torture of his existence. This was no less than he had wanted then. He could leave this life behind with honor. The irony was, now he didn't want to die this second.

The first attack brightened the shadows of the tree with a blinding blue explosion when Joaquin had apparently taken more time than Diego was willing to give. Energy pulses blasted against the trunk as Joaquin leaped for safety. Limbs and branches swayed and cracked as he raced upward, Diego following, driving him further from the hidden house.

chapter three

THE PEACE of early evening was torn apart by an explosion. It ripped through the trees as though they were paper cutouts, simultaneously flattening several robust shapes with the obliterating strength of the blast. The last tree toppled with a splintered, cracking crash less than five hundred yards from the cabin. The wave of the aftershock rocked the entire shell of the small home like it was made of matchsticks and no more than a child's toy.

Terrified screams erupted through broken windows as glass shattered and fell from window frames, splintered like sparkling mosaic crystal leaves. Lily shot out of her bed like the largest demons of Hell were after her.

Because they were.

The floorboards and walls shook around her, vibrating under her bare feet as though a runaway locomotive raced right outside the walls. She fought to stand, flipping covers out of her way. Lurching to reach Tabitha's bedside in the bedroom space they shared, she ruthlessly yanked cords from the machines to free her from their forced immobility.

Houston cleared the doorway only a second later, his gaze cold and resolute. He jerked his head over his shoulder as he held himself steady with a hand on the doorframe when another shudder rocked the house. Fury made his voice sharp and commanding. "I'll carry her. Go with David."

She nodded, not arguing a second, snatching her jeans from the bookcase where she had tossed them at night and fled the room in her nightshirt. A sharp, whistling sound overhead seared the deafening silence of the wounded night, and she flinched as recognition hit her mere seconds before another explosion rocked the ground. She bit her lip to swallow her fear, searching in a near panic to remember how to get out of the little cabin, suddenly unable to remember a single thing about where she was. Amy and Kathy flocked in front of David in the hallway when she reached the bedroom door, no less terrified with wide, unseeing eyes, but they hadn't been asleep. It felt as though she were walking through a fog with the floor tilting precariously under her like a funhouse floor made of rolling barrels. Hearing Houston's sharp bark to move, Lily jumped into her jeans, then hurried in front of the trio in the hall, snapping into the now to race out the front door to the outside world.

The motor of the diesel specialty bus cranked to life with Laney in the driver's seat, her cheeks taut and pale, her eyes fearfully searching the smoke-filled sky as she prepped the gleaming monster to run and run hard. Houston jogged from the house with Tabitha folded securely into his arms, David bringing up the rear, herding Amy and Kathy.

Fires raged deep in the trees where the explosions had happened, seemingly stopped by some sort of wall, not reaching them and not getting any closer. Thick smoke billowed up, obscuring what was left of the sun's rays on the western horizon.

"Where are Diego and Tani?" Lily shouted, whipping between Houston, desperately searching the demolished windows of the cabin for any sign of them from inside the bus. There was nothing to see in any of the powerless rooms plainly visible through the gaping holes. She wanted to run out the doors of the bus to search for them, but couldn't without trampling right over Kathy and Amy.

"They can catch up. Don't worry," Houston said, rushing to put Tab on the bed. It had been specially outfitted for her to travel at the rear of the bus. "Floor it, Laney!" He snarled the order as soon as David was in and the door slammed shut.

Laney didn't hesitate a heartbeat, maneuvering the converted bus through the overgrowth covering the driveway, leaving the lights off and trying not to use the brake.

"Why are they f-firing at us?" Amy stammered.

"Because they can't get close enough to actually touch you. Their weapons can't either. Diego set up a perimeter line no one and nothing can cross without him allowing it." Houston reconnected the important lines for Tabitha, an IV and a standard monitor, then strapped her down with secure belts to keep any jarring from tossing her right off the double-sized bed as they bounced over the uneven ground.

"So they're flushing us out?" Kathy gasped, her eyes rounding as a noticeable squeak took over her voice.

"They may think they are," Houston muttered. "Diego is going to kick their asses for this. He loved that cabin."

"Lily!"

Lily's head snapped up from where she numbly watched Houston taking precious care with Tabitha. Her gaze went unfocused as the sharp shout entered her thoughts.

"Joaquin!"

"Santa María." The grateful benediction was no more than a whisper in her mind. *"I am with you. Diego has engaged your attackers."*

"What is going on?" She silenced the fearful sob with sheer willpower of steel. She would not let her fear leak into her thoughts.

"I don't know. I'm on the wrong side to see what is happening." Real apology rumbled in his words.

"Joaquin!" She almost shouted for real when she felt his voice create a void of emptiness that told her he had withdrawn. What could Diego do? Where were they, and where was Joaquin? What was happening? Who was attacking them?

There was only one person who would dare. Tenorio had found them, and he wasn't the kind of man to let his escapees remain free. The knowledge that they had been found so quickly and easily chilled her.

"Lily, Diego and I are not far away, but we can't come to you right now. The way out will soon be safe. Stay calm. I can talk to you easier than the others." Titania's collected and confident tones soothed her. Lily nodded. It was up to her to tell them what was happening outside where they couldn't see. Tani's faith in Lily filled her as she did what had to be done to get them safely away.

"Tani knows where we are," she informed the others inside the bus with her. Lily noticed the stretched and fearful tension filling the luxurious space wall to wall for the first time as everyone who could, snapped their attention to her. A total silence had filled the bus as they all waited for the next inevitable moment, knowing death waited for them. "Diego is with her."

Everyone knew Tani and Lily had connected by their telepathic talents so no one questioned her information. Amy and Kathy sat on the floor, shoulder to shoulder on the carpet. David was near the front, watching from one angle as Houston did the same to their rear, searching through viewing portals in the thickly covered, tinted windows. Most of the walls were solid, like a tour bus.

Dark shadows seemed to bleed from the sides of the path to engulf the night and the bus as they crawled down the thin road that led to the only pass out of the woods. Another roaring rocket erupted in the distance to their right, sending a shower of debris high into the night. Desperate whimpers rose, but everyone stayed quiet and as calm as possible. Kathy and Amy both closed their eyes and waited for it to end, the same as Lily did.

JOAQUIN felt only a brief frustration when he encountered the wall of protection that he'd missed the night before because he hadn't dared get as close as he was now to the cabin. Diego allowed Joaquin within the energy boundaries to meet the bus, the invisible shield dropping immediately. There was no doubt those same barriers had been ample to keep the intruders at bay, feeling them against his mind and skin as Joaquin physically neared them. He was as sure those same barriers were why the attacks weren't on the mark and could get nowhere close enough to do physical harm. Whatever Diego was, his strengths were deep and strong.

He landed with light feet on the roof of the bus, immediately scanning inside the moving vehicle, and found everyone who should have been, inside. Relief was deep, knowing no one was harmed.

Whipping his head toward the flow of anger and determination in the distance, he snarled to the depths of the woods, sending the rush of his own anger into the shadows as Diego unleashed a huge power surge against the forces that had sent the first attack. An attack which had happened only moments before full nightfall. Blue light lit the woods as though the trees themselves were wrapped in chilling fluorescent flames. Another explosion rocked the night, but this time, it was Diego's kill—a large vehicle and all its ammunition exploding. Not an aimed missile targeting the people beneath him.

Lifting his hands, Joaquin pulled in more of the nighttime darkness, masking their size in a nebulous blanket of shadows. Driving past outstretched limbs, the sharp whip of branches felt like fire-stoked lashes against his chest as he kept his position on top of the bus, steeling himself against their inflicted pain. The created concealment never wavered as he focused, all the while biting back the skin-stripping sting as each strike flayed into his chest and legs. The thick cover of shadows muted their noise and hid their heat.

Diego had alerted him their attackers were using heat and night vision gear to snare their quarry. A quarry now protected by a tentative alliance between the two vampires. One who had the ability to crush the invading force of ammunitions and men, and Joaquin, who could direct the night to do his bidding in a way he'd rarely done, commanding a strength he'd seldom, if ever, needed before tonight. His lowered hands hovered flat as if controlling the rocking spine of the diesel-powered beast beneath him as he concentrated his attention to keep them all hidden.

His soul had snarled in shock, demanding retribution for this attack against Lily the instant he'd awakened. Once above ground, he'd raced to the cabin, uncaring if a welcome was given or not. Nothing would hold him back. Diego, already on his way to face the worst of the threat, unexpectedly had taken him into his confidence, giving him the situation in detail. As soon as he understood the direness and offered without provocation to help, Joaquin had felt the first seeking wave of energy roll over the treetops in the direction of the incoming vehicles. The ensuing explosion was what had lit up the night sky with another burst of heat and light.

"Lily, are you all right?" Joaquin asked, his gaze unblinking and focused on the murky road ahead of the bus's nose. There wasn't a single flicker of moonlight making its way through the churning clouds of roiling smoke filling the sky. Joaquin weaved the heavy gray and black clouds effortlessly to his advantage.

The chatter of her fear was perceptible even through her thoughts. "*I'm okay, but I've been better.*" Inside, he wanted to smile at her determination to be strong, but didn't dare, fearing a drop in his concentration would break the cover he controlled within his hands. They weren't out of trouble yet. The sound of engines growled like lumbering animals ahead. There was movement and lowered voices discernable to him. Whatever lay before them was moving in their direction, directly across their path to try to stop them.

"More vehicles are lying in wait at the branch of the roads." Diego's voice thrummed through the vacuumed silence surrounding Joaquin on top of the bus, confirming what he'd detected beyond the darkness. *"I cannot remove them to allow you safe passage. I cannot reach them in time."*

"I will see them safely through," Joaquin swore. The barrier Diego had constructed had held the forces several miles from their goal, infiltrating their human minds with a sense of inescapable horrors to be found if they forced their way forward. The strength it took to create such an impenetrable force, and maintain it, especially during daylight hours, was not lost on Joaquin.

"Then in you, I entrust them," Diego intoned, shifting out of Joaquin's attentions to his own battles, trying to stop the forces from congregating further and freezing their escape entirely.

"Lily, there is a trap ahead. Diego will come when he can, but we can't stop."

"How will we get through?" Adrenaline ratcheted her fear, making her voice rise high even in her thoughts.

This time, his smile was a little harder to restrain, looser with confidence. *"With a little help from overhead,"* he answered cryptically. Lifting his hands, he relished the feeling of his powers seeking out into the night, absorbing the sensations of the world around him to command them to his will. Clouds quickly gathered as lightning spiked and slithered against the tumultuous billow of black swathing thickening in the sky. "*Tell whoever is driving to maintain this speed. Don't use the brakes. My concentration is divided, and I can't hide them.*"

"*What are you doing?*"

The tremor of fear and uncertainty was easy to catch in her words. He knew her greatest fear was that there was no hope to escape from the terror surrounding them.

"*Literally? Hiding you in plain sight,*" he replied, maintaining the shadows surrounding the bus while commanding the fires of nature to strike and boil in the night skies like a witch's cauldron of old.

LILY sank down on her knees on the carpet next to Laney to be close to her and still be able to see out the panel length windshield. Her attention zeroed in on the road before them as she listened to all the voices she had to blindly trust. "Just drive. Don't slow down for anything." Branches whipped like they were possessed in the growing winds.

Laney nodded, her hands steady on the wheel to keep them on the winding shadows of the path that wasn't even a real drive. "Where is that storm coming from?" She licked at dry lips, her voice quivering as her gaze jerked up then to the track ahead of them.

Lightning struck a few feet in front of the bus a heartbeat later, illuminating in a blinding blast the path that wasn't any larger than a track for two tires.

Lily blinked to clear the sudden streaks flashing in front of her eyes. Rain fell in the next instant, raging in rivers from the sky. Whimpers echoed from the rear of the bus.

"Don't slow down!" Lily reached up when she felt Laney react to the weather, almost letting the bus drop to less than a crawl.

"Right," Laney replied, firming her lips, pushing onward. Lily settled again, her attention riveted on the outside world. The wipers made little headway on the waterfall of rain as it hit the flat windshield. Water ran in building rivers in front of them, pouring like a dam had given way down the pathway to disappear beneath the bus.

"Shit," Houston swore a few tense moments later. "We can't get past those."

Lily saw them too. Three large military-green carriers sitting like vultures along the road and tucked into the trees, their shapes blurred through the falling deluge. Tarps covered the rear of each vehicle, but didn't hide their cargo. Large guns sat poised, ready to fire in two of them, aiming right at them, down the throat of the bus. She held her breath.

Yet nothing happened as they neared. Not a person moved within any of the carriers, the bus inching closer every second. Fear created an icy tremor down her spine as her blood pumped mercilessly against her ears while those hulking shapes loomed out of the dark.

"Lily, you can do this. Give her my directions."

Lily sucked in a deep breath and let it out. "Track to the right. That's it," she encouraged when Laney found the rut, following the voice and images flowing through her mind, pushing her own fears right out the window. There couldn't be room for any fears. How Joaquin could see anything in the pitch black night awash in a lightning storm like she'd never seen, she had no idea. She wasn't even sure where he was, but she was blindly putting her faith into his view of the world outside in that torrential rain. She knew without any other light, she was as blind as Laney trying to drive through it all.

Another flash of lightning struck at their side, illuminating the wilderness with a bright ball of light. Where it looked like there was not a single foot of space, they barely slipped past one of the large covered trucks lying cross-wise over the road, leaving just enough room for the bus and maybe a prayer. The vehicle they were avoiding had actually done them a favor by shoving its way into its position, knocking some of the closer foliage down or away. A brash, scratching-hiss sound reverberated through the length of the bus, like nails on a chalkboard scraped down the side, making her cringe in anticipation of capture, but it drew no attention from outside.

"You're doing wonderful." The gentle encouragement warmed her, even though she couldn't stop from boring the night ahead of them for more dangers, expecting the soldiers laying in wait to jump out at them at any second.

"Keep going, Laney. We're almost clear." She could see the open path ahead of them in her mind's eye. A path that would widen into a drive of sorts, leaving no room to doubt the help, or why. Or how. For the immediate moment. There'd be time for that later. Much, much later. When they were all safe again.

Laney nodded in answer, her hands gripping mercilessly around the wheel until her knuckles were bloodless. Every little nudge of the steering wheel moved them. Every moment took them a little farther from those behind searching for them in their wake.

"A little further, then you can increase your speed."

"How do you know?" He sounded so sure when she still couldn't see more than a few feet into the swirling mess outside.

"There aren't any more trucks left in front of you. Diego has halted the remaining vehicles on the other side that were waiting to cut off your escape. He has removed those which could harm you at long range. Once you were free of his barrier, their long-range guns would have reached you too easily. He'll be able to catch up soon. I'll keep you hidden until you are safe."

She shook her head, mystified. *"How did you manage that? How did you keep us from being seen? Where are you?"*

"You called them gifts," he replied, adroitly bypassing the majority of her questions. She heard

the whisper of his voice low and deep, the first hint of exhaustion weaving through his words as he spoke. "*For the first time, I can also.*"

"*Your curse?*" she asked with a shiver of awe, unable to comprehend what he had done to protect them. Yet, there had been no mistaking the way the night had made way for them, embraced them, cloaked them in the swirling murkiness making up the drenched view of the pathway ahead of them, soaked with rain and shadows. It was a heavy blanket of darkness and moisture and she could only guess it was what had kept them invisible. Those same shadows continued to circle around the road and the front of the bus, almost like an amalgamation of shifting ghosts and darkness swirling and circling them ceaselessly. The rain thinned to a mere downpour.

"*That and many more.*"

Wow, was her first thought, and he chuckled in answer.

"*Just a few more minutes to make sure you won't be followed,*" he cautioned.

Lily touched Laney's leg, daring to feel a brief flare of relief at his latest news. "We're almost clear. When we are, speed, but no lights. Not yet." Laney nodded in understanding, her attention not faltering once. She'd handled the bus with finesse and skill, every inch precious in their escape.

Miles rolled beneath the bus tires, leaving the mess of the cabin and several confused truckloads of men behind. It would take them time to know they'd missed their quarry by not just a little, but by hours and miles by the time they realized they could finally reach the cabin. They would also discover they had accumulated dozens of unaccountable casualties and losses caused by some force none would be able to explain.

When the way opened up in front of the bus, headlights flicked on and Laney put the bus into a new gear, widening the gap of their escape by even more.

JOAQUIN sank to his knees on the bus's roof, trembling hands catching him when he collapsed forward. His head hung limply as he rode the silver and black beast while it gained speed, the rain he'd called flying in the wind behind him in streaming rivulets off of his head and shoulders. He was soaked to the skin and couldn't find it in him to care. He was too drained to change his shape right then to leave the bus behind anyway.

The second he released the shadows, Lily told the driver to turn on the headlights. Now, speed was the most important thing. Dizzy from expending so much energy, unused to being taxed in that capacity, he simply sagged on his hands and knees, weaving with the lumbering motions of the bus as they cleared the hidden dirt tracks for paved roads, then highways. He felt the burning trails biting into him from the thin branch ends that had sliced against flesh, tearing at his clothes as he'd kept his vigil over the people in the bus. He pushed the remaining pain out of his thoughts, their razor-sharp bite already beginning to fade as his body sealed the thinnest cuts. His fangs had extended long ago, craving to replenish his drained and wounded body, having awakened already in need. Yet, beyond the hunger and exhaustion, he felt exhilarated, felt *alive* in a way he hadn't felt in centuries. And he would do it all again if needed for the caring beauty behind Lily's voice, to know she was safe.

He became aware of the vampire's arrival as a pair of black boots landed at his shoulder. The boots, thankfully, were worn by probably the only other vampire Joaquin would care to meet in his weakened condition and not worry about his safety.

The rest of the clouds ceased to tumble and roll overhead, a few splitting into fluffy charcoal masses as the fury and energy Joaquin had used dissipated, the same as the rain itself faded to mist, then nothing.

A strong hand lowered and grabbed firmly, yet respectfully, around Joaquin's arm, hefting him to his feet once more.

Diego stared at him in silent contemplation for a moment or two, showing no sign of his thoughts in his bright eyes as they locked on Joaquin. Then, with little warning, and with Joaquin too exhausted to care to fight and not greatly worried over the outcome, Diego simply lifted him off the rear of the bus and carried him into the night.

chapter four

LILY slipped from the tiny bathroom on the bus wearing a clean band logo sweatshirt from the drawers to replace her nightshirt, feeling a little more human. David sat at the foldout table next to Laney, talking with Amy and Kathy on the opposite side. Houston had taken over driving, giving his wife a break after the stress of the escape. It wasn't hard for Lily to figure the bus had been one of Tani's tour buses for the band.

Not long after their rescue, Titania had explained about being kidnapped, as well, by Albert Tenorio. Their band had had to cancel the second half of their tour, essentially vanishing from the public eye to keep the girls safe. Titania had never once whispered a word of condemnation for the change in her plans. It sometimes struck Lily out of the blue that so many people would change their entire lives for the four girls they had saved from the clutches of Hell. It surprised her more how much she thought of them as her friends now when she'd doubted ever having any such freedom in her life again. Lily crossed her arms over her body, leaning to stare out the slit that made a window between the side wall of the bus and the bedroom partition where Tabitha lay ignorant of the world around her. Night had fallen thick and dark as far as she could see. She had no idea where they were.

"How long will it take to reach the new house?" Amy asked. Lily listened, but didn't join the group. She felt too keyed up to sit.

Laney shrugged now that she was sitting with them and everyone was a little calmer. "I imagine between twelve to sixteen hours depending on how hard it is on the mountains."

There was a collective sound of relief.

"We're just leaving ahead of schedule," David quipped with a light joking tone, trying to downplay the seriousness and help them all relax.

Lily glanced at him, then swept away before he connected with her gaze. She was pretty sure the lightness of his tone was forced, however well it was hidden. David hadn't been left unscathed by Tenorio's hands. She wasn't entirely at ease around him regardless that he was Titania's drummer and one of her best friends. Something about him just didn't *feel* right. For the most part, Lily could ignore it, but she was completely tied into a knot at the moment. In the confined quarters, it was harder to fight the twitch reflex to avoid being close to any man.

Lily remembered the story she'd heard from them. With Tenorio trying to draw Titania out, he'd kidnapped David and had taken him to the compound where Diego and Tani had then found the girls also being held. David's tortures were well hidden, most of them healed beneath his own clothes, the same as hers now were. Only hers covered her entire body, a winding, slashing tapestry of thin cuts, lash scars, and gouges.

"At least Nathan is already there. The security will be in place and it's even better camouflaged than the cabin was." Lily wasn't ready to accept any place would be better, no matter how positive David sounded.

Kathy's expression was pensive. "How did he find the cabin?"

Silence pervaded the small space of the interior cabin. Lily closed her eyes against the threatening rise of bile, her fears surging to the front. Tenorio had found them, and a lot faster than any of them had anticipated. He could do it again. A hidden location was no guarantee of safety. Even if she had to remain on the run for the rest of her life, she'd never let herself become one of his test subjects again.

"I don't know," Laney said, interjecting some soothing warmth into her own words. "Diego may know by the time he catches up with us."

"Are they okay?" Lily asked, speaking for the first time. It had been hours since she'd felt Joaquin's withdrawal. Tani hadn't said a peep in as long. After relying on both of them, it bothered her that they'd left her in silence since the last words she'd shared with Joaquin.

Laney focused on her clutched hands on the table for a moment. "I feel them. They are okay, just not real close."

Lily wished Joaquin would say something, but didn't want to reach out to him, unsure about her sudden depth of shyness or her unordinary craving to connect to him. He was a block of unanswered questions, one she feared finding all the answers to.

Like *how* had he kept them from being seen? How had he created a storm, any storm, of that magnitude? Why did she want to feel his touch, hear his voice in her thoughts? Why did she feel any level of comfort whenever she spoke with him? It only happened when she was talking to him. No one else. How could she feel at ease with him now, when even the thought of being near David left her feeling clammy and edgy? She didn't feel quite so threatened by Joaquin any longer, but why? She was wary. That was an irrefutable fact, but now she was also intrigued by him, by his gifts. She hadn't actually met him, yet he'd risked his life to help them escape the sneak attack on the cabin simply because he'd heard her yell at him.

Where is he now? Her eyes drifted shut and she let her confused mind relax, calming the tumultuous heaves of her stomach, all delayed reactions to the last few hours. Fear had become such a constant in her life. It felt surreal to realize she had unbelievably begun to live outside of that box of fear in the last few months. It should have been no surprise, then, that when the source of those known fears reared up like a demonic specter and dumped a backlash of pain and fear on her lap, she felt like the same person she'd been when they'd first rescued her.

Beaten. Broken. Scared to breathe. Tipping forward, she rested against the cool glass, watching the reflection of the stars in the glass flicker as they swayed along the imperfections of the highway. She regained her equilibrium a heartbeat at a time.

The sensation of the bus slowing a little later startled her and she yanked her pensive gaze forward to the front of the bus. "What's happening?" Her mouth suddenly felt dry. Had they hit something? Was something wrong with the bus?

Houston slowed and pulled cautiously to the side of the road. A moment later, he opened the door to what appeared to be an empty highway.

"Someone order takeout?" she heard Tani say with a cheerful lilt in her voice as she clambered on board, her arms full of bags and cartons as she appeared through the split doors. "I hope you guys like Chinese." Lily felt the tension leak out of her shoulders, trying to relax, and finding it to be a lot harder than she would've imagined.

With her on board, Houston closed the doors and started moving forward again. Lily let out a breath seeing her, almost wistfully, searching beyond her to the door, half hoping that... The truth smacked her with a dose of reality.

No. She wasn't. She didn't...couldn't. Could she? Was she really looking for Joaquin? Was she expecting him to be with Tani? Did she want to meet him? Was she ready to see face to face the man who she'd connected with, the man who had done so much to help them escape? Unable to answer herself truthfully, she focused on what Tani was saying instead.

"Sorry I couldn't catch up sooner. Diego wanted to take some time to slow down any chance of pursuit. We're all clear now."

"They were from Tenorio's compound, weren't they?" Kathy asked, a panicky twitch causing her to wrap her hands together.

Tani set the aromatic bags down on the Formica table with David lending a hand to help her spread them out for everyone to enjoy. "Unfortunately. We're still searching how they found us."

Lily caught Tani's automatic inclusion into their problems. They were all in this together. The truth of hearing it eased Lily's apprehension a little. Returned some of her waning strength that she'd lost in the last few hours. She knew they wouldn't turn their backs on them because Tenorio was heating up the hunt, but her realm of experience was short and warped anymore when it came to steadfast friends.

"He'll find us again," Lily stated, her gaze raking the group, then returning to stare out the small window she'd claimed, hoping she never saw the extremes it would take to lose her closest friends.

"He'll never give up." She had no doubt to that, none in the least.

Motions slowed, then ceased, stilling the preoccupied drag of Styrofoam across the table with all eyes finding her once more. Then, Titania purposely flipped cartons open and produced plasticware to eat with, not letting the dire predictions deter her intentions.

"No, he won't, which is why we're trying to find out as much as we can from the men who were sent tonight. Diego is searching them now, looking for the people behind the orders. If it goes straight to Tenorio, we know who he is. We only need the chance to find him. Nathan's last report was that he hadn't returned to California yet. If it was someone else who ordered this attack, then we will know, and can protect you better."

Tani sat down on one of the long cloth benches, her hands lying easily on her lap as she continued. "We never promised this would be easy on any level, Lily. We did promise you protection and stability to heal."

Lily's shoulders shrunk in. "I know." She looked over her shoulder, catching the other woman's almost blank blue stare. "I can't go back, Tani. I can't. And I won't." No one would understand the terrors Lily had seen. Tabitha would know, but she laid silently, no more than a breathing corpse barely feet from where Lily stood. Not even Amy or Kathy knew the deepest atrocities Albert Tenorio had inflicted on his 'subjects'. They hadn't been there as long, less than a year each. Tenorio hadn't begun to do his worst to them. They should be thankful.

Tani stood and approached to stop at her shoulder. A tender hand swept a wave of red hair away from her shoulder and face. Gentled, her voice lowered to make the conversation private between them. "It won't come to that, Lily. Tenorio will be stopped. He beat us to the first punch. It's an advantage he won't be able to exploit twice. We just need to find out what gave him that advantage."

"You believe Diego can do that?" She desperately wanted to have that same blind faith in her benefactor, and almost could, but she'd, at best, rarely seen Diego and had spoken to him even less. It was like he was doing his best to not overwhelm the women. He was a very imposing, intimidating figure when he looked a certain way, which was fairly often. It was his nature. He was a leader, undoubtedly the one who protected them all. Being considerate and soft of his charges was unusual for her to see. He was the protective force, while Tani was the caring part of the pair. His kind had been the vicious type she feared the most at the compound. Silent stealth and strength, and there was no way to win against that fear.

Absolute conviction warmed Tani's usually pale features, bringing a brighter sparkle to her dark blue eyes. "I believe Diego can do anything. I've seen him do the impossible. Just have a little faith in your future, Lily. It's just beginning. Don't let it slip through your fingers so soon."

"I know." Lily nodded, but wasn't sure she believed it yet.

"Come eat something," Tani offered, beckoning toward the table where other conversations were about anything but their near escape. "I brought plenty to get us through to breakfast."

Lily cast a glance at the table full of people, but even them and the scents of orange and cashew chicken couldn't help her drum up even an interest of an appetite. "Maybe later," she answered, swinging around to look sightlessly out the window. "I'll check on Tabitha."

Tani's expression was understanding, giving Lily time to find her feet again after the rushed departure from their cabin. No one else may have known how shaken she felt over the near escape, hearing the shattering whistle of the incoming missiles that had been meant for them, and their total destruction. There had been no subdue and capture in their plans. Refusing to let the chilled knowledge escalate into something she wouldn't be able to keep at bay, she turned and opened the bedroom door to disappear into the private mini-room where Tabitha lay.

The room was draped in dark colors, since it had once been a sleeping quarters for whoever had been on the bus at the time, with one window on each side thickly tinted to the outside to look like it was, in fact, black glass. There were other accent colors in the bus, some deep russets and blues, but in here, it was dark. Period. Lily was actually kind of grateful for the simple lack of anything in the room to remind her of the outside world. She could lose herself in the cavernous feeling of the room, the only real intrusion being Tab's monitor and lines attaching her to them.

"At least you didn't have to hear them coming," she said flatly as she sank down to one side of the bed, careful to not make Tabitha move. She brushed Tab's short, fringed locks out of her eyes, even though the wispy blonde strands wouldn't bother her. Her hair had been much like the rest of her, the same as Lily, abused and ignored. New haircuts and tons of soap and water. At least on the outside, they looked like average people.

The inside was a different story.

"I wish you would wake up," she murmured, stroking the cool smoothness of Tabitha's skin with tender fingers. Houston had pulled up the bed blanket to her waist, covering her where her nightshirt didn't when he'd settled her into the bed. Testing the belts, one across her thighs and the other across her stomach, she found they were snug, but not overly tight. She refused to allow the first impulse to take root—to tear them from her body. The bed was large enough for her to too easily roll around given the chance. Even a hard turn on a highway ramp could do it. Lily understood their purpose, but she didn't like seeing her friend restrained any more than she, herself, would have wanted to be. "Just until we get to the new house." She said the words out loud, as much for herself as for Tabitha, lying so unawares on the bed beside her. Then, she began to talk, to push the remainder of the last few hours even further away.

"You're going to love the new place, Tab. You'll see. I've seen the pictures. It's beautiful, out in the wilderness like Diego's cabin, but right next to the mountains. Like you can reach out and touch them. Laney said the rooms are huge, so we won't have to share anymore. Not that it was a real hardship, staying in the room with you. You were the best roommate I've ever had," she chatted, forcing lighthearted cheer into her words, hypnotically smoothing the sheet and blanket covering her friend beneath her fingers. "Believe me, after living in a dorm for two years, you get all kinds of experience with roommates."

Mentioning her dorm brought thoughts of if her family knew she was missing. Had the school contacted them? Probably, when the dorm rent came due again. Had any of them looked? Had they assumed she'd run off with some hunky California guy? Would her mother and father have even looked up from their lives to blink at the news? She hadn't thought about her family in at least two years, not since she'd realized there was no way out, utter defeat and hopelessness killing her inside. She'd given up hope after realizing she wasn't ever again going to see the outside of the cage she called home at the compound. Lily had prayed with every breath she took, every moment of every day, that someone would realize she hadn't simply taken off. Leaving home to go to the West Coast to go to school had, if anything, taken a burden of one away from her parents. Lord knew they needed all their attention on her older sister and younger brother.

She blew out a breath, releasing the ancient frustration. She was the only balanced child of the three. Of course, her parents knew she'd disappeared, she rationalized, but knowing them, there wasn't much they could do other than place a missing person's report and hope she turned up. She'd always been the steady one. She would turn up. Come home.

If she only could.

Raking stiff fingers through her hair, she pushed the old hurt away. It was part of what had driven her to go to school so far away from home, and you couldn't get any further from rural Nebraska than West Coast California. She'd been there endlessly for her parents, and for her brother, who had been born with a mental deficiency. She'd been able to do her own laundry by the age of ten. Was cooking and cleaning up after herself. Took responsibility for her homework and excelled. She'd fought tooth and nail to keep her grades up, rather than acting out for attention. At least her parents had attended her graduation. It was one night her sister had already been in jail and they only needed home care for a few hours for Brian.

Lucky for Lily.

"It's going to be okay, Tabitha," she whispered, believing fiercely it was time for things to change.

The process had already begun. She wanted to see her family again, but could wait. She didn't want to endanger any of them by reaching out too soon, letting them know she was safe. The scare she'd given herself over Joaquin was plenty for the moment. She missed her parents so much, even with all the differences and neglect she could see in her childhood. They were still her parents. They weren't bad people, just preoccupied with Brian's handicap. Lily was almost positive his illness wasn't an illness at all, but was actually telepathic ability in excess. Even her sister, Susan, had temperament issues she felt were caused by it. She'd never been able to connect to either so there wasn't any proof, only a general belief from her own experiences. She'd never been able to really discuss it with her parents either. A few mentions had only garnered her wide-eyed, ludicrous stares. Before Tani, she'd heard only quiet, vague, unfocused voices. Then, there was Tani, Diego, and now, Joaquin.

Maybe she'd been looking in the wrong crowds. The thought brought a twitchy laugh to her lips.

The future was getting better for them, all of them. Tenorio's attack tonight had been luck and timing. She did believe Tani when she said Diego was going to find out how it had been done to prevent it from recurring. They'd come this far. She refused to dwell on the what ifs. She'd lived in fear for too long already to start living that way now when they were free.

All the girls, which was a miracle in itself, were free. Were protected, and safe. Lily wanted desperately to believe things would only keep getting better. Maybe the longer she told herself to believe in that fact, the more her life would improve. She never expected easy. She'd never really known easy.

She came from solid, middle America stock. Her mother was Irish and then some, born in Chicago, where both she and Susan had been born. Her dad was a Pittsburgh man, all the way, but had moved his family to Nebraska for a job. She looked like her mom, except for her stature. She got that from her dad. Five-eight was intimidating only until the ninth grade. She'd played high school basketball and had gone to college to study family dynamics with hopes of flowing into a child psychologist. She adored children. She always had, even her own pain in the ass brother. He wasn't a rotten type of male, just in need, and she'd never hated him for it. She *had* resented her parents for their limited attention spans, which seemed to only occur for Brian, or whenever Susan was doing something again, like getting thrown in jail. Her sister had seen the inside of a jail more times than Lily had seen a full moon. Proving to be the least troublesome, they'd relied on her stability to give them the capacity to care for the two who needed them more. Only Lily had needed them too.

A slow breath slipped out between tight lips, her hands moving again to stroke Tabitha's forearm with tender care. A distraction that was powerless against the coming tide.

That life was over for her, whether she was able to see her family again or not. Her education had lapsed, there had been no boyfriend at the time she'd accepted Tenorio's offer to participate in his study, and she was as sure any trace of her existence had been wiped clean where it could be, if he'd had any say in it. There was little doubt her life had ground to a stop on the outside of the compound. What kind of life could a person non-grata have anyway? She couldn't go home until the threat of Tenorio looking for her was gone. She had her doubts there was anything at all for her to return to considering what she knew, and how long she'd been missing.

Lily had been swimming in and out of cresting waves of rage since the rescue from the compound as she came to grips with her freedom. Curbing the rushes of resentment brought by the reality of this new situation, and knowing that there wasn't much she could do to change any of her past, was a full time effort. Like spirals, the emotions twisted and spun, tightening under the weight of her memories until common sense or real life stepped in and proved she was safe now, safe within the company with which she'd shared the little cabin.

It hadn't taken long for her to discover, once in Tenorio's hands, there would be no escape from the compound. She'd never even known where they were being held. Every person in contact with them made sure that the prisoners, whoever they had at any given time, knew nothing about their location. All she remembered was visiting with Tenorio one evening at his mansion to interview for a place on his study and, once she'd confirmed her ability to his satisfaction, she never saw the outside world again. She promised herself she'd never feel that powerless again.

She knew it was part of the healing, to get to the other side of what had happened, but there were moments she wanted to scream, or cry for hours. Silently, she had. More than once.

Lily had once had dreams, ambitions for her life, had expected to graduate and have her career, with a family. She'd had a plan and knew what she was doing to get there, but the horrific direction her life had taken had stripped her of that control, stole the chance for both. Ripped away any kind of life to be anything other than a breathing shell of the person she had been before that fateful meeting.

Her desire for children had dwindled with each passing moment of her imprisonment. She doubted she'd even be able to conceive, much less carry a child after what she'd suffered through. Not all of the blood she'd lost had been by needle. *Not that it matters*, she silently berated herself.

Who would be able to stand to look at her now with her entire body a menagerie of scars? Who would want a woman who looked like she did? She'd never thought she was a beauty pageant contestant with her flaming red hair streaked with a deluge of colors. Sunlight had always played havoc with the tones. She was broad in the shoulders and tall. Not petite like Tani or Amy. What her mother had kindly called solid even though she'd been trim. She didn't have Amy's sweet looks either. Being Midwestern-bred did have its benefits. Amy was what Lily knew a fourth or fifth generation Midwesterner would look and act like, since she'd gone to school with so many from her early years through high school.

That wasn't Lily.

Jagged lines scored her jaw where pummeling fists had left their mark. She couldn't stand to look at herself in the mirror and hadn't bothered since the first scar, given to her not long after her capture. It was only the tip of the iceberg.

Her body was a worse nightmare beneath her clothes, hiding the signs of her imprisonment every day she breathed. Long, jagged rips, or lash marks, or scalpel slices. There were so many. She knew every one. So how would she possibly interest anyone who would have to deal with not only the damaged mind, but also the destroyed body of the woman?

She pried her hand loose from the bedding when she realized she'd clenched the blanket covering Tabitha into a nearly bloodless fist. She dragged in deep breaths, refusing to wallow in the pain for longer. She knew enough about pain, all kinds, to know holding it close was toxic. She was a stronger woman, a fighter, or she would have succumbed to Tenorio's cruelties long ago.

All he needed was their physical being. The one thing he hadn't counted on was their own mental blockades and strengths. They had to be willing to let him probe their minds, and he soon discovered they weren't. So he probed everything else, taking and taking, or having his men try to convince them they were only causing their own pain, doing for him what he couldn't do as a single person—debase and defile them.

Hate-filled images flared against her vision the deeper she delved into the past. The remembered neck-snapping strikes led to blistering pain-filled explosions on her eyelids. Constant rapes, held immobile and defenseless with straps nearly identical to the ones that held Tabitha safely to the bed. As if she could feel their tightness strangling her flesh, she ran her hand around her wrist, rubbing away the sensation of hard leather and cuffs, feeling her heart pound in answer to the reawakened memory.

She shook her head, her hair swirling madly with the jerked motion as she fought the memories, wanting to be free of them. Blood pounded against her eardrums with a harsh thunder as the anger and emotions swamped her with merciless disregard. The rush of the night's escape, the fear of never being free, and the flare of anger that she tried to fight every second from taking her under in its powerful undertow had her catching her breath in a vicious sob.

Without any idea of where it came from, a soothing blanket of calmness infiltrated her wildly rampaging thoughts. It encircled her body and her mind like a velvet ribbon until she felt securely embraced in its calming comfort. She wanted to lose herself to the consuming sensations. The feeling was like being wrapped in heavy flannel in front of a blazing winter fire.

"Breathe," came the single, crooned directive.

Only it was a masculine voice reaching out to her, not Tani, the one person who she would have expected to be the first to brush against her thoughts to offer a hand out of the quagmire of her pain. Just like she had done in the past.

There was no doubt this was not Titania.

Tender and consuming, she was swept up into a cocoon of gentleness, drawing her away from the pain as if each excruciating thread simply drained away from her thoughts. She sucked in a deep breath when she heard his voice again, comforting her, pulling her closer to him and away from the memories.

Vivid, nightmarish images were pushed away. Just like the picture of the leaves he had shared with her the night before, breathtaking visions filled her mind. Her vision burst with pictures of tranquil waters, of the shimmer of the moon over the lapping edge of the ocean. Grabbing another breath, she thought she could actually find the tang of the salt in the air, feel the coolness of the sea breeze on her skin. Her eyes fluttered closed as she welcomed the diversion, for the moment singularly trusting him as he displaced each raw feeling with something simpler, gentler, and she let herself fall into the feeling, craving the peace he offered.

"*Thank you,*" she replied a few moments later as her body went pliant and the last of the pain flowed away, as though the thoughts themselves were being blown away by a firm summer wind.

"*You should have never known such pain,*" his voice whispered into her mind. "*You are an amazingly strong woman to have suffered so much, yet care even more deeply about your friend's welfare before your own.*"

Her gaze flicked to Tabitha, sleeping unaware on the bed. "*She suffered even more. If any of us have the right to call it quits, she does.*"

"*Maybe,*" he intoned, as though withholding judgment. "*But what I have sensed, the strength you have, is yours. And right now, you are my only concern.*"

"*So you don't know what I was thinking?*" Rising to stare blankly at the rear wall in front of her, she waited for his answer with a knot in her stomach, wondering if it were possible. And fearing the answer.

"*No. It was the sheer sharpness of your pain and anger I felt.*" There was a pause, but he was still there, a lurking warmth, a long-lasting hug kind of feeling when he imparted, "*Whenever you feel it becoming overwhelming again, reach for me, call my name, and I will find you. I can help you. Don't let yourself suffer alone again. Promise me."* The deepness of his tone, the seriousness, felt real, that he meant what he said, what he was offering. Unfettered aid.

Could she rely on this person, someone she hadn't even met yet? Could she trust herself to him like this? Somehow, she actually found herself wanting to, wanting to move forward on the road he presented. He'd helped her the night before, like tonight, without question, without hesitation. What she was really asking herself was, could she trust him?

"I promise." It was the beginning of a deeper healing.

chapter five

MUFFLED voices floated up the stairs to Lily from the first floor. She'd slept for several hours when they'd finally arrived at the new house they would be calling home, unable to do more than heave her exhausted body into a bedroom and pass out. Then, she had kept Tabitha company, reading most of the afternoon until she first heard someone in the front room. Now, she stood inside Tabitha's bedroom door, trying to hear without being obvious, but couldn't well enough to know what they were discussing. Considering the lowered tones, it couldn't have been good. Considering how they'd had to flee, leaving the danger behind, she knew it wasn't. Leaning a little closer to the frame, she tried to hear more, reaching for even a snippet of conversation.

"Hi, Lily."

She whirled. Her heart shot into her throat.

Nathan held up his hands, freezing to the floor a few paces away. “Sorry. Didn’t mean to scare you,” he said with complete earnestness.

She gave him a shaky attempt at a laugh, dismissing the hard thumping of her heart, or trying to. “It’s okay. I didn’t hear you.” Of course not. She’d been too busy trying to eavesdrop on what was happening one storey down.

“How’s she doing?” He tossed a glance over Lily’s shoulder into the room behind her where Tabitha lay unconscious.

“No better.” Despondent over that very fact, her shoulders sagged a little.

“Hey.” His voice dropped, rich with concern, flowing around her with understanding. “She’s going to make it.”

“I wish I shared your optimism.”

“You do. You don’t recognize it anymore. You’re the most dedicated friend I’ve ever seen. If you believed she didn’t have a chance, you wouldn’t sit with her every night.” Boyish charm flitted across his features, then disappeared as if his words embarrassed him. Except, if she hadn’t known any better, she could’ve sworn she caught the slightest sliver of sadness in his gaze before he turned on that grin. The same grin that had been one of the constants of their freedom. Nathan was one happy kind of guy.

“I’m on my way down,” he said, giving away nothing of his thoughts.

"It's about the attack, isn't it? What they're discussing?" She felt her heart thud against her ribs, awash in layers of trepidation, but she had to know.

He ran a hand over his spiky blond hair. "Yeah, and if Diego was pissed by the attack, this is going to make him furious."

"I want to know." She could protect herself better if she understood what was happening. She already knew her pursuer intimately. She refused to let herself be at that bad of a disadvantage ever again.

"I don't blame you," he told her, not sounding in the least surprised. He looked directly at her, seeming to debate his next words, then finally saying, "You should know. Joaquin is here."

She blinked and stared at him, her body trembling now for an entirely different reason, and dread was nowhere to be found. Her mouth suddenly felt like it had been stuffed with cotton balls. "He is?"

"He arrived with Diego today," he explained. She'd been unaware of what time any of them had arrived because she'd slept for so long.

Instantly, her thoughts were tumbling, racing, and confused. He was there? Why? Had he followed her? Them? She didn't believe he was intent on jeopardizing them—he'd ensured their escape the night before. Then, why was he there?

"Well, that's easy enough to answer. To meet you."

She managed to stifle the gasp of surprise in her throat, but her widened eyes snapped to the stairs as if drawn to the one man who lay out of her sight. "*Quit that!*" His rebuttal was a low, rumbling chuckle.

"Come on," Nathan invited with his easy going smile and a rolled shoulder, apparently unaware of the discussion happening between her and that mysterious, disembodied voice. "You're awake. Might as well hear it, too."

She nodded, suddenly wary of Nathan's news. His jovial attitude didn't hide the apprehension or concern over what he was about to share. Cautious of the coming moments, and the unknown man downstairs, she left Tabitha's door half closed and trailed behind Nathan.

JOAQUIN felt the need to hold his breath, but hadn't breathed out of necessity in centuries. He was going to meet the owner of that lovely voice. Finally. Since the first words, the shout that had stunned his mind enough to freeze him, he'd wanted only this. Every word had heightened this one need. Someone like Lily had never happened to him in his long life. The world that was unveiling before him was as unexpected as she was.

Last night she had been incredible, a strength to admire, giving him a focus within the bus without hesitation to keep its immense size ensconced in his whirled shadows. The storm had been extra, but had done its job, forcing visibility to be nonexistent.

He'd fed to replenish his weakened body not long after Diego intercepted the bus, then with Tani safely with the travelers, the two men had wreaked a nightmare of havoc on the force of soldiers. The night had passed with a grim satisfaction. There was no real enjoyment in destroying traces or proof, only in the knowledge those men would never see the dawn again. Diego had destroyed all the electronic equipment with a power that had shocked Joaquin, a strength he'd never seen, and was too thankful he'd never felt the need to turn it fully on him. He'd learned in no short order to respect the other man's depth of powers and knowledge as they worked side by side, silently slaughtering the ones who wanted to find the women who, even then, were asleep over his head. He knew for certain at least three were.

Though, the only person he was concerned with who wasn't asleep stood partially hidden behind another vampire a few steps from the bottom of the staircase. Joaquin made no move to approach her, even though anticipation made it hard for him to stand still, eagerness buzzing through his blood like an unending burst of energy.

Delayed shock and disbelief infiltrated his scrutiny when he realized there *was* another of the Brethren on the stairs. He slanted Diego a look. Just how many Brethren were involved in this? In his long life, Joaquin had never seen two for any length of time. Yet, here he stood with Diego holding Titania protectively at his side, and now this young blood. He was as close to baffled as he'd ever been.

"Nathan," Diego greeted the young man as he neared.

"Good to see you made it," he said with a chuckling laugh that seemed to lighten his youthful, swaggering steps. This vampire was too young to have such a travesty happen to him. To have been transformed to Brethren. It wasn't a situation he would have wished on any person.

Nathan swung toward Joaquin. "Hey." He greeted him as if he belonged there.

Joaquin was still unsteady in this situation and could only wait to see what happened next. He merely dipped his head in answer.

"You cool with this?" Nathan asked Diego, inferring with a shrug whether or not to include Joaquin in the discussion.

"He is welcome," Diego replied. "He may not take on the fight, but he is a friend."

Nathan shrugged, apparently eased with the declaration.

"Come on, Lily," Tani encouraged, beckoning her to join them. "You could be a huge help on this. You remember the most from your stay with Tenorio."

She rolled her shoulders, stiffening her spine with an indrawn breath, then walked the rest of the way into the living room. "I'll help you no matter what it takes," she told them, her gaze as clear as her voice. "You know that."

"This is Joaquin," Diego said, watching their reactions, unmoving in his scrutiny.

Lily stopped only a few feet from him, illuminated in the light, her eyes wide and unblinking as she finally put a face to the voice, the same as he.

And her face was beautiful.

Thick waves of russet and sunset hair flowed over her shoulders in disobedient curls. Eyes the color of ocean-kissed sand watched him, and when she parted her lips on a slow breath, they reminded him of the summer tulips he'd seen during travels through Europe. She was tall, which was probably the largest surprise. He hadn't expected her to be voluptuous, or so lovely. His own preconceived images were nothing compared to the real woman's beauty. At that moment, it was a good thing he didn't breathe.

She would have stolen it from him.

Two casual paces forward stopped him well short of her space, and he simply bowed. "It is an honor to meet you at last, Lily. You will never know what hearing your voice two nights ago did for me, but I am forever and always indebted to you," he said with a total lack of pretentiousness, stating nothing less than the truth. This woman should never know the whispered sound of a lie ever again.

She moved forward, narrowing the gap even more, and held out her hand, her eyes never leaving his face. "Thank you for your help last night. We never would have had a chance without it."

Delicately, as if holding a precious bloom, he gathered her hand, the smooth skin pressed deliciously against his own. "I made a promise to you. I do not break promises." Then, before the tremor he felt against his palm could become too noticeable and expose the fear he felt all but arcing off her skin, he released her with a lingering brush of warmth. What surprised him more was the sensation of her skin against his. He'd known she would be special, but he hadn't expected to this extent.

"Tell us what you found, Nathan," Diego said bringing everyone's attention to the moment at hand, the request more an order. By his expression, Diego wasn't expecting anything good.

Nathan sat down when Diego did, his hands hanging limply between his knees where he slumped. "It's not good. Those two screens you brought were GPS navigational trackers." Diego nodded as if he wasn't expecting anything different. Joaquin watched them all, keeping an eye on Lily as the tension continued to ratchet higher and higher with Nathan's report. She sat quietly, staring directly at Nathan as nearly indiscernible flashes of horror darkened her eyes and paled her cheeks. "The screens themselves couldn't tell me much. I did, however, discover what they were tracking."

Titania tucked herself tighter against Diego as he nodded, ready to hear the worst.

"One of the rescuees has an embedded GPS chip somewhere on their person. They both read the chip's location to within less than a hundred feet in radius. We may have set him back but..." He flashed Lily an apologetic look. "We're sitting ducks again."

"Is there any way to find out who it is?"

Joaquin studied Diego's expression. Firm, controlled. He would do anything to protect those under his care. It raised him higher in Joaquin's estimation. The confusion he'd felt was slowly dissipating. Just because he'd never encountered a situation like this changed nothing. The fact was, Brethren were living with, and protecting, humans whom they had taken into their care. He didn't let his attention for Lily drop even so.

"We can send them all to different locations and see who has it. The problem is, whoever it is, is already here." His face tightened. "The location is already in someone's hands."

A gasp whipped his gaze immediately to focus on Lily once more.

"We need to remove it," Titania said. "But how? If we take it out and drop it someplace, will they think we're moving again?"

"It's possible."

"How do we find out which of us it is?" Lily asked. Joaquin didn't hear a single break in her voice even though the strain of it was apparent in her pale features. A remembered pain flashed briefly, then as quickly disappeared from her tawny eyes. The more he watched her and the way she interacted and responded to those in the room, the less he believed Diego to be behind her pains and fears. Everything about this was all so unusual from what he knew. Even though he doubted Diego's culpability, he still silently vowed to watch over the redhead sitting ramrod stiff on the edge of the nearest couch, well away from everyone—and him. His first duty was to Lily, and her safety.

"X-ray or MRI would be the best way to locate it, but we can't take over a facility to do it. Whatever it is, it has to be tiny. Injectable." He let out a rough sigh. "Practically undetectable, if at all, would be my assumption."

"A time bomb," Lily whispered with a grimace, her lips thinning as she said it. "That is definitely his style." She met everyone's gazes, even his for a brief second. "Tenorio is one sick man. It could be any of us. We've all been injected." She shivered once, but regained her composure. "Maybe even all of us."

"Is that possible from what you got out of the trackers?"

Joaquin's gaze went from Lily to Titania and her question, her brow tight with tension and worry, equal to every person in the room.

Nathan shook his head. "It's possible, but I only found one signal."

"Then that only leaves one thing to do." Diego ran a hand over Titania's shoulders at a comforting pace. "We have to stop him before he gets here, and if we cannot, remove the beacon leading him here."

"How are we going to do that?" Lily asked, sitting up straighter, her hands clasped in front of her. It wasn't enough to hide their trembling from Joaquin. "Do the GPS systems work in reverse?" she asked Nathan hopefully.

"Unfortunately, no," Nathan replied.

Her shoulders slumped at his answer.

"Diego," Nathan said with deliberate warning in his tone. "We can find out who it is; we may never find the chip."

Silence fell across the room like the emptiness of sound after a death knell has been rung. Joaquin was sure he heard leaves falling outside in the darkness it was so quiet within the walls of the home. Watching each, it was clear everyone came to their own conclusions about the direness of their situation.

Diego shared a look with Titania, catching Joaquin by surprise, never expecting such an intimate gesture from the silent and undoubtedly intimidating leader of the group. Then, the warrior stood. His usual, even expression was drawn under the strain of the evening. "We know where Tenorio can be found. We will start there."

For some reason, Joaquin was almost sure he could also hear the tick of that time bomb along with the fall of the leaves.

"Houston and Laney will stay to guard the house," Diego continued. "Nathan, are you willing to go back with us?"

He shrugged. "I'm free." Joaquin wondered at his quipped return, but didn't judge him when his gaze was flat, yet his voice wasn't. It seemed they all had secrets. Joaquin had no room to judge. "I'll make sure the security is up. Houston knows how to work it." He tossed a glance toward Joaquin. "Is he staying?"

Suddenly, all the eyes in the room were pinned on Joaquin.

"He is a welcome guest. It is up to Joaquin." Titania offered a kind smile, a smile of warmth, welcome and friendship. He swallowed, feeling and witnessing more in the last hour than he had in so long. The last memories of his emotions were nothing more than dust.

"It's not only up to me," he silently shared with Lily. *"If, sincerely, it would not disturb you, I will gladly offer to stay."*

"I can be of help," he told the others in the room out loud to further his chances of acceptance, so he could be near if Lily needed him. She was, and remained, his sole reason, but he understood the dangers they faced were not to be minimized. Those affected everyone in the house. "I am at your disposal," he directed to Diego with a note of respect. If Joaquin was allowed to stay, he would accept Diego's law and rules. A mutual understanding was returned. That only left the one person who mattered, who hadn't said one word yet to leave a clue to her thoughts.

Lily's quiet, yet calm tones floated to him from where she sat. "I don't have a problem with it." She let out a fast breath, as if steeling her words. "I trust him." Then, she met his gaze and impaled him with a true, if only slightly, tremulous smile. She stood from her seat, stepping forward, and he rose to meet her. He restrained himself from reaching out and touching her, shaken at the swift rise of want spurring the sensation of feeling her skin within his again. There was an inner strength in the soul of the woman before him, a strength he honestly believed wasn't recognized beneath the depths of her pain.

"Thank you," she said. Inside, he bathed his soul in the sound of her voice, but knowing her fears were very close to the surface, he allowed none of it to show in his expression. Her trust was fragile. He wouldn't threaten their tenuous link.

"Then Joaquin is welcome. We will not leave before everyone in the house is familiar with his presence, but we cannot delay for long."

"Agreed." Nathan echoed Diego's consent.

"Tomorrow night then." Titania stood, her smaller frame all but enveloped beneath her husband's long embrace. The fact that they did consider themselves husband and wife still rocked Joaquin's perceptions of what he knew about the Brethren.

"I need to check on Tabitha," Lily said, turning, saying nothing else to climb the stairs.

"I guess that leaves me to give you a room," Nathan said to Joaquin. Diego led Titania out the front door without another word. Joaquin's place had been decided. He was welcome, and for the woman disappearing up those stairs, he was staying.

Joaquin's gaze followed her as she ascended the stairs, jeans wrapped around long legs, and a dark blue sweatshirt under the fall of her hair. The rolling waves reached to the middle of her back, the red and golden hues glinting in the light from overhead. The vibrant curls seemed to gather the light and play with it, sending the glittering beams out into the world in a plethora of color.

Just when he thought he had reached the end of his time on earth, redemption for his failures appeared out of the darkest night. He could help Lily. He could ensure her safety, her happiness. He could do for her what he had failed to do for Angelica. And when she was safe, he would walk into the sunrise, as he was meant to do, what he should have done long before now. He hadn't been looking for redemption in this life, believing the penance he had paid over the centuries had been payment for his sins. Maybe he had finally proven himself enough to accept this challenge, accept his true redemption, which was currently disappearing through a doorway on the second floor. Or maybe even this was his reward for paying his debt to his wife's death. Either way, he had heard Lily's pain, the same way she had heard his. He couldn't turn his back on her now.

She had given him purpose again. After centuries of his own kind of hell, something inside of him was reaching out for this woman who had truly suffered. Her pain was her own. He knew he could ease her life, protect her.

He had limitations during the sunlight hours, but the nighttime was his. It was his world, in all its dark and ugly colors. He knew how to walk through it, how to live in it. If this threat she feared should come looking for her again, none would live. That was his silent vow to her.

Except for that softest caress of her skin, he had not tasted her, yet he knew her scent, her voice, her thoughts, and it seemed to grow only stronger with each touch of his mind to hers. She thought he only knew her thoughts when she actually spoke to him, but since the first musical sound of her on his soul, he had been no less than a shadow to her own musings.

"Dude," Nathan said with a low growl of warning, now at his side.

Joaquin gave his attention to the younger man.

Meaning snapped in his eyes. "Hurt her and you're dead."

"I've already heard that warning," he mused, not at all offended. "I mean her no harm whatsoever."

Nathan tipped his head in the pugnacious way that the youth of this time seemed to understand. "Just don't forget it." He walked up the stairs and Joaquin followed until he paused at a door in the hallway. "We all have rooms," he said as he opened the door. Joaquin walked in and Nathan shut the door behind them, leaning against it. "I guess you've figured out we don't use them."

"I wasn't sure. There is a hollow beneath the house." He mentioned it offhandedly, not expecting anything other than what he knew he'd hear.

"That's Diego's lair. Trust me, you don't want to mess with him. I think he'd defy the sun itself if something threatened the girls. Anything less doesn't stand a chance."

He looked at the younger man who stood with his arms crossed, staring coolly. He never looked away. "How do they not know?" he asked, knowing what he inferred wouldn't be misinterpreted. It was one of the questions that wouldn't leave him.

Nathan shrugged. "The girls were a wreck. It took them weeks to even understand they were free. I don't think they would even really care, to be honest. They've all seen real monsters. We're tame in so many ways in comparison. Houston and Laney know. Don't mess with him either. He bites, and not in any way you'd like." Nathan flashed him a laughing grin, the one he'd seen downstairs. "He plays hard too."

"None of you use the humans?" A raw stillness sank into the room. *That* was the question he had to know. The wrong answer and he'd take Lily away without a single bone of remorse.

"None. We all leave to feed. Diego takes care of Tani. Just remember," Nathan said, laying the ground rules with a firm note. "No fun stuff where they can see you. Always scan ahead before popping in somewhere. The girls are getting used to their situation, but don't take it for granted. They still have nightmares and spook easily. No walking through walls or changing shape near the house. The grounds are safeguarded for about five miles in all directions, but Diego let you in, so they won't affect you."

"He has that kind of power?" Joaquin asked. Was that the barrier he had encountered at the cabin? Was that how they had managed to slip away, undetected by the invading forces, because they hadn't been able to get any closer because of Diego's strengths? The possibility of that much power in one being was boggling. The reality was almost frightening because, if he'd really wanted to, Diego could have killed him without lifting a finger in effort.

Nathan snorted. "Dude, you don't ever want to see the *kind* of power that man has. Let's just say, it's a good thing he's on our side."

Joaquin wasn't surprised to hear that. Nathan only confirmed it. He had a feeling what he'd seen the night before was only a fraction of what Diego was capable of. "I appreciate your help."

Nathan turned and reached for the door, pausing to look over his shoulder. He shook his head. "Dude, I'm not doing it for you. Lily would fall apart if Diego had to destroy you. Whatever happened, meeting you has done something to her. She's stronger. I can tell. She won't let anyone touch her, but she reached out to you. And she smiled. I don't think I've ever seen her smile."

A moment later, Nathan left him alone in the room to...what?

Only time would tell him if he'd made the right decision to listen to an angel's voice. What he didn't know was if this angel would lead him to his redemption, the one he truly needed, or to his own personal Hell.

chapter six

LEAVING his room to begin his nightly routine, Joaquin paused in the well lit upstairs hallway, right outside the half opened door to Tabitha's room. Lily's clear voice drifted to him as she read ceaselessly to her friend. Just as she had every night since he'd first heard her voice. Her voice wasn't musical or light. There was strength and depth in her tone, feminine but firm, a rich sound that embraced the listener. He fell under her magic charm nightly. It still caught him by surprise the same as when he'd heard her the first time, the way he felt himself become, for no better description, spellbound. She would read for hours. It didn't matter the book, or the words. It didn't matter if the woman lying in the bed didn't move. Lily read. Every night.

Catching every word, he could listen for as long as she would read. Lily was dedicated to Tabitha's recovery, and her voice was one of the sweetest sounds he had ever heard. Tonight, she was reading

Shakespeare. He leaned against the doorframe on a shoulder, not intruding to listen.

Diego, Titania, and Nathan had left only two nights before searching for Tenorio, hunting to remove the chance of any more attacks like the one at the cabin. His acceptance had come the night Nathan had explained the tracking and the embedded chip, but it was with only a very thin line of trust from Diego that he remained in the house. There was a grudging consent to leaving Joaquin behind in their place, and he had received his fair share of warnings before they had departed. Understanding the birth of their mistrust, he didn't take offense. He would have likely done the same in Diego's place. His protectiveness toward those in this house was genuine. In that, he and Diego were the same.

Joaquin woke every night as he had for centuries, except now, he awakened aware he'd been given a second chance at deliverance for his mistakes so long ago with Angelica. His purpose was clear now after he'd spent a few nights in her company. Lily must be kept safe. No matter how difficult or impossible the task seemed, it was his purpose now. Where he'd failed before, this time, there was no room for it.

The bitterness he should have felt was cold and faint when he thought of his long lost wife. He'd suffered for long, soul-numbing months after the wreck of the Manila Galleon *Nuestra Señora de Ayuda* in 1641 off the Catalina Islands. Barely surviving the wreckage, he had reached the mainland physically drained and emotionally destroyed after watching his beloved wife wither and perish on the long, arduous journey across the seas. Then, when there had been no life, no reason to continue, he saw death coming and had welcomed it. He had wept, thinking he had finally been forgiven and he would soon be in his *Angelita's* arms again.

Instead, the Devil had played with his soul and had made him pay for his sins and failings in the worst imaginable way. To live as he was, a monster, the undead creature of timeless fable, the kind told to children when they did not want to listen to their *Doña* at bedtime. He paid for his sin every night, for allowing his love to die on that journey. He should have taken better care of her, kept her safe. The guilt never left him, no matter how hard he tried to forget.

He should have died, not her. She'd had family in California, expecting them both to join them and start a new life in the new world and untamed country.

Neither had ever arrived at the *rancho*. She was gone, and he was the myth of nightmares, walking when he shouldn't be. Paying for his failures as a husband and as a man to the woman he loved for all eternity. And here he was, circled back again to weigh the want to end his life as a soulless wraith, or to remain, to learn how deep the perfection he saw in Lily ran.

Watching Lily care for her friend, he knew her perfection ran deep. The sorrow and pain he felt when she spoke to him, when she let her defenses down enough to link her mind to his, was hard to hide. He knew it was there. Diego had been firm. It was her choice to tell him what had happened. No one, none of the women or David, were to have their privacy invaded for any reason. That was unquestionable. He remembered clearly the discussion they'd shared before Diego had left.

"Do others invade often?" Joaquin asked after Diego had taught him the intricate wards camouflaging the house within the embrace of the wilderness surrounding them. Diego's ease with the magic created more questions, but he withheld them for the moment. Remembering the protections was the important thing, not curing his curiosity.

Diego moved with a fluid, confident kind of grace, the black leather trencher he wore swirling around him. He was a commanding figure. Joaquin stood at just over six feet and Diego was taller still. The man carried himself with a regal bearing, an assurance in himself Joaquin knew only came from hard earned experience. There was no doubt Diego had once been a great warrior. Considering the battle he'd witnessed during the invasion on his home, he still was.

"No. We are far from the major cities to keep the girls safe. It is paramount they heal."

"What happened to them?" Joaquin had known there was something hidden in Lily's deepest thoughts, wrapped tightly in a blanket of fear, something in her past that affected all of them. Learning Diego had not been responsible for it compelled him to understand her deep seated fear better.

"It is not my place to tell you," he replied after a deliberate pause. "Do not pry at Lily. It will be her choice to tell you, or not."

Joaquin heard the hidden truth in those words. Lily needed control in her life. "I will not." And he'd upheld that vow, even though every part of him ached to ease the pain she suffered from. His one intrinsic ability. The one gift that had given him a remarkable ability to calm horses, a love of his and his wife's. He'd been an exceptional breeder and trainer.

He swallowed the cruel memory down into the pit of his history. *Had been.* Now they wouldn't let him near without mind manipulation. Most prey animals wouldn't. They knew a predator when they saw one. He'd had no need for his one special gift in his silent world. Until now. The ability he hadn't needed made him very sensitive to Lily's flares of anger and pain with this unusual bond he'd formed with her. Especially when he was close to her.

The night they'd fled the cabin, distance had made the thread between them weaker, stretched, yet he'd still felt her intense trembling as though he sat right next to her. It had frustrated him that when she had almost imploded on the bus, the single embrace of comfort was the most he could offer.

Even now, he didn't feel it had been enough. Those fears and angers were held tight, behind a locked part of her mind she hadn't let anyone into. He didn't blame her for not wanting to pull them up to be examined or extinguished. The little he'd already unintentionally stumbled across had churned his stomach with its viciousness.

Her strength, her determination to go on after living through so much agony, awed him. Humbled him.

Because he had wanted nothing more than to die when he'd heard her voice. Yet, she would defy any threat to live, to stand beside her friend and keep her alive. Joaquin had never met her level of resilience in any other person, man or woman, ever.

His perusal of Tabitha's room showed it was similar to the one he had been given, except for the medical equipment. Simple in style with pale colors on the walls and floor, even on the curtains to give it an airy, welcoming feeling. Large windows opened to the wildness outside, currently showing a brilliant sky of glittering diamonds in a cloudless sky. A sky he had just visited on his return from the closest town to fulfill his waking needs. It felt odd, but somehow comforting that when he returned nightly, he slipped through his bedroom window and unlocked his door to emerge as the nighttime watcher as though he'd been in that room all along. All signs of normalcy were given to make himself and the others seem human. Gifted, but still human.

Movement brought his gaze to Lily as she closed the book to set it aside. She brushed blonde hair away from Tabitha's face even though its shorter length was in no danger of causing her problems where she lay so still on the bed.

Then, Lily spoke. "You know, I never expected to see the outside again. I honestly thought I would die in that cage."

He straightened from his casual pose, letting his arms relax to his sides. "You don't have to talk about it if you don't want to." *Cage?* Just what had she lived through?

"I just want Tabitha to wake up," she said with a wealth of emotion clogging her throat, making the words hoarse. "I think if I thought I was on the verge of drawing my last breath, that I was going to die the next time someone touched me, it would be hard for me to wake up too." She took a steadying breath. "I know I can't give up on her."

"Your care, and the others' will help her heal, Lily," he offered, unsure what kind of comfort she needed or how much to give. Except for the one handshake they'd shared, he hadn't touched her. He believed she'd drawn the strength to allow his touch because she had been surrounded by friends, and he hoped he'd never given her a threatening sensation. He hadn't let a single flicker show that he'd felt, sensed and tasted her fear in that simple, congenial contact. He hadn't touched her since, and had given everyone ample space to never feel crowded or encroached upon. It was taking time to ease himself into the rhythm of the home, but the others were growing accustomed to him. Patience was one thing he did have in abundance. And time. It didn't insult or anger him when Kathy or Amy raised a questioning stare in his direction. He was what he was, but he was still a gentleman and he treated them all with respect. He hoped, in time, they could all find the peace that they deserved. After what he'd encountered from Lily alone, he knew they were due.

She nodded at his words. "Tani said she only needs time. I know she's right." Raising her hands upward, she tugged the waves of hair where it had fallen to cover her cheeks, hiding her away from him. "But it doesn't make it any easier to watch her like this night after night." Desolation darkened those tawny eyes when she finally rose to look in his direction. "I think she's given up. Just when things are improving."

"Titania is right. She will have time here. She is in there." He flicked a look to the woman sleeping on the bed, sensing her, but not seeking or intruding as he'd promised. "She is tired, and scared. She will have to find the strength to wake up to see if her world has changed on her own, to decide what she'll be able to do with it." It only took a moment longer studying her in return to realize why Lily was so distraught. "You've been trying to reach her, haven't you?" he asked gently. In her own world of pain and fury, she was trying to reach out to her friend. Just like she had with him.

Her head wobbled as she admitted it with a stilted, guilt-laden movement, avoiding his searching looks. He walked close enough to see her face and noticed the shadows under her eyes for the first time. “Have you been sleeping?” A dismissive shoulder roll was her reply. He wanted her to answer him on her own. He meant what he’d said. Only if she wanted to. It would be her choice whether she revealed herself to him or not. He enveloped the words in a soothing timbre, wanting to do more, wanting to wrap her into a safe ball of cotton to keep the world from hurting her more.

A hesitant catch in her voice drew him a step closer. “No, I haven’t been sleeping.”

Joaquin remembered what Nathan had explained to him that first night. *Nightmares*. He was sure they all suffered. Being a vampire, the most he lived with was a vision on his mind that he could wake with when the sun set. There were no dreams. Not any longer. Slowly, he watched her relax as he did what he could, exuding the comfort he knew she needed, managing to not touch her in the process, even though he wasn’t prepared for how hard it was not to touch her, to help her the way he intrinsically knew he could. Physical touch would have expedited the aid. In the end, the result was the only thing on his mind as he poured himself into helping her.

The small clock on the dresser ticked while the strain apparent in her body and on her features seemed to melt away. Lifting her hands, she scrubbed them over her face, then drew a deep breath. "How do you do that?" Wide eyes met his when her hands fell. "It's almost as if you can take it all away."

"Almost. It's the one gift I was born with." The only one he'd actually thought of as a gift until he'd been cursed, and then, even his gift was useless. Until now. Until Lily, he'd never even known humans responded to it. He'd always directed it to the animals he'd trained. Three hundred years ago, he wouldn't have ever considered using it on another human being. When he'd helped her the first time, he'd done it in instantaneous reaction. Without thinking of if it would work, without thought to repercussions or worries about if it would backfire. Simply, he had to help her the only way he knew how. Keeping her talking, she hadn't been aware of his subtle touch. Now that he knew she did respond to it, he would do anything to help her. No one deserved to exist in the living hell he knew she kept hidden from the world. A hell he'd caught in glimpses. Considering how close Lily was to the woman on the bed, it was a miracle she hadn't fallen into the same mindless non-existence to escape her pain. He didn't blame either woman for their personal answers to their suffering.

Only, he was drawn to the one before him in a way that confused him, thrilled him, and made him feel alive for the first time since he'd died.

"Your gift," she mused. "It must be."

"Must be what?" he asked, seeking her expressions again, the planes of her cheeks, the studying gleam in her eyes. The parted softness of her lips. He found it difficult to look away from her open guilelessness.

"Must be why I can be here with you and not feel threatened." She tilted her head, obviously examining him and that very fact. He remembered their meeting, when he had held her hand, and knew she was remembering as well. Breaking down how she had managed to do it when she had wanted to run the other way out of reflex.

"I can't stand to have any of the guys touch me." A shudder visibly slid over her frame. She went on as if it hadn't happened. "It's hard for me to be in the same room with them, no matter who else is there. No one or everyone. I know I'm safe, but..." The words trailed off, and he wasn't going to press.

"Do you trust that I won't hurt you?" He'd never thought anyone's acceptance would matter again, but hers did.

Like a breeze lingering in the room, he felt the brush of her gaze as she looked into his eyes, followed her as she searched his face and saw everything she needed to know right in front of her.

"Yes," she finally answered him. "I do believe you. You're different." Moistened lips came together, her eyes glistening as her mind worked.

If you only knew how much. The caustic thought never reached her, but he couldn't restrain it either.

The next three nights, he followed the same routine. Walking out of his bedroom to saunter down the hall to lean and listen to the woman next to the bed as she poured her strength into Tabitha through her words.

Thick, red hair fell like a waterfall against her shoulders and back. He found himself drawn to the colors more and more until he realized why. Those colors reminded him of the brilliance of the sunset he'd never see again, shades of deep red and gold, a natural blending much like Mother Nature's artwork. With the length cascading around her in ripples and waves, the richness was breathtaking. Discovering what was prompting the comparison only drew him to the vibrant colors more. She was a work of art from the colorful curls of her hair to the sandy tones of her eyes to the cream lightness of her skin. Lily was not frail, nor was she anything less than feminine. He hoped some day to share his visions of how he saw her with her. He knew she would never believe a word of it now.

He listened, unmoving and silent, until she stopped reading, then Joaquin stood away from the wall.

"How are you this evening?" he asked.

She stretched, rolling her neck. "Better. I can't remember the last time I've slept so well, but the last three days have been incredible." Marking the page in the book, she placed it on the table by Tabitha's bed.

He hid his pleasure and his smile. She didn't have to know he'd been helping her. She needed the rest to heal. He couldn't ignore her need, and resisting his desire to help her was futile.

"No nightmares?" He didn't bother to hide all of his concern. He found himself honestly caring for her answer.

She blinked, then focused on him. "No. Not one," she answered, a little surprised, as if realizing she hadn't had one in several nights.

He nodded. That was all he needed to know. Since he couldn't follow through on his first impulse—to take her away from the threats and danger, he ensured she could heal. There was also little doubt, after watching her the last three nights that she wouldn't willingly leave her friend behind. There was a forged bond between them. A bond he could respect, a survivor's bond. The deep bond of soldiers in the battlefield. So he did the only thing he could. He stayed, and helped.

Lily just didn't know it.

"I need to walk outside," he said, making his voice neutral. He'd already searched the surrounding woods and knew it was quiet. It appeared to be the perfect opportunity to allow Lily room to reawaken to the world surrounding her. "Would you like to join me?"

Tension stiffened her shoulders. He didn't say what came to the tip of his tongue. That she could trust him. That he would die before he would hurt her, or any of the women. The choice had to be hers. She had to find the strength, and realize the truth. That she was safe.

"I haven't been outside yet," she replied, her voice subdued. Gradually, the tension in her shoulders lessened without his involvement.

"The skies are clear. You should be able to see quite a few stars."

A wistful shadow flowed over her face. "I haven't seen them in years. I've been watching the sunsets and sunrises every day I can." A fierce streak of courage glowed in her eyes, hiding the pain of what the truth of those words meant. "I missed too many."

He gestured toward the stairs with a gallant bow. "After you, then. I see no reason to miss another night."

A spear of pleasure pulsed through him as her lips lifted in answer. "I think I'd like that."

Conscious of her need to not feel crowded, he followed a couple paces behind as he let her lead the way downstairs.

LILY heard the door close, separating her from the rest of all she knew. She jerked to a stop on the front porch, her gaze sweeping from side to side, taking in every detail. Shadows shuddered beneath the trees, a slow breeze weaving and rocking leaves and limbs. At a glance, those shadows held an eerie, apparition-like quality, but a blink, a heartbeat later, and they were nothing but shadows, nothing but the sway and swing of the trees in front of her.

She released a slow breath, twisting her neck to relax. There was nothing there that wasn't there during the day. There was nothing there that hadn't been there the day before.

"Is this the first time you've been outside?" he asked, stopping a pace or two away on the next step down. His consideration to always give her ample space wasn't lost on her. Where he stood below her, the light from the house illuminated his features. Midnight dark eyes with jet black lashes encircling them. Masculine, though thinner, cheekbones, a firm set to his lips that spoke of willpower and strength while every word relayed his gentle nature. He was several inches taller than her, long legs and narrow hips with an athletic body. There was no doubt he was a man of strength hidden within the sinewy length of his frame. She was just as positive he would die before he ever entertained the idea of harming her or anyone else in the house. His patience as she came to terms with being outside for the first time was proof. He wasn't prodding her to move in the least. She calmed the surge of her heart with only a little effort. It was getting easier to find a calm as each day passed.

"Since we've been here? Yes," she replied. "It took a couple days to get organized and settled. Stepping out here didn't seem very important."

Drawing a deep draught of the cool mountain air, she could taste the pine on her tongue it was so fresh. The air itself held an invigorating strength, filling her lungs with pure nature. "It is lovely out here," she said a moment later, relishing the languid relaxation of the moment.

"There's a clear spot a short distance from the garage where you can see miles of open sky," he told her. "It's beautifully breathtaking. Even the mountains are crystal clear." He tipped a shoulder in light coercion.

"I'd like to see it." What surprised her was, she meant it. She wanted to do things, enjoy the freedom she had now. She never wanted to take it for granted again.

He nodded and walked to the bottom of the steps, letting her join him at her own pace. The nighttime was beautiful in the wilderness. There hadn't been much time to enjoy it, or daytime for that matter, at the cabin. She refused to acknowledge the tremors of nervousness or let them get a grip on her, a chilling fear that could make her falter.

Tabitha wasn't the only one who needed time. At least now, she really felt she'd have a chance to get it. She was free, no longer staring at inch-thick steel bars. She detested those bars with every ounce of her being, despising the men who had kept her locked within them.

"It will get better."

"You're in my mind again." She shot him a reproachful look, but she doubted he'd seen it from where she followed, nearly behind him. The sway of his straight black hair kept pace with his even stride, swishing evenly over his shoulders. He cut through the shadows of the trees as though he'd done so numerous times, her words not even slowing him.

She followed his steps through the shrouded undergrowth of the woods.

He shrugged without apology. “You can do the same. I’ve offered myself freely and openly. You only need to look to see what I am thinking, or feeling.”

Her first thought was that walking over his thoughts was something she couldn’t do, then realized she had, more than once. “Why would you do that?”

“Simple. You can’t trust what you can’t examine right now.” He paused his stride and turned. He lifted a hand between them, casting a curious look at his flat palm. “Like this. Your first expectation would be my intent is to hurt you, to strike you.”

Dark and sincere, his eyes found hers. There was no condemnation in them for her fears. She stiffly nodded when she couldn’t deny he was right.

“I have never, nor would I ever, strike a woman. You don’t know that.” With a delicate touch, he formed his palm around her jaw, caressing her skin in the coolness of his own. “I know how hard it is to stand there and accept this, even when it is meant only in friendship. I felt your terror when you let me hold your hand the night I met you. I see it now.” Eyes that swirled with the shifting light of the surrounding shadows never blinked. “That is why I hide nothing from you. If you don’t want me to know your thoughts, you can always erect the barriers you have in the past. I will not force them.”

With a gentle stroke, he brushed his thumb across her cheek, then let his hand fall away. Her breath left her in a slow pulse of sensation when he did stroke her. She had forgotten what true tenderness and empathy felt like. It burned she was so hungry for it.

Resuming his pace, he began to stride again through the thick stand of trunks and wavering limbs. They'd taken no more than a few steps when her words stopped him.

"And you expect me to just believe you?"

"I don't have any expectations," he replied evenly. "You will do what you must."

She froze and raked a hand through her hair, causing the full waves to cascade around her in disarray. "Joaquin, I can't be the person I was before I was caged." There was no way to hide the stammer in her voice.

"I know." The wind rustled the leaves again, punctuating how absolutely silent the darkness was. When his voice reached out to her, she felt the way it wrapped her, cocooned her in his complete understanding. "But you can be the beautiful woman I see right now, the woman who helped an absolute stranger. The same who has stood beside her friends. You don't recognize that woman because you haven't acknowledged her yet. You fear the woman you have become because she was forced upon you. When you do, you will be free, the way you were meant to be. There is no shame in being the woman you are today."

Those words whispered away on the breeze and he started walking again. She had to blink to hide the tears his faith had dragged up unexpectedly. As much as she hated to think she was vain, it wasn't his compassion bringing tears to her eyes.

He had called her beautiful.

When she reached his side, she didn't once think about how close he was, how they almost brushed arm to arm. "I don't want to be scared, or ashamed, of what I am," she said so quietly, the words seared her throat with their brusque heat.

He looked at her, lifting the hand he'd touched her with to catch the tears off her lashes. "There is nothing to fear." One by one, he captured her tears. "The shame is not yours, lovely. It is theirs. You are strong. You never broke." He glanced away. His body tightened.

"What is it?"

"Shh," he breathed. "Listen."

She tried and couldn't hear anything but the soughing of the trees all around them. Then, she heard it. An almost silent sound, a pace, a swish. In instinctive reaction, she pressed closer to him.

"Do not fear it."

There was something in the woods they couldn't see and *he* was telling *her* to not be scared. She wanted to scream at him that he was insane, but couldn't find the words. Without warning, he twined his fingers through hers and simply walked forward. Stunned and absorbed at the same time, she followed without question.

Seconds later, she heard a low growl. The clench of his fingers wouldn't let her turn and run. In fact, he kept her moving forward toward that ominous sound. Her throat was so dry, each breath felt like she was deep in a blistering desert. She couldn't tell one tree from another. She would have only gotten lost had she tried to run. Instead, she stayed a little closer to Joaquin.

She stopped when he did. "Watch," he said close to her ear, his voice practically nonexistent. A heartbeat, two, passed. Then, she saw it as it seemed to slink out of the shadows. Her eyes widened even as her jaw tried to drop to the leaves beneath her feet.

"It's a cougar." *A large one!* The size of its paws alone would have covered her hand easily.

"A young male hunting," he confirmed.

She stifled the squeak. "Hunting? And we're standing here letting it watch us?" Scratch that. It was *nearing* them!

"Stay calm," he advised. "Let him approach. He is only curious."

She couldn't run. Her legs had turned to water when her eyes latched onto the threat bending through the fallen shadows like an apparition brought to life. "I thought wild animals avoided humans?" she whispered, leaning closer to him as the giant cat approached. A fierce-looking face tipped up, sniffing at the air, but didn't make any threatening moves or sounds. It simply picked its way forward, as if it was of no concern to cross a mountain lion's path.

"He is cautious, but not fearful. He's been around humans before. I don't think he's entirely wild."

"That's so sad. Someone will hurt him if he doesn't know to run like hell." Her fingers tightened around his as the cougar's clawed paws brought them within feet of each other. The last thing she would have wished for any creature, human or otherwise, would be to be captured or caged. Or worse.

"I am helping ease his natural wariness," he explained.

Together, they watched as the large feline sank to a haunch, then rolled to his side, offering a single grunt of unconcern. With a tender tug, Joaquin pulled her down with him when he knelt.

"Move slowly."

With a little direction, he placed her hand on a thickly furred shoulder. Shock, then wonder rifled her system. She sucked in a gasp at the muscular strength, the rich feel of the velvet coat as Joaquin let her fingers slide free from his to run over the length of the animal.

"Amazing," she said breathlessly, awed at the experience. Moments ticked by without notice as she ran her fingers up and down the cat's solid length, curving over the unmoving head. She even dared to run her fingers over richly tufted ears. The feel of a racing heart beneath her fingers when she reached ribs reminded her that this was a flesh and blood creature. Long claws unsheathed and dug into the ground as the animal arched into her caresses. He didn't purr like a housecat, but the animal didn't seem strained under the touch of her fingers either if the way his paws curled was any indication.

"He needs to be free. It would be a crime to let something happen to him because he's gotten used to prowling through people's trash."

"I fear you are right. That is what he has been doing." Joaquin searched the darkness, but for what she didn't know. "I think he's followed the small game this far with winter not too far off. Hopefully, it will be enough to spur his instincts to cease what he's been doing."

Together, they stood, giving room to the magnificent creature on the ground. The cougar rolled to its feet, then shook its tawny coat with a fierce shudder. With hardly more than a fleeting look, it bounded off into the trees.

With the cat out of sight, Lily practically bounced on her toes. "Wow. That was incredible! That was just...amazing! I've never done anything like it, not even petting zoo style. Did you see what he let us do?" Now that it was gone, giddiness made her voice pitch high.

He reached out for her. "Come. I promised you the stars tonight."

She pressed her hand into his without a qualm or a twinge of fear. She didn't even have the attention to give it a second thought. "Have you done that before?" she asked. Joaquin had been so relaxed about it. He had to have known the effect he would have on the animal.

"In a manner of speaking. In many ways, I am like the wild animals."

"In what ways?" she asked, overwhelmed with curiosity and the stolen pleasure of experiencing the cougar up close.

"Some day, I will tell you." His tugs were gentle, keeping her close to him.

She caught fleeting glimpses of his smile as they walked and knew he'd enjoyed the mountain lion as well. Joaquin was unlike many of the men she knew, and worlds apart from the men she'd spent the last three years despising. He never hid his intentions around her; every move was a deliberate action. Like the gentle touch to her face. She'd known what he was going to do, even when her nerves screamed to run because she feared what her past had taught her to expect. He was the unexpected. She didn't know when it had happened, but she was walking with him, her hand curled through his, relaxed, enjoying the darkness, a moment stolen out of time. She looked up, wondering how much further the clearing was he had told her about, when she realized, with the cougar, they must have been outside a lot longer than she'd guessed.

Watching where she was going once more, her hand in his, she asked him, "Why is it taking so long to get to the spot?" She wasn't sure how long they had been walking, but it did seem they'd been out long enough to at least reach the garage. She thought she knew where it was in comparison to the house. Or thought she did. Now, she wasn't so sure.

"My duty is to search the grounds every night for any signs of problems."

"Have there been any problems?" She searched the shadows with him, instantly becoming more attentive, but couldn't see more than a few feet into their thickest, no matter how hard she tried.

"No. I want to ensure that doesn't change." The pressure on her hand became a gentle squeeze. "Have no fear, lovely. We're almost there."

A few minutes later, she spotted the outline of the large frame garage where the bus and two of the cars used for general purposes were kept to her left. Beyond the garage and the drive winding through the trees to access it and the house, she spotted a sprawling clearing.

"Through there?" she asked, pointing. She hadn't been outside and had no idea what the terrain looked like. This was all new to her.

He nodded and led her across to stand in the middle of the clearing where the trees literally opened up as if throwing their limbs wide to show off the night sky. Trees stood as clumped sentinels around the large clearing while late fall blooms lay lost in the weave and wave of the lush grasses.

This time, her awe was no less inspired, but certainly more reverent. Stars were tossed far and wide across the night sky. Black velvet sparkling with a timeless glitter.

"Beautiful," she breathed, turning a slow circle to take it all in with her head angled up to see every twinkle, every shining diamond. "I can't remember the last time I saw so many."

"You should see them every night," he told her. "You deserve every night, forever."

chapter seven

VIBRANT red hair swayed against her back as she tipped skyward to bask in the pearlescent shimmer of the night sky. Joaquin had never encountered anything as enchanting as her absolute enjoyment in these reawakening discoveries. The luminous glow of her skin bore the radiance of the stars she admired while her lips parted in wonderment, lost in the delight of the moment. Like the joy of a young child, her every expression and breath were innocent, entranced by the multitude of timeless stars and their brilliance.

For him, they held not even a little interest when he could watch her like this. Her hand slid from his so she could turn in slow circles, to find the wide open sky above the tips of the trees in the distance.

“That’s beautiful!” she breathed, awed. His gaze followed hers. The peaks of the mountains cut like giant carved arrow points into the sky. They were several miles away, yet couldn’t compare to her as she stood under the stars’ warmth. “Almost like you could reach out and touch them." Filled with a quiet admiration, she continued to spin in small increments to take it all in.

He took an intentional step to create space between them before he followed through on his impulse and reached out for her. He knew how hard it was for her to have physical contact—he felt the tremors of fear every time he held her hand within his own. He still craved to feel her in his hold regardless, to caress the silken smoothness of her cheek, to find the alluring delicacy of her scent flowing through her hair, or her taste on his tongue.

He was aware enough to know what it was he ultimately longed for from her. A kiss. A kiss unlike any he'd tasted in centuries, unlike any he'd hungered for in his endless life. Desire, as a man desired for a woman.

There was no explanation, and he had no right to these new feelings. She was wounded. He was a walking wraith, no more than the shadows filling the boundaries of the clearing where they stood. He had no right to feel this desire, but not having the right didn't sway his hunger for her, either.

There had been no one since Angelica's death. There had been no one who had stirred his needs, made him burn with her nearness.

Yet, Lily did. He'd been drawn to her since the first sound of her voice. Not even Diego's attacks had deterred him. Now, he awoke every sunset seeking her, needing to hear her voice, to feel the beat of her heart through the bond they shared. A bond he still had no explanation for. Every touch of their minds made it stronger, brought him closer.

He watched her now as she marveled at the clear breadth of the sky, or the way she sought to simply soak up the raw majesty of the mountains in the distance. Red hair shimmered in the moonlight with hints of gold and russet as it tumbled down her spine. She wore a plain black sweatshirt and jeans, the sweatshirt making the moon glow and stars lighten her features even more.

"I never thought I'd see this again," she said without inflection, a cool, emotionless voice. It hid the reality of her feelings on the surface, or so she thought. There was no hiding from him. Not any longer.

Her tawny eyes drifted closed. "You've given me so much tonight." When they opened again, she faced him, pushing her fingers into the front pockets of her jeans. "I can be the woman I am, starting tonight. I can see it now, I can see me. I can't remember when I wasn't terrified of everything, of every single touch. I don't want to be like that any longer. I want to be me."

He hated hearing the anguish in her words, her innocence savagely stripped in a way she never should have known. He stepped forward until there were only a few thin inches between them.

She raised her chin, allowing her gaze to rove over his entire face. Reaching out, she found one of his hands and held it cupped within hers. A shiver of awareness slid up his arm to curve over his shoulders until the hunger he'd been battling settled at the base of his neck. For a man who rarely felt any temperature other than what he created for himself, he felt flushed.

"This. Even this was impossible for me."

"What do you feel?" He knew what he was feeling, but refused to let her know what her innocent discoveries were doing to him.

"I don't feel fear. I don't feel disgust. I feel..." The tawny orbs of her eyes found his once more and he wanted to fall into them. He'd never hated his not-living state as much as he did in that moment. "I feel kindness. I feel concern. I feel friendship." Glancing down when she did, her thumb stroked him, as if cataloguing the unique textures of their combined touch. "I feel, Joaquin," she finally said in a low voice, her eyes locked on their joined hands. "That is an incredible gift, and because of you, I am strong enough to embrace it again. Because of what you have shown me, what Tani and Diego and Houston have shown me, I can move forward again."

She was killing him, so slowly, so wonderfully. Without thinking about what he was doing, he cupped her cheek again with his free hand and luminous watchful eyes shot up to his.

He knew without asking this time what she felt. There was surprise—it was in her gaze. There was a hint of wariness in the rapid pants slipping between her parted lips, but the outright fear and terror he had witnessed on the nights before had faded into a place where she could either control it, or dismiss it.

The gentle sway of the breeze through the trees created a timeless music. Chirps of the nighttime insects filled the swollen silence between them, the two of them lost for a breathless moment.

Creamy skin slid beneath his thumb when he grazed her cheek, the same as she had done to his hand. "*You're incredible. Beautiful.*" The words were no less of a caress than his touch.

She blinked, breaking the connection, dropping those spell-spinning eyes to look down once more. "I'm not beautiful. I'm a wreck, Joaquin."

"You're wrong. I see courage and that makes you beautiful to me." Holding her chin firmly, he raised her, making it impossible for her to avoid his gaze.

"I'm scarred," she stated coldly, twisting out of his hand to expose them. Anger glittered now in her eyes. Anger and pain brightened by a thin veil of tears. He wanted to annihilate the men who'd caused those tears with an intensity that shocked him.

With a subtle touch, he traced the myriad of thin lines crisscrossing her jaw and down her neck with the tips of his fingers until he stopped at the top of her collar, right over her pulse. She didn't move at all. If it had been possible, he knew he would have felt dizzy, touching the delicious pounding of her heartbeat beneath his fingers. There wasn't an actual hunger prodding him. That had been relieved as soon as he'd awakened. Touching her now, right there in this secret moment stolen out of life, created something deeper within him, clawing at him to discover this new treasure. To make them complete.

He yanked his attention to the moment. He had vowed to Diego as part of his tentative allegiance to never take from her. He would never jeopardize his salvation, or hers. “I knew they were there, lovely. They matter little to me.”

She jerked away from his touch, but held his hand still in her own, gripping it painfully in emphasis, turning to avoid his stare. “I’m like this everywhere, Joaquin. There isn’t a part of me that isn’t scarred.”

“Do you really think they are all I see when I look at you?” he chastised her gently. Sliding his fingers into the wealth of her hair, he stopped her retreat. “I see them as much as I see the burning red of your hair, or the brightness in your eyes. They are nothing to fixate on, no more important to me than your own fingers.” He purposely caressed and curled around the hand holding his until she relaxed. “If I were covered with scars from my life, would it make me a different person than the one who is here now?”

“No!” She was quick to deny it, whipping up to pierce him with her total conviction.

“Then why do yours control who you are?”

Lashes lowered, hiding her thoughts.

He tilted her face again when her answer never came. “Lily, they don’t. They do not *make* you the person you are. Their meaning would have been no different than if I’d been dragged by the horses I trained.”

If her face could pale more in the bright starlight, it did. The heat and anger coursing through her blanched her features until the depth of pain she lived with daily was nothing but a glitter of hard diamonds reflected in her eyes. The first wave of her memories almost knocked him off his feet when the sudden release of the vile atrocities poured free of her restraints.

"I was belted down and sliced, Joaquin. Chained and whipped." Black rage made her snarled words sharp, savage, cutting through the night like the emotional dagger they were meant to be. "I was raped, too many times to count. Needles, belts, knives, fists." She ripped her head up, dislodging his hand completely, her mouth a twisted slash against the whiteness of her skin. "That is how they happened. I was a prisoner. A lab rat."

"All because of this! Because I can talk to you with my mind."

"I think that makes it a hell of lot worse than anything else concocted on this planet. I was *forced* to endure, not by accident." A heavy silence fell with her rage, vibrating around them like a mirage heat wave in the air.

"That is what they freed you from?" Joaquin found he could barely speak, his entire being locked in shock under the weight of her truth. He stood, frozen, overwhelmed by the avalanche of her tortures.

His anger ripened as her pain, her assaults, crashed into him with no barriers, with no walls of preservation keeping her memories behind locked doors where she had been hiding them. Like the opening of Pandora's box, everything surrounded him with a sudden impact without warning, without surcease. Images of blood, waves of screams that shook his mental stability. Every instance of pain was replayed in detail, every moment freed for him to witness with the steel control she'd wielded completely stripped. Tortures Joaquin hadn't even thought still existed had been used on the woman before him. And she carried those memories with her every day.

"That, and more. So much more." She whimpered, beaten once more from the inside out.

His life was forever changed because of what she'd held so deeply inside. He'd never had a clue, respecting Diego's wishes to not pry, and not delving where he felt Lily wouldn't appreciate the invasion. Being right wasn't helping soothe his inability to strike out at those who had hurt her so savagely, when even he had never guessed the depths of her pains, hadn't even been close to knowing the agony she'd lived through, lived with. And he felt powerless to help her in the way she needed to heal. There was no way he could avoid the boil of her fury as it rose up, suddenly free of her constraints, or the rise of his own anger with her explanation sitting like a giant venomous snake between them, ready to strike either of them. Now he knew why Diego had insisted their privacy be kept. Horrors like these demanded retribution. A punishment he would gladly pay back for her.

He'd been so focused on his own liberation, on his own goals, he'd arrogantly dismissed the kind of hell she'd seen. Helping her heal was one way he could help her. He wouldn't stop offering his support, but the fact remained, it was a selfish means to an end. Now, when he knew the truth, he wanted to destroy those who had laid even one finger on her. The urge to find each and every one and slowly torture them for the cruelties she'd suffered made the retribution to the force that had attacked the cabin a simple night of practice. Now he knew what it was that tortured her every waking and sleeping moment, what he'd felt those nights when he was too far away to do more than give her his strength. A resurgence of a pain no person, man or woman, should ever be made to endure.

Slowly, she slackened, her hand gentling where she clutched him. He hadn't even noticed the bite of her nails slicing into his skin with the pulsating flood of emotion surrounding them, shackling them together within the nightmare of her past. Lifting her free hand, she pressed it flat to his chest as though supporting herself against his frame, too tired to stand alone. Or maybe to push him away, but there wasn't any force in it.

Without another word, he slipped his fingers into her hair again, releasing her hand to embrace her shoulders, tugging her into his body without an ounce of strength, the need subliminal. She didn't resist his gentle urging. Her weight cradled willingly against his chest with her cheek pressed to him. He gave thanks she hadn't looked up at him again. There was little doubt the fire of his anger was blazing in his gaze. It nearly consumed him, yet his hold was nothing less than tender, protective. Not a hint of his emotional battle was revealed in his stance, in his touch. If she had any idea how much he was hiding, she wouldn't have been so acquiescent in his hold.

Several moments passed with her curved into his body, her heat rolling over him, and he soaked it up as though his body thirsted for it. Another new sensation he only wished he had the time to examine. He didn't. Battling the influx of angers—his and hers—made it difficult to separate anything other than the immediate moment before him.

"You are stronger, Lily," he affirmed in a raw whisper over her head. "You know you are free. Time. That is all you need." With effort, he pushed away his own rages. There was little he could do about them. The important person stood like a gift within his embrace, seeking solace as much as he wanted to give it.

Dipping down, he pressed a single kiss to the crown of her head in comfort, freezing as soon as he touched her. A second of time raked over him, chilling him with the liberty he had taken. She said nothing, didn't flinch, didn't move. Painstakingly, he searched her thoughts and felt no paralyzing fear, no fury like what he'd experienced through her. She was relaxed, drifting through the moment.

At the same instant he realized she wasn't reacting violently to his touch, or the brush of his lips, her sweet scent filled his senses. Her hair smelled faintly of vanilla and cinnamon and his desires exploded against his control again. Not just to feed, to cure his nighttime hunger with Lily's blood, but to savor, to relish, to worship. All it would take was one shared taste to make their connection complete. Instinctively, he knew it would solidify the bond they had created, the inexplicable bond borne out of his desperation and her tortured agonies. Sharing blood had created the link between himself and his creator. Some things were never forgotten. He refused to commit that sin with Lily even if he felt he should with a longing and need that struck him as brutally as one of Diego's power bolts.

He'd been careful to not get so close to her, resolutely giving her all the room she needed. It didn't matter she'd reached for him first. Not tonight, or the first time he'd ever heard her voice.

Joaquin closed his eyes and rested his chin gently on top of her head, burying the hunger to make that connection in the depths of some lost well in his soul. He knew she had breaking points. Tonight had been a roller coaster for her. Her exhaustion was apparent in the slack way she bowed into him, simply standing together. The fact that she did lean into him, stood preciously folded within his arms, was not lost on him.

It felt to him as though she had scaled one of the largest barriers of trust between them, or maybe she had simply lowered the wall enough to finally make the single leap over it. Either way, it was a triumph. It would take time for the exposed wound to heal, but it was a beginning. He would ensure she had every opportunity to have any amount of time she could need.

"Close your eyes, lovely," he soothed, letting her fall deeper into her own self-hypnotic relaxed trance with a little help. "Hold on." Her arms locked obligingly around his frame. Keeping her mind in a languid state, he defied gravity by reversing his weight balance to gradually float upward away from the ground and over the treetops. No sense in scaring her with what she wouldn't understand. Within minutes, he set them down near the front of the house. He usually wouldn't have manipulated her memories, but she was worn out after her adventures and outbursts, mentally drained.

"Go inside and rest. I'll check on you before sunrise." It was a gentle order.

Golden lashes fluttered to reveal slumberous eyes watching him through an unfocused haze. The effect of having her body next to his, her lips beneath his, so close, so tempting, was volatile. She swept common sense clear away. The globes of her breasts pressed into his chest tighter when she arched in invitation, and he answered before he could question why she would, or tell himself why he shouldn't.

There was no fear resting in her mind. He found nothing but absorption in the moment. A natural reaction to a mutual desire that was gradually beginning to rise out of the ashes of her pain. The reality of their shared attraction made him ache in places he'd forgotten even knew how to feel.

He leaned downward, a slow inch at a time, until he rested over her mouth. He touched her, a mere tease of his lips to hers, and waited, each breath a faint flowing caress against his skin. A heartbeat, two, and he closed the space, sealing her to him.

Intense, scorching heat filled him. Though, as it consumed him, he changed nothing of his actions or touch. It flowed inside of him and sank into every cell. It flared within him, and he drank in each pulse like the sweetest wine. The sensation of her against him was divine. There had never been a heaven for him in this world.

Until now.

Sensitive to her every thought, he closed his eyes and kissed her, losing himself in the rapture of feeling, the giving return of her lips on his. Nimble fingers pressed into his sides in answer. His palm slid down the back of her head, cupping beneath her ear, his thumb stroking the smooth silk of her throat. So easily, he found her pulse, the hard tattoo of it pounding into his palm.

With tight control, he sipped at her lips, waiting for her to open for him. He could so easily lose himself in her kiss, desperately wanted to. The merest chance he could frighten her kept him from moving too fast, or pushing for too much. A ravenous hunger for the temptation at his fingertips gnawed at him, but he refused to answer it. He would never take from Lily.

With learning touches, he flicked the tip of his tongue against the arch of her upper lip, then the corners, seeking the sensual heat within. He traced her with only the slightest weight of his tongue, felt the warmed shake of her body, the rising heat of her blood as she responded, as she awakened to him. Restraint. He never imagined himself capable of it at this magnitude. But for Lily, there was no other way. He willingly gave it.

Tentatively, her rosy lips parted and he found the bottom one, nibbling its softness tenderly between his teeth, then stroking away the sensations. Pure energy zinged into his bloodstream with each tender sip. She tasted like honey and cinnamon, like the memory of a summer dessert, and he wanted to devour that sweetness with all the abandon of his childhood behind it. A shudder struck him blind at the hesitant touch of her tongue rising to meet his, learning him in the same slow, seductive dance he'd just performed. A low, growled groan rose as her actions became more sure, more teasing. More Lily.

Electricity pulsed along his skin, burned him where she touched him skin to skin. Sweet like a delicacy and as memorable as his last sunrise, he feasted on her kiss. The abundant wealth of her hair wound around his fingers as he massaged her neck, the strands like rich woven cotton as they slipped under his hand.

The craving to have her touch on his body as he fed on her sweetness, to have her kiss in unbridled passion, clawed at him. So was the want to have more, more of Lily. To feel her like a woman. For her to be a part of him.

To claim her.

He stopped the kiss, stunned, releasing her lips with a final taste of their heaven. He had no idea where that want, the instinct to do something so unknown to him, had materialized from. He was careful to keep his thoughts guarded. From the kiss he shouldn't have started to the thoughts borne from their kiss. More than he'd ever hoped to find, and shaken at the enormity of what he was feeling.

He straightened, gazing down at her with her hair wild in his hand and her eyes glazed with a need that shocked him as much as it called to him. A passion had awakened in this woman of strengths, calling to him. The same deep, untapped passion he had thought dead to the world surrounding him. It called to him like a woman's siren call to a man.

"Go." He firmly pushed this time. Another kiss like it and he'd never let her out of his sight. It was tempting to take her away as it was, damn the consequences.

She nodded in answer, then turned to climb the front steps leading to the large porch running along the home. The door closed between them, separating her from him. It almost killed him to not follow.

"Joaquin."

Diego's voice reached out to him and he stilled, no longer shocked by the other vampire's abilities. The other man's voice was as effective as a sheet of ice water being dumped on his racing thoughts about the redhead he'd just kissed, though. It was best to lock them away for the moment to be savored at a later time.

"Sí?"

There was a warning edge in Diego's voice as he communicated on the semi-private path all vampires shared if they attempted it and personally knew the one they sought. The communal path was broad and wide open, much like a broadcast radio signal. Anyone available could hear. It also meant Diego was aware of every detail of what had transpired between himself and Lily in the last few hours. Joaquin should've known Diego would never leave those behind completely unwatched, no matter how far away he had to go. The proof Joaquin was right was in the man's next words. He knew perfectly well Lily had exposed the darkest, wounded parts of her soul tonight. Whether he approved or not remained to be seen. The repercussions or punishments would have to be worried about at a later date and time.

"We have found another of Tenorio's holding prisons."

Joaquin's eyes narrowed as Diego relayed the visual of the site. Several cells of steel bars barely large enough to walk across. Cold iron chains wrapped through rings on walls with more welded to the legs of metal beds. No natural light. Only one door in or out. It was a prison not unlike the barbaric prisons of his long ago life and gave new meaning to Lily's pain. That was the life she'd been freed from? He asked his conscience, knowing the answer immediately. He strengthened his vow she would never know that kind of torture again.

"If he was holding people here, he moved them some time ago. All the electronic equipment has been removed or disabled. There is no information in them any longer."

Joaquin felt the frown develop at that news. A dead end. "*What are your plans?*"

"We will return tomorrow night. Have there been any problems?"

Joaquin knew what he was asking. "*No.*" The beacon had, as of yet, not brought them trouble.

There was a short pause before Diego's rumbled tones reached out to him again, proving Joaquin was right with his statement. Nothing else mattered so long as he protected one and all, including Lily. Joaquin didn't break his promise to Diego to keep them all safe, and he also kept his promise to Lily. The road she took to heal was a road only she had the right to choose. Trusting Joaquin tonight, trusting any man, was a choice only she could make.

"I do not think we have a lot of time before that will change. Nathan will stay behind to track Tenorio and his movements. We have a new name to work with–Ron Hawthorne." The bite of anger was modulated, but not hidden. There must have been some sign of this man to raise Diego's ire.

"Do you think he was behind the attack on the cabin?" Joaquin blended into the trees to continue with his nighttime watch, doubling the wards as Diego had shown him to lend his strength to their protection. He wasn't as adept, but allowed, Diego had a couple hundred years of practice on him.

"I do. We will share what we learned when we return."

Joaquin nodded, then the discussion ended. He got the feeling the news would not be good at all.

chapter eight

LILY Turned over in her bed, nuzzling down into her comforter and pillow, taking a deep breath of the scents. Cotton, warm and clean. It brought so many memories, good memories this time, of her family and her home. It was one of the few moments in her day when she knew exactly where she was and knew she was safe. The blinds were drawn to keep out bright sunlight so she could sleep during the morning hours. She loved to watch the morning sunrise before she went to sleep and wake in time to see the setting sun. The same sights that, before her imprisonment, she'd taken for granted. Now she didn't want to miss a single one.

She showered, then with a towel around her hair and ignoring the bathroom mirror's reflection, dressed to join the others and spend some time in Tabitha's room.

A knock followed by an excited squeal at her door before she was fully ready grabbed her attention.

"Lily! Are you up yet?"

She opened the bedroom door and found Amy bouncing on her toes. Electricity popped on the air she was so excited. "She's awake!"

Lily felt the immediate hard press of joyous tears at the news. Amy could only mean one thing. Tossing the damp towel on the bed, the two women raced down the wing to Tabitha's room. David and Houston stood outside in the hall watching the scene. None of the guys ever entered her sanctuary. After the tales of their imprisonment, no one would jeopardize Tabitha's health by making her feel captured again, or threatened by any male influence, if it could be avoided.

Kathy sat in the chair, holding Tabitha's hand. Tears shimmered on her cheeks, but the broad and glowing smile was impossible to mistake.

"Is she?" Lily choked out a controlled sob of happiness. She began to shake with all the pent up emotions she'd held for Tabitha's hopeful recovery.

Kathy looked up and nodded. "She clasped my hand! She's waking up."

Lily rushed to the side of the bed and sank to her knees. "Tab? Honey, can you hear me?" Her voice shook. She drew a fast, hard gulp of air to calm the waver in her voice.

Tabitha's chest rose and fell where she laid, the coverlet keeping rhythm with her breathing, an uneven tempo that betrayed her silence.

"I know you can hear me, Tab. Squeeze my hand if you can hear me."

Kathy gasped and shivered as her gaze snapped up and Lily stared. "She can hear you!"

"Hallelujah," she heard Houston say with heartfelt sincerity from several feet away.

"That's wonderful!" Her vision dropped to watch Tabitha's reactions again. "Okay, honey. It's time for you to come back all the way. You're safe. We're all here. Kathy, Amy, and me. We're all together and we're free, Tab. Open your eyes. Please."

She held her breath and waited.

"Needles," the injured woman breathed, her voice coarse and rusty from not being used.

"It's vitamin supplements, Tabitha. Healthy junk food for you."

"Needles," she said again, harder, clearer.

Alarm escalated quickly when she realized what Tabitha was getting at. Lily leaned in, adding firmness to her words. "Tabitha, I know you can hear me. You are *safe*." She punctuated the word. "Tenorio is gone. There are no drugs. You have been very sick. The needles have kept you alive. You are safe," she repeated, then waited for another reaction.

"I think she passed out," Kathy pointed out, holding a limp hand in her palm.

"We'll have to watch her, make sure she wakes up coherently enough to not cause herself damage by trying to strip the lines," Houston warned them from across the room. Both the other girls nodded in agreement.

Laney walked up in her robe, rubbing her eyes. She stood with Houston who curled an arm around her waist. "What's happening?"

"She's coming out of the coma, and she's very incoherent. She thinks she's still being drugged because she can feel the needles," Houston explained. Worry gave them all grave expressions.

"We'll watch her," Amy said. Kathy laid the hand she held on top of the covers with a last squeeze and a concerned look at the woman who had suffered so much.

"Of course we will," Lily replied firmly, searching the faces closest to her from where she knelt next to the bed. "She's a fighter. She's come this far. We all have. She will make it."

She refused to believe otherwise. There had been a long road before her and she knew the strides she'd made. She met the other women's gazes and all reflected the same thoughts. There was no way Tabitha wouldn't improve if they had anything to say about it.

"I'm going back to bed," Laney said a moment later. "Wake me when they get home." She looked up at Houston and, even though his expression was somber, he nodded, offering her a quiet kiss.

"Go rest. You need it."

Lily looked closely at the blonde and noted she had a pale glow to her complexion. She'd been scarce the last two days.

"You're not sick, are you?" Lily walked up with Amy and Kathy trailing, concern growing when

Laney dropped her eyes with a tinge of guilt wafting in the air surrounding her. Getting medical help all the way out there was hard enough as it was. Getting it anonymously was next to impossible.

"No, not sick."

"What's wrong?" Amy asked, usually the quietest of the four women.

Laney and Houston stepped out to give the trio a chance to join them in the hall. Lily took the hint and partially closed Tab's door. Laney looked to her husband, then at them. With a lopsided, guilty grin, she told them, "I'm pregnant."

Lily gasped while Amy and Kathy gave quiet shrieks of happiness. It was a surreal moment out of their nightmares for all of them. All three gave hugs to her, except Lily immediately knew why it bothered the tall blonde more than elated her.

"Are you going to stay?" She looked at both, receiving an arched brow from Houston and widened eyes from Laney at her directness, but knew they weren't offended by it.

"We both want to," Houston explained with a nod of agreement from Laney. "Diego and Tani are coming home tonight." Houston shifted his weight, appearing less tense now that neither he nor Laney had to hide the truth. Even Laney relaxed a little more into his one-armed embrace. "Tani's my best friend and Diego is almost like a brother to me now. We, neither of us, can leave them with all of this hanging over you girls." He shook his tawny head, his worried, somber look returning. “We couldn’t do it to you.”

Lily sniffed and quickly blinked to stop the sudden burn under her eyelids. She’d never felt more blessed than when they did or said something so selfless.

“We just weren’t expecting it. I’ve been on the pill since we married.”

“Nothing is foolproof,” Kathy remarked.

Houston snickered. “Thanks.”

Kathy blushed, but grinned.

“Come on. Let’s go have some tea or something,” Lily offered.

Laney nodded. “I think I’d like that. I can sleep after they get here and we all powwow. It’s more fun when I’m coherent to watch Diego’s fireworks, anyway.”

Kathy and Lily chuckled while Amy shook her head, although the petite blonde smiled with a silly happiness that almost made Lily think everything was going to be all right. Maybe for a few moments, she could even let herself believe it.

ROUGHLY forty-five minutes after sundown, the front door opened and Titania entered with Diego closing the door behind. Not ten seconds later, Joaquin came down the stairs to meet with everyone and hear the report about their visit to one of Tenorio’s compounds.

Lily cradled her mug, the steam rising lazily from her tea as she settled into one of the overstuffed chairs, tucking her legs beneath her. Like always, Joaquin took up the sentinel position behind her chair, holding up the wall with that formidably solid body of his. The same body that had held her with surprising gentleness and understanding the night before.

She blinked, her cup freezing on its rise to her lips. *Solid body?*

Moving the cup the rest of the way to hide her expressions, Lily took a few minutes while Diego and Houston talked between themselves to dissect the previous night before sitting to address everyone.

The moments at the clearing. The shared conversations and the fact she'd so openly bared her nightmare with Joaquin, and he hadn't been repulsed, hadn't reacted in any of the ways she would have expected. No disgust, no anger at any perceived weakness in her. Only an endless wealth of support and kindness. Warmth suffused her when those facts rose up, inarguable. There was no anger at her for what she'd suffered, no sneering belittlement. She hadn't known what to expect, long ago giving up on any crumb of compassion to be offered to her from such an unexpected source. Lily was getting used to those around her, but a week ago, Joaquin had been an unknown. Last night, that fact had been obliterated, and in a way she never would have dreamed.

She smiled, remembering the tender and equally explosive kiss he'd given her before he'd left her at the front door. More than once she thought she'd only dreamed it, but knew even her wildest dreams weren't that...tender. Even exhaustion couldn't have created that kind of hallucination.

"It was no dream, lovely."

She blinked, gulping down the sudden rock that seemed to have materialized out of the chamomile tea in her mug. Just how long had he been lurking in her thoughts? She felt the need to groan, or even to demand he stop doing it, but knew, somehow, his deeper needs weren't to invade her privacy, but to ensure her happiness and peace of mind. Minutely, she shook her head, wondering, when had she become so important to him? Or better yet, when had she begun to care either way? Lack of an answer made her reply abrupt.

"You're in my head again," she scolded him.

She sensed an impudent shrug. *"I like the way you see me."* Surprisingly, there was no male vanity in his thought, only a simple pleasure in the factual truth. Having him shadowing her thoughts should have made her nervous, edgy, but she discovered she wasn't. It was like having her protector with her always. It was comforting in a way she never would have dreamed only a few short months ago. Not invasive, not restrictive, not even intrusive, only there if she needed. The truth of his desires to help her in any way he was able struck her as one of the most considerate efforts she'd ever experienced.

Glancing up, she noticed Diego had stopped talking to Houston. His features were fierce and Lily waited for the shoe to drop. A blanket of warmth, of tenderness, wrapped her up in a cocoon and she rolled her shoulders to let it fill her, cover her in its invisible gentle touch. The silent promise within it—she was safe. The same promise he'd offered the night she'd heard his voice, a promise strengthened and held unquestioningly every moment.

"Tenorio has hired reinforcements. A man by the name of Ron Hawthorne, an ex-militia man with exceptional expertise." Diego didn't pull any punches as he explained what they'd discovered. "There was little left of the compound we uncovered from the information taken from the force that attacked the cabin. We believe he was the person who planned the attack. Tenorio has sunk into hiding for the moment." His silvery eyes glittered, a heavy pause filling the room as he touched on each of the three women present. "We also believe he has more prisoners like you four."

Lily's knuckles tightened on her mug and her stomach twisted, picturing what any prisoner of his would suffer through. A soothing touch flowed down her hair to caress her neck, but she knew without looking, he hadn't moved.

"Any idea where?" Kathy asked.

"Not right now," Tani replied, a worried frown knitting her brow. "There was nothing at the holding compound we found this time. We think whatever was going on there was stripped before the attack on the cabin happened."

"How many places can he have?" Kathy said with a low snarl. Amy rested a hand on her shoulder and Kathy let out a slow breath, gathering her calm around her, then asking, "So now what?"

"Nathan is searching for Hawthorne, and following any sign of Tenorio. We need to find out who has the chip." Diego's eyes settled on all of them. "We have no choice. We must find out who has it and remove it. As quickly as possible."

"How?" Lily sat up. "Nathan said it could be any of us, and pinpoint small." Silence fell throughout the room as anxiety colored the air.

"I think if we join our strengths, we can do it," Tani said. "We discussed the possibility of at least trying before returning. Something that doesn't feel right, or that sounds off in our bodies." Diego held her hand tightly when she sent him a glance, his devotion immediate and apparent. "You weren't the only ones who had injections." Her voice turned brittle and her shoulders sagged, but Diego held her close. "I had forgotten, but he had knocked me out with a tranquilizer that almost killed me. It could have been the only one. It was just as likely not."

"Too bad Nathan destroyed both the trackers finding out what they were following," Kathy muttered without rancor at the situation. "Would have saved a lot of guess work."

"Will it work?" Lily lifted her mug only to find her tea had cooled to a tepid sourness when she sipped at it.

"We can try," Tani answered, her resolute tone hiding her obvious uncertainty. "If we find it, it will have worked. There really is no other option but to try."

"Then let's start." Lily placed her cooled tea to the side. "I can go first. Should I lay down somewhere?"

"Let's try the couch." Tani motioned to the couch opposite where Amy and Kathy sat. Everyone stood and Lily strode to one of the long couches. Meeting Joaquin's gaze and seeing his unshakeable calm, she sat, then stretched out. He came and knelt right at her side. Without an ounce of fear, she reached for his hand.

"Relax. I think I know what they have in mind," he whispered to her in comfort while he twined their fingers together. She forced the tension out of her body.

"I'm ready."

"Make a circle around her." Tani joined them when everyone took up their positions.

Diego explained. "Envision your inner energy as a source outside of yourself, a part of you that you can control to the smallest detail. Focus until it is sharp, an exact point of energy. It will move outside of you, but will never truly desert you. Stay relaxed, Lily. Nothing should hurt."

She nodded and waited. Grounding herself with those mysterious, swirling midnight eyes, she held herself still. The lights in the room seemed to dim around the peripheral of her vision as she focused only on the man next to her.

"Do you feel anything?"

"Not yet, but I can feel the energy building."

"This is new. Diego explained to me what they were wanting to do. I know it is safe, just unknown to you."

"I trust you."

The slightest rise of pleasure warmed his watchful gaze, but he stayed silent. She hardly blinked, never releasing his hold, even when the warmth invaded. She almost giggled at the sudden touch, something so light, so feathery, it did startle her, except it was on the *inside*.

It took several stretched moments until she felt it recede. The miniscule point of *something* had traced her entire body.

"Whew!" Kathy said with a sharp cry. "That was incredible!"

"Was it hard for you?" Lily asked, turning for the first time since they'd begun to look at the others surrounding her.

Both Amy and Kathy shook their heads. "Once we got the vibe, Diego controlled it."

Tani nodded. "If you can do it to yourself, it's a good thing to learn to do."

Lily sat up with Joaquin's attentive help.

"It helps us to heal," Tani said.

"Really?"

Tani blushed and Lily caught the scowl Diego shot her. She didn't look up at him before she nodded with a guilty jerk.

"Next," Diego ordered before Lily could ask any other questions about what Tani meant with her healing comment. It took her a moment to get the 'vibe' Kathy had said she'd felt, but she wasn't kidding when she'd said Diego controlled it.

Floating within her thoughts, she sensed in a way that almost made it visual as she coursed within Kathy's body. She felt Joaquin, Diego and Tani acutely. Amy was there, but more like herself. There was even strength from Houston and Laney. It was an indescribable stream of power that fluctuated between and through them.

"Remarkable," she breathed when they were done. It took time, but with each gathering of their energies, it became more natural to feel the sensations, to feel her way, to meld it all together.

Tani was the last, and immediately, she felt Diego's attention, devotion and worry deepen. She also noticed Tani had no real heartbeat and didn't seem to be breathing. Little facts lodged in her mind, but under the pull of the gathered focus, she couldn't deviate from their intent to examine any of it.

Together, they released their focus. Tani sat up, brushing her length of hair behind her. "Nothing?" A darkening frown appeared when Diego shook his head.

"Does that mean it's none of us, or that this isn't working?" Kathy wrapped her arms around her middle and leaned a hip against the edge of the couch as Tani rose to stand with Diego.

"If that wasn't strong enough, I'd be surprised," Lily retorted. Joaquin stood behind her and she almost leaned into him, seeking a comfort from him that still caught her off guard. She shook herself mentally to clear her thoughts.

"That only leaves Tabitha and David then." Amy frowned. "She may fight it."

"I think she'll listen to me if she's awake enough to hear what I say. I can reach her inside. I can at least try, and maybe it will keep her calm." Lily found drawn expressions on everyone, their worry right on the surface.

"Where is David?" Kathy asked.

Laney rolled a hand toward the stairs where the basement door was hidden. "He's been in the basement a lot. I think he misses his drums."

"I'll go get him," Tani offered, but was stopped with a halting hand on her shoulder.

Diego's voice was flat. "He's not in the house."

"Where would he go? I haven't seen him, but he wouldn't take off. I'll be right back." Houston turned to march up the stairs.

"I haven't seen him either," Lily interjected. "But I rarely do because I do the night shift."

Kathy and Amy looked at each other then shook their heads collectively.

Lily immediately knew this was not a good thing, feeling the flare of worry and fear like a slide of ice down her skin. When Joaquin stepped up behind her and put a comforting hand on her spine, she welcomed his touch before she could consider why she shouldn't, why she should be wary. Or why she longed for his comfort when she could barely stand anyone else's physical touch. When only a moment before she'd been unsure, she wasn't, needing the stability emanating from Joaquin. Tani barely raised an eyebrow, but both Amy and Kathy looked at her oddly, both confused at her open acceptance of not only a male, but of his touch. She didn't avoid their stunned stares, but didn't owe anyone any explanations for her actions either.

Houston jogged down the stairs with a sparking glare popping in his eyes. "Half his stuff is gone."

"Crap!" Titania exclaimed.

Diego tugged her closer, soothingly. "You have a way with words, *cara*."

"Now what?" Tani asked.

"Wait." Lily blinked, wondering if it was possible. Of course it could be. "What if it's him and he knows it, or even suspects it? He wasn't treated any better in the two days he was there." Everyone knew what Nathan had confirmed through the two trackers, that someone was indeed carrying nothing less than a tracking device to bring hell down on them.

"Show me."

She did without a qualm, letting Joaquin see the horror she, herself, had witnessed, and had endured. The flash of whips, the thud of hard-hitting fists. Cruel words, and crueler abuses.

He never moved, but she felt the protective charge of his will envelop her, embrace her. "*Never again.*"

"*I know.*" She returned with a wash of her faith in his word. Belief, faith and trust had to start somewhere.

"We have to find him," Laney said, openly trying not to cry. "The dork did it on purpose. I know him." Tani nodded in agreement.

Houston raked a hand through his wavy hair, muttering a curse under his breath. "We'll have to spread out."

"I will help," Joaquin said without hesitation.

"So will I." Lily quickly offered her help in any way she could.

"Lily," Joaquin said with an immediate bitten disapproval.

Tani held up her hands to stop any further bickering. "Look." She rubbed her eyes. "This is turning into one big steaming mess. We can't have everyone flying out of here on a manhunt. If it was David, then we're not going to be the only ones looking for him."

There was silent agreement and several disturbed nods.

"Laney, I love you like my sister. You and Houston stay here. You can't afford to get roughed up now anyway."

Laney gaped, then laughed at Tani. "How long have you known?"

She smirked, but with love said, "That doesn't matter. It would tear Houston apart to be separated from you with you carrying."

Houston didn't deny it, instead pulling her a little closer into his body.

"I think I see what you're getting at." Kathy dropped her arms from around her middle, avoiding looking at Lily, or more likely, Joaquin. Lily couldn't help in any way to encourage their trust of him. They all had walls to surmount when it came to their past and moving forward. "Amy and I can take care of Tabitha. Between us and Laney, we can."

Lily felt Joaquin's displeasure growing behind her as her determination firmed, and Amy and Kathy gave her the opportunity to join in the hunt. There was some kind of argument happening between Diego and Joaquin. It was something she could almost hear, but it was like listening through two walls.

And it drove her insane.

"If you're going to argue about me, do it where I can hear it!" she snapped.

Three sets of eyes turned to her, but she didn't back down. Diego's frown deepened. "My apologies, Lily. I was not aware."

She snorted, and as a statement, stepped away from Joaquin in rebuff. "I got that."

"We only mean to keep you safe," Tani explained.

"But I *can* help." Lily let out a breath. "I couldn't hear you two clearly because you have walls up. Most don't. I can hear voices as well as I can talk telepathically. I chose not to. I'd go nuts in a heartbeat if I let it all filter in."

"It's not that we don't want your help," Tani said with an evasive tone, her blue eyes meeting hers, then sliding away.

"Then what is it?"

"We're not human, Lily."

"What?" She shook her head at the lyrical sound of Titania's voice between her ears. "I know I didn't hear you right." Diego's ever present scowl deepened at Tani's explanation.

Without a glance, Amy and Kathy left the room, walking up the stairs. A moment later, their bedroom doors were heard opening and closing.

"Why'd they leave?" she immediately demanded.

"I sent them to bed," Diego said without apology. "There is no need for them to hear this."

"Maybe we should sit?" Houston offered. "This could take a few minutes."

Lily shot him a look of dawning comprehension. "You know, don't you?"

Houston and Laney both nodded without remorse. Lily rubbed a hand across her brow. "Fine. Explain how you're not human." She plunked down on the couch where she'd lain, crossed her arms, and waited.

chapter nine

"IT'S VERY simple, really. We're vampires."

Lily smiled with sarcastic humor at the woman sitting across from her. "Please. Vampires don't exist. Just tell me the truth."

Diego gave Tani a glance and a nod. Then, Tani opened her mouth.

Lily stopped breathing. She knew that those—that it wasn't possible, but she wasn't imagining it either. "Oh shit," she managed on a strangled croak. "Where—How—" Pushing out her hands, she steeled herself with a good shake. Then, opened her eyes to focus once more. "Show me again."

This time, when Tani smiled, her teeth were normal, pearly white and straight. "Now watch." And without warning, two teeth lengthened, becoming noticeably sharper by themselves than when lined up. "It's an illusion. It's what you expect to see, so they are normal. They're always pointed now," she said, filling in the question blank. They withdrew much the same way as they had appeared, once more showing her a straight line of gleaming, pearl white teeth until she determinedly focused. Then she could see the jagged tips as clear as Tani's nose on her face.

Lily's breathing staggered painfully.

"It was better and easier to not explain, to not cause any of you more stress by letting you know the truth."

"Nathan is like you too?" She watched the other woman expectantly. She *knew* what she would likely find out, but hearing it... She couldn't ask Joaquin. Not yet. Maybe another explanation would present itself before she'd have to face that truth. She could hope. Unreality had officially become a part of her life.

"Yes." Titania drew a breath, rolling her shoulders. "He's like me, actually, quite young in vampire terms, and facing a lot of turmoil. He came about it rather cruelly, and has lost everything he had."

"Like all of us." The connection was clear for Lily.

Titania nodded. "Yes. That's why he is adamant in helping as much as possible. His life was stolen, much like yours and the others. He believed he was being mugged, and was converted."

Lily's eyes widened. "Oh my God! Why? Who?"

Titania placed her hands within Diego's, twining their fingers together, taking her time to answer. "Why? Because a vampire lives to create havoc, to encourage chaos. They are cruel and hateful. It's a single pleasure for them to cause hysteria and pain.

Conversion is the worst kind of all of that." She opened her mouth, but seemed to think better of explaining it more. "As for the other, it's hard to say who. None of them typically leave calling cards when they do attack, or bother to explain why any one person was chosen over another. Diego knew because it was his once best friend. I was an accident Diego inadvertently started before he realized what had happened. He never intended for me to become like him."

"But..." Lily sat dumbfounded by the reality. She almost didn't know where to start. And Joaquin... She couldn't look at him yet, though she knew he stood behind where she sat, still there, still giving her his unconditional support and comfort, regardless of her ultimate decision to his future.

Titania lifted a pale hand, and Lily felt her jaw all but snap shut with questions. "Let me tell you a few things first. We don't keep you for ourselves. Know that up front. We leave every night and Diego takes care of me and my needs. Your health and care really are of the utmost importance to us. We don't kill to survive. In fact, it takes very little for us to live on. Not the way most bodies do. And it doesn't harm—"

When Lily felt herself blanch of color, Titania blushed, breaking off and changing direction. "Sorry. I just wanted to put your mind at ease. You are not here for any reason that has anything to do with what we are or how we survive. Please believe that. I saw what Tenorio had planned. I touched that evil place and I never want to again. Now we know there are more of us, gifted people who are being held, tortured, killed. We will find them, and somehow, he will be stopped."

Lily pinned Diego with a stare that could melt carbide steel. "You too? You 'made' her?"

"It was a turn of events that brought us together," he stated without apology. "The conversion was, in fact, an accident."

With aching slowness, as if she moved through some sort of sludge, she stood. Facing Houston and Laney, she told him, "You're not. You're up during the day. Are you human?"

"Yes and no. I'm not a vampire, but I'm not purely human in the same sense."

"It's okay," Laney coaxed when he stopped with a hesitant and heavy pause.

Houston's smile was lopsided. "I'm Jahehn. I come from a Native American line of shifters. My grandfather was pure Jahehn. When it skipped a generation, they thought our line had lost the calling. My mother could have killed my dad when I did get it."

"Shifter?" she muttered. God, she could barely breathe. Her world spun, or flipped, or something, but this was not the one she thought she knew.

"Wolf," he tagged on when she could only stand gaping at them all.

"But all of this"—she swept a hand to encompass all of them, including Joaquin, who had stayed silent and still—"it's myth!"

"Not really." Laney's calm voice helped slice through her disbelief. "You're telepathic. Myth or reality? For us, this is our reality. I've known Tani for several years. Houston's known her since she was fourteen. Our friendships kept us together when her world fell apart. Your friendship is keeping us together because we are all different. We need each other." Curling into Houston's shoulder, she continued with an iced fear growing in the words when she passed a comprehending look over Houston. "Our child will be different. And if you think you're terrified of them finding you, I'm as terrified of what my child will face in this world. We could leave it behind, but then we'd be risking our child, just like you were risked in the normal world. Just like Amy, Kathy, and Tabitha. Do you understand?"

"I think I do," she finally managed through numb lips, to be heard over a heart thudding with incredulity. With the strength she had left, she faced Joaquin. "And you?" He nodded, but she felt such a wealth of misery in his admission wash over her, it made her eyes burn. She shivered once with the enormity of what they had divulged.

The truth hit her hard and fast. "You're in as much danger of exploitation as we are."

Tani gave her a look of complete agreement and understanding. "And not just by people. If any one of the science fields got their hands on one of us..." She visibly shivered. "The Brethren, the core of the vampires who don't exactly live by a badge of honor, they don't like us, they hate those like us. Friendship among the Brethren is never going to happen. Diego had no idea until he found me that there was any other way to live. He had been alone for a very long time. Nathan was the same way.

"It's a two front battle, three now with Tenorio. It would be hysteria if one of us were captured. Proving our existence has been a challenge since the beginning of time. The Brethren have fed that incurable curiosity with their games and man's own imagination to fill in the gaps."

"You're different?" All three nodded when she met each gaze. "How?"

"None of us has ever killed to survive. We respect life, and for some, it hasn't been easy to not take that step." Titania shared another compelling look with Diego, a look of sheer understanding. "Brethren have no respect for the living, the very beings they need to sustain themselves with. Killing during feeding makes them fall into a soulless, maniacal, cruel darkness that can't be reversed, and it's as strong a pull as any addiction to fight their entire existence. Those who succumb are the vampire of myth, the vampire of today who is sought and hunted. To our knowledge, we're the only ones who are not like the Brethren."

"Oh my God!" She whipped around to gape at Joaquin. "That is what I felt when I first heard you." *An absolute desolation.*

"I was at the end of my endurance," Joaquin replied with only a small flare of shame, though he never dropped her gaze. "I was ready to face the dawn that night. I did not lie. You saved me, and my sanity." He stood as still as stone, accepting whatever her decision would be.

She gripped his arms, giving him a commanding shake. "Do not apologize!" Centering herself in her topsy-turvy world suddenly gone wild, she asked everyone without looking away from Joaquin, "How can I help? We need to find him. I had no idea..."

"Shh." She didn't argue when he wrapped his arms around her and tucked her beneath his chin.

Now she realized why Tani had no heartbeat. Neither did Joaquin where she pressed against him.

Vampires? Real vampires? It was unbelievable on so many levels, but Laney was right. This was the world she was in now. How much was real and wasn't was no longer governed by the same rules she'd known her entire life. She drew a slow breath, absorbing what Tani had told her, understanding what it meant for Tani and Diego, and for Joaquin. Even Houston was different. This was the reality she lived in and, in many ways, it explained so many of the little things, like Diego's strengths and talents, never seeing any of them during the day, even though she could've sworn she'd seen them. It had to have been a cover. When it came to being a vampire, though, it couldn't have mattered less to her. It wasn't like these mythical 'monsters' were truly the monsters she would have expected to find herself living with and around. She'd stared real monsters in the face and felt their cruelties, all the time while they were disguised as a normal person like any other.

"You've never, you know...*bit*...me, have you?" she asked low enough for no one else to hear from where she curved against Joaquin's shoulder, praying that she knew this answer. When he replied, her relief almost had her sag into his embrace.

"No. I vowed I never would." The steel in his words left no doubt he wasn't lying. She knew the determination behind his vows.

"Your help is part of the problem. I believe you would be invaluable with your telepathy. Diego and Joaquin fear for your safety. And you can't change your physical presence."

Diego stood, Tani following, expressing it was time to leave to find David.

"I'd slow you down." She frowned at the bitter truth. It only took a couple seconds to come to her decision. "Go. I can talk to all of you. You can go unseen and search faster than I could."

Relief was so strong coming from Joaquin she wanted to smack him. Because he'd won.

"Only with this. We still have things to talk about." She made sure he heard it loud and clear.

"Lily, I will tell you anything you could ever want to know, so long as I can keep you safe."

She stepped out of his embrace only so far, feeling the caressing weight of his palms fall to her waist when she reached up to cup his face. "Just come back." Vampire or not, she wanted him there.

"I will. I have every reason to." Before she could guess his next move, he leaned down and kissed her, a passionate, brief melding of lips that left her off kilter. And on fire.

LILY sat beside Tabitha reading, trying not to think of where Joaquin was, of if he was in danger. She knew if she worried too much, he would hear her and he didn't need the distraction in their search for David.

Vampires.

She still wanted to roll over and laugh. It was like being in some crazy movie. Vampires, wolf shifters, parapsychology gifted people.

The only thing they were missing was magic. Toss in a witch or two and she'd know she'd somehow left her world completely behind.

Tani had informed her not too long ago the three had to split their search when David hadn't been in Parks. He could be in any direction. Houston had searched his room for any clue to where he had gone, but there was nothing, only proof of his leaving with gaps in his closet and a few other things mysteriously vanishing. Like Houston's Ferrari.

Lily couldn't deny she'd felt drawn to Joaquin, had felt his pain and his loneliness during their first conversation. It had been the unignorable pull reaching for her. That desolation. She knew that pain, how deep it sank into the body and soul. He could infuriate her without trying, but never be mad at her because of it, or for any of her reactions or feelings. The deeper knowledge was, she missed him.

No matter how hard she tried to ignore it, there was something about Joaquin she felt drawn to. She couldn't explain it. She didn't understand it, but there was something about him. There was a calmness that almost seeped into her from him. As though he knew the right things to say, the right things to do to keep her calm. Even through all the shocking discoveries and surprises, she'd never once felt threatened by Joaquin. It was, simply, the man himself.

"Lily?"

The croaked whisper snapped her entire focus to the woman on the bed before her. She didn't look away for a single second. "Tabitha? Can you hear me?" She quietly placed the book down, bringing the rocking chair closer to hold one of the hands in front of her. "Can you feel me?"

Air staggered in and out of Tabitha's chest, rifling the bed sheets.

"Tabitha." She repeated her name, slowly, calmly. "Focus on my voice, Tab. Wake up."

Restraint kept her glued to the seat of the rocking chair when she really wanted to scream and jump up and down in joy. The road ahead would still be a long one, but with Tabitha waking, nothing looked impossible in that moment.

"Can you hear me?" She clutched the hand before her, waiting, anticipating.

Lashes fluttered, revealing turquoise, sea green eyes.

Lily felt the wet streaks as they raced down her cheeks. “Thank God,” she choked out. Tabitha worked her jaw and Lily offered her drops of cool water. “Better?”

She blinked and sighed, then her eyes closed again.

“Are you still with me?” she asked, worried she’d passed out again.

The hand in hers tightened and the rise and fall of her chest deepened. “Feels weird.” Her voice was rusty and raw from not being used.

She’d been warned to not overload her if and when she regained consciousness, so she went with the basics.

“You’re in a bed, resting. We were rescued.”

“Rescued?” Tabitha frowned, her brow drawn so tight a V cut into the sunlight yellow eyebrows over her eyes. “Rescued?” It seemed to be a foreign idea to her.

“Yes. All of us. We’re all here. Kathy and Amy are down the hall asleep.”

“How long?”

Lily tried to remember. “At least nine months now. We’re safe.”

Tabitha’s voice dried out and Lily gave her some more water, using a dropper to slip it into her mouth.

"You're weak. You need time to heal. Time is all. You need to rest." But happiness for her friend brought tears rushing forward without restraint.

Tabitha flexed a hand and grimaced. "The needles?"

"Vitamins. Fluids to keep you alive."

"No chemicals?"

"Vitamins and fluids. Nothing more." Relief made her voice tremulous.

Tabitha relaxed in stages on the bed. "It feels different."

Lily released her hand and splayed it on the cotton sheet of her bed. Tentative fingers ran over it, learning the texture.

"A sheet!" she exclaimed weakly, shock vibrating in her voice at the sensation.

"Open your eyes, Tab. The room is beautiful. No bars, no guards."

Her lids fluttered open. She squinted. "I-I can't see." Distress made her sob, her eyes slamming shut as a fresh wave of pain flared over her face.

"Shh. It should pass. Your body has gone through a lot. We're here to help you."

Time fell open and the thickening silence made the room shrink, made the air oppressive to breathe as Tabitha gathered her strength. One word blurted from her. A word torn from the depths of her anger, her pain, and her soul.

"Why?"

Lily froze, staring at her friend. "Why?"

"Why didn't you let me die?"

The pain in her voice was bottomless. Lily had to bite her lip to not whimper from the anguish in the single question. “Because you were strong enough to live then, through it all. You’re strong enough to live now. It *will* be better, Tabitha.”

Silence again. The overwhelming sense of despair was hard to fight.

The brush of fingers, a bare touch of a feeling, floated past her cheek in comfort and she turned into it, seeking, but there wasn’t anyone there.

She knew instinctively who it was. Even with miles between them, he was with her. She knew it as surely as she was breathing in that moment.

Lily swallowed and closed her eyes for a brief prayer of thanks for her friend. Calming her tumultuous heart, she stood. “Just rest, Tabitha. We’re all here. You are safe.”

The deep, easy breathing beneath the sheet told her Tabitha had slipped into sleep again. Lily’s fingers trembled when she lifted them to wipe away the persistent tears clinging to her lashes.

“She is confused, lovely. Soon it will be easier for her.”

Lily wrapped her arms around herself, walking to the closest window in the room, Tab’s bed behind her. The moon had slipped behind the trees. It was only a couple of hours until dawn. *“How do you know? She is so angry, so weak.”*

“Because she has you to guide her. Like you did with me.”

She pressed her forehead to the window, and said the first thing that came to mind. "I wish you were here."

"I will be. We will find him."

She felt the weight of all of her frustrations and despair lift from her shoulders, not surprised any longer that he would do it. He would take care of her no matter how or where. She was beginning to accept that she had become his world. Somehow, some way. "I don't have any idea what I'll do with a vampire, Joaquin."

"In time, I will show you."

The teasing remark was given with a meaningful, sexy chuckle. She rocked her head against the pane of glass. She wasn't quite ready to play along with that assumption. That would be admitting to too much too soon. A concept that lingered in the recesses of her mind, but she hadn't had the strength to pull it forward to examine it either. Not yet. "Just, please come home."

"I will. Té adoro, corazón*."*

She lifted her fingertips to her lips, and for an instant, thought she had felt his kiss. It made her shiver with a new anticipation, a wanting that was as new and unexpected as a spring rain to her senses.

What surprised her more—she didn't fear it.

"I FOUND Houston's car." Joaquin heard the direct message. Changing his course, Joaquin met them, alighting on the roof where they waited. They

were miles south of the house. It had taken them hours to find any sense of him. Aware of the night in an innate way since his first rising, he noted dawn wasn't far off as they converged. They'd come a lot further than he believed either Tani or Diego were expecting. It only meant David had intended to leave before they'd ever realized, long before anyone would think to look for him, or stop him. Joaquin also noted he was moving east as well as south, away from California and Tenorio.

The three owls changed their shapes, landing to sit with their legs hanging over the edge of the building. "Why here?" Across the street, the car was parked at a plain motel. There weren't many cars in the lot, and only a few signs of life in either direction. Joaquin guessed he had stopped for the night. There were no lights anywhere in the rooms. At that hour of the morning, he wasn't surprised.

"Why did he leave at all?" Tani asked. "He didn't have to."

"We will only find out one way."

Diego stood. They stepped over the edge and floated to the ground, striding down the sidewalk, following the numbered doors until they reached the one before the nose of the car. With a cautionary look, Diego became mist and slid through between the door and the frame. It only took him a moment before he returned, and he didn't walk out the door with David. "It is his room, but he is not here."

Titania put a fist to her hip and grumbled. "I'm going to give him a piece of my mind when we do find him."

"I do not think it will be possible."

Her eyes flew to his. Even Joaquin knew the flat mercury of his return gaze was only the beginning of the bad news.

"There is blood on the bed and it looks as though he struggled."

Tani gasped. "They have him already?" She whirled to pace with harsh stomps. "Damn it! It was him. This isn't fair. We don't have any idea of where he could be, or even how long he's been missing. He didn't do anything to anybody."

Diego swept her against his chest. "I am sorry, *cara*."

"We can't give up," she bit out sharply from where he held her, her shoulders rocking with shudders. Joaquin heard her quiet sobs easily. "We can't."

"We will not, but there is little we can do tonight."

"What about the car?"

Diego stared as he debated. "Leave it. It is time we separated ourselves as much as possible from the world Tenorio knows us to be in."

"Houston is going to kill you," she warned him.

Diego only shrugged. "I am sure he will see it my way."

Joaquin wisely chose not to add his opinion.

chapter ten

"SO, DO you have to sleep in the ground?"

Joaquin smiled inside at her inquisitive question. He would not make it to the house before sunrise. None of them would, but he couldn't leave Lily wondering. She hadn't been happy with the news about David. He'd left out the worst details to spare her the shock. She'd immediately understood what it meant when he told her they hadn't been the first to find him.

"It isn't uncomfortable. It ceased to be a problem a long time ago." He flew over the tops of trees, trailing Diego and Tani. The moon was gone and the world beneath him was dark, a flat black that gave little comfort. Focusing forward, he knew where his comfort was.

She fell silent, but he realized she was only thinking. He hadn't corrected her when she guessed he hadn't been sleeping in the room at all. He would still maintain the charade for the others in the house. Lily had been very open to the oddity of their all sharing one house. He wasn't sure enough about the others to make that assumption. Kathy and Amy, while not uncomfortable, he knew their trust was still fragile. He knew his attention to Lily, and her openness to him, confused Kathy.

"You had said before that Diego always knew when we were talking."

"He was concerned for you. I was an unknown."

"Is he still?"

Joaquin glimpsed the larger owl ahead. *"I do not believe so. He is still capable, but he is being polite."*

"You can do that?" Wonder filled her voice again.

"It's unusual for our private thoughts to be overhead, like you did with me. Vampires can hear between themselves the way I can with either Diego or Titania. Personally knowing who you want to talk to does make it a bit more foolproof. A blood bond makes it stronger, like the bond I had with my creator. Imagine a community phone line. Everyone can hear on one phone, but if you have a singular line, then only the person you speak to can. It works both ways. There is a community way to hear which is broad and open, and a private one."

"And the bond?" she asked with a tremulous hesitation. *"Only with blood?"*

"What are you asking, corazón*?"*

A moment passed, then two. *"I don't like people listening in, if you want the truth. It feels wrong."*

"You need to control your privacy. There isn't anything wrong with that. No, it isn't the only way.

We can block as well as hear. Right now, it's just you and me," he offered soothingly.

He pulled in his wings with slower drafts, aiming for a tree as Diego and Tani left him behind. Some habits were hard to break. Not giving away your sleeping ground was one of them. He would meet them again at sunset. A flicker of acknowledgement rolled across his consciousness, and he knew he was alone with his thoughts, and with Lily.

Sitting in the tree gave him the memory of the very first night he'd heard her voice, and he smiled. He wasn't sure what he was going to do from one minute to the next when it came to the spirited redhead. She was unlike anything he had ever expected, and growing stronger and more sure of her world every day. He was cautious of examining his growing feelings too closely. Especially at times like this. When talking to her gave him feelings he hadn't experienced in too long, sharing in her company like he was even if they were still miles and hours apart.

Leaning into the trunk, he stared upward through the trees, catching the glimmer of the stars. He remembered her exuberance the night before in the clearing at seeing their timeless beauty. Through her eyes he was seeing them, almost for the first time, bathing in their breathtaking beauty.

Settled into a corner of her mind, he knew she was in her room, brushing out her hair on the bed, and he wished he could be there to see it, to feel it, to do the light strokes for her and feel the thickness in his hand again. He couldn't stop the urges of want. He felt everything, too much of it, when it came to Lily. He'd do anything to never let it end.

"I feel it too," she whispered against his mind.

Joaquin blinked, taken by surprise. She was in his thoughts?

"Of course, the same as you are. You said I could at any time. Just because I never said I wanted to didn't mean I couldn't. I meant I wouldn't, but I feel differently about it today. I feel closer to you, somehow." Her words drifted over him like a spring shower, a whispered sweetness against his soul.

He closed his eyes to center his energy. He felt light enough to float right away from the tree. *"I don't understand what is happening between us, Lily."*

"Don't you?"

He shook his head at her cheek. Oh, he feared he knew, and he knew how badly it was doomed between them. She was growing stronger and braver by the day, especially to openly acknowledge this connection they shared without a trace of fear.

There. He felt it. Her smile. A secretive lift that made his blood pulse with need at the sensual innocence she exuded. The remembered warmth of her body, the silk of her skin, the honey of her kiss, the craving of her taste all layered on that pulse. He found he hated being so far away from her.

"Go to sleep, lovely. I will see you soon."

"Goodnight."

He relaxed into the boughs of the tree, letting her warmth fade as she drifted toward slumber, until he knew she had finally fallen asleep. It was an all-encompassing sensation he took to ground with him, the one he wanted to wake with.

LILY waited for him on the porch when they arrived. There was no denying the pride he felt seeing her there, accepting him for what he was. Together, the three owls soared then arched to land, changing their shape to settle on the ground.

She clutched at the rail, her golden eyes wide and unblinking with only a touch of disbelief and worlds of wonder. The rich fall of her hair cascaded down her back, being lightly ruffled with the slow breeze of the evening. With parted lips and her eyes on no one but him, she reminded him of those sirens of old that he knew no man could ignore. The beautiful witches who had stolen hearts and lives from many sailors in those tales.

"Wow!" she breathed. "That was incredible."

The ache in his chest grew with the breathless sound of her voice. He hid it, but it was harder and harder to keep from her. He feared the enormity of what he felt would frighten her, especially with everything that came with those feelings. Most were nothing less than carnal.

He knew her pains, her fears. Knowing didn't stop the wanting. It was a multi-layered desire, stronger, and impossible, to ignore deep down. Not only for the woman, her taste, her sweetness, but for the rich wine of her blood. He'd been fighting the depth of his hunger since the kiss that had stolen his air and then his soul, since the first impulse to make her his, all his, only his. It wasn't possible. That crying hunger wound throughout his body, seizing his soul in its unforgiving grip. There was only one way to appease it, by doing the one thing he swore he'd never do. He'd paid his penance, and Lily was his salvation, his one chance at redemption. As Nathan would have said, he didn't want to blow it.

He reached for her and he felt a surge ripple up his arm when she didn't hesitate, slipping her hand into his without a stray tendril of fear anywhere.

"Any ideas where they took him?" Standing with him in the clearing in front of the house, Lily faced Tani and Diego, worry pinching her features taut.

"I have sent Nathan to search for him. We all feel he was taken to California, but to serve what purpose we cannot say."

"Do you think they followed him because he did have the chip?"

Tani nodded, looking miserable. "He knew one of us had it. My guess is he wasn't taking any chances, and he left thinking it was the only way to not have what happened at the cabin happen again."

Joaquin sensed Lily's frustration. Pulling her closer, he wrapped her into his side, his only want to comfort. She flowed against him and his heart beat in answer. The reaction stunned him. She was getting further and further under his skin every moment.

"How did he manage to get through the wards?" Joaquin asked. He knew the power was a repellent as well as a protection to guard the people within its boundaries.

"Those within are not affected. Those wishing entry who have never left would suffer the wards, and it would be a painful attempt."

Joaquin could only shake his head at the design of the protections, to be that exact. He barely understood how they worked to camouflage the property and maintain the secretive aura surrounding the entire home.

"Now what?" Lily trembled against him, and he tightened his hold reflexively, wanting to protect her from the world at large.

"We wait." Diego's expression was flat. "Nathan will tell us as soon as he has any idea if he was taken to California. If not, then we wait for David to return. He still may."

Joaquin knew it wasn't easy for the man to accept he couldn't do anything to help David. They all knew David returning on his own was a slight chance at best.

A moment later, Diego and Tani turned and disappeared together into the woods, leaving Joaquin and Lily alone in the muted wash of light from the front of the house. He knew they would return in a short while. They always checked in before dawn, the same as he did.

"Do you think he'll be back?" she asked him, searching for any sign of hopefulness, expecting honesty. He couldn't ever give her less.

"No, I do not." He tucked her closer. "What he did may have saved everyone, or not."

Silence hung heavily between them, broken only by the slow breeze through the trees and the occasional chirp of crickets and creatures that lived best at night.

"Joaquin?"

He hummed against her hair, absorbing the fragrant nuances of vanilla and cinnamon again, a scent he had missed. The paleness of her skin against his was a lesson in contrasts. His was the natural shade of warmed honey, hers looked like cream. The vibrant red hue of her hair spread like a sunset across her sweatshirt. The black length of his fell to his shoulders, straight where hers was a riot of curls and waves. The tawny golden brightness of her eyes, so unlike many he had seen, glowed with her acceptance as she stared at him.

"Take me to see the stars again."

Holding her closer, he pressed a light, caressing kiss to her temple. He couldn't refuse her anything.

"Hold tight." He knew she didn't want to walk. She clasped her hands around his neck and he looped her waist, pulling her flush against him. The feeling of her along his length was a heady sensation. He forced the groan down into his chest. "If you're scared of heights, don't look down," he warned her. She nodded, pressing into his body instead.

"Don't let me fall," she breathed against his neck.

An amused chuckle rumbled from his chest at the notion. "Never." She stayed calm, her breath warming the side of his neck where she rested, simply accepting that he would keep her safe. Accepting whatever he did to fulfill her wish. Something warm invaded his blood, then invaded his heart with the simple act.

His intentions to keep her safe, to find his redemption through her salvation, were changing, morphing into a new world of meaning and he didn't know how to stop the changes from happening.

As he floated upward, doubts that he would be able to let her go at all appeared, whether it was he who faced the morning sun or her to a new life. No matter that he knew it was impossible, that she was human when he was so far from it. The facts didn't seem to matter any longer. Drawing a breath for the sheer pleasure of finding her scent, he knew he was losing the battle. A happiness he hadn't tasted in centuries sang through him like a beloved melody. A craving he was finding harder and harder to fight pounded in his body, and in his blood. To have her, all of her, as his.

He ensured his thoughts were blank as he battled inside with his own desires while they traveled over the treetops, pointing them toward the clearing. It didn't help his conscience or his restraint that Diego and Titania were a perfect example it *could* be done, but risking Lily in any way tore him apart. Titania had been an accident. An accident gone right. Over Lily's head above where she would see it and worry, he frowned. The risk was too high. He refused to impose on Lily the injustice that had been forced on him. She deserved the life laid before her, a life that was much improved, no matter that she would one day die.

He hid the internal wince at the pain-filled thought.

Setting them into the middle of the clearing, he relaxed his hold enough to reach for her and brush a kiss to her temple. "The stars are yours."

"I didn't feel it at all," she replied with a pleasurable gasp, filled with astonishment as she glanced around then looked up into his face. Moonlight gleamed off the fairness of her skin. Supple and pink, her lips glistened and her eyes sparkled, reflecting the tiny flames of the stars overhead. He couldn't remember seeing a more bewitching sight. If there was a God, he was torturing him because in that moment, the only thing he wanted was to taste her kiss again when he knew he shouldn't, when he knew he didn't have the right. Desire clawed up his frame, emboldened by the endless wants she created within him. He kept his lips shut, hiding the worst of it from her. There were a few wants and reactions he had very little control over when it came to the woman in his arms. He didn't want her to fear any part of him. Looking beyond her, over her shoulder, he fought his demons down.

He won, but only barely. Shivers rocked him anyway when her fingers slid down his shoulders as she released him.

"Who is the woman you mourn?"

He blinked, stunned by her question. She pressed tender fingertips to his mouth even though he couldn't think of a single way to answer her, taken too thoroughly by surprise.

"Don't be upset. I've seen her in your memories. She's beautiful, but so distant. I haven't tried to pry, but you think of her often."

Offering his hand, she twined them without hesitation, both turning to walk in any direction. An owl hooted off in the darkness. "She was my wife."

"Your wife? What happened?"

"When we were young, we left Portugal for California. Her uncle had a *rancho* and had offered us a home and work. The world was still very untamed then," he explained, although a little wistfully, pondering on the advances he'd witnessed since then and not all of them good. "The journey was long and hard on her. She didn't survive being at sea for so long and, shortly after she perished, the ship wrecked. Only a few survived."

She wound her free hand around his arm, offering support. "It must have been awful watching her die."

He bathed in her compassion and she gave it without hesitation. "It was the worst time of my life, until I was attacked." His voice grew cold. "Then I learned I was wrong."

Lily paused and stepped in front of him to study him. "You *look* young, until I look into your eyes."

"I was thirty-four the year we boarded. I'm not quite as old as Diego, though," he told her with a playful grin. Her dark, fawn eyes sparkled up at him with the shared humor.

"You don't sound like him. You do have an accent, but you talk different. More like everyone else. Until you're worried," she tacked on with a knowing glance.

He chuckled, urging her to walk again, admitting his one secret no one else would ever know. "I found one invention that stumped me when it was created. Television. For almost four years straight I tried to imagine why and how the people could be inside. I listened and watched. I used to try to mimic John Wayne and a few others. The whole process fascinated me. Eventually, I discovered the reels, the cameras, and it made sense. The last movie I saw was a few months ago, but it still seems incredible to me. It's a long stretch of evolution from the time I came from."

"You watch movies?" That seemed to take her completely by surprise when she didn't just stop, but jerked to a halt.

"Haven't you?" He arched an eyebrow, then lifted a hand to sweep her hair away from the side of her face so he could see her expressions. He loved watching the rise and fall of her thoughts on her features.

"OF COURSE." Lily shook her head, a very rich laugh rising from her. "You are not what I would have expected if someone had jumped up and yelled vampire." She pressed into him, lifting her face with her eyes closed to feel the butterfly brush of the breeze against her skin. A too short moment later, she began to walk again.

Movies? Never saw that one coming.

Lily strolled next to him, enjoying the crisp feeling of the mountain air, her thoughts rambling to all sorts of topics. The clearing was easily a mile wide, and she could see the tops of the mountains in the distance. Boulders and fallen trees lay to one side, like the mountain had at one time shaken and that was where everything loose had landed. It was a beautiful place to be and partly why she had asked to come there. The rest were reasons that she was still trying to fathom and come to grips with. Decisions she'd been weighing, actions needing deliberate thinking.

She'd been skirting around the real questions all night. Whether he knew or not that she was avoiding something, he didn't let on that he knew. The firmness of his arm beneath her hand was solid, warm and supportive. The hand entwined with hers was gentle, cradling. Shivers rocked her every time he stroked his thumb across her. It kept bringing his kiss to mind. The one that she couldn't forget. The one that made her want more.

She knew she had to be going insane. He was a vampire, for all that was holy! Silently, she cursed and swore, not that it helped her any. Her body still went up like a flame when he touched her, when he held her. She knew her whole body had ignited when he had kissed her. It wasn't frightening to her that it had been him, a vampire, to make it happen.

What frightened her was that it could end. The thought of anyone else getting close still disturbed her to the point she knew she was allowing her fears to have too much control. But she didn't want to test her theory only to find out she wouldn't ever be able to stand anyone else's touch again either. She wasn't an idiot—most days. She knew she was attracted to the contemplative man next to her. Knowing all of that about herself didn't stop the fears from rearing up, though, wanting to slice through any happiness she may have. The last three years had left a mark on her soul. There was no way to outrun it, no way to separate herself from it. The progress she had made was something to be proud of. She was walking with another person, a man who was quickly becoming a friend unlike any other when, right after the rescue, she could scarcely stand to look, talk or move for anything or anyone.

A wolf howled in the distance and a second matched its cry, both carrying over the trees with a beautiful night song echo that had her turning to hear it better.

"I bet this kind of wilderness is like what it was in your time."

He rolled a shoulder. “Some. It does bring back the memories, but they are old. Many things are simply gone.”

Sadness. It was still lingering on him, as much as her fear lingered on her. She drew a breath to ask her next question. “If I had not happened, would you have gone through with it?”

She felt his twitch through the hand she held, giving away his surprise at her query. Proof he wasn’t hanging from the rafters of her thoughts tonight. Her eyes misted a little at the effort of privacy when she knew it was almost a need, like breathing was for her, for him to know how she was doing and how he could make it better for her.

“Yes.”

This time, when she stopped, she planted herself in front of him. “Do it.”

“Do what?” His eyes widened and he looked at her, absolutely lost.

Her intention became clear when she tilted, swiping her hair clear from her neck. “I’m thrusting my fear to Hell,” she said, her throat raw as emotions bombarded her. It made perfect sense to her. “I entrust you with my life, Joaquin. The same way you put yours in my hands that night. You said a blood bond would make a concrete connection.” She lifted her eyes, seeking his, then dropping them, baring her neck, and her soul. “I offer mine to you to make that connection real.” Then, she stood still and waited.

The last thing she was expecting was for him to shove her away.

"No!"

Devastated, she couldn't grasp what she'd said to create such an explosive rejection. Her heart shriveled as her insides turned to ice. *The scars.* They were everywhere. Agonized tears filled her eyes. She'd blissfully forgotten about them with the way he looked at her, with the way he kissed her, forgotten how truly broken she was. How could she have forgotten? How could she have dared to move above them when she would always suffer for them? Pain and anger rose from her past, blinding her to the hurt in his eyes.

She ripped her hands through her hair, making it fly in all directions. "You're right. What was I thinking?" she nearly shouted, rage filling her in the chilled and agonized depths where she could still feel, shriveling beneath the reality that she'd blissfully, if mistakenly, been able to forget how she looked. "I'm damaged, scarred."

"No! That's not why—"

Fury flashed against her clenched vision until she swore she saw lightning bolts wreaking havoc in the sky. "Isn't it?" Sobs racked her as memories shackled her around her throat and shook her. Roaring filled her ears and she slapped her hands over them to try to stop the wailing shrieks and cruel words. She sank to her knees. "Make it stop!"

"Lily!" Firm hands tugged at her wrists, but she fought him, fought the pressure, clawing at the person in front of her, fighting for her life.

"No! Don't touch me!" She screamed, seeing nothing but the faces of the men of her past as they mocked her, held her down, pinned her and abused her. She whipped her head in remembered pain with the feeling of a lash slicing her back.

"Lily!"

She heard nothing, too encased in the memories as they swelled and crashed across her vision and attacked her body. Memories she'd spent hours of every day, days of every week, trying to forget, trying to move beyond their hideous stranglehold. Memories of so much pain, so real she felt the sharp slice of each cut to her skin, every brutal fist and degrading touch. Tumbling deeper into a well she'd almost managed to control, she trembled violently, lost to the remembered tortures.

A single touch on her forehead swept it all away with a blanket of nothing and then she fell slack to an utter silence.

chapter eleven

HOLDING her like a cherished gift, Joaquin cradled her to his body like the fragile heart he knew she was as he approached the house. The front door opened before him and he ensured it closed with a bare thought to the outside world. No one was downstairs to watch him, or they would have seen the complete devastation he couldn't remove from his features.

In her room, he laid her down with tender care on the bed and lovingly brushed the hair away from her tear ravaged face.

He had done that to her. Somehow, he had caused her to relive the pain of her imprisonment. Through their bond, he had felt every single sting of the whip, every painful violation of her body as they overwhelmed her. It was no less than he deserved.

"Forgive me, *corazón*. I never meant for you to suffer." He knelt and closed his eyes to silently beg for the forgiveness he didn't deserve.

It had been a knee-jerk reaction to push her away because he had been fighting that very hunger since their kiss. Call it a need, an urge, a clawing driving force—they all could be used to describe the way he craved to do just what she wanted. To solidify the bond they shared.

To make her his, unquestionably.

He wanted her like no one else. He desired her with a depth that obliterated any memory. The want to touch, taste, please, worship was an endless ache of hunger in his blood, in his body. Hiding his reactions from her had become a full time torture, his only respite was when he had no choice, when the sun was high.

The flutter of her hand landing on his cheek startled him. He hadn't realized he'd been kneeling with his head pillowed on her stomach.

"I'm sorry," she whispered, her voice graveled and raw from her outbursts.

"Do not apologize." He said it firmly, fighting to make the words happen, so close to tears himself he wasn't sure he could stop them. Lifting to see her clearly, her hand followed and he cupped her hand to his face, grateful for the simple contact. "I hurt you. The last thing I would want on this earth is to cause you more pain."

"I know." A slow breath made her body rise and fall in front of him. "I'm tired," she murmured, turning away. Tawny eyes opened only briefly, flat and devoid of any of the life and energy he knew was the woman he'd unintentionally hurt by trying to protect her. Not just from herself, but from him.

A light tug told him to let her hand go. He did, feeling the chasm of her silence as it broadened between them. He stepped away, guiltily hiding his presence from her to watch her fall asleep, to ensure the monsters of her past did not return.

He had to make this right. Slowly, as he watched over her, the beginning of an idea formed. He could only hope it was enough to prove to her how special she was to him.

LILY closed Tabitha's door after another night of quiet reading. The woman was hurting, and mostly hiding. Lily let her have her way. She felt battered, herself, torn and emotionally ravaged. She was utterly useless to help Tabitha the way she felt. She knew Kathy and Amy talked to her, giving Tab all the support they could.

The problem was, Lily was running on empty.

Joaquin had disappeared.

She hadn't called for him outright. She could, but something stopped her cold. Shame was hard to hide from considering the way she'd lashed out at him. She knew he was somewhere. He would never go back on his word to Diego, but she didn't feel him in her thoughts anymore. Like he had disappeared out of her life only.

It hurt. Not in the same way her relapse had hurt her. This pain was deeper, cruelly dragging the life out of her in a way she couldn't explain, and she knew no way to stop it. She'd never thought she'd miss anyone on this level, where nothing held any joy for her. It was a day to day existence, and this time, she couldn't even blame her past.

Simply put, her heart was dying.

When she dragged her feet to the kitchen for her nightly tea, her gaze landed on the silhouette at the bottom of the stairs and her heart tripped before her brain recognized the man standing as still as a picture. His eyes were focused on her and nothing else, their dark shadows openly exposing his acceptance of the blame he suffered for the pain he'd caused her. After five nights, she couldn't make herself care anymore. She didn't even know she was going to do it when she jumped from the third step to land in his arms. He caught her with a whirled grace.

"Where have you been?" she demanded into his embrace, too overjoyed to make it remotely accusing.

Setting her on her feet, he reached to cup her throat, his thumb running delicately against her skin. His eyes glittered, seeming to reflect her thoughts back to her in their mysterious depths. "I've been right here. I wasn't sure after…" He hesitated, and she saw his gaze flicker to her lips. "I missed you."

Before she could note if they were alone or not, he was lowering to her lips, claiming them with a tenderness that made her shiver and almost weep. Every apology she heard was rasped for her ears alone as he begged for her forgiveness and understanding. He'd never meant to hurt her. He would die before he would ever let her past rise up again and destroy something as beautiful as she was. That he adored everything about her. She was not broken, and he'd never meant for her to think that was why he had rejected her.

She could forgive him anything in that moment.

The warmth of his lips lifted from hers and, reluctantly, she opened her eyes.

"I want to show you something. Will you come with me?"

She nodded, having a hard time finding her voice. Her thoughts swung to Tabitha, worried about leaving her alone with her having longer moments of lucidity.

She followed him when he turned for the door, opening it as he said, "She is safe, asleep. We both will know if she wakes."

"You're sure?"

He nodded. "We won't be gone long."

"What are we going to do?"

"It's a surprise." He gave her a quick look, nearly playful, and held her close. "Hang on."

"What are you doing?" Her hands swept up and clasped behind his neck in reaction, already knowing what to expect and anticipating the surprise.

"Taking you on a date."

Her mouth fell open. Then, she laughed, feeling buoyant for the first time in almost a week. She rested her head against his chest, amazed all over again at Joaquin's ability to reach inside and make her melt. She never felt her feet leave the ground.

HE HAD hurt her. He would do anything to take it back. He couldn't. So maybe he could just make it right. It had taken him more nights that he never wanted to spend alone again to think of a way to fix it. Each night he'd burned, smoldered with his need to be with her, but he hadn't trusted himself. He feared he would forget his own promise as high as his desires were raging for this woman. He'd stayed away as long as he physically could. Tonight, his resistance had shattered finding her at the top of the stairs and feeling her pain. Yet more pain he was causing.

He curled his fingers through her hair, letting her look up now that he was where he wanted to be. He hadn't wanted to frighten her with the distance they had come. He'd hazed the journey for her.

"Where are we?" she asked, looking around.

"In town. You told me you haven't been." He wanted to show her the world, give her wonderful memories that would eventually bury the pain of her past if he couldn't completely obliterate them.

She shrank into his body, cowering in the shadows where they stood, too shaken to lift from his embrace where she tried to make herself smaller. "I want to go home." The terrified whisper in her voice made him ache to comfort her. Her fear was instant, a thick and tangible wall between them.

Her face filled his palm as he cupped her chin. He felt the way she shivered and held her closer. "Lily. You are safe. No one will see you."

"There could be people here, looking for us. David is still missing," she hissed. The anxious tremor in her voice almost made him change his mind, but he shook his head.

"No. Listen to what I'm telling you. *No one* will see you." He wrapped his arms around her, not moving from the alley where he had landed. He wouldn't push her, but he believed she could do this. He knew she wanted to. "Do you understand? No one will see you, or me."

She lifted her face to search his, her cheeks pale. She stared at him with burnished gold eyes. "Wha-What do you mean?"

The stark terror in her eyes tore him apart. Somewhere in those eyes was the brave woman he knew she was, yet here she stood, trembling and terrified to walk down the street with him.

"You know I am not human," he said, swallowing when his voice was laden with emotions. "I can protect you, Lily." Lashes hid his view of her beauty when looking into those same golden-brown eyes became impossible. The things he wanted from this woman... The ways he wanted to touch her made his entire body ache with a rushing need he'd long ago forgotten. Five nights had dulled nothing.

"I trust you, Joaquin." Four whispered words, spoken in true honesty. His heart rose with a swift punch into his throat. He'd feared she never would again. She nuzzled deeper into his embrace, her cheek pressed against his chest. His arms tightened automatically. He breathed in the essence that wove through her hair. After a moment fighting his own reactions, he nodded.

"Just relax." He tipped her face up and brushed a sweet, molten kiss to her lips. Everywhere she pressed against him, everywhere she touched him, left him on fire. He slid his arms from around the feminine curves of her body and clasped a hand in his, threading their fingers together, taking a single deep breath to ground his thoughts. It was an odd habit for a vampire, one that stuck, especially when he breathed by choice, not out of need, but at that moment, he needed to center himself somehow. His thoughts were in a chaotic turmoil and he needed to control them for her sake. For both their sakes.

He took a step and she followed, albeit with a low shiver he could feel through the interlocking skin of their fingers. He lifted them and kissed her knuckles.

She stayed close once they cleared the corner of the alley, both strolling in an unhurried way. Gradually, the clutched rigidity of her hand in his relaxed. He caught her gaze and offered a smile. Streetlamps spilled light across the sidewalk as they passed by storefronts and she began to look around with interest, peering into windows, or watching as people flowed around them like water over rocks in a stream without even a glance in their direction.

"They can't see us, can they?" she whispered, leaning close to be heard.

He shook his head. "They can't hear us either."

"Incredible." She calmed in increments next to him, the ease of her grip in his giving her away. Pedestrians were few, but the occasional passerby or car on the street still made her pause. The sudden sound of her breath catching, or the weight of her anticipating discovery at every turn, soon faded. He let her stop and investigate to her heart's content at whatever struck her fancy—window dressings, posters of movies, anything at all. Even the stuffed animals in the window of a children's store.

The simple pleasures of her joy filled him. Soon her lips were curved into an engaging smile and her eyes sparkled with her newfound freedom. Time wasn't marked, but most of the stores were closed and locked for the night.

"This was wonderful," she quietly remarked with absolute fascination when they reached the end of another block. Street lights brightened the night with their changing colors. Cars drove by without a single hesitation to wonder about the couple walking after dark. They were invisible to the passing world. The thing that broke his heart was the way she refused to look at any reflection of herself, or at any clothes. Tonight, as always, she wore a plain sweatshirt and jeans, covering any part of her that would otherwise be visible.

His fingers tightened for a heartbeat. To him, she was beautiful, from the golden earth color of her eyes to the burnished sunset and cinnamon of her hair. The texture of her skin, the taste of her on his lips, burned into him. The feel of her lush body called to him, stronger than ever. Absence had done nothing to cool this fire she alone created. The desire raging through him was unlike any he'd ever experienced. A dragged breath shot a liquid shudder through his body as he lived with that forbidden pleasure, just for a moment, in his own mind.

He looked away to try to control his thoughts, but try as he might, the feel of her succumbing to his desire drove into him like a spike of lightning. The craving for her was impossible to ignore. And with his craving was a deeper one yet, a hunger he'd ignored, fought and denied since meeting this woman. Craving the flavor of life that only she would have.

He hungered for her. Completely.

"Joaquin?"

He snapped around to look at her. Wide eyes caught his stare, worry dimming their sparkle. Want. Desire. He couldn't deny it any longer. When he thought he'd be able to walk away when the time was right, he conceded there would be no leaving her behind. Admitting it made everything a lot more complicated. He couldn't have her, yet he would never let her go either.

He forced the argument to cease. There was no other way. He had no idea how to be with her and not make her *his* prisoner. She was human. She would age. She deserved a life. Feeling like a selfish bastard wasn't helping him find a solution or leading him on the right path to take, but at the moment, it was all he had. She was all he had.

He paused on the sidewalk as a blankness permeated the air, oozed toward them like a sludge on the wind, interrupting his inner turmoil very effectively. They were invisible, but others of his kind would know he was there. Energy pulses could be felt in the surrounding wind. It was taking energy to shield them from human eyes. He scanned, surprised another of the Brethren would be in the area. They were not lying thick on the ground, as he'd heard some say, or to even find another this close to Diego's territory. Only rarely had he found his own kind. Now it was too late to try to leave. If he fled, he would draw this unnamed Brethren to the house, endangering those living there. Here, he could protect himself and Lily.

"What's the matter?" she asked, automatically leaning toward him, searching him and the surrounding street. It was mostly quiet now.

"Nothing." He deliberately pulled her closer, away from the lights into the shadows of the closest alley. He searched the sky, and listened for the newcomer. The unknown vampire was either being cautious, or wasn't any more interested in meeting than he was.

That soon proved to be wrong.

"She's a hot one. Let's share," crowed a crass voice as a form appeared on the street before them.

Joaquin didn't care for the way he eyed Lily at his arrival, like a trophy. Lily was no one's prey.

"Be quiet!" It was an order, and he had no chance to explain either. He pushed her behind him, facing the owner of the voice. It was worse than he'd thought. He was sure he was facing an imbecile.

Putrid odors reeked from where the other stood only a few feet away. Lily buried her nose into his shirt. This one apparently liked the environs of the local dump as his hiding place and hadn't learned or didn't care that he could erase the stench.

"I am sorry, lovely. Running would have lured him into a chase. Here, it is only he and I. Do you trust me?"

"Kind of not the time to ask that now, don't you think?"

"I believe I will take that as a vote of confidence."

He heard her impertinent mental groan loud and clear, but showed no sign of it on his face.

"Come on," demanded the other vampire, waving a hand to make Joaquin move. "Pass her up. I'm hungry." He rubbed his hands together, as if waiting for a lavish feast.

Joaquin made sure to block their immediate surroundings from any who could become interested in the men talking in the shadows, keeping all three invisible to any idle curiosity. The later hour and absence of business patrons helped considerably without him spending a lot of energy on the effort. "We can be gentlemen about this. It's rude to discuss this on the street."

That seemed to make the other vampire pause, standing straight and eyeing Joaquin with confusion. Then, he grinned. "Oh, you're one of them fancy talking ones, ain't ya? Where're you from?"

Lily coughed into her hand to not gurgle her laughter. Joaquin doubted the other vampire had a clue she was laughing at him. "That isn't really important, is it?"

"When I tell you to, take two steps back from me."

He felt her nod against him. "You and I both know what we really want, right?"

"You ain't kidding! I haven't had a good, hot one like her in weeks. All a bunch o' hags. All that seems to be out at night anymore." Dark blue eyes began to blaze at the thought of what he was about to indulge in, and with whom.

Joaquin clicked his tongue as if in sympathy for the uncouth and unwashed creature daring to continue to stare at Lily like a prize catch. "I can see how that can be such a disappointment to one such as yourself." Joaquin couldn't understand how this one had been turned. He was not aged, and by his manners, it appeared he may have been half-witted as well. It was like Tani had said, there was no rhyme or reason to those who were chosen by their creators. This was proof someone in the Brethren was not being at all conscientious about his chosen 'children'.

"I know!" he agreed with a robust grin. He scratched his crotch, apparently so recently turned he still retained many of his human expressions and gestures.

"I will make you a deal," Joaquin lied. "She is special to me. I will share." He raised a hand to pause the other's advance. "However, you will do the proper thing and take her into the shadows. Agreed?"

"Oh shit, yeah! Man, I'm gonna have me a time with her."

"I bet you are," Joaquin muttered under his breath. He gestured to the alley a few feet behind them. "Shall we?"

"Name's Kurt, by the way."

Joaquin rolled his eyes. Didn't anyone tell this one the Brethren didn't get along?

"Joaquin, there's something false about him."

He followed the approaching vampire with an untrusting gaze. "*What do you mean?"*

"I mean he's not an idiot! Look out!"

The warning saved his life. He may have been large, and inordinately insufferable, but Kurt was not a moron. The entire discussion had been a ruse to allow Kurt the chance to get close enough to make a lethal attack, something Joaquin would have never allowed if he'd been alone and not protecting Lily.

The attack was swift as a huge, meaty fist swung around, forming into a large claw at contact, knocking Joaquin away from Lily's side with an unexpected strength and dagger sharp claws that curled into rending hooks as they tore into his shoulder. Apparently, Kurt was not really in the mind to share. The act had been nothing less than a distraction from his intent. She was vulnerable and completely exposed.

Joaquin released a hiss of fury. Large, raw punctures bloodied the shoulder of his shirt.

"That was the wrong thing to do, my friend," Joaquin growled, every word coated in menace. Anger made his voice thick. Putting on speed from where he'd spun from the force of Kurt's attack, he wedged himself between the blood lusting vampire and Lily. He'd never had any intention of letting him near her. Joaquin's only goal had been to avoid witnesses to the coming death that would be a swift and enjoyable punishment for threatening her.

Lily evaded one grasping hand as Kurt reached beyond Joaquin for her hair, uncaring of the wall of Joaquin's body in the way. Kurt continued to work around him as if he didn't exist.

"I'll give her back when I'm done," Kurt drawled without concern. "Come here, honey. I'm hungry."

Joaquin watched in horror as Lily froze. It was something he had not counted on, not against Lily. Kurt was manipulating her, invading her private thoughts to do his bidding in thrall, but completely aware of what was happening to her to terrorize her further. That meant Kurt wasn't paying attention to Joaquin. It only took a short-lived second in time for him to reach Lily. Then, Kurt had his hand on her, pulling her toward him, his long teeth dripping with a ravenous hunger Joaquin had tasted and had managed to step away from.

Joaquin's vision became a field of red.

He launched himself against Kurt, tearing Lily free of his repugnant hold. He pushed out to her, cocooning her to soften her landing on the hard pavement of the alley at the same time he found flesh with a rammed shoulder. The impact met Kurt's rather large body mass. It made finding a place to strike difficult. He must have fed often and frequently to maintain it. Overweight issues weren't usually problems for the Brethren.

Snarls filled the alley like a pack of ravenous dogs had been set loose. Kurt dug into Joaquin's wounded shoulder while they grappled on the ground, both looking for the upper hand. "That's for reneging!" Large claws widened the wounds, and Joaquin's jaw clamped shut, ignoring the blistering pain that radiated to fill his upper body. With a vicious kick, Kurt tossed Joaquin off and lunged for Lily, watching them both in dazed horror from where she lay crumpled, unmoving on the ground.

Joaquin only had one choice and would have to face the consequences after. He wouldn't be able to end this one by strategy alone. He changed his form, embracing a large wolf's shape as he lunged once more, hearing her scream behind him as he did so. He didn't want to hold anything back from her. He was what he was, and right then, he had no choice but to protect her the only way he knew how. He was not a skilled fighter. He relied on the creatures that were. He lunged up the other vampire's body with powerful legs to dig his teeth into the flesh at his neck, snapping his spine between powerful jaws.

Kurt collapsed in a mushy bag of bones, roaring in pain on the ground. He flopped like a huge, banked fish, trying to take a shape to repel the next attack, with no time to heal such a major injury. Joaquin never gave him the chance. While he held him pinned to the ground, a single claw grew saber sharp. With a deadly motion, Joaquin sliced his head clean from his body. He saw Lily wince and turn away, and regretted with every breath he took for showing her this part of his world. It was the ugly reality she didn't need to know. Not yet, not ever.

It didn't take long before the body disintegrated, skin, flesh and clothes turning to dust. Joaquin concentrated once, more commanding sharp winds into the alley and shot the ashes upward to be carried in all directions by the surface breezes over the buildings.

Silence permeated the air, the faint sound of life beyond the alley filtering in now with the battle over. Exhausted and weary from the fight, he was even more leery of the coming moments, facing Lily's disgust and horror over what it was that made Joaquin a vampire. The hunger, the bloodlust that was a fine line before him every single night he opened his eyes. The violence that, even at the best of times, couldn't be helped. He'd never wanted to expose her to any of it. Tonight had gone horribly wrong on so many levels. When he'd wanted to prove to her how special she was to him, that she was safe, that he could protect her to give her room to heal, he'd failed.

When every trace of Kurt's existence was gone, and unable to find a way to procrastinate any longer, he walked to where Lily sat huddled on the ground and sank down next to her.

chapter twelve

"WAS HE for real?" she gasped, stunned and shaken, clamping her jaw like a vise to not let her teeth chatter. She stared at the ground where the body had been splayed. There...then gone. Nothing left any indication he had been there at all. No blood, no ash. Just...nothing.

Joaquin barely moved from where he collapsed next to her, leaning against the wall with his head resting on his forearms supported by his knees. Exhaustion radiated off of him.

"Unfortunately. I am sorry."

She jerked up straight at his tone, studying him. "For what?" There was rued apology in his words. She knew Kurt's appearance wasn't his fault, just as she'd caught those brief glimpses of his wife in his memories and knew her death was not his fault. He held the blame when there was none. Although she'd be the first person to admit to being a converted believer in the impossible now. She was getting used to the idea of Joaquin being a vampire, and Tani and even Diego. Kurt was the type she never wanted to meet again.

"It was because you are with me he found you. He sensed the energy—" He pinched his lips, silencing his next words with a clipped sound.

"Hey. You saved me from him. You can't hide like that anymore." She looked into his thoughts without thinking twice and shuddered when she ran right into the pain radiating from his shoulder, and his exhaustion. It surprised her more to discover he was blaming himself because he had been using so much of his own energy to keep them from view. It had led Kurt to them like a beacon. She pushed his hair away from his face and sucked in a deep breath to not cry in alarm. "You're pale!"

He only shrugged.

She grabbed his arm and shook him. "Look at me, Joaquin!" She shook him again to add emphasis to her order. Her lungs hurt when he did and met her searching gaze. His skin was taut and he was deathly pale. "How often do you have to eat?" She studied his face, waiting and watching. She knew Diego took care of himself and Tani nightly. "How long has it been?" she demanded when he refused to answer her, belying the order with a tender sweep of his hair from his features.

"Two nights. It's not important. I will see to myself soon enough." He let his head drift to rest against the wall behind them, his eyes closing. She wanted to groan loudly at his answer.

Now she understood why Titania was regularly wanting to strangle Diego. She suddenly had the urge to do exactly the same thing to Joaquin. It was too late to yell at him for not taking care of himself. She shifted to her knees, and cradled his face in her palms. "Joaquin, you haven't seen yourself. You *need*...whatever it is you need to do."

"I will not leave you," he said in denial, rocking his head back and forth to punctuate it. "I will take you home."

She ground her teeth together. "And then what? Hope to find someone out on the street at this time of night when you're done making sure I'm safe at home?" Which was exactly what he would do. She wasn't sure she wanted him finding just anyone. The idea of it bothered her. She shook her head, unsure why it did, and unable to name the reason behind it. "Look, I know you didn't want to before, but Joaquin, you have given me so much already. This is completely different. Let me do this for you," she entreated him.

His eyes popped open. "No. I won't do it. Not to you." Tenderness was woven through his words on laces of steel.

She swallowed, wondering at her own sanity, at the direction her thoughts were taking her. Looking at him, the sharpness emphasized in his skin, she knew she had to. He wouldn't ask either, which left her no choice. She pushed away the uncertain feeling threatening to rise inside. She had been frozen with fear seeing Kurt stare at her, those long fangs of his shining in the night like daggers.

I'm not thinking of really doing this, am I?

No more than I did a week ago, she mocked herself. Looking at Joaquin's face, though, apparently, she was. He needed her. She took a steadying breath, not dropping her eyes from his, and made up her mind. This wasn't the same thing as the bond she'd thought she wanted. This was straight survival. If what she had could help him, heal or cure him in whatever manner they needed, then there was no other option. Not for her.

She studied him for several silent, stretching moments. He remained stoically quiet, hardly blinking. "Titania said it doesn't take much, right?" she queried, albeit a little on the wobbly side. She swallowed to shove the feeling far away. "Enough to give you back your strength would help, wouldn't it?"

"I will not take from you," he said, his face growing stiff with the strength of his own will. "You have suffered. I will not do this to you."

She pictured her hands around his throat and made sure to send him the image. She was trying hard not to get mad at him, but it wasn't working very well for her. His expression never changed, and it appeared his eyes may have glittered even more in defiance. Implacable was a word that suited him well.

"You haven't seen your face," she repeated. She purposely flipped her gaze to the blood stain on his shoulder. She couldn't tell if the wounds were still bleeding, but she knew the punctures, as much as his not taking care of his needs since her breakdown, were causing him problems. He needed this. It wouldn't be a far off the mark guess to believe he didn't like to leave the perimeter of the house after what had happened between them. Just because she'd never felt him, she was more than positive he'd rarely left.

She sighed and sat on her haunches, creating a small space between them, pushing her hair away from her throat while she watched him. He might as well have been carved from stone. He didn't so much as twitch in acknowledgement of her movements. "Joaquin, you have given yourself into my care. You are the one who made that promise and I am caring for you. Now get over whatever sense of self-loathing you are trying to hide from me for needing this." She leaned forward until she was practically touching noses with him, meeting his gaze with a resolute one of her own. "You did not cause this. You did not cause my pain. I was wrong to put your face to my pain. I can help you. Now, damn it, do something about what you need." Then, she tilted until her throat touched his chin and, with her eyes closed, she waited.

She expected him to push her away again. She expected pain. She expected a new kind of agony for her offer and was prepared for it. She knew what vampires were. The one thing she knew for certain was Joaquin would not kill her. It was really the only thing she was confident in. She knew what they needed, what Kurt would have done had he gotten so far, and knew she was putting her life in his hands. She knew a lot.

She realized, as the seconds ticked past, she knew nothing.

His hands reached around and cradled her tenderly, as if she were a precious gift to be treasured, to be handled like exquisite jewels. He pulled her into his chest, giving her space to become comfortable, supporting her on his lap. "You are amazing," he breathed against her throat.

She shivered at the warmth of his touch, felt as it cascaded down her skin like a single caress. He braced her to rest against his body, and she clenched in anticipation, and a little fear.

What she felt was not pain. She felt kisses. He dropped them everywhere, tender brushes of warmth to her temple, her cheek. He murmured soft words into her ear as he gifted those honeyed kisses of his along her jaw. She felt herself relax, becoming almost languid in his embrace.

Shivers started and ran along her spine when he slid his mouth down the length of her neck. Sparks seemed to follow in his wake and her skin tingled.

"Do not fear this. I can block the memory."

"Don't you even dare! I'm not scared." Okay, just a little lie, she conceded, keeping the thought as tucked into her mind as possible.

She felt his smile against her where he pressed those decadent kisses and she knew she hadn't stuck the little lie deep enough, but he didn't stop anything of what he was doing, or change his method. The rasp of his tongue ignited nerves she didn't know she had when he gently laved her pulse. Those sparks grew into bright lights of color, exploding all along her spine. She gasped sharply at the sensation, arching into the feeling. A tossed arm circled his head, holding him closer, unwilling to let him stop.

A slow groan rose from deep inside his body, vibrating her skin where he suckled. The near-tickle of a sharp tooth poised over her, rubbing, enticing, seducing, and she shivered with a new want. A heartbeat later, a pinpoint pain made her cry out, but it quickly transcended into a pulsating heat, something so electric she felt herself go up like a hot flame within his touch.

Nothing in her life had ever felt like this, so all-consuming, so decadent. Lily pulled him tighter. She couldn't help herself. She'd never felt anything like it. After years of pain and agony, she'd discovered pure bliss.

JOAQUIN'S world exploded with the first drop. Her skin was warm, pliant, sweet, and he savored every caress he gave her on his lips, wanting to remember this moment forever. When his teeth broke through her skin, he knew his dead heart exploded into action. She was everything he had envisioned. Sweet as the forbidden fruit he had believed her to be. Heat and desire sank into him as he absorbed her selfless offer. It was as if stars were lit behind his eyelids, as if there was lightning coursing over him, over skin and nerve alike. There was so much energy, so much compassion in her, it was wrapping around him and holding him to her as tightly as any chain ever made. He had never experienced this while taking what had, since the beginning, been nothing more than the filling of a physical need. He was in awe of what he was feeling. He was in awe of the woman in his hold.

There was no denying it. With Lily, there was something *more*.

The raging need to claim her reawakened with a vengeance and attacked him ruthlessly with her taste flowing over his tongue and filling his body. The same reaction he'd had when he'd first explored her kiss. The same crying demand to make her his. The urge brought his hold a little closer, wanting to hold her as tight as he could, to never let her go.

It wasn't right. She needed things he wouldn't be able to give her. She deserved a freedom in her life that had been maliciously stripped from her. A chance to find what had been stolen from her. All the longed for things he'd found within her deepest recesses—her family, her past, her future. He fought the urge down, hiding the depth of his fight from her.

He sipped gently at her pulse, not wanting to mark her, then tenderly ensured there would be no sign on her fair skin. He had not taken as much as he truly needed, but he had taken enough to see them both safely home. The depth of her concern for him, to make sure he took care of himself, tingled with an unusual warmth near his heart. The slow realization that she was special was no longer in doubt. Unfortunately, he still didn't have any answers to the swarm of questions that grew in leaps and bounds with every touch, every kiss, with every screaming desire that would remain unfulfilled for the angel in his hands.

He tilted her face up to him and caressed her lips, feeling their luscious warmth beneath his own. He knew her fears and wanted to be gentle, but right at that moment, desire and passion filled his veins as much as her blood did. It was impossible to simply hold her and do nothing. He tightened his restraint. He had seen beauty within her at first sight, but had not thought of her as a woman, as a man would see her, and want what he held. Want to cherish her, to caress her, to feel her. To please her. She made him hunger in more than one way, and it wasn't easy to keep it under the surface, hidden behind his control. That need to control himself had pushed home how vulnerable she was, and with her vulnerability, how much she *was* trusting him.

Kurt's arrival had forced her to face more than he had ever wanted to pressure her with. Yet, she was staying with him, solid in her belief of him, and even though she feared life almost every day, she didn't let her reality make her fear him. There weren't enough words to describe how he saw her. And she had demanded he not dim what he was doing. She was an all or nothing type of woman, courageous without even knowing it.

The thought made him smile while he continued to nuzzle her skin and drop gentle touches anywhere within reach, which was quite a bit of her warmed neck.

She sighed at his continued ministrations and he wanted to catch her sigh again. So he did.

He lifted his palm to her face and held her, his eyes feasting on the way hers grew luminous, watching him. "You are beautiful," he whispered, dipping lower to hover over those lips he craved. He craved them almost as much as he knew he would now hunger for her taste. "Never doubt the way I see you."

He hesitated only a brief moment, to make her aware of what he was going to do. She was not lost in the mindless thrall he usually instilled on the ones he needed. He couldn't remember a single time he had not blanked a mind for feeding. She was coherent of every motion, of nearly every desire swarming through his heated blood. Her welcoming reactions made his gut clench even tighter, her innocent expression of desire enrapturing him. Not a hint of fear colored her gaze, and the beat of her heart was steady, and building. Anticipation. He allowed himself to indulge in it, to savor it as he had not allowed himself when he had first shared her kiss, too shocked at the riot of intense feelings and sensations from those first stolen moments. Now, a different kind of hunger had invaded him, a desire he had believed had died with Angelica.

When he claimed her lips, this new heat filled him, pulsed along his skin, and the first thing that entered his thoughts was that he had found heaven. The temptation to have more was strong and lured him closer, brought her nearer as he delved into the sweetness of her mouth. Everything about her was sweet. Addictive. From the sweet essence of her life's heartbeat to the beguiling little whimpered gasps of pleasure that slipped from her lips beneath his.

He cradled her tighter into his arms, weaving his fingers into the richness of her flaming hair. The red of a courageous heart. He traced her welcoming mouth, sipping at the sensitive flesh of her lips as he memorized every little moan passing between them.

He wanted to plunge his hands into the thickness twined over his fingers and devour her sighs, but he reined in the heightened volcanic boil of his desire to a simmer, keeping it under the placid surface he knew she trusted. This explosive level of desire, of wanting, was not what he had expected from her kiss. The reality of his passion had been dead for centuries. How could a single kiss make him feel so much?

It was like a new world was opening up for him. He was seeing all of it through her eyes. Colors and scents. Life all around them. She was giving all of it to him. The sensations bombarded him, growing and layering on the last. Everything that had once been barren was now verdant, his soul spread wide open like an offering to absorb the light she shared with him, obliterating any lingering darkness within his heart and mind. The gentle slide of his lips over hers created a fiery friction spurring his desires as much as her blood had only a moment before. Sipping at them when he wanted to devour drove his desires higher. When she opened for him, he slipped between her teeth and fed on her kiss like she was the finest ambrosia.

It was too much for him. After so many bleak years, he felt close to overloading, and he refused to fail her, not now, not there. He had brought her to town to make his point that she was safe no matter what, especially safe from and with him. Instead, she had given him yet another gift, her trust, her belief, and now her own life's blood.

He had to pull himself away from the temptation that she was. Her lips were a glistening petal of softness. She had perfect lips for kisses. She made him feel, made him want, and he had no right.

But he knew that wouldn't stop him. Not now.

He brought her closer, simply soaking up the warmth of her skin, tracing her jaw with his lips. She purred, caressing him almost restlessly, brushing against his chest with the taut peaks of her breasts wantonly. Even beneath her sweatshirt and through his own clothes, the touch of her own rising desire seared him through.

Her fingers snaked upward, filling with the weight of his hair, holding him tightly in answer.

"Lily," he said between touches and tastes. "Delicate and as beautiful as the flower."

"And I swear you're blind," she teased him, smiling up at him from where she rested on his lap. She seemed completely unconcerned with her position, or their location.

"I could take eternity convincing you," he said on a slow breath near her ear, tenderly licking at the pink shell. Daring his restraint, he shared his wishful image with her, opening his mind to her with his deepest desires pushing him.

Moonlight played over them both in the meadow he knew she loved, the small valley hidden between the peaks of the nearest mountains where it created a beautiful haven of solitude and natural beauty. In his mind, he held her close, held her tight as he kissed her. Not just the light kisses he'd shared with her, but deep, passionate kisses that enflamed them both. Kisses that left them both yearning and craving and demanding fulfillment in a way tender kisses would never give. It was impossible to hide the truth, how deeply he craved her, wanted her. Needed her. And he didn't try. Not now, yet here, in their shared moment out of time, he could show her, share how he saw her, desire her the way he truly felt and wanted. In his shared vision there was a measure of safety. A safety that still challenged his sanity.

"I want it all," he breathed into her thoughts, even as he held her protectively on his lap, sharing the make-believe dream with her. She shivered, but not in fear or revulsion, but in wonder. He heard the

sharp rise and fall of her breathing, the swift intake of surprise as he continued with his seduction.

With tender hands, he removed the light dress he imagined her in, sweeping it over her head, baring her like a fiery headed goddess to his view. Her body was perfection. Firm breasts filled the touch of his palm, sleek legs he craved to feel wrapped around his waist. Cinnamon curls covered her sweetest treasure. He knew her taste. She would be as sweet as she was everywhere else. He swallowed, barely able to restrain himself, even in the shared dream. This was for her, her pleasure, her enjoyment. To share without fear.

There was no logic in how deeply he wanted this to be real. He nuzzled her closer in his arms, pushing his limits with the dream seduction, sharing his every touch, his every caress, through the images in his mind.

Gentle hands slid up her body, against the bared skin he envisioned, pulling her tighter until she pressed with seductive heat against his chest, skin to skin. He felt aflame from the heat of her body pressed against his, from just the image. He shuddered, realizing the real thing could very well set him ablaze with heat unlike anything he'd ever experienced.

His lips flowed over her shoulder to the pulse of her throat, kissing her there, thanking any god he could think of for the beauty of endless courage beneath his traveling lips. A shudder shook the woman in his arms, the one he held and the one he seduced. She was as entrenched in the fantasy seduction as he was. There wasn't a whisper of fear, only anticipation and need swelling and swirling around the pair.

With intent filled motions, he drifted lower, caressing the gentle slope of her breast with a seeking tongue, trailing a damp path over their flush softness. Her fingers delved into his hair, holding him tighter, her fingertips massaging his scalp in encouragement. Then, he lapped at a taut, rosebud peak and she gasped, arching and writhing, a breathy moan slipping from her, a sound that ignited him even more. Before he could tell himself it was going too far, he took that hardened nub between his lips, enjoying the feel of her full breast as he worked his tongue over her flesh, sweeping to draw her deeper, then lightly letting her free to repeat the torture. Her head fell back, lost in a sea of brilliant sensations.

A low growl escaped from between his lips as he suckled and tasted her sweetness on his tongue. He wasn't even sure which 'he' had made it as deep as he was in his own fantasy. Her body beckoned to him and he had to obey.

"I want you Joaquin," she panted against his throat. Everything within him froze.

That wasn't the Lily of his mirage dream who had spoken.

The dream vanished in a cold slap of shock. He shook everywhere with repressed desire racing through him like a volcanic river.

He pushed it all down with a vicious hand of control. "I'm sorry, lovely. I shouldn't have pushed you." God, how he ached. What had he done? He'd lost sight of what he'd intended with the sharing. He buried himself against her, fighting for that thread of control he always had when he was around Lily.

Gentle fingers slid from his hair, following his cheek, holding him. Her voice floated across his ear. "I want you, Joaquin. I know what I'm saying. I wanted it before, but my fears and my past were still able to confuse me. Not now."

The gaze he found when he finally dared to open his eyes speared him through. Joaquin stilled, searching the fiery vixen in his arms. He wanted her. He wanted her the way she was, lying so trustingly in his arms, lost in passion. He wanted all of her.

"Belong to me," he told her before he could call back the words.

She lifted up passion soaked eyes to stare at him. "What do you mean?"

He stood, not answering, urging her to stand with him, desperate to tear the words out of the air. "We need to return."

She arched an eyebrow at him at his abrupt change of direction. He shut his thoughts to her gentle prying. How could he explain it when he didn't know what he meant by it either? Those uttered words had been nothing less than the admittance of his greatest failing—wanting her too much. He couldn't have her, yet the wanting, the *hunger* he felt for her didn't lessen in the least.

"How is your shoulder?" she asked him.

"Healing. Hang on," he answered, bringing her closer her as she buried herself into his chest. He rose from the pavement of the alley without a sound.

For a second night, he set her on her feet near the front door, battling with what he had done, with what he wanted, and cursing what he knew he couldn't have.

"Joaquin." Her voice reached out, reached up to him, and he searched her face. "Yes."

Tumbled thoughts roared and rippled. "Yes?" He watched in fascinated wonder as the tip of her tongue curled over her lip, leaving a moistened trail behind.

"I want to be yours."

"The bond?" The chill of the meaning dragged down his lusts, but only a little.

Shame darkened her eyes for a split second, then the woman he knew behind those amazing, expressive eyes warmed beneath his hands. "I was wrong in my reasons. The night I asked, I saw myself after and..." She looked down and he hated losing the wonder and warmth of her attention. Gathering her strength, she went on. "You are not and never will be an escape from my past. I am the woman I am, the one you've always seen, the one you've never let me hide from. You accepted her long before I did. At that moment, I was hiding, wanting it, but for the wrong reasons. I did want to escape because you make me feel I am worthy. It was an easy escape, and I was wrong. I am worthy. I am that strong woman, the woman they created, true, but beneath, I'm still the woman they never broke," she told him on a steeled whisper. Her fingers trailed along his skin, brushing over his neck. "I'm not hiding anymore."

He had accepted her because he'd always seen the strength she owned. Knew the compassion she shared selflessly with Tabitha. She was a remarkable woman, a woman who he was honored and humbled to know. Joaquin would always cherish her. The ring of the words burst through him like the bells of St. Anthony's. The last of his resistance was blown away like the fall of the autumn leaves with a single gust. Quick and unstoppable. With a moan as strong as any wind, he swooped down and claimed her lips. If he was to be lost, then let him be lost with this one woman.

SHE SUCKED in a quick squeal when he scooped her up. She never saw the door open, hardly noticed a thing about the house as he carried her to her room. With a quiet thump, the bedroom door closed behind them and locked them away from the world. It amazed her how quickly his eyes darkened with desire, yet burned so brightly with that same desirous fire at her words. She had no idea what she was going to do with a vampire in her life. Not right this moment. She was willing to hang on and fight for him with both hands, and figure it out later.

"Lily," he groaned, the sound torn from him, pained with restraint. "If I do, I don't think I'll be able to let you go. You deserve more than I can give you. You deserve the life you haven't yet received." He cradled her face in his palms, holding her like a delicate creation. She was positive the trembling between them was all hers.

What kind of a life would she have with him in it? What would she do with a vampire in her life? She didn't relish the thought of losing him. It hurt imagining him not being a part of her world, vestiges of the last five days showing her the anguish she would be facing without him, alone. She couldn't imagine letting anyone else touch her, either. Not having Joaquin's innate ability to soak into her conscience and keep her calm whenever she needed him to be there was frightening. She knew it was him. No one else felt the same. No one else had been able to touch her. It was because of him she was beginning to feel normal again.

"You don't understand, Joaquin. I need you," she explained, feeling empowered that she did know that about herself. Epiphanies were wonderful things. Because of him, she felt she could move forward. She didn't want anyone else, either. "I don't want you to let me go."

He stilled as unmoving as a dark statue, his eyes trained on her, an insatiable hunger in them that was blinding in its intensity. The sight of him made her blood pulse with hard ticks against her skin, making her feel electric from the ends of her hair to her fingernails. The rich sound of his voice resonated through the room. It caused her heart to dance to an erratic rhythm for a new reason. "Belong to me, heart and soul and I will provide for you. Give yourself into my care and I will protect you."

She didn't need any time at all to make up her mind. "Yes," she answered, a needy whisper of longing for only what Joaquin could give her.

JOAQUIN found her lips, gently caressing them, trailing his tongue across their fullness. As sweet as the spring breeze, as beautiful as the moon on the rolling seas, she melted against him. He'd never imagined he would feel this way again. Hot and cold. Breathless. Blessed, yet even as he rejoiced in each new discovery, he knew it was as much a curse as the one he'd lived with for centuries. This joy would come with a price.

He lost the battle to stop, to tear himself away, looking into her eyes and seeing a wanting so deep, she almost brought him to his knees.

There was more than wanting, deeper in her soul. Something so ageless, between one beat of her thundering heart and the next, he was lost.

He'd never imagined the fire he felt beneath his fingers when he stroked them through her hair, feeling its warmth wind sensuously over him. Pressing kisses to her lips, he slid his fingers deeper, holding her as closely as he dared, as close as he craved. Supple like a reed in the wind, she accepted him, meeting his passion, dueling with him as he tasted her.

Slipping from the intoxicating heat of her lips, he suckled adoring kisses to her jaw, licking at fragrant skin. She shivered beneath his touch and he brought her closer in answer, nearly lifting her off the floor with his arms wrapped around her. Sensually addictive, the feeling of her fingers on his body brought his fires raging higher. The silken feeling of her beneath his lips made his heart trip, made it beat unaided by him with a wildness that made him ache.

The pulse of her heartbeat beneath his touch enticed him. Lifting the heavy fall of her red hair away, he skimmed down the sleek offering of her throat. Shivers vibrated her, traveling from her to him along every inch of touching skin. There was no strength left to resist temptation when he stroked his tongue with a languorous movement over her heavily racing pulse. The shuddering moan that erupted from her stole his sanity. Her fingers clutched at him, digging for purchase as he made their world spin.

"Belong to me," he whispered like a dark enchantment into her thoughts. With a gentleness created by his very need for the woman in his hold, he teased her skin with the merest tip of a fang, stroking, seducing. *Wanting*. Wanting like he'd never wanted before, knowing this time it was for keeps. No argument on the planet held sway at that moment. He'd tried, fought them all. And lost.

Unlike in the alley, he knew there was no going back. He knew this went deeper than a healing need. Joaquin knew he didn't deserve the angel in his arms.

He knew he didn't have the strength to pull himself away from temptation a third time in one night.

The urge to claim her, to leave his mark on her, rose up with a fierceness that rocked him stronger than ever when he discovered the pulsating beat of her vein beneath his lips. He'd die if he couldn't fulfill its demand. His body's tension coiled as though a cobra had wrapped around his spine. She arched, pressing herself against him, and her moan sounded like a siren's bewitching song when he finally took what she offered, cursing and hating everything he was when the first taste of her heated essence hit his tongue. *"I tried, Lily. Please know I tried to give you the freedom you deserve."* Her heartbeat throbbed in answer and he absorbed her offering like a true gift, from her to him. She writhed, shuddering in his arms when he finally succumbed and instinctively made her his, leaving his mark on her for every other male of their kind to know she was treasured and cherished above all others.

Looking into her thoughts, her mind was a kaleidoscope of brilliant colors, pleasure and a euphoria of sensation careening wildly through her. Affection, trust, arousal; those and more swirled through her thoughts.

With tender licks, he closed the pin-sized holes in her throat. The love bite would be far more noticeable. He winced when he saw the bruising on her fair skin, but it was done, and he couldn't find the power to regret it. Floating in that aroused euphoria, he tipped her close, every motion endearing her to him tighter. With a command borne out of his driving need, his shirt ripped away with a sharp tearing sound to hold her flushed against his bare chest.

"God, how I need you."

He moaned at the understatement. This had surpassed mere need. With a single lengthened nail, he flicked a strike against his chest, directly over his heart, watching the first drops form with something raging inside of him, demanding he not stop. Something innate telling him this was right, even when he feared it with every cell of his body.

"Belong to me. Be mine, forever in my care. I give myself to you, heart and soul." His voice choked on a quaking gust of air at the first touch of her inquisitive lips. His head snapped back, staring unseeing at the ceiling, seeing nothing but the flashes of euphoric explosions before his eyes. Lightning struck his body to roar down his spine, tearing over his shuddering length with the force of a raging tsunami wave when her tongue flicked with teasing licks, then her mouth formed to suckle the thin slice like she had found a rare candy.

Rapture. He fell into it, and knew from that moment on, he was lost.

chapter thirteen

HER LIPS trembled when he tasted their warmth after sealing the slice, drinking in the essence of her soul, of her beauty. And felt the power of something so elemental, so wondrous, he feared he was imagining it.

How could he care this deeply for another person again? He knew the taste of it, as unique as the warmth of the woman he held, but had never once imagined he'd have the chance. She stood trustingly in his arms and, with the beauty of her soul reaching out to him, he knew there was no illusion to the emotion.

He slanted, deepening the kiss, thrusting his tongue, delving to find the sweetest nectar. She welcomed him, opening to accept his kiss, meeting him with daring little thrusts of her own, tempting him to the edge of his sanity. Together, they drifted to the bed, his arms around her as he worshipped her lips, nipping and tasting silken skin. With slow movements, his hands drifted down to her stomach, passing over the mounds he desperately wanted to taste on his tongue. Always aware of her every thought, her every doubt, he moved with infinite gentleness, awakening her desires to a pitch he wanted her to live and breathe, through him.

Unhurried, he lifted her turquoise sweatshirt, drawing it over her shoulders. She dropped her arms to cover her body as soon as they were free. Rising over her, he gifted delicate kisses at her shoulder. "Let me see your beauty," he coaxed. "Perfection is in the eye of the beholder, and to me, you are perfect."

Little by little, she relaxed beneath the traveling of his adoring mouth as he licked across her collarbone to the hollow of her throat. Trailing a hand down one arm, he lifted it from its protective position over her stomach, skimming her with the tips of his fingers. White and mottled scars crisscrossed her body and snaked down her arms. Some were vicious and snarled, thick and obvious reminders of the pain he knew she'd lived through. Others were exact and thin, as though someone had taken a blade to her skin, the kind of wounds that hurt the most for the least amount of effort. Regardless of their creation, they covered her body, leaving not a visible inch unharmed.

Tenderly, he laid a palm across her abdomen, wishing he could absorb the agony of all of those moments from her body and from her memory. Without warning, exposed to the marks of her imprisonment fully for the first time, the fathomless rage he'd felt when she'd bared the truth of her past consumed him. He closed his eyes and dropped a kiss to her stomach, hiding his turmoil from her as best as he could. The man who had done this would pay. If there was ever a being Joaquin would kill without a qualm, it would be any man who had hurt Lily.

"It is over, Joaquin." Her voice floated to him and he realized a single tear had fallen from his eyes to her skin.

"If I had known, lovely, you would not have suffered."

The sensation of her fingers combing through his hair soothed the angry feeling of injustice. "I know."

He released a breath, consumed by her compassion and understanding. Before he could give any of the bitter emotions a chance to rise again, he delved into her belly button, and she giggled in reaction. Tension leaked away from them both as he learned her body a caress at a time. Each stroke meant to tease, arouse, pleasure in a way he knew she'd never experienced. She watched him closely when he undid her bra, removing it with the same reverent care he'd done everything else. He didn't purposely avoid the scars, but they ceased to be a singular area of attention. Not when there was her entire body for him to worship.

Free from their confines, her breasts drew his attention. Full, soft and tempting, he swept his tongue around the hardening peak of one and heard her hiss in answer, arching into the wicked sensation of his mouth on wanton flesh. The taut bud puckered and teased him. He swirled it over and over, slowly nearing the pink nipple, dragging his tongue over the heat of her flesh. She moaned and gasped, then whimpered when he drew her completely into his mouth, lashing at hot skin with his tongue as her whispered moans entreated and deepened. He never lost his awareness, constantly searching for any sense of fear, constantly in her thoughts as each new touch reawakened part of her, all of what she'd been forced to shut down to survive. Warming his hand against her body, he caressed and stroked when he switched his attention to her other breast. She moaned in sweet little gasps of pleasure.

Each motion was deliberate, arousing as he moved downward, sliding to the edge of the bed. The first sense of unease happened when he touched her waist. "*Focus on my touch, lovely. You know you are safe.*" She relaxed again with an exhale of tension, becoming boneless again. He didn't move any slower or any faster. The snap came free on her jeans and he ran his tongue across her pelvis, suckling at the uncovered pale treasure of her body. With a restrained touch, he pulled her jeans free and she lay bared before him on the bed. She trembled delicately, unsure, but hungry for his touch.

Joaquin knew by the horror of her memories what she feared. He took excruciating care to never make her feel trapped, or forced. Only pleasured. Dropping kisses along her body, he caressed and massaged her, moving in languid circles closer and closer to the heat of her center. He filled her mind with images of her lost in rapture, building them over and over as she became reacquainted with her own body and the pleasure it—he—could give her. Images of him pleasing her, of both finding exquisite release with each other, filled their minds.

"You are a treasure," he told her, inhaling and finding the intoxicating scent of her arousal. He dipped in and flicked his tongue against her core. She nearly screamed, but not in fear. In bliss. She shook with it. *"Feel me, hear me, know me."* The words fell from his thoughts as he suckled and licked at her inner heat. She arched, clutching at the bed, rocking her head back and forth with each touch. She rose higher and higher on pulsing waves of energy.

He flicked and delved, coaxed and teased, taking her to heights she'd never known. Shudders rocked her body. He never relented, bombarding her with a mixture of his physical touch and the images in his mind.

Her release was shattering when it hit, consuming them both in the conflagration of ecstasy. Sparks ignited behind his eyes as the shared connection erupted in a passionate firestorm. Harsh gasps filled the room when he stood, completely naked. He lifted her effortlessly to the center of the bed and rose over her. He ached, he was so full, eager to feel her body, dying to claim her as only a man could claim a woman. He licked a trail from her hip to her shoulder, his palms on either side of her head as he rested his hips between her thighs. Heat from her body swamped him and he clenched his muscles to not succumb to the temptation too quickly.

Her eyes snapped open at the first press of weight against her body. She stiffened, staring at him wild-eyed. He froze instantly. "I would never hurt you," he told her, deliberately saying the words to bring her focus to him. She looked wild. Flame and cinnamon red hair spread beneath her, framing wide and anxious golden eyes. No one was as beautiful to him. Changing his intent, he laid down on his shoulder beside her and stroked her side with a loving touch, cupping one of her breasts with gentle fingers until she relaxed again.

She turned and found his stare. The image he shared was self-explanatory and completely up to her. Her breasts rose and fell with panting breaths. He stayed still as she made the decision, aching but patient, knowing she needed to make the next step.

It didn't take her long to feel in control once more. Pushing against his body, she easily rolled him onto his back, pressing slow, wicked kisses to his chest as she took the initiative. He groaned like a dying man when he felt the heated dampness of her mouth on his neck, her lips sliding with silken heat across nerves that hungered for her touch. Instinctively, he arched into the sensation, tilting until he was an offering for her exploration. It was his turn to fist the covers into knots as he fought the rolling urge to bellow his desire, loud and hungry for her. He had never felt anything as decadent in his lifetime as the heated torture of her mouth on his own neck, against nerves that were screaming for release.

She trailed up and down his throat, pausing to nip and twirl her tongue against him until he had to close his eyes to the colliding stars in his vision. The groan of pleasure was unstoppable when she found the tumultuous beat of his body, suckling against its pounding as he had done to her. Ecstasy made him shake until she released him, willing himself to stay still, to give her all the control she could want or need. Sparks rose when the billowing length of her hair razed his shoulder, draping like a red curtain across his body. She was deliberately taunting him, knowing he wouldn't move an inch while she held him spellbound. She only laughed when he growled once in aroused frustration. There was no misunderstanding. The way they shared each other's thoughts and pleasures didn't leave room for it.

Straddling his hips, she slid down onto his length, gasping as new pulses of pleasure struck them both. "Joaquin!" Lily's head snapped back in ecstasy. He gritted his teeth to not move too soon. Shudders racked his body with the strength of his restraint.

Lily was killing him. She enveloped him. Tight. Fiery. Passion consumed him. A fire he'd never touched raced over his body, between them, until he feared he would be next to go up like a flame, out of control. She slid along his shaft, clenching him within her body like a silken fist. Her short nails scored down his chest as desire rode over them both. Everywhere she touched came alive with a molten burn.

He coaxed her down to blanket his chest, finding her mouth and devouring her kiss. Absorbed in sensation, he lifted his hips, thrusting into her welcoming body and she cried out in endless pleasure. Control was quickly slipping to a point neither could maintain. She flexed, meeting his thrusts, stretched above him. The fire within rose like a wall of flame, scorching him from the inside out. Sharp, pleasure-filled cries filled the room. Her breasts swayed above him and he lifted, lapping at a succulent nipple, and felt her reaction clear down to his toes.

Wrapping his arms around her, he rolled, pinning her beneath his weight. There wasn't a glimmer of fear in her thoughts, everything about her absorbed in the sensations between them. And absolute trust. He'd never experienced a more pure gift. Her thoughts were wide open, like her body, welcoming, sharing. Joaquin opened his thoughts, letting her see the vision she was.

She was beautiful, her face flushed with desire, her eyes glinting with passion. She stole his breath when she caught his gaze. Her expression was guileless, absorbed. Finding her lips, he kissed her, wanting to take her within his soul and keep her there, safe and his for eternity.

She shuddered in bliss and arched her neck when he finally set her lips free. "*I know what you need. Take what I offer.*" Her eyes drifted closed even as her body held his length tight, unrelenting.

"My lovely flower, my Lily. You accept me like no one ever has."

Her mouth grew supple as she smiled, her fingers caressing his shoulders. "*I can for you. When it is you and me, it feels perfect, right.*"

He knew exactly what she meant. He'd never felt anything so right in his life. There was no physical need this time. It was more, deeper, compulsory. He had taken earlier when he had been wounded, and just a few drops moments before, sealing her to him forever. Need didn't play a part in her offering. It was instinctive, maybe even primal, to claim her in all ways. And thoroughly impossible to resist.

He dipped to brush a tender kiss against her mouth, savoring the delicate sensations against his own. He sipped, sliding against her body in sheer bliss as he filled her over and over, her body accepting him as eagerly as her heart and soul had. He groaned, feeling her leg running up the length of his calf. Drifting down her jaw, he drew her earlobe into his mouth, toying with the bit between his teeth, nibbling playfully. She reacted, her entire body arching against his in passion. Quick pants and clipped moans reached him. The sharp rake of her fingernails against his body drew his eyes closed in heightened arousal.

His next thrust moved his hands under her shoulders and he pierced her, the richness of her life flowing over his tongue even as her release erupted past his ears with a sharp cry. Passion drove him. She writhed and clawed, the sharp rake of her nails on his back as potent as her taste. He filled her body over and over, claiming, taking, pleasuring. Lightning pulsed along his spine and he craved the sensation, drove himself toward more, toward the ultimate ecstasy. Sweeping against her throat, the surge grew, clutching at him until there was no choice but to answer her call. He held her tightly, losing himself in her body. Losing himself to her heart.

Her cry met his, ecstasy gripping them both as eternal pleasure sent them careening beyond the wall of fire.

LILY'S eyes drifted open, feeling languid and relaxed in ways she couldn't remember. Hazy, late day sunlight patterned by the slats of her blinds brightened her room. This morning she'd missed her first sunrise in weeks.

Because Joaquin had loved her continually until she'd fallen asleep in his arms. She didn't even know when he'd left her.

Stretching out a hand to the other side of the bed, the spot he'd lain in was long cold. A sigh left her. She might as well get used to it. There were some obstacles they weren't going to be able to get over.

No matter how much she loved him.

Her hand stopped its meandering pattern through the sunrays splashed across the covers. The hard rasping beat of her heart told her she wasn't asleep. And proved she'd really had that thought. Shocked, she blinked, but couldn't deny it was invigorating, couldn't deny it was true either. She was in love with a man she barely knew, but trusted implicitly. A man who had seen the world and had suffered. He was a vampire. She almost giggled, but stifled it, sticking her head into a gripped pillow to force her thoughts in line.

In control once more, she lifted herself and turned toward her nightstand. According to the clock, it was after five. About time for her to get out of bed anyway.

Pushing blankets out of the way, she padded to the bathroom and actually made herself look in the mirror, studying her reflection, something she'd done very little of since she'd been rescued from the compound. What did Joaquin see? She wasn't some classic beauty. She had freckles over a lot of her face. Glancing down, she saw the scarred reminders of her past beneath her chin and beyond. She traced a finger over the ones on the top of her breast, knowing she'd felt revulsion before at the hideous sight. Now she felt Joaquin's trailing touch. They were still obvious and ugly, but she almost understood his words, that they were a part of her as he knew her. They weren't important to how he saw her. And he thought she was a gift to him. The stunning realization made her smile.

She lifted the swath of her hair away from her body, exposing the hickey on her neck, and she grinned, remembering every detail about how she'd acquired it. Lily covered the mark with a palm, pressing against it, and swore she felt his touch, his lips as they caressed her. She shook her head and dropped her hand, feeling silly for the self-indulgent thoughts. The weight of her hair covered it well when she let it fall again. It wouldn't do for Tabitha to see it. She wouldn't understand. Two weeks ago, she wouldn't have understood either.

Thinking of her, Lily quickly showered and dressed to see how the other woman was doing today. Amy took the morning shifts after Lily went to bed and Kathy would sit with her until late afternoon. Tani would usually take half the night, but with her and Diego hunting for some sign of David with Nathan, Lily had spent most of her evenings with Tabitha. Last night had been an exception. Regardless of what had happened, Tabitha was going to need time to regroup, get her strength back and adjust. Lily believed Tabitha was more resilient than they were giving her credit for.

There was a strength in Tabitha that was buried, abused and hurting. She really wanted to see that strength in her friend again. It was her strength that had shown Lily that Tabitha could be telepathic if she tried for it. It just wasn't an easy task for her. It was that same strength Lily hoped would buoy Tabitha through the coming months of her recovery. She was going to need all the help she could get.

An eerie quiet filled the house when she finally stepped through her doorway into the hallway. Looking into Tabitha's room, she was resting, but alone. She turned to look over her shoulder, wondering where the odd, wary, tingled finger of warning sliding down her spine was coming from. Lily released a breath to calm her edgy nerves before she turned the corner into the woman's bedroom, but a sound stopped her.

"Houston?" No answer. She called for Laney, hesitant to knock on their door with her getting used to being pregnant. She'd done nothing but sleep all week. Backtracking, she knocked on Amy's door, then Kathy's to get silence from both rooms.

She cast a worried look into Tab's room again, then jogged downstairs to see if there was a note. Maybe they had gone to town to buy groceries. Maybe the other two girls were in the basement.

Maybe she wasn't as alone in the house as it felt.

The sun was still high on the setting horizon, hours from sundown. That limited who could be there, lurking, by several. Searching the kitchen, she didn't find a note. Whirling from the counter, she searched with a sweeping look, nervous energy making her jumpy. She knew she'd heard something.

"Who's there? Amy? Kathy?" she called, hoping like hell if it wasn't one of them, it was just a tree outside making noises along the side of the house somewhere. *Damn it! Where is everyone?*

Diego, Tani, and Joaquin wouldn't show up until sunset. That was a given. So it wasn't them. They didn't slink around the house in any fashion to begin with. Quiet, yes. Sneaking like silent ghosts, no. With cautious steps, she exited the kitchen and searched the front room and the living room. Everything looked the way it was supposed to. Nothing looked out of place. It didn't matter. *Something* was wrong.

Shaking her hands out, she drew a breath. She was creeping herself out. There was nothing wrong in the house. So *everyone* had left her. She could handle it.

Her heart hit her ribs when she heard it again. A thud. Had to be a tree branch hitting the house. Nothing moved inside. She knew it was just her and Tabitha, for some reason, somehow, they were the only two in the house.

When a hand shoved a rough cloth against her mouth and a harsh, stinging liquid seared her lungs, she knew she wasn't alone at all.

"I'M SORRY, LILY."

She blinked, but there was only a blurred, watery light from everywhere and it was slicing her brain in half. She snapped her eyes shut, trying to focus, too disoriented to manage more. She felt like she was in her own body, but it definitely wasn't acting like it was hers. Her nerves felt numb and her entire body felt sluggish.

"You have to believe me," the voice said. The light passed and it was dark. Then it happened again, and passed. *Streetlights? Where am I?* There weren't streetlights anywhere near the house.

She tried to speak, but couldn't. There was tape over her mouth. Rolling her head weakly, she turned and squinted at the person next to her. After two seconds, she closed them again, unable to keep her stomach from rebelling, and vomiting with her mouth sealed was a death sentence. Sucking air through her nose, the deliberate actions began to sweep away the grogginess of whatever drug it was he'd knocked her out with.

She opened her eyes at some point when she thought she could handle it and tried to see who was driving.

Shock sent ice cascading through her veins. David? It looked like him, but he looked like he'd been through a meat grinder. Scrapes and cuts across his face showed he'd been brutally attacked, and one eye was bruised a deep mosaic of purple and blue. Trying to shift her weight seemed harder than usual, until she realized she was bound. Gagged and bound. Lovely. And no clue what was happening. Or why.

"I'm sorry," he said again. Remorse and pain were woven deeply into the apology. "But I can't let them hurt my sisters. I can't take the chance that they will," he entreated. He lifted a hand and ran it under his nose, wincing at the motion. She spotted more caked blood on his arms. He shook his head, running a hand down filthy jeans, then gripped the wheel. What she could see of him was a wreck in every sense of the word. He had yet to look at her.

"Nathan was right. There is a chip. I have it. They told me so. That's how they found me at that roadside rat's nest. I fought like hell to remember what had happened when they got me the first time. I was scared," he admitted, choking hard to not crumble. He moaned once as remembered pains surfaced of when they'd abducted him, rocking him with shudders of agony, then, "Oh, yeah. I remembered." He cursed and banged the wheel with a fist, his voice filling with rage and more pain. "Five hours and they would have been there. They would have been right on top of us! Because of me!"

He flicked a glance, apparently not surprised she was awake enough to listen. "They threatened my sisters. I made them a deal."

She wanted to cry. He had to know they would come anyway. He'd led them right to the house! She forced a sharp bark through her immobile lips. It was no more than a muffled grunt to her ears.

"I know! You think I wanted to do it?" He wiped his nose again. She realized he was crying, and fighting it, too enraged to be reasonable. "They can't get near the house. Something happens and their scouts wig out, then disappear off their radars completely. Their sensors can't pick up anything about it, like it's some kind of black hole of space on the ground. I didn't know they'd even been trying or I would have stayed. They might have missed the house, even with this stupid chip. Instead, I ran. They found me." White knuckled, he twisted his fists on the steering wheel.

Lily tried to breathe deeper to help clear her thoughts more. Diego and Nathan had been removing scouts? She shivered, realizing it had to be true.

"You know, if Amy and Kathy had been there, I couldn't have done it. But shit, I show up and no one is home. Where was everyone? Didn't they miss me?" She couldn't feel sympathy for his wounded feelings. *They're probably out looking for your sorry ass* was her thought, but she wasn't able to put it to voice. She had no answer either to where everyone had been when she'd awakened.

"I swear, ever since Tani hooked up with that watchdog of hers, she hasn't been the same. Never around for anything!"

He was rambling now, alternating snarling with that pathetic whining. It wasn't hard in the least to hear the bite of jealousy in his complaints. Unrequited love, and Tani most likely had never known it.

"They probably don't even know I'm gone," he bitched.

Oh, they know, all right.

She wished she could talk, ask him questions. Find out where he was taking her, though that was probably a foregone conclusion. She shivered, although she fought to ignore it.

"All I know is fuckin' Hawthorne better leave my sisters out of this." Her eyes widened. Was that where she was going? He was taking her right to Hawthorne?

"Lily!" Joaquin's voice was crystal clear and so welcome.

"Oh God, Joaquin." She almost wept in relief as she sagged in her seat. Lashes covered her eyes as though she were drifting in and out of consciousness if David looked. His misery went pretty deep. She doubted he'd taken two glances at her since he'd trussed her up for the car trip. *"Took you long enough."* As if she'd never doubted him—because she hadn't.

"I know, lovely. I couldn't reach you."

"I was knocked out with some drug. I can feel you!" She reached for him with every ounce of her willpower and was rewarded with a wash of tenderness so strong it was beyond anything she'd felt from him yet. Steady and calm. She was beginning to feel his influence spread throughout the coldest parts of her that were still shaking with fear and uncertainty.

"I'm with you always."

Hearing him, the relief was immeasurable. She didn't have the time to analyze why things felt different, stronger, or why she suddenly knew what he was doing down to the last drawn breath. *"I think we're heading south. He's taking me to Hawthorne.*

It's David," she added, wishing it weren't, knowing how this news would kill Tani and the others. "*They've threatened him and his sisters. He's desperate.*"

"*Taking you was not an option,*" he replied, sounding far too composed about it. There was a chill in his words that told her his intent. He was coming for her. David, and anyone else, would pay.

She looked from beneath lowered lashes across the console to see David run a hand through his hair, then across his nose again. He seemed to be getting himself under some level of control. "*Is everyone there safe?*" she asked him.

"*Yes.*"

"*Let him take me to Hawthorne.*"

She knew the instant she made the suggestion, it wasn't going to have a snowball's chance in Hell in July. Then, she turned it around on him.

"*Trust me.*"

JOAQUIN soared up over trees like a rocket possessed through a night daring to turn muggy, racing in the direction of her heartbeat, hearing her thoughts and feeling her absolute trust and faith in him. She'd never doubted he would find her.

Even though he had failed in keeping her safe. Neither Diego or himself had guessed David would come home on his own, and not like this, to kidnap someone.

"Hawthorne is one of Tenorio's commanders. We can learn more if I make it into his camp."

"I will not risk you." She was determined to make it even harder for him to keep her safe by walking right into the lion's den.

"We know he's been tracking David. He knows the vicinity of the house, but hasn't been able to breach Diego's protections. That can't last forever."

They would if Joaquin had anything to say about it. "*Then I will take you away.*"

"I can't leave Tabitha behind, Joaquin," she reminded him gently. "*Arguing about it isn't going to do much good.*"

"No, because I will win."

He felt her grin, knowing she was remembering when he'd won the last 'battle', then a hopeless echo in his mind told him things were about to go from bad to worse.

"Not this time. We're here."

Joaquin lowered his head and put on the speed, following her distinct trail, weaving over the landscape as miles fell beneath his wings. And for the first time in too long, he prayed.

chapter fourteen

"JOAQUIN, do you need assistance?" The intrusion was subtle, as if he might have been surprised at the offer. He shook his head to the other man's voice, but answered nonetheless.

"Where are you and Nathan?" He never dropped Lily's welcoming embrace, homing in on her like a falcon on scurrying prey. He didn't bother to relay the situation. Diego knew everything that happened within his protections, and Joaquin had found that now included him as well. With the complexity of this new set of circumstances, it was taking time for him to adjust. For a man unused to friendship, least of all from the very ones he'd ceased to trust, being accepted into the world Diego ruled with a fierce protectiveness was very unusual, and not in a small way, unsettling. Family was something he thought he'd never have again. It looked like he was going to be proven wrong, all because of one fiery woman who owned him body and soul.

"Near enough if you should have need. We are searching another of Tenorio's offices, looking for information on his current projects."

"Any new information?"

A touch of angst flowed on the mental link. "*Not here, not yet.*"

"I will update you soon." He sent the thought, cutting the thread off as Lily's fears spiked, making his worry for her safety crest with a rush. It was like a blind game of charades, but knowing to the detail what was happening because her reactions fed it all to him like a physical touch.

A snarl rose up as the tape was ripped from her face. He felt the flare of anger, the heat of the pain, and wanted to snap the man before her in two. "*Don't antagonize them,*" he pleaded, knowing she was seconds from unleashing her fury on them and fearing the severity of the retribution she'd receive. The remembered images of her abuses made his body tremble. The situation had, indeed, gone from bad to worse. He pushed himself like never before to reach her.

LILY glared at the man before her, thankful, at least, for them untying her feet if not her hands. The tape had hurt like hell, but she could breathe now, a stale, flat air she could have lived without ever knowing again.

By the time they'd arrived, she had been aware enough to make out some details when David had been given access through gates lit by floodlights bright enough to make the entrance look like a prison. How many places did Tenorio have to hide his projects? She shivered, wondering how many people had been tortured, how many were still missing, and how long this had been going on. When the car stopped, she barely had time to blink before the door was opened and she was yanked out. Someone sliced the tape around her feet and shoved. She didn't have far to go. Through one metallic door after another into the belly of the beast.

She was now sitting in some drab, gray claustrophobia-inspiring room nearly alone, but not nearly enough. A man dressed in fatigue pants and a puke green T-shirt prowled in front of her where they'd dragged her to sit, his expression menacing, his gaze bitingly cold. The chair wasn't comfortable by any means. Somehow, she didn't think the decorator had comfort in mind.

"Oh goody," she muttered scathingly. "Interrogation one-oh-one."

A cruel fierceness darkened the man's features. She refused to show a single twitch that his intimidation was working. "*Good girl.*" The proud praise came and she felt stronger.

A door opened in the wall behind her. "Sir. All signs show he was not followed." She fought the smirk. Not followed in any way they'd be expecting.

"Good. Escort him to his quarters. We may need him again. He's the only key we have to reach that damn site." Poor David. Lily knew better than to think his sisters would be safe with just one recovery. Their escape had struck a hard blow to Tenorio. Sadly, now, David had proven himself capable of doing what none of them could do. Reaching the house and getting to the girls. He was screwed.

A clipped heel behind her signaled a salute and then the door shut, leaving an unfriendly silence between them.

"Hawthorne," she sneered. There was no doubt as she studied the man before her.

He dipped his head in a mocking show of congeniality. "I'd say welcome, but I know you've been a guest in the past. So maybe," he drawled with cutting condescension and a raised eyebrow, "welcome back."

Lily rolled a shoulder in unconcern. The hit came from nowhere, snapping her head on her neck painfully. The snarl was so loud she would have said he was already in the room. Except she was the only one who heard Joaquin's growling rage.

"Calm down. I can take a lot worse."

"I knew this was a bad idea."

She sent him a glorious smile and a cascade of adoration, even while she licked at the drops of blood pooling in the corner of her mouth, finding and keeping the dagger sharp gaze of the man before her. *"I will be fine. This is my chance, Joaquin. This is my fight. There's a world of difference between being hit for fighting back than them wanting to destroy me. I can control it."*

"A fair fight is when both *can defend and attack. Remind me to show you a demonstration when I get there."*

She barked a laugh, enjoying their conversation too much to care what the bastard in front of her thought.

"You thought that was funny?" He braced himself with his palms on her chair, corded arms caging her, lowering his face to be right in front of hers. She almost told him what he'd had for lunch, but pushed it off of her tongue, managing that much restraint.

Joaquin groaned at her wayward thoughts. "*Remind me to wash your mouth out with soap.*"

"I find it funny that you're going to die." Calm and without a grain of worry, she informed Hawthorne. "Who else are you holding?" she taunted. "I can't be the only *lucky guest* tonight."

Her bravado wavered when he snapped straight and motioned to the door. She hated not knowing what was behind her. A window, maybe. In the door or in the wall, or maybe a camera. It gave her an idea of what kind of security measures they had within those gray walls. That was good information, along with what she'd seen outside. She passed it on. Joaquin would come, but he'd be prepared for the possibility.

"Where are the others?" he demanded, growling like a rabid dog. "Who rescued you? Where did they take you?"

"I'm a little tied up this evening. Can we reschedule?" she asked in a pleasant voice, batting her lashes coquettishly, as though he'd only stopped in to chat over tea.

He lowered to taunt her with a cruel smile again. He was no different from the men she'd suffered under for the last three years. At their souls, they were empty. The door opened with a snarled signal, capturing her gaze to make his intentions clear. "Take her to the cages. I'm sure her memory of them is a sweet one. Maybe after a few days there, she'll be more willing to cooperate."

At the mention of the torture chambers, she almost balked, but then found the strength to smile up at him again without a care in the world. "Club Med."

This time, the fiery clash of flesh left a sharp ringing in her ears when his fist connected with her aching jaw. Two dressed as soldiers appeared and dragged her bodily from the room—she'd be damned before she'd *help* them imprison her again. The dull ringing in her ears faded, but didn't go completely away, and she wondered for a split second if he'd damaged her eardrum. It was a small price to pay in her mind, and she would heal. She'd survived all their abuses and tortures too many times to count already. She pretended to hang her head in utter defeat, but searched the corridors and corners, opening her mind to absorb every sound, every thought of every soul within its walls.

She almost screamed as the sounds crashed into her all at once, clenching her jaw tight to hide the vicious pain. Voices, emotions, intentions. She heard it all. She hardly felt the chains when they were each locked around her wrists as her head rolled, then listed, her mind being drenched in the world surrounding Hawthorne. Trying before had been futile in an effort to escape. Like now, it hurt in ways a human wasn't meant to experience to open herself up to so many influences. And the last thing she wanted was for Tenorio to learn how deep her telepathy ran. He'd never had a clue.

"Lily! Stop!"

"I... No. I'll...be fine." That was when she felt Joaquin's terrified realization for her adamancy to be taken into the bowels of Hell.

Because she had the very gift to find out everything they needed to know. She prayed it didn't drive her mad in the process.

"LILY!" He felt her conscious mind respond, but she was so deeply smothered under the bombardment of every person's thoughts surrounding her, she didn't react for several minutes. He kept breathing strength into her to bolster her efforts, to keep her from drowning under it all.

"I'm here."

A whispered acknowledgement. It didn't ease the strain he felt, knowing she was feeling it a thousand times stronger. He reached out to divert some of the pain, hurtling as fast as he could through the night to reach her side.

She was in pain. She was hurting, but she didn't stop, ignoring his pleas when the striking of all those voices rose like storm tossed tidal waves to pummel against her mind with tsunami strength. It was tearing his insides apart. All that pain. He knew what he felt wasn't nearly close to what was bombarding her every second. The way she forced each voice to override the cacophony as she endlessly searched for the one, or few, that would tell her what she was looking for struck him at the depth of her ability and her strength. He couldn't see how she had ever thought herself to be weak.

He knew he was getting closer to her with every passing minute. The intensity of anguish flooding over her was impossible to push away, impossible to not feel in every pore of his being. David had several hours head start, being able to drive in sunlight. It was proving to be the greatest disadvantage Joaquin had at the moment. Each second it took to reach her was another second she was in pain. And he couldn't stop it. She wouldn't let him.

"Lily." He reached out to her again, forcing his way past her barriers to shoulder some of the effort, relying on his own strengths to pick up some of the overflow. The blast of pain was crippling when he broke through those barriers, shaking his concentration so hard he almost lost his form for the

second time since he'd met her. He shuddered at the impact. "*Enough! Stop. You must stop!*"

Her answered words were faint, dragging and slurred. "*For now.*" Several heartbeats passed before the whispered sound of her voice reached out to him again. "*I didn't find anything, but I will.*" It was a vow to not fail. He feared how far she would push to gain that success, to find Tenorio's whereabouts, or to locate the other project prisoners. To have her chance to fight back, but at what expense to herself?

"*Rest,* corazón. *You need to rest.*" He hated to impose his will on her, but he pushed the compulsion on her before she had an inkling of his intention. It had to be done to keep her from searching for too long. Exhaustion emanated from her in pulsating waves.

He only wished he'd had the ability when Angelica had been so ill. Then he would have done anything to save her. His once precious wife, more precious to him than the air he had once breathed so normally, taken for granted.

Never again. He would not fail Lily. She had become the very reason he could relish each rising for the first time in his endless existence, the only reason he needed to push on through a life that should have ended so long ago. She was his soul, the light to an endless drifting in a world of darkness. If he had once longed for redemption for his sins, then he would suffer for an eternity upon eternity in penance if anything happened to Lily.

The bond they shared had solidified into a thick and unbreakable cord that reached out to him from her on every level. What she felt, he felt. What she thought, he could hear, sense or feel. Unless she kept him out...

He groaned with sudden insight. She had been blocking him. It was undoubtedly conceivable considering how often he had to seek her to hold her, to help her, to offer his strength to protect her. That's why he had to continually push his way into her mind to help her shoulder the agony of the intrusiveness. She had been protecting *him*. He could only shake his head at her stubborn nature, finally coming to the fore when he'd known all along she had the strength to be the person he'd seen the entire time.

He just hadn't expected to meet that woman now, when he wanted nothing but to keep her safe at his side. Deep inside, she was a gentle creature, a tender being who couldn't hurt anything or anybody, but she owned the strength of an entire army in her soul. He'd tasted it, felt it. It was her reborn strength that filled her now. She needed to strike a blow to the ones who had taken so much from her. Her need battled his urges in a determined confrontation. Joaquin wanted her out of that place, needed her standing by his side. Safe.

Lily wanted retribution. If not in blood, then in a way that would leave a mark on all of them. But she was suffering, and it reawakened all the guilt and raging agony of his failure to protect Angelica, rising from his past like a voluminous ghost. He hadn't been able to protect his wife, and now, here, he couldn't protect Lily.

Rage hazed his vision as the sum of it all hit him. She was his in every sense of the word. His to protect, to cherish. Nothing would stop him. She was putting herself at risk to save them all.

Without warning, two more owls joined his harried flight. He hadn't asked, silently accepting he'd never had to.

The rumbled tone was unmistakable when it flitted through his mind. "*You will not reach her before daybreak.*"

He couldn't bring himself to answer, knowing Diego was right and he'd have to let Lily live another day in their hands. It was what he hadn't been able to share with her, not wanting her to lose faith. He would save her. There was no failure.

"You have shared blood."

The carefully directed statement caught him off guard when it hit him, deliberate and very private between the two men. He wasn't sure how to respond, or what Diego would do knowing Joaquin had done what he'd promised the other he wouldn't do—take from Lily.

"Yes." There was no point in lying. No reason to deny what Diego could obviously sense too easily now.

"Are you claiming her?"

The bite of the question was a warning. The wrong answer would probably be the last thought he'd ever have. He knew the only answer he could give.

"I am. She bears my mark."

Diego fell silent, leaving Joaquin to wait, prepared to fight for her, praying he wouldn't have to. He knew Diego could destroy him with hardly any effort.

"This is unprecedented. We will have much to discuss once she is with us again. Are you prepared to stay? She will not part from Tabitha."

"I am. I have offered myself to her, and in doing so, to you and your fight."

Joaquin sensed the unspoken approval from Diego. They spurred on to their destination. Toward the light that warmed him and glowed from the inside out.

His only light.

Lily.

chapter fifteen

THE ACHING tension between her shoulders woke her up. She stretched, well aware of why she felt like she'd been hanging from a taffy pull. She lifted her head until it rested against the bars she knew would be behind her. There was no comfort knowing she was right when she found the cold, biting steel at her back.

"Joaquin?" The silent call of his name faded away, leaving her cold.

There was no answer. An emptiness she had never experienced made her eyes water. The weight of the silent barrenness tried to crush her like the memory of his absence from her life after she'd hit her lowest. He would come. There was absolute faith in that knowledge. It had to be daylight. It was the only reason he *wouldn't* answer. She drew a deep breath, burying the rush of loss she'd suddenly been hit with. She wasn't alone, just for now. She wasn't forsaken. He would come.

There was no light in the cages. Their only light came from weak fluorescents recessed within the hall ceiling several feet away. She counted a total of six of the torture cages. She'd spent enough time in them to know what they were. Which meant they also had containment cages. Lab rat cages to study them. To imprison them.

Drawing her strength inward, she carefully opened her mind again, waiting for the bombardment to hit.

It did. A split second later. She snapped taut, grasping the chains attached to the cuffs on her wrists in bloodless grips, stifling the urge to scream. Within moments it became manageable, but those first few minutes were always the most agonizing of her life.

"...boots are polished..."

"...the movie last week..."

She sifted through them, one by one, seeking, searching, and by God, prying like a thief. She didn't care.

Then, what she hadn't expected to hear at all—a female voice. A voice praying, sounding hopelessly lost and bereft. A voice that had nothing to do with the machinations of the compound surrounding her.

She followed the sound of that one voice, seeking its owner. Long, agonizing moments later, she relaxed, withdrawing her energy, allowing a very small, victorious smile. All she had to do was wait for nightfall. That would be a cakewalk.

THE INSTANT he snapped awake, his first reaction was to connect with her, reliving her pain with no warning. Searing and throbbing along his back and behind his legs. He hissed as the striking agony invaded his nerves and muscles, clenching and screaming in reaction, only an echo of the torture she had been dealt. Dirt exploded above him with a vengeance, spewing for yards in all directions as he shot like a lightning bolt clear of his resting place, wanting to scream out the sheer agony that stripped his skin. A red curtain blinded him for several seconds as he fought to calm himself. Similar earthly upheavals happened in the distance. Joaquin didn't think twice, knowing they were rising to join with him. For the first time since his conversion, the three had lain to rest within knowledgeable distance of each other; a lesson learned, broken. And there was no stronger statement of unity.

"She's been whipped." Two sets of grave eyes flattened at the news when they neared. "She's tired from blood loss, but not giving in." He glanced in her direction, feeling her awareness, sending her comfort. Her relief was impossible to miss. "She knows we're coming."

"Then let's not disappoint her," Nathan said with a smile that belied the defiant heat in his gaze. The three bounded upward, changing their shapes on the fly.

"This won't be like the compound," Joaquin cautioned. He relayed the layout of what she had seen to the other two.

"Doesn't matter. She won't suffer another night in their hands."

Joaquin could do nothing less than agree with Nathan's determination. Joaquin's vow had not changed. She would be rescued without fail.

"She has found at least one more," he told the other two flying with him.

"Focus on Lily. We will find the one she heard." Diego's intent became clear. They would disable those at the compound and rescue Lily and the woman she had found.

"How are we going to keep them from finding the house? Lily says they know where it is and have been searching for a way to reach it, but haven't been able to get close enough. That's why they tricked David." Joaquin sent the problem on the community wavelength he'd once described to Lily.

"Nathan?" Diego asked.

A mirthless laugh echoed on the wind. "*In that, some things will be exactly like the compound. I doubt they've changed much of anything in their procedures since they never would have found what short-circuited their alarms system.*"

Agreement circled all three.

Joaquin reached for her again, pouring strength into his voice, his will. "*Lily?*"

"I'm here." Exhaustion thickened her words, but her voice was so comforting to hear at all. "*I'm cold.*" He sent a wave of warmth to her without a second's hesitation. "*Thank you.*"

"I can see the buildings now," he told her.

"Be careful. There are guards everywhere."

"With you?"

"Outside, and in the hall where the cages are. I think there's only one there, though."

He knew the more he talked to her, the more her strength was flagging. As he drew closer, he was better able to study the damage their lash had done and was sickened into utter silence.

"Why did they hurt you more?" He would've cried if he'd been in his own skin.

"Tried to make me talk. They tried," she told him with whispered pride. *"They failed."*

He cocooned her in his own strength, letting her lean on him even when he was still too far away to actually touch her, too far away to take away the pain of the multitude of cuts. She was fading, drifting in and out of consciousness, no matter what he did.

Together, the three landed on the sprawling building directly over her head. It was all he could do to stay there, calm and patiently observing when he wanted to claw through the roof beneath him to get to her.

Crouching, they took a moment to take in the layout of the compound and study the activities on the ground. Nathan spoke first. "The computer controls are in that one." He pointed to a short block building with only a few windows. There were none at all in the structure beneath them where Lily was being held.

"This is getting to be a habit," he drawled with that youthful insolence Joaquin had seen only once or twice before.

"We need more than a diversion this time." Diego crouched low on his haunches, studying every aspect of movement around them with a keen gaze. "This must stop. The offices we searched were nothing more than his place of business, the man he pretends to be for the world. He had none of his private enterprises on his computer or where it could be discovered." He gave both a thoughtful look. "I managed to destroy his entire computer bank at his private residence. This"—he waved a hand—"is likely his solution to that destruction."

Joaquin ran a hand over his face, trying to concentrate, knowing Lily was directly beneath his feet. "Then there's Hawthorne. He knows at least of David and Lily, and knows David can get in when he can't."

Diego nodded. "I know." He frowned.

Joaquin was getting impatient. Lily was growing weaker, colder.

"Patience, friend," Diego told him, sliding a mercurial gray look at him. "We will not let her die. She already shares blood with you. Her path has been set."

"What do you mean?"

Diego glanced away. "She only has two choices left to her. She will need to share blood again, and suffer the conversion the same as we did. Or die. There is no in-between in this."

Joaquin almost fell from his own lowered crouch in stunned shock, but managed to grab himself in time. "Titania's accident?" he uttered in bewildered, slow-dawning shock. Diego only nodded. *What have I done?* Chills slid down is spine to form ice in his stomach.

"I do not understand why it is happening anymore than I understand how we are different from the Brethren who created us." He shrugged. "But we are. I also believe once we find the one who completes us, we become stronger."

"Explain," Nathan demanded, his eyes widening.

Diego narrowed his attention, watching as men paced and circled below them on the grounds. "Before I met Titania, I had certain controls of magic. The energy pulse is one." He seemed to be counting. "Once we...joined, there was no question to it. I could control it, and more. Much more."

Joaquin considered what he was hearing. "The bond? It has made us stronger together?" Was that how Diego managed to maintain the protective barriers around the house? Because with Tani, Diego had found something more? Joaquin wondered, only to have his thoughts interrupted.

"Yes. Once she survives the conversion—you and I know there is no easy way around it." Both Joaquin and Nathan nodded in agreement. "Then you become complete in a way that is significant to the both of you.

"The search we did for the chip? It was Titania's suggestion, but it was easy to do once I understood her intention. The same with healing. I could heal myself, but learned when she was attacked I could reach out to her as well." He seemed to fall into a silent introspection for a moment. "She is telling me to mention her strengths have also increased. When it is the right person, the benefits are twofold."

Joaquin finally understood what he was saying. "Lily is this person to me?"

"She believed it almost immediately. I had my doubts, but you understand why." He tossed a snarled look to the military precision below them. "This is what they all came from. It is because of Titania I did not kill you outright."

"I owe her many thanks, then."

"So, there is hope?" Nathan asked, looking for all the world like a child needing reassurance.

"There is, but I cannot say when." Diego held his chin in a firm hand, his attention fully on their situation. "Wait a few more minutes. I will search for their munitions. I am sure this force has an even greater holding than the last. Nathan will corrupt and destroy their computer banks, disengaging their alarms and their cameras. Once that is done, we will find everyone being held. Crippling Hawthorne should slow down Tenorio from pursuit for a very long time."

Joaquin nodded, albeit grudgingly. For the minutes wasted, Lily was still suffering. Diego placed an understanding hand on Joaquin's shoulder, finding his gaze as a sense of brotherhood flowed between the two men. "I know David would not have hurt anyone under different circumstances." Turning the other way, he told Nathan, "Be sure to erase any information on the house, on us, on the girls. This cannot continue."

Nathan nodded, his expression firming once more. Then, like silent harbingers of death, they separated. Joaquin watched as they melted into the shadows, Nathan on his mission and Diego hunting the armory.

Moments later, one by one, lights blinked out, causing immediate shouts from the ground. *"Cameras are down."* Joaquin didn't wait. Not one soldier saw the mist that slipped beneath the vent lip to slither to the floor below. All the bars made him shiver with revulsion, feeling the echoes of pain and horror that had been suffered inside that building. He approached Lily's cage, easily sliding between the bars before solidifying his body once more.

Finding her brought fury rising with a sharp, volcanic boil. She had been stripped naked and spread eagle to be whipped mercilessly. Her head hung and only shallow, shuddering breaths showed she lived at all. Blood pooled on the ground where she had been left to bleed, her weight held on the balls of her feet, her arms pulled overhead by pulleys.

It was all he could do to croak her name on an anguished gasp, then snatch one hand brace in a cold hand to squeeze the iron. It crumbled into dry dust in his fingers. Holding her weight, he repeated it on the other shackle until her limp form fell against his shoulder where he caught her. Holding her tenderly, he braced her to crush the ankle chains, then created a long shirt to cover her body, knowing the welts on her body were oozing again because of the unavoidable movement.

"I'm so sorry," he choked out, breathing in her scent where he nuzzled her temple. "Why, lovely? Why did they do this?"

She pressed into his embrace. Even though she was weak, her heart was beating strongly. "For escaping." Her breath warmed his skin where she touched him. "They thought I would tell them how to reach the house."

He pressed into her hair, hiding the anguished tears that fell.

"Don't cry for me."

Groaning, he could barely talk, outraged at her condition. He needed time to help her, especially if what Diego said was true and that Joaquin would be able to heal her.

Chilled but tender fingers lifted and drifted over his cheek. "I knew you would come. They couldn't break me."

"We're getting out of here." He mouthed the words against her skin. Waves of warmth soothed her pains as he absorbed as much as he could, easing her torment. Immersed completely in the blinding intensity almost brought him to his knees, proving her strength once more. He had no choice but to steal an extra moment or two to wade through her agony and ease her pains in the process. He couldn't let her go on in her current condition. Then, with as much gentleness as possible, he lifted her into his arms, carrying her weight as if she weighed as much as a butterfly.

Before he could take two steps to reach the gate, a shuddering explosion rocked the building and shook the ground beneath his feet with a horrendous quake. He smiled knowingly. Score one for Diego.

"Woohoo!"

He almost laughed out loud at Nathan's gleeful reaction.

"And we forgot the marshmallows." There was a definite playful whine in the young man's complaint.

"What are marshmallows?"

"I'll show you some time," she answered drowsily from her position in his arms. Her mouth brushed his neck when she spoke and it sent a raw shiver down his body.

He didn't spare another moment, simply cupping his hand over the gate lock and pushing. The steel door flew open with a harsh, grinding, metallic snap.

"You're pretty handy to have around," she teased him.

"Just don't be kidnapped again. My heart can't take it." He strode through the mangled gate and aimed for the one door.

"Your heart doesn't beat," she pointed out.

"Some, not as much as most normal humans. I can make it beat a natural rhythm."

She shook against his body, laughing, trying to hide the winces even that little movement caused her. Holding her like the treasure she was, he prayed she laughed for him for a very long time. "Hold on," he told her, concentrating to do the same to the steel door before him that he'd done to the cage gate.

It shattered outward, a warped metal plate sliding on the concrete floor, leaving sparks in its wake. He didn't think twice, lifting his hand and forcing a hard wind ahead of him. The guard running toward them was lifted and slapped into the opposing wall. He fell slack with a resounding crack of bone.

"Let's hope they're too busy to worry about their prisoners."

"Did Diego find her?"

The response was swift in answer. "*I have her. She is not in as bad a condition as Lily, but she has been here for far too long.*"

Lily nodded, relieved. "I heard him through you, didn't I?"

He pressed a loving kiss to her forehead. "You did." He wasn't sure how or when he was going to break the real truth to her, that she was becoming as much like him as she was human. He had to get her out of there before anything else could be decided.

Nathan's determined tones reached out to him next. "*The computers are in a series of meltdowns. The only thing they're going to have left is a lot of steel cases and garbage. I'm going to get David.*"

Joaquin nodded, marching with his precious cargo through the labyrinth of corridors making up the building where the cages were. He didn't put another worry toward the other two, knowing they were perfectly capable.

Diego met them at the door to the outside. He held in his arms a limp, tallish brunette. "She was the only one I found any signs of." Diego had put the woman he found under a mental command to keep her blissfully unaware.

"I only found one voice," Lily said without lifting her head. Her disappointment was unmistakable.

"She will not be left behind to suffer more. That is one less for Tenorio's experiments."

She nodded to acknowledge she'd heard Diego, but kept silent, conserving her strength.

"Then let Nathan locate David and meet us on the other side of the plateau."

Oblivious to the two walking men holding their precious burdens, soldiers raced back and forth searching for the cause of the fires, trying to extinguish them even as more seemed to ignite and detonate all around them.

Shadows leaped and jumped in front of the roaring yellow flames, spreading to four of the lower buildings. The munitions building was completely engulfed in a riotous conflagration of heat and bursting spires of flame. Dust rose and swirled in the jarring wind currents from the raging heat as the speeding vehicles and men raced to douse the flames that refused to die, almost as if they were fighting to continue their path of destruction through the compound.

"Nice work," Joaquin stated watching intently as yet another building, one that appeared to be barracks, erupted with a *whoosh* sound.

"The less left, the longer it will take for them to regroup."

Joaquin couldn't argue with that logic. Not for the first time, he wondered what kind of man Diego had been before in his life, because the man who stood with him now gave new meaning to the word 'relentless'.

Diego turned his back on the snapping blazes and marched away from the worst of the eruptions while Joaquin followed. They lifted effortlessly and cleared the high wire fence with little trouble. Ahead of them lay miles of open desert and rock formations. The compound had been nestled in deep dunes and arroyos, hidden from the natural world. The closest sign of life was still miles away.

"Houston has left to meet me before sunrise. He will take our new charge to the house." Diego looked toward the compound and frowned. "David and Hawthorne are missing. Nathan is searching, but thinks they are gone."

"That's bad, isn't it?" Joaquin studied Diego's expressions.

"It is not good."

Joaquin lifted Lily higher and a cool hand spread against his chest. She was resting, but hardly coherent. "She needs care." He knew they would not reach the house in time either.

"Houston can ensure she is safe. He can take her as well, if you wish, and see to her wounds."

Joaquin curled her tighter into his frame, unwilling to let her out of his sight again, even though he knew she would receive the best of care with her new family. When he didn't reply, Diego continued, understanding Joaquin's reticence without a hint of condemnation for his feelings. Joaquin didn't doubt Diego would have done the same for Titania, care for her, hold her, protect her, if their roles had been reversed.

"There are places to hide in the canyon where you both will be protected." Large, feathered wings protruded from Diego's shoulders, moving with a graceful lift as they stretched and rose above him and over his head. "Take the time you need, friend. We will welcome her as one of our own when you both return." His somber countenance became less strained for a heartbeat. "Titania is anxious for her and sends her prayers. She will not be alone."

Joaquin was grateful for the unequivocal support from the both of them. "Tell Tani I am in her debt." If it weren't for her, he would have been vampire toast at their first face off.

"Good luck." Then, with a nod, Diego launched into the air, a majestic form carrying precious cargo.

Looking down at Lily's pale face, everything else melted away. "Let's go, lovely."

chapter sixteen

JOAQUIN knew the caves and cracks Diego meant. They were closer than the house, but still took time to reach. The entire time as he made that journey, his thoughts tumbled. There were memories, however distant, of his conversion and he knew the pain he drew from her now was nothing compared to what he had unintentionally forced on Lily to have to endure.

When the devil had attacked him, he'd been bereft with his loss, welcoming the end he'd thought he'd earned. Suffering the catastrophic, painful tragedy of the wreck, awash in the guilt and loss of watching his wife die. It was an end, but not the end he'd believed. The creature who had 'made' him had played with him, alternately diving against Joaquin's throat as though he was his last supper to then leave him weak and defenseless in the wilderness of the new world. He'd been too exhausted to fight off the attack, then too weak to escape.

There was no memory of the first drink for him. The Brethren who had made him had jumped between cold and calculated to nearly maniacal in his treatment of Joaquin. To this day, he didn't even know the man's name. He knew at some point, his creator had perished. There was an infinitesimal prick of knowledge, like a light bulb just going dark, and whatever had tied them together in his creation had ceased to exist.

He did remember his conversion. There would never be enough time and distance for him to ever forget it. The humiliating pain, an absolute loss of his own body and its functions. He'd never faced a higher form of degradation or forgotten the feeling of being ripped open to be shoved ruthlessly into his own skin, inside out. He'd gone to ground on pure instinct. His creator had abandoned him before he'd even begun to lose his humanity. The absolute vacuum of the 'living death' had disconcerted him when he'd awakened to find inches of soil over his head. He'd panicked, bursting through the barrier. It took him three nights to realize when he woke, he wasn't going to suffocate. He didn't breathe unless he wanted to. It was an afterthought in his new existence.

He had almost died irrevocably the night after his conversion, so stunned and disoriented erupting from the earthen bed he'd burrowed, he'd stumbled along the nearest road searching for help, any answer, or his creator. He'd found none of what he searched for.

Someone found him, though. Horsemen who thought to take advantage of a lone man, obviously unsure of his place, and even more unsure of what he was doing. He did have the presence of mind to defend himself that night.

The horses reacted the worst, screaming and fighting to flee the terror they instinctively recognized. The men were not as astute. Two had drawn swords, flicking at him with the razor-sharp edges. They never touched him. Speed was his first discovery. Strength his second. Then, it became his fight as, one by one, the five fell beneath his hand.

For a man who had never killed a person, fighting for his very life changed it all. Death was only another step into the life he'd been shoved into. The scent of blood from one of the injured was the brain-numbing shocker.

Fangs unlike any he'd ever seen burst forth, making him freeze like a statue to examine the change, the urge and the cause. Nearing the fallen man, he stared at him through dispassionate eyes, where the fallen no longer seethed with the bravado of his friends and their malicious objective. He watched Joaquin through eyes glassy with pain and shock. A quick assessment showed he'd damaged something in his fall from his horse. Even though his hands moved, his legs did not even though he scrabbled to get away any way he could.

Joaquin knelt next to the man and let the urge, the hunger, guide him. There was no escape for either man. He recognized penance when he saw it. If this was his for Angelica, then so be it. He would pay his debt to his love.

The first rush was a shocking bliss. Remembering too well the abuses his creator had forced on him, he placed a hand over his provider's eyes and let him rest, taking from the pounding vein in the man's neck, guided by some unseen, unknown hunger. He didn't try to fight the horror of this new hunger. He knew what he faced after spending countless nights as another's victim. The man's life would end by someone else's hand, a merciful hand to end his injuries. Not because of Joaquin's needs.

Something stopped him from gorging as the heat and life filled his limbs. A knowledge, or a warning, he didn't know then, and he'd never once dared to challenge it. Never once wished to see what the outcome would be for crossing that line. Never once fed to end a life, to steal away the soul, the beat, of another. He had to live this way. Joaquin had never delivered the fatal blow that would end their existence as they knew it.

Until now. Looking at the beauty in his arms, terror knifed him.

He had done this. Despair like he'd never known trapped him in a heavy fist. Lifting her, he buried his nose into her hair, so fragrant, redolent with the scent of cinnamon. Ahead he saw the first place that would work, but passed it, knowing he needed a deep hideaway.

Because come daybreak, Lily would be completely alone. With a dead man.

HER BODY ached. Tingles of awareness brought her up from the fog she'd been drifting through. The tender lapping of a tongue against her thigh made her jerk completely awake.

"I better know you," she muttered while her hands clenched into something scrumptiously comfortable layered beneath her.

"You know me like no one else."

She grinned, hearing his voice and floating along the river of sensation he was giving her. She winced, flinching when he found a slice over a nerve.

"Relax. This will help." The warmth of his caresses continued.

"What are you doing?" It felt like...he was...licking her. He couldn't be, but the velvet heat repeated with slow, lingering swipes. What was worse—she was enjoying it. His touch was making her heart speed up, easing the sting of the cuts and slices in her skin, drawing her attention further and further away from the pain.

"Salving your cuts."

"That doesn't feel like any ointment I've ever known."

He chuckled, his warmed breath flowing over her skin, making her tremble anew. "Better than any ointment, love. Just lie still." A tender kiss followed. "You have a lot. I don't want to miss one."

She opened her eyes. And blinked. It was pitch dark. How could he see a thing? She couldn't see her hand in front of her face. Beneath her, she felt a thick pile of something cushioning her along her front.

Other than that, she was completely naked. She couldn't find it in her to really care too much, though. His ministrations were heavenly, distracting her from her unclothed state. Tilting, she lay her cheek down, too tired to think too fast.

"Where are we?"

"In the Grand Canyon." Another swipe higher on her inner thigh. She twitched, swallowing the automatic groan. He was slowly melting her into a mass of quivering need with his attention to detail.

"I take you to mean that literally." His laughter warmed her and she smiled. "I can't see anything."

"I'm sorry. It's too confined for a fire. I can see. You are safe."

"What are we doing here?"

"Tending to your cuts."

She hated to complain about that part, even as wonderful as it felt. It was so unusual. Her mouth snapped shut when he found a particularly sensitive one. The groan was impossible to hide this time. She clenched her hands again, feeling velvet and more. Pillows?

"How did you manage pillows?" she wondered aloud, the unexpected sensation of their plushness distracting her away from his apparent ministrations.

"It was the only thing I could think of at the moment. These needed to be cared for, you needed to be cared for," he purred, dropping another decadent trail along her buttock. "Do you want something else?"

"Hmm? Oh, no," she breathed, shuddering as he moved again. "What *are* you doing?"

"I'm healing you."

It was so matter of fact that, for a moment, his words didn't register.

"Wait. Healing? How?"

"The same way I can heal my bite after feeding. The ones I've already done are beginning to show improvement. By the time I'm done, they'll be mostly gone from all over."

"Amazing." She lay there, entrenched in his touch, his lips and his tongue as he laved and lapped a slow moving trail up her body. The stroke of his fingers on quivering skin a moment later had little to do with healing, and she told him so.

His voice was as sensual against her skin as the velvet beneath her. "It's hard to ignore your body, *corazón*. It warms beneath my touch like the hottest fire. You're so soft, silky everywhere I touch. And delicious." She knew he was teasing her; the flutter of his fingers matched the lowered lascivious voice.

She laughed. Pressing her face into the pillows, she endeavored to stifle the giggles she knew would echo through the cave, or wherever it was he'd hidden them away. Between his touch and his teasing, it was easier to forget why she was hurting, knowing she was safe again.

"Ah, Lily," he crooned. "I love hearing you laugh. It was taken away from you for too long." Her breath caught, and she tried to roll over, but his hands stayed her. "Not yet."

The caress of his fingertips teased as much as the wandering of his tongue where he stroked against her body, time after time. The drag of his hair on sensitized skin sent sparks up her spine in a rush while the touch of his body next to hers, so close but not where she needed, where she craved to feel that searing, passionate touch, drove her insane.

She wasn't sure how much time it took until he was satisfied. She, on the other hand, was a riotous knot of wanting, writhing with barely controlled restraint into the pillows. She wished she could see. At least she wasn't claustrophobic.

What felt like an eternity later, but may have taken less than an hour, he lifted the length of her hair free of her neck and kissed her there, below her ear, blowing gently against the shell. She shivered like a leaf in answer.

"Lily." Her name was a wrenched groan from his lips. "My lovely Lily." When he said things like that, she felt so cherished. She wanted to wrap up the feelings and keep them close. Forever. His caresses changed, deepened, revealing his own hunger, his own desire. His lips slid down her neck to her shoulder, nipping and teasing at skin. She moaned as he suckled, finding sensitive spots where she didn't know she had spots.

She opened her eyes and fought to make out a shape, any shape, in the darkness of the cavern they were in. There was absolutely no light at all. She trembled, unable to restrain it.

He stopped instantly. "What is wrong?"

"I don't like not being able to see." She didn't mean to make it a complaint.

"Hush," he soothed. "You're not complaining. This is foreign to you." He sat up and lightly tugged her body up until she rested comfortably against his chest. She realized he was as naked as she was. She couldn't even say when he'd undressed.

"I don't have a way to make it brighter in here," he explained. "The cavern is deep in the wall of the canyon."

"Why down here?"

Sexual tension stiffened his frame where they touched. "Because in a few hours, you're going to be as close to alone as it can get, and I wanted you safe." His voice had dropped the sensual purr. He was dead serious.

"Alone?" Her voice rose with the news, snapping up to try to find his face in the darkness. It was a lost cause. "Where will you be?"

"I'll be right here, but I'll be asleep and I won't be able to hear you if anything happens. The path to this cavern is very difficult to find and harder to traverse for normal humans. I had to make sure you would be okay first."

"Not able?" He wasn't making sense.

Tender concern flowed on the air between them. "Lovely, I'll be dead during the day. I didn't want you to face the sunlight hours alone. There was no way we could return to the house in one night." God, she hated when he could say it succinctly and sound normal. "Down here, you are hidden, safe from the sun's heat and everyone else."

"Dead? As in, really dead?" she asked, hating the chirped squeak in her voice. She made it a point to loosen the clutched grip she had on his body. Not even a flicker of discomfort had moved his muscles in argument to her relentless hold. She had no doubt she'd left marks.

"Yes."

She tucked herself into his shoulder, her thoughts running in all directions. Dead. *He is a vampire, dummy,* she chided herself. *What did you think he'd do? Get a room at the local Holiday Inn?*

"You'll be safe here. I promise you." He started to nuzzle her again, brushing light lips to her temple.

"It's not fair that you can see and I can't," she pouted. She didn't want to think about later right now.

"Then feel," he breathed, sending a rush of warmth cascading down her body to make her quiver in anticipation. "Feel me the way I feel you. Need me the way I need you." His voice, that rich timbre of exotically accented sound, drew her closer until she succumbed.

He groaned when she gave in, her body bending and arching against his in answer to his caresses. As though he were afraid to break her, he laid her down on the lush pillows, their softness a contrast to the solid hardness of his body. All contours and angles. Her hands roamed his body, tracing, learning. From the smooth arch of his neck to the broad strength of his shoulders. She learned the planes of his chest, gasping at the heat of his skin in her hands, feeling the way he reacted to her touch as she glided across, up and down.

He wasn't as tall as Diego or as broad as Houston, but solid in a way she longed to touch.

"Then please, touch me."

She sent him a reproachful look, but only felt his total absorption in what she was doing to him. Someday she'd get used to having him hanging around in her thoughts.

"Share them with me. See how I see you." He lowered to find her lips and her world exploded in a beautiful flood of color.

What she saw amazed her. Shocked her, because she didn't recognize the wanton creature that opened herself up to Joaquin like a gift.

"You are a gift, a precious one to me. A gift I will protect until even the nights have ceased. You are the beat of my heart, the joy in my life."

Her lips trembled, overcome with emotion at his sweet words. "*Love me,*" she entreated.

"I already do."

Without a single pause, he sipped away the tears as they fell from the corners of her eyes, kissing her face with such gentleness she could barely breathe. He rained those kisses on her cheeks, her eyes, her forehead, then moved to nibble and adore her throat, nipping at the smooth pulse spot beneath her ear. With as much attention to detail as he'd used caring for the slashed cuts in her skin on her back, he adored her body. Shivers of desire flared outward with every touch.

There was no restraint in her cry when his mouth touched the taut peak of her breast. His hair slid like fine silk through her fingers, thick and plentiful, her only anchor as her world soared and tilted. Air slid furiously through her lungs as she fought to keep up with his attentions. Every touch sent her higher, soaring further. Her shoulders bunched as he drew her deeper into the pleasure he created with his mouth on her breast.

She found she didn't need light. Being enveloped in a sightless void, her senses grew heightened, her skin becoming a living, hungry part of her that craved his decadent kisses. Whispered words fell in sensual clouds on her ears. Every movement, touch and brush of his lips against her skin sent a volley of sparkled shocks over her nerves. Every stroke created a maelstrom of light behind her lids, stars exploding with brilliant color as new sensations and pleasure like nothing she'd ever known sent her careening wildly, bucking and pleading for anything and everything. The tentative pressure of his hand against her core didn't make her flinch or retreat. She answered his question, opening for his searing touch, and was rewarded. Nothing had ever prepared her for the pain of imprisonment. Nothing had ever prepared her for the pleasure she now found with Joaquin.

She greedily soaked it in, wanting more, craving everything and, in answer, he delivered until she screamed in ecstasy.

Gasping, she barely registered his weight above her. The smooth feel of him poised at her entrance, not rushing, not forcing, only waiting, almost had her in tears again.

"Joaquin," she whimpered, lost and clinging to the only thread of sanity she had left. Then, he was inside her, every part of him, filling her. With slow, methodical movements, he stroked against her. She arched in answer, every pore crying out in need, in a deep hunger she'd never known.

Sounds echoed to them from everywhere. Tender words of passion slipped from his lips as he dropped kisses, rising to find her lips, tasting her, then delving within with his tongue, claiming her mouth the same way he claimed her body.

"Mine. Always." The thoughts whispered through her mind, swirling wildly with the beautiful patterns of light he'd given her.

"Yes," she answered without hesitation.

"Be mine, Lily. Be mine for eternity."

Her body tightened in answer to his decadent words, hot and slick with moisture as he drove into her.

He arched his spine, a slow hiss of pleasure breaking his mental seduction. "Do that again."

She did, flexing her hips and holding his length in a steel grip. He groaned, so shaken he quivered over her. "Lily!" He shouted her name, plunging into her. "I have to have you."

Grasping her shoulders, she felt the heat of his breath on her throat, teasing and licking at her. Even in his most possessed, he still restrained himself, wanting her allowance to take the only thing he couldn't live without.

One hand moved down her body, cupping her hip, his thrusts never stopping, never slowing as he buried himself into her over and over.

Electric shudders spiked her when he swirled his tongue over her pulse. Trembles erupted on her lips under the impact of all the raging sensations. She tilted in answer, no compulsion, no argument. She could never deny him.

"You are the greatest gift," he whispered against her throat. Then, she felt the heated suckle of his mouth, arching with another cry as pleasure hit her bloodstream, flaring all along her body in wondrous detonations. There was a brief pain, but she was so swept into the sensual storm he had created between them, it was forgotten before the pain had even registered as a discomfort.

His body dominated hers, rising and falling with a growing ferocity. He no longer scared her in any way. She wanted him, all of him. Joaquin's passion was unmistakable. Even at its highest, when he was most able to hurt her, he couldn't. She felt the heady pulls against her skin. The bone-melting pleasure of his mouth on her neck was making her turn to liquid and throb for more at the same time.

He rose over her, curving her body tight to his. She wrapped herself around him, taking him, welcoming his passion and giving him hers. He took it all, lowering to kiss her. Time stood still. Tension wound her tighter and tighter like a coiled spring.

Then, her entire world erupted in a kaleidoscope of colored rapture.

DROWSY kisses warmed her shoulder. She burrowed into the pile of pillows, large, sultan sized squares of velvet and satin piled to cover at least as far as she could reach a hand, and likely further. She felt like she could sleep for a week. She was exhausted, but surprisingly, not hungry. Realizing she hadn't eaten, she tried to remember to how long it had been since she had, and was worried at the answer. After thirty-six hours, she should be ravenous with hunger, but honestly, the idea of food left her stomach feeling unsettled. Had Hawthorne injected her with something again? Using her for one of their many questionable tests?

She shifted and the arm across her stomach glided lower. The motion brought her body closer to his, delightfully closer.

"Mmm," she purred, arching into his steadily seeking kisses.

"Have I ever told you, you remind me of the sweet summer desserts I used to have as a child?" His voice was far away, lost in a memory.

"No."

He tickled her skin, his nose planted beneath her ear as he inhaled. "You do. Vanilla and cinnamon. Intoxicating." He nipped as if he wanted to eat her right then and she giggled. "How are you feeling?"

"Tired, but what a wonderful kind of tired." She heard his low masculine chuckle.

"No pain from the whip?" Concern made his voice attentive even when his lips were being single-minded.

She shifted, stretching, and found none. "Nope."

He grunted softly. "I will kill the man who did that to you."

She blinked. It was said with the ease of saying he'd buy bread on the way home. "You're serious, aren't you?"

He pulled away and, even though she couldn't see him, she knew he lay directly in front of her. A hand rose to brush at her hair, proving her right. "No one will ever harm you again." It was a statement in stone.

"Joaquin, it is done. I know there wasn't anything you could do. You did the best thing. You came for me. I don't want anyone else's blood on my hands." Unerringly, she found the curve of his face and stroked him with her palm. *Who needs light*? she thought.

She felt the warmth of his breath, then his kiss in her palm when he turned against her. "For you Lily. Not because he doesn't deserve it."

She stroked his ear and the loose strands of his hair. It wouldn't be long until sunrise. She hoped she could sleep through most of the day. She wasn't sure how she was going to handle sleeping next to a dead body. Just the idea of it gave her chills.

She shivered when the fact became larger than life.

"What's the matter, lovely?"

"Just thinking." She felt his worry surfacing. "I'm worried about how I'm going to deal with today, while you're, you know—dead."

"Will you have problems feeling trapped without any light?" His worry climbed higher. She realized he hadn't thought that far into it, but she could ease his tension just the same.

"No, not just because it's dark. I can live like this for a few hours."

Again, his fingers combed through her hair. "My brave little flower."

She snickered, knowing she was blushing and so thankful he couldn't see it. She felt the heat of it bloom across her face as his touch wandered more.

"Lily, there is something we need to talk about."

"You mean other than you being a vampire and the fact that I'm in love with you?"

Stunned silence.

And it kept going.

And lengthening. New chills rose on her skin and they had nothing to do with the coming day.

"I shouldn't have—" His kiss was a scorching heat, unexpected when she knew the only sound she'd heard for minutes was her own breathing. His arms encircled her, yanking her passionately against his body, feeling every inch all along her front. There was no way to hide his throbbing arousal. Her body melted to liquid with his body touching hers inch by demanding inch.

He released her only when she had no choice but to need to breathe. He pressed his forehead to hers. "I never expected to find someone like you, Lily. I never thought I'd feel whole again. You give me life, Lily. My only intention was to see you safe, cherished and healed, to move on, to have a life when I first met you. My redemption for failing Angelica." He paused, seeming to gather his thoughts as tension flowed up and down his frame in waves. "I never once believed I'd feel this way again, and I never expected it to be returned." Gentle, life-giving lips settled on hers, worshiping her in such a beautiful way that she had to pinch her eyes to stop the dampness behind her lids from growing. "I never once thought I'd love you. I think I have since that first argument."

She had to swallow twice to make her voice work. "How long until sunrise?"

"Soon," he answered, sipping hungrily at her lips and cheeks.

She wrapped a hand over his head and pulled him with her when she rolled, kissing him with all of her heart. "Then let's not waste the time talking," she murmured against his throat, feeling his entire body harden more with the innocent caress. He groaned and answered her with a kiss that burned her down to her toes.

chapter seventeen

ROUSING unhurriedly, she blinked, not thrilled it was still as dark as the deepest black sea all around her, but knew without question she was safe. She also knew it was daylight somewhere beyond where she could see. As a guess, late afternoon. The air was still and just warm enough for her skin not to chill with being asleep. Was it something he'd taken into account when he'd taken her there? She could only shake her head in wonder. He would do his very best to ensure her comfort and care. It sent a shot of sappy warmth right to her heart.

She'd been beyond exhausted when she'd finally curled into Joaquin's body to drift into the best sleep of her life. Without an ache or pain. Just a wonderful, peaceful lethargy. Rolling, she jumped with a startled gasp when she found the lump of cold next to her. Shaking her head at her own ridiculousness, she settled her racing heart down to a reasonable pace.

It was only Joaquin. She *knew* that. And that was probably the very reason she'd been caught so off guard. He was *right next to her*. They'd drifted into a tranquil state and she'd fallen asleep. Of course he'd stay right where he was. Did she think he'd rise to the ceiling and hang like a bat?

She snorted a laugh. *Bad joke, Lily.* Daring herself with her curiosity growing, she trailed the back of her hand along his cheek, feeling the absolute chill of his skin on her fingers. Wondering, she moved further until her hand rested over his chest. Not a single movement. Nothing. And still ice cold. Lifting her hand, she shook off the shivers with a quick chastisement.

He'd stayed close so you wouldn't be alone, idiot.

The realization warmed her even though he couldn't know how much it meant to her. He obviously had done something that was as foreign to him as hiding in a lightless cave was for her.

Because he'd never make you face something he wouldn't do himself. She knew he'd slept alone every night since he'd changed. Centuries of no blanket wars, of no dreams to share, no nightmares to soothe.

She laid down without a hesitant bone, pressing herself along his length like a living blanket, knowing her body's heat would do nothing for him, but it would be the first thing he'd feel when he did wake.

That meant everything to her.

JOAQUIN neared the campsite with a stealthy prowl, spying two hikers enjoying the canyon's wonders. They would suffice for his needs. He had little time to waste. Lily was asleep in the cave, a little extra behind it to keep her dreaming happily so she wouldn't wake to find him gone. His skin still felt the lingering shock of waking to find her heated body draped lovingly over his own.

It had been a shock, but such a wonderful one it had taken him a full fifteen minutes to even think of disturbing either of them. His skin had burned beneath her, as though a single fire danced between them, back and forth, warming them as his body became acclimated to not being alone, absorbing the feeling of her silken skin along his from his shoulder to his foot where hers had hooked him in her sleep. Those sensations weren't the only things his body seemed to respond to either. Her scent soaked into him and desire rose to meet it, soaring at an unruly speed to reach out to her with a vicious need. He ached with wanting to feel her again, so full and hard he almost groaned at the speed with which it overcame him.

But he needed to feed. They had things to talk about. He had to tell her what they'd done. He prayed she would still love him after. There was no way he could live without her. Not now. Those moments had slipped through his fingers nights ago. He hoped by the end of tonight she would come to him willingly.

In his deepest soul, now he understood what Diego and Titania shared, and felt doubly blessed to be given this chance. A second chance at life, with love and friends.

The sun had set not too long ago and the men he watched sat near their campfire on a forgotten river log, relaxing from the dinner they had eaten and an extensive day exploring the canyon. Thankfully, with the two, he wouldn't have to leave either weakened. The canyon was a rough environment even for the heartiest of beings.

Checking one last time for any signs of anyone else, human or Brethren, and finding no one, he glided out of the shifting shadows and drew the young pair to him. Two strong men. He'd sensed their close friendship in their words as he'd studied them and the night.

Bringing the first into his arms, he closed his eyes and pictured Lily, her succulent body glowing and replete as she had been the night before. The feeling of her fingers, of her skin as he had touched her, pleased her, made his heart beat with a hard rhythm, one he didn't have to prod. He swallowed, keeping the groan inside. He swept the wounds closed with hardly a thought. With her on his mind, it was easy to stop himself from taking too much. There was so much he would have to learn about having a life partner, a mate, as Diego had called Titania. His wife.

The slap of wanting came out of nowhere, so strong he almost broke his enthralled hold on his provider.

After he took what he needed from the second, he sent them to their site with orders to sleep the night. They had water to cure their thirst in the morning. Satisfied they would not come to harm from his needs, he whirled and burst into the sky, dropping his shape to create the streamlined body of a hawk. Every cell demanded he return to her. Even this little amount of time, of distance, was enough to make him edgy. He had to know she was safe. The strain of her abduction and tortures would not be quickly or easily forgotten.

Soaring through the star-speckled night, he zipped into the cave opening, hidden from most eyes because of the angle of the canyon face. It was easier to see from above than below, and there was no place at the edge to look down.

He found her where he'd left her, curled delectably on the pillows like a red-haired goddess. All that warm, fair skin glistened against the rich jewel tones of the velvets. The image made his body throb again. His instantaneous reaction had him wondering if he'd ever outgrow his burgeoning need for her. He hoped on every moon he'd seen the answer was no.

Kneeling, he scooped her into his arms, then turned to make the reverse journey through the winding splits forming the only way in or out. Long, jagged cracks in the canyon that had happened millions of years ago.

Dropping easily from the height, he landed in the scrub of the canyon floor, striding to take his precious cargo to a bend in the riverbank where the surface had smoothed out. Boulders lined the canyon between the river and cliff face.

Picking a nearly flat one, he hopped up and sat, holding her in his lap. With a little thought, he prepared rousing her by giving her a pair of jeans and a top, but instead of the unflattering sweatshirts, he created a long sleeved silk blouse with lovely buttons that would be a delight to slide free. Her breasts rose and fell against the material with an alluring rhythm, making his already tight and needy body swell with hunger. He couldn't care less what she wore. Nothing was a prime choice, but he knew she was still very self-conscious over the proof of her imprisonment on her body. Lastly, a simple pair of sneakers like the ones he'd seen her wear, and he lifted the sleep curtain on her mind.

Giving kisses on her face, she tilted and turned, welcoming every touch. "Wake, lovely. Open your eyes slowly. It may take time for your eyes to adjust to light again."

Golden lashes fluttered, heeding his warning even as he did his best to distract her from everything else. She purred wantonly and curled tighter against his chest, comfortable in the cradle of his arms. The needy groan was impossible to hide. Thoughts tumbled and whirled like a windstorm, dangerously erotic with promising images dancing across his mind.

They were coming from her.

He tipped back and laughed, too happy to care about anything else at that moment. "You little minx," he playfully accused her, swiping her hair away from her face.

She lifted her eyes, looking through her lashes at him, a wicked smile playing across her lips. "Yes?"

Joaquin dropped a quick kiss to her pouty mouth. If he asked for more, he'd take everything. "Can you see all right?"

She rubbed a hand over her eyes, blinking to clear them. "Yeah, I think I'll be okay." He nodded, then let her slip from his hands to her feet. "Walk with me," he coaxed, twining his fingers through hers.

"Shouldn't we get back?"

"Soon." Questions colored her gaze when she caught his. He wasn't trying to be evasive, but he had no experience with 'making' another vampire. "We need to talk."

Those same tawny eyes gathered the stars as they began to sparkle with mischievous remembrance peering up at him. "I think we tried to last night and something seemed to interrupt."

"Ah, my lovely," he breathed, grinning, remembering too well what had happened. Tugging her close, he walked along the river.

She ran a hand over her stomach, a confused frown rising, then fading from her features.

"Is something wrong?"

"I was thinking. It's been two days since I ate, but I'm not hungry. I feel mostly okay. A little tired, but not deprived. I've been worried why."

Joaquin nodded, his own concern matching her frown. The tumble of the river was soothing as it raced its endless path alongside them. "You haven't eaten in two days?"

She shook her head. "No."

Now that was something to worry about. They'd bonded two nights ago. With a sinking feeling, he realized it had already begun. She was living on borrowed time until her body gave out, or they successfully completed the conversion. There was no thought of failure that she wouldn't survive it. He'd done nothing but pray for the last two nights. He knew he'd only begun to renew his need in his faith. "Lily, there's something I have to tell you." Heaviness made his entire body feel like lead. Fear of her rejection. Fear of failure. Fear of losing her. It all attacked him mercilessly.

"O-kay," she replied, a touch of anxiety reaching his ears. Her fingers twitched within his grasp.

"When we bonded..." He lost his nerve. He tried again, knowing he had to take whatever punishment she gave him for it. Take it and move past it. He wasn't going to let her die. "When we bonded, something happened."

"Oh?" She paused, turning to look up at him. There was no censure in her gaze. No condemnation. Not yet.

“You remember Titania telling us she was an accident inadvertently started?”

She nodded, listening astutely.

“She never explained what it was that had been the accident.” He glanced away, then faced her, unable to say it without seeing her reaction. He wasn’t a coward. “You and I did the same thing.”

It took a moment for the truth to become clear to her. Her cream pale skin whitened to snow, making her eyes too bright and too large for her face. “No.” She choked on the word, her eyes widening more. “No!” Trembles rocked her frame. “You’re wrong!”

“I wish I was,” he admitted. “You and I are forever, I meant that.” He raked a hand through his hair. “But I didn’t mean it like this. I was going to live your life and let you go. I would die without you, but I never intended for you to... For this to be the way,” he finished lamely, reeling from the pain rolling off of her. It swamped and choked him like the bitter dust of the river bottom surrounding them. He deserved every evil, disgusted thought she could throw at him. He had a few himself.

“What did you do?” Fury made her eyes spark for a whole new reason, brighter than anything he’d ever seen. They narrowed as her hands curled into fists.

“When I accepted you into me, I shared with you. You carry my blood in your veins.”

“I...drank your blood?” Revulsion and horror made her waver, her eyes closing. Instead of bloodless, she looked a little green. "Oh my God," she breathed. "I think I'm going to faint." She spun and walked to an even spot and folded bonelessly to sit. Haggard breaths lifted her shoulders as she cradled her head. "This can't be happening," he heard her mutter. "I thought..." She swallowed, taking huge gulps of air. "I thought it was for now. For us, yes, but..." She whimpered. "I wasn't expecting eternity to mean *eternity*!" Her voice carried down the canyon as she shouted out her growing rage at him. The golden fire of her eyes split him in two.

He approached and knelt before her. "I know."

"Damn it! I can't drink blood! I don't want to be a vampire!"

Joaquin couldn't deny her pain, or her rage. It was no less than he'd suffered. It made no difference it was as unintentional as Titania's conversion had been, an innocent attempt to keep them safe. The intensity of her anger was killing him, a little at a time.

"It takes time to get used to—"

"I'm not going to get used to it! I'm not going to do it, damn it!"

"It can't be reversed," he informed her, damning himself for every word he'd ever uttered to her, for every emotion he'd dared to let himself feel. He'd done this to her. There was no one else to blame. Joaquin's worst nightmare had come to pass. His redemption had become a living hell. "If you cannot do the conversion, you will die."

Cold. Her eyes were actually so cold, he shivered. He swore he saw her words form as ice shards in the air, there was so much coldness in her, so much pain. She was frozen. He'd done this to her, hurt her so bad, her soul had frozen solid.

"Then you have killed me. Even when Tenorio couldn't, when Hawthorne couldn't break me, you have." She stood with little warning, looking beyond him. Through him. "Take me home, Joaquin."

Pain sliced him down the middle with her judgment, because she wasn't wrong.

Gathering her stiff and unyielding body against his, he tipped her into his shoulder and soared upward. He tried only once to reach her, touching her gingerly with his mind.

The slam of the wall was so fierce, he felt the reverberation down to his toes.

SHE DIDN'T look at him when he placed her on her feet. "Lily?" She shook with rage, completely ignoring the heartfelt plea. Neither had spoken on the way. No sense in starting now. Anger still made her shake inside. She marched straight up to, then through, the front door. She would've slammed it, but knew people were probably asleep.

Her life had been turned on its ear yet again. Stolen for the second time. She was hurting inside, bloody and bleeding. All she wanted had been stripped away. Control over her own life. A fragile chance to have a real life. A normal life. Gone. She knew she was just as responsible. She'd asked for him to do it, but she hadn't thought he'd... She couldn't even finish the thought. She'd meant the bond with every fiber of her being. She knew what it meant for him to take from her, but *from him*? How had he done it? She didn't remember a thing.

"Lily!" Whirling, she was nearly knocked off her feet by Kathy and a quickly swooping Amy. "You're back!"

She hugged them both. Overcome with the welcome, she let her previously raging emotions melt away.

"I'm glad to be home." She said it, then realized she meant it. This had become her home. These women, and the others surrounding her in her life, were her family. She hugged them fiercely, too happy to see their faces again.

"We knew they'd be able to rescue you," Kathy said, her lips trembling to restrain the tears, then swept them away when she couldn't. "Diego told us a little bit ago what happened when they found you and Claire."

"Claire?"

Amy and Kathy both nodded. "The girl they found at Hawthorne's. She is resting upstairs, still in shock, but so happy to be out."

"Like all of us," Amy said quietly.

Lily forked her hair with her fingers, sending it rolling around herself in a wild wave.

"They also told us they didn't get David. We'd gone into town with Laney and Houston to look into some baby stuff. Normal stuff," Amy added, regretfully because if they'd been there, David might not have been able to get away with what he'd done.

Kathy wiped another tear away, saying, "I can't believe he'd do that to any of us."

"Did Diego tell you why he took me?"

They both shook their heads. "Why don't we get some tea and I'll tell you? We also think Hawthorne still has him. He wasn't found when Diego and Joaquin arrived." She didn't stumble over his name. Amazing. At least she was able to keep her anger at him out of her voice. She'd have time later to figure out what she was going to do about what he'd done. There had to be a way to reverse it.

There had to be. She didn't want to have to suck blood for the rest of her—supposedly now very long—life.

Both Amy and Kathy sat asking very few questions as she gave them her rendition of her capture and rescue. When she was done, they sat in contemplative silence. What was left to be said? David had paid the price trying to protect his family. It was a futile attempt. No one was safe with or from Tenorio.

She lifted the mug to her lips and sipped, instantly putting it down, unprepared for the sudden volatile reaction from her stomach.

"Is it too hot?" Amy asked.

"No." Lily swallowed, fighting the hard roil her stomach had threatened her with—a distinct message. Usually, the warning right before something unnatural and very unpleasant was about to happen. Breathing through her nose, she calmed the constrictions tightening her body like a vise. It took a few minutes. Cautiously, she tried again to sip at the drink, savoring the taste to encourage her stomach to want the flavorful tea.

She lurched from her seat and spit it into the sink, gagging and coughing.

"Lily!" Kathy was beside her, rubbing her back. "You're not feeling well and we've kept you up to talk. You probably need to sleep. It's shock or something."

"Yeah, or something," she sputtered, sucking in air to calm her stomach. Well, that explained why she wasn't hungry. It wasn't going to ask, and definitely wasn't going to take anything she stuck in it. Lovely.

She ran the back of her hand over her forehead, confused and feeling more tired. "I think I will rest for a while. Is Tabitha doing okay?"

"She's fine. Been sleeping almost nonstop. She needs it more than anything."

Lily nodded. "All right, then." She nodded, giving a fake smile. "If you need me, just come get me. I'm sure I'll still be awake." Especially if her stomach kept this up.

Once inside her room, she closed the door and leaned against it, the first unbidden tears falling free. "*Joaquin, what did you do?*" Covering her eyes with her hands, with her back pressed to the door, she sank down.

Lily never heard him. Gently, strong arms lifted her off the floor. She formed a fist and hit him on the chest, then did it again as Joaquin crossed the space of her room to lay her on the bed. He didn't try to stop her as she pounded out her misery on his body.

"Damn you," she cursed at him. "Do you even know what you've done?"

"With every bone in my body."

She sobbed once more. "You have to reverse it, Joaquin." She couldn't look at him, her head turned away even though she knew he stood right next to the bed. His fingers were drifting down her cheek, chasing the tears on her skin. "There has to be a way."

Silence stretched out. When he finally spoke, it was with a grave finality. "I've talked to Diego. It can't be undone."

Curling into a ball, she turned her back to him, sobbing into the blankets beneath her. "I promised I'd never lose control over my life again, Joaquin. I lost so much. So much. I have to be the one to make the decisions. I have to be in control. Otherwise, what am I?"

"I know, lovely," he soothed contritely.

"You stole it from me. You *ripped* my life from me."

He walked to the other side of the bed and climbed up to sit against the headboard, then found her shoulders and pulled her into his body.

"I hate you," she bit out. Then hated herself more when she arched into his stroking touch, to give him a better angle. Her body had turned traitor.

"I love you," he replied. "I would still live your life and be eternally grateful for the chance, but Lily, this will kill you. I'm sorry I'm being selfish, but I don't want you to die if you don't have to."

She sniffled a little longer, then, "If I become like you? Like Titania?"

He nuzzled the top of her head with his cheek. "Yes. You can still have what you want. You'll just get to live a lot longer to do it."

She snorted, uncaring if she sounded like a stuck pig or not. "Not a great trade-off. All the control I could want, if I suck blood." She shivered, unable to hide the repulsed reaction.

"I can help you," he offered sincerely. "I would take care of you."

Damn it! She wanted to rake him over the coals, wanted to flay his ass alive for what he'd done. It wasn't going to be that easy, though. She was just as guilty. Accepting that, though, didn't make the bitter truth any easier to handle. "I'm half to blame for this. I told you to do it." Begged him. She wasn't so proud of that fact now, but she hadn't expected to *drink* his blood. She'd only known, at that point, she couldn't lose him. She was only a knocked head away from realizing she loved him.

And still did.

"Yes and no. Neither of us had much control of the situation." He was still nuzzling her. "When I held you, it was like my life had started over. All the years before were the path to be here, now. For you. I knew when I did it, I wouldn't be able to let you go."

Kisses were beginning to fall where his cheek had been. Kisses that burned with his need, burned with his own angst and regret. "The need to make it a complete bonding was impossible to fight. I had to do it. It was tearing me apart to make you mine completely and holding back. I belong to you as much as you belong to me." His tender words were wrapped in the remorse she knew he felt. A deed done that couldn't be undone. So close to him, no longer hiding from his thoughts, or hiding hers from him, she knew every thought, every punishing recrimination he'd called himself, and likely more that she couldn't find. "If you don't, then I will die with you."

She snapped up to gape at him. "Why?"

Midnight dark, his eyes were limpid pools and, looking into them, she found herself reflected back. "Because everything I am will die with you."

chapter eighteen

"YOU DON'T have long before your body will begin to suffer. Another day, maybe two." He wasn't going to let her die. She may be undecided, or think she had a choice. He regretted with every bone in his body he'd already made the choice for her, for the both of them. She may even hate him more before it was all done. It wasn't an easy way to live, or not live, depending on who he asked. He couldn't let her go. He was selfish. A bastard. He wasn't going to let her die. He would prefer her to accept what had happened, but if she didn't, then so be it.

"What about Tabitha?"

There wasn't any surprise that her next worry would be for the other woman. Lily had been putting a lot of her own issues purposely somewhere far away so she could care for her. Now it was time he cared for Lily.

He ran his fingers through her wavy hair, unable to not touch her. He had to have her in his hands, feel her on his skin. Drawing a slow breath, he drew the lingering scent of cinnamon into his lungs. "You will still be able to care for her, the same as you have. I wouldn't take you away from her. I will provide for you and keep you safe."

He knew what he was asking of her. He had once been human. A man with a world, a wife, a life. He also knew her fears weren't going to be enough to stop him. They were real; he wouldn't belittle them or her, but fears could be tackled, banished. She was strength personified. He doubted she would ever cease to amaze him. Which is why he knew she would survive. Lily wasn't the kind of being to give in when things got tough.

Sliding down onto the bed, she followed, albeit stiffly and not entirely convinced. "Trust me, lovely." He whispered into her hair, dropping kisses wherever he found a place. There were a lot of places.

"I can't do it," she whimpered, shivering, abhorrent to the very idea. Wrapping his arms around her, he pulled her to rest on his shoulder.

"When it becomes the difference between life and death, the human body and mind can overcome almost anything," he replied. Brushing her hair away from her face, he found her eyes were closed. "I didn't have the benefit of a teacher when it happened to me. I was left to fend for myself. No one to show me the way. I won't let that happen to you, Lily. Titania is also here. Maybe talking to her would help?"

"Why is this even happening, though?" Her hand slid across his body, pulling her tighter against his frame, seeking comfort, seeking solidity in a rapidly changing world. His hold tightened, relishing the length of her against him, pouring out any reassurance she may need unselfishly.

"I don't know. Diego is just as puzzled. This has never happened within the Brethren."

"Brethren? The society of vampires as a whole? This has never happened?" Disbelief echoed in Lily's voice.

"No. Not with so many of us finding each other whole and sane, and then finding you. Two pieces to a puzzle we are just beginning to see."

"What does it mean?"

He shrugged. "None of us know. There is something happening, though. We are being drawn together, even if it is only by accident."

Joaquin knew she was thinking. "What if you are, but aren't, Brethren?"

"How do you mean?"

She lifted to rest her chin on the back of her hand, cushioned on his shoulder. "Well. You were created the same, but something in all of you kept you from going off the deep end. Even Nathan has been able to hold on. He's young, but determined. Then Diego found Tani. Somehow, I haven't staked you yet."

"Low blow, my dear." He tugged lovingly at the ends of her hair.

She shot him a withering stare. "I owe you one, or twelve." He would have sighed if it would have helped. She hadn't forgiven him yet.

Taking the prudent path, he didn't remark on that. "So, what are you thinking?"

"I'm not sure yet. I want to talk to Tani and Diego. Get their impression on all of this."

"Lily." He pressed a kiss to her forehead. "There isn't any way to reverse it." He knew he'd hit a point when she narrowed her eyes at him.

"You don't know that." She turned away from him, but didn't move off his shoulder.

"Lily." He tipped her face up with a finger beneath her chin to look into her eyes. What he saw was a world of pain he'd caused. "I'm sorry."

Reaching down, he pressed his lips to hers, feeling the way they trembled and quivered even as he warmed them with his touch. Lingering over the softness of her lips, he fed his hand into thick sunset hair, relishing the weight of it against his hand. He didn't want to fight anymore, not tonight. He didn't want her anger.

With a gentle push, he rolled her beneath him and braced his hands on either side of her face, lowering to drop butterfly kisses on alluring skin. Tonight, he wanted the woman who owned the fire her hair warned the world of, wanted the strength behind those sea-tossed, golden-as-sand eyes. Craved the passion in her hands.

"No more, lovely. Not tonight," he whispered against her mouth, licking at her lips like she was the embodiment of the cinnamon confection he'd described to her. There was more than one way to win an argument. Or simply, not allow it to happen.

This was a much better use of their time altogether.

"I haven't forgiven you," she warned him even as her lips answered his.

"I know." Then, he didn't let her say another word. Her hands felt like brands as they slid up over his shoulders to twine through his hair. Her skin was like a delicacy, to be enjoyed one thorough sip at a time. The scents he found warmed his blood as he inhaled beneath her ear. She shivered in answer. The reaction made the ache under his skin double. Made him crave her and her taste as though she were the sweetest wine. "You are perfection." He blew a light stream over her ear and she quaked deliciously.

Rising over her, he held himself still, sliding the first button free on her shirt. He swirled his tongue over the exposed gift of skin. All along his body he throbbed, pulsed, hungered. Another button slipped free and the rise and fall of the tops of her breasts drew his attention to their softness. He couldn't resist the playground, licking over exposed, flushed skin. She gasped as he delved between them, tasting the valley of flesh. With deliberate motions, he slowly released each button, letting the fabric of the cream shirt gradually gape open with a teasing view. She'd never wear another one of those of nondescript sweatshirts around him again.

Every time he looked upon her, all he could think was how lucky he was, how beautiful she was to him. Running his fingers up over her stomach, he inched over her ribs, feeling the way she trembled beneath his touch. It only took a quick twist of his finger to slice the lace of her bra with an elongated nail. He groaned as her breasts fell free. The cherry tips peaked in the cooler air.

"You drive me wild," he told her before he drew a taut nipple into his mouth, swirling his tongue over it, tasting her. She moaned, arching into his pulls. He answered with a harsh groan when her fingers kneaded against him. Claiming her, he hooked a leg over hers, leaning on a hip, caging her beneath his weight. Her feminine curves fit into him as though she were made for him. He didn't try to hide his arousal, the turgid length pressing into her hip like a hot brand. He wanted her to know how she affected him. Wanted her to know he couldn't live without her, without her touch, without her voice. He doubled his efforts, moving to the breast being warmed in his palm. Her entire body shuddered in pleasure.

Fire pulsed in his blood, under his skin, heating his hunger to greater heights. Quiet whimpers and gasps escaped her with each new exploration of her body. The feel of her fingers mimicking him on his own shirt made him lift but only an inch or two. Shivers rocked his chest as the protection of his shirt gave way. Then, it was his body being explored, touched, tasted.

The unexpected bite of her nails running over his chest made his head snap on his neck in rapture, fire and lightning raging like a wild tempest within the depths of his soul. She shoved the shirt clear of his shoulders and he shrugged it off, throwing it behind his shoulder. Her fingers splayed, hungrily drawing patterns against his skin. Her lips beckoned to him and he worshiped them.

Shudders racked his body as the sensations of her nails running gently over his nipples hardened them, sending arcs of desire soaring through his body with each touch. A lightning bolt that singed nerves and skin alike. Delving between her lips, she met his thrusts, teasing him with a passionate mating.

Catching her bottom lip between his teeth, he growled once, a low, possessive sound. Dropping a final kiss on her sweet mouth, he slid down her body, his tongue leaving a trail that burned, the same way he burned for her. The catch on her jeans was less than a thought and he pulled them off as he lowered, removing everything with impatient tugs. Then, she lay before him, and his desire reached new heights.

Kneeling beside the bed, he brought her to him and drew her knees over his shoulders. There was no hesitation this time, only a single-minded purpose. Her pleasure. She quivered with anticipation, not fear; with wanting, not worry. Nipping the soft flesh of her inner thigh brought forth a light squeal and he grinned. "Ah, lovely," he breathed, finding the scent of her essence permeating the air between their bodies. Overcome with a deep surge of wanting, he couldn't contain the lusting shake of his own body.

Then, he touched her with his lips and she cried out, tension rocketing up and down her body on the tail of the pleasure comet he'd released. Moisture pearled on her skin. Sliding along plump, feminine folds, it soon coated his tongue where he lapped. Licking his lips, he savored every drop of the sweet juice of her ecstasy. Finding the taut nub of nerves, he suckled on it and her body jerked. Every nerve was tuned to her, every need was seeking her, plummeting them both into a maelstrom of rapture. She came apart with a sparkled joy beneath the onslaught of his mouth.

With a lasting, moaning cry fading into the room, he stood. Destroying the last barriers of clothing, he lifted her in steady hands, finding his heaven within her arms, surrounded by her body. Thrusting deep, he took them both over the edge of sanity.

There was no other moment in time. Everything around them stopped. There was nothing outside of that room, nothing beyond those walls that mattered. And there was no other woman for him. He would forever crave the fiery woman in his arms. The passionate creature who stoked his own fires, his own passions, to a place he couldn't remember and dared with his very soul to embrace. Feeling her heated skin sliding against his sent shots of electricity into every nerve.

Clutching her firmly in strong palms, he sent them careening into that wild pleasure. Her uninhibited cries filled the silence of the room.

Shafts of moonlight sliced the darkness into a rainbow of glitter, glistening off of her creamy skin as though she were an angel from heaven. He was mesmerized by the beauty of her body, illuminated so lovingly in those white moonbeams.

That was when he accepted there was no option. Stubborn or not, hate him or not, he wasn't going to let her die. The conversion was her only chance, their only choice.

Like lighting a fuse from a bonfire, he felt his body winding tighter and tighter, striving for utter completion when he felt her explode all around him. Rearing back, he filled her one last time, arching as he plummeted to his own release.

HE COULDN'T stop touching her. It didn't matter that they'd enjoyed each other with cataclysmic results; he wanted her again. His body throbbed with it. He wondered if this same urgency would follow them after the conversion, waking next to each other, sharing the skies of glittering stars like a private midnight showcase. What if it increased? Was that even possible? The very idea made his heart thunder against his ribs. Because he wanted her like his last wish on earth as it was.

The memory of her body lying so sweetly next to his when he'd awakened told him it was very possible. He'd awakened to find his body already craving, his lips already wanting to take every whimpered moan from hers.

Wandering fingertips stroked her side, her body rising and falling in languorous relaxation. He could still taste the heady honey of her pleasure on his lips. Her body was ripe with pleasure, and he ached to pick the fruit.

"Why are you looking at me like you want to eat me, big bad wolf?" she teased him in a throaty purr. Tulip pink lips curved upward and her eyes glittered with humor when they found his.

"Because I do." He drew near to nip her shoulder to prove his point.

Laughter, rich and playful, was made sexier by the smile on her lips. "You need to work on your poker face. The idea is not to be so obvious."

Joaquin arched a brow. "Really? But why would I want to do that when it is the truth?"

Her laughter deepened, then she stretched her arms overhead and relaxed, leaving him a splayed playground to explore and enjoy. The sound of laughter slowly died and her eyes became watchful, studying his movements. He couldn't seem to stop touching her. He didn't want to.

"You really don't see them, do you?" she asked a little wondrously.

"See them?"

She gave him an irritated look. "Don't be obtuse. I know you aren't like that." She propped herself on her elbows. "The scars." Loathing etched her face when she looked down the length of her body. "I'm a walking roadmap."

He lowered and kissed her stomach. "Ask me if I care about the color of your hair, or these adorable freckles you have." He lapped over a few that were strung like a comet's tail beneath one breast, causing her body to squirm. "One is natural, one is not. I understand that. Others may not see what I see. The beauty of you. I don't care about what they can't see."

Golden lashes lowered to hide the reaction he felt nonetheless. Then he leaned forward, touching her lips with his. "Lily, you are perfect." Tenderness welled up, nearly clogging his throat as he sipped at their luscious softness. She was fragile while she was strong. She was beautiful even though her body had been abused. She was wild, yet could be so gentle. She was a woman of contradictions. "I love you," he said against her mouth, sharing the enormity of what it meant through his touch, his thoughts, his heart. Wave after wave of emotion rolled over him, sweet warmth drawing him tighter, closer to the angel beneath his lips.

Maybe through all those dark years of loneliness he'd paid his penance and this was his reward—a soul to love again. All he knew was he had been blessed. Death no longer beckoned to him. Life unlike any he'd known lay before him. He was going to grasp it with both hands and hold on tight.

Letting his hands roam at will, they found the valleys and peaks of her body, caressing her until she relaxed and bowed wantonly for his touch. He envisioned the joy of loving her every night. So sweet, so tempting in the moonlight. In the wild grasses. On the sandy beaches beneath a full moon. He groaned seeing it, and wanted it all.

The sharp drag of gentle nails scored his chest, roaming to his shoulders and his arms, drawing his hungers higher. A drawn hiss of air slipped out, his jaw tight as sparks rose in the wake of her touch. Everything about him tightened with wanting. Leaving her kisses behind, he slid lower, making a measured path to the curve of her chin, licking and kissing with engrossed attention, filling the craving of her tantalizing taste on his tongue.

He noted the texture of her skin, feeling the way she heated beneath his touch, instead of the roughness of it. She trembled with awakening desires, her body writhing in undulating waves of desire. There was no way to pretend the marks crisscrossing her body weren't there, but they didn't change his view of her either. While some were obvious, most were fine and faint. Her breasts were still full and round, with a trim body and gently sloping hips that fed into sexy legs and delicate feet. Where she saw ugly, he could only find beauty.

Gliding along her body, he worshipped her the only way he knew how. A little at a time until the only thought between either was the wonderful rise and fall of their desire. The darkness of night cocooned them, two bodies, two hearts. There was enough light from the stars outside her open window to see every flicker of pleasure that flitted over her face. He could hear her low moans and the sharp gasps, and he strived to create more for her.

Everywhere he touched, she shivered. Everywhere he tasted, he found sweet heaven.

He rolled her onto her stomach, and she moved with hardly a resistant whimper. Then, he licked the length of her spine. All her latest cuts had healed, and not one would scar. The patterning of abuse on her back was denser than on her front, and it was hard to let go of the rage that crushed him when he looked at what she'd suffered. He closed his eyes to not let the wash of anger distract his intent. Soon, the men who had hurt her would pay, whether she said otherwise or not.

With gentle pressure, he lifted her where he kneeled, finding her heat. Her gasps were stronger, growing needier, hungrier by the second. There was absolutely no hesitation, and there never would be again. She was completely his. Caressing her, he took her, filling her body as deep as he could go.

His shoulders bunched as heat and tightness enveloped his length. The blankets bunched into her hands as she rocked with him, following his pace, his strokes taking them both higher than ever before. Shudders rolled down her body when he raked her with arousing nails and she groaned and mewled, as absorbed as ever.

"Joaquin," she whimpered, a heated plea. She rocked into him and he felt his control slipping.

"Are you sure?"

"God, yes!" She twisted hard, wiggling against him, pulsing all around him.

With a handful of her hair in his palm, he pulled her taut against his pelvis, grinding against her body. She cried out in passion, delirious with sensations.

"No more gentle," she begged, pushing harder, needing. Hard gasps were the only sound in the room.

He didn't argue. He didn't wait. With a commanding strength, he took her over the edge. Her entire body twitched, aching. Needing. Over and over he thrust into her until he felt the tremors of her release building. They grew, and together as one, they shook. Her hands were clenched to the bed, his hands pinning her to him as though he feared she would disappear. He spiraled higher with each enraptured thrust, being carried on the ecstasy of sensation traveling like a livewire between their two bodies.

He jerked when she cried out. Her entire length locked on his shaft, pulsing around him like a velvet glove as she flew over the crest of the mountain. With a low roar of sheer bliss, he followed right after.

chapter nineteen

THE NEXT NIGHT, she read to Tabitha like she did every night. She hadn't spoken again to Lily, and if she was awake, she wasn't letting anyone know it. With a sigh, Lily left her friend, more worried than ever, but unable to do more for her. At least she knew she had friends nearby and help if she needed it. There had to be something for Tabitha to live for. She hoped they found it soon. She was refusing to eat anything substantial, refusing even broths, and Houston made killer soup.

She licked her lips. That *almost* sounded edible. She decided she'd snoop in the kitchen and see what was available.

"Where is everyone?" she asked Tani when she reached the kitchen. She wrinkled her nose at the leftover scents of chicken parmigiana, wanting to backpedal out of the room like something had died in there. No luck for soup. Or anything else if her stomach's opinion was to be counted for anything.

"Nathan came back tonight." Tani walked out, leading them both into the living room, which gave Lily a respite from the strong aromas. "He couldn't find David, Hawthorne, or Tenorio. They're doing reconnaissance around the house."

Lily shook her head. "Sounds like some bad military movie."

Tani nodded. "I'd have to agree with you." She sat down and offered a spot to Lily, studying her with a worried frown. "How are you feeling?"

Lily blinked, then pushed her hair from her face, not prepared for her directness. Lily guessed it wasn't hard to figure out Tani knew what had happened, and was happening, to Lily. "More tired tonight. The smell of dinner wasn't agreeing with me. I should be starving, but if that was dinner, I'm screwed." She couldn't stop the slump of her shoulders. She *was* tired.

"This hasn't been easy on you. Stolen from one life to be thrust into an equally foreign one. Have you tried any juice? That helped me."

"I've managed some water, but that's it. I can't even stomach tea." She leaned back, holding out the waist of her jeans. "My jeans are getting loose! I'd complain, but it's almost a good thing in that regard."

"Stop it. You are not fat."

She inwardly groaned. "*Quit listening in! Hello! Private conversation going on here.*" Her miffed tone carried quite well between them. A wave of support and adoration bathed her, then she knew he'd left her alone. Unless he was being especially sneaky, or she wasn't expecting it, she always knew when he was in her thoughts now. Which was pretty often.

Tani put a hand on Lily's arm. She didn't jerk, hardly noticed it as out of the norm. Was she becoming more balanced? Able to withstand touches from a friend without wincing? She hoped so. Right now, she needed a friend badly.

"Lily, you're running out of time. I know you are mad at Joaquin. I was furious with Diego. It's not an easy way to live. Not to be punny, but at times, it just sucks."

Lily giggled and Tani shrugged with a disparaging smirk. "There's a lot you will be giving up. No one will lie to you about that. But there's one thing you will have for a very long time." Tani paused, her hand squeezing with warmth and understanding on her forearm where she still held on, offering strength and support. "Joaquin's absolute love. He's not going anywhere without you, and you aren't ready to leave us. We don't want either of you to leave either. Except maybe for the honeymoon."

"Honeymoon?" Lily squeaked. This time, she plopped to the back of the couch, boneless.

"Well, adjustment period sounds so...cold."

Lily felt herself blanch. Searching the ceiling, she asked, "Was it hard?" She hoped she was ready to hear the truth.

Tani curled up for a little girl talk, facing Lily, her feet beneath her. "At first, yes. I haven't even had a year to come to grips with this. But, Lily, the only other option you have is to let your body die."

"What about what I'm doing here? Kathy and Amy? How do you keep them from learning the truth?"

"It's the only lie we've told, and before Joaquin burst in on you, you were part of it. No one not directly affected knows the truth. We..." She lifted a hand and ran her fingers stiffly against her temple, then let it drop, acting a bit too cheerful to hide the guilty look in her blue eyes. "We blur the truth. Amy, Kathy, and now Claire, believe without a doubt our room is at the top of the stairs. They see us go in and out of it all the time, but in truth..." She drew a breath, a seemingly more natural affectation for her than for Joaquin, she noted. "We hardly, if ever, step foot in that room."

"You don't eat anything either, do you?" She'd watched them and eaten food at the table with them plenty of times, hadn't she?

Tani shook her head. "Diego can stomach it better than I can if he has to. Age, for him, makes a difference."

"So all of it was, like, a mirage? Something we only think we're seeing?"

"Yes. We're very careful around all of you just the same."

Lily fell silent, her thoughts running like sparrows, skittering from one side of her mind to the other, an endless barrage of questions and worries. "And how do you..." She couldn't even make herself say it.

Tani was again considerately supportive. "Honestly, Diego had to help me in the beginning. I think it's really a natural aversion. None of us just *fell* into the *I vant to suck vour blood* lifestyle." Lily laughed behind her hand at Tani's exaggerated Boris Karloff attempt with the raised hands and haunting expression to go with it. "He couldn't do it, Nathan couldn't. I couldn't. I don't know Joaquin well enough to ask, but he seems pretty even keeled. He probably didn't wake up just knowing anymore than the rest of us." Her expression fell serious. "Diego thinks that's one of the keys to the difference between them and the Brethren as a whole. You either wake up starving and go bonkers for it, or you don't, and stay sane."

Lily snickered. "Kind of simplistic, don't you think?"

"Yeah, but I've always wondered why there were differences. At least for as long as I've known Diego." Her eyes shuttered for a moment as if thinking, then cleared. She continued. "You probably don't know this, but I met Diego's 'maker'. He attacked me."

"No!"

Tani's expression went to abashed pretty quickly. "Well, it was after I attacked him first, but it's where I first noticed the differences. Brakka was repugnant, absolutely vile to touch, to talk to."

"So there are differences," Lily said, her mind grabbing onto the discussion problem in front of her, also remembering her not too distant introduction to Kurt, not quite ready to tackle her situation en masse.

"Diego and I discussed trying to find out what they could be, but then David turned up missing, and we found all of you." She waved her hand to include Lily.

"I want to help. I can do this. It's actually one of the things I was studying in college. Micro and macro dynamics fascinate me."

"Like goldfish in a bowl?"

Lily laughed, completely relaxed again. "In a basic way of explanation, yes."

Tani's blue eyes brightened. "That is cool! It would help us immensely, especially, if for some reason, more like Joaquin trip over us and decide to stick around. Can I help?"

"Of course! It was your idea first." Lily crossed her arms, leaning again to stare at the raised ceiling. "But that means I have to go through with it. Or die." An inelegant sound escaped her throat. "Not much of a choice." She let out a suffering sigh. "No more hotdogs, or sunrises. No more ice cream." She sat up with a snap. "Oh no! No more chocolate." She couldn't help the pout, smacking the couch with an annoyed movement. "Man, I loved that best about the holidays, more chocolate and desserts than you could shake a stick at."

"If it helps, you won't actually crave any of it," she offered with another warm hand squeeze. "They smell like anything else, cut grass, a sun-baked beach, chocolate torte." She rolled a shoulder for emphasis.

"Don't ever equate chocolate torte to a beach," she shot back, aghast, albeit not entirely meaning it. Sinking into more worry, she drew on her bottom lip, pinning it between her teeth for a moment. "How long do I have?"

Any frivolity was dropped like a lead weight out of the air.

"It takes three exchanges. The next will give you a boost, but will also begin the physical changes. Your timeline is shortened. You'll begin to feel the differences sooner. They're more noticeable, too."

Lily rubbed a hand down her face, chilled and unsure, but not seeing any way out of making the necessary, if not the only, choice. "*Joaquin?*"

"Yes, lovely."

"You're one hundred percent positive you want to be stuck with me?"

"I'd be the luckiest man I know if I could have you."

"For eternity? You're a glutton for punishment."

Rich laughter flowed over her. "*Eternity would be a nice place to start.*"

She rolled her head to Tani, aware she was more fatigued than she'd thought. It was frightening in a lot of ways to know she was, quite literally, dying. "Thanks, Tani. I'm glad I got to talk about it at least a little."

Tani rose up on her knees and opened her arms. Lily fell into them willingly, wrapping her own arms around the petite, raven-haired woman. "I'm glad to have you as a sister. It sucks being the only girl vamp in all of the Brethren."

Lily leaned slack, utterly shocked. "Really? The only one?"

She nodded. "None of them even knew we could be. Men seem to be the principal offspring."

"Wow. Does that make you, like, a queen or something?"

Tani blinked. "Good God, I hope not!" Then, they both burst out laughing.

LILY stumbled out of bed the next night, holding a hand to her head as the room spun. Closing her eyes, she collapsed on the edge until everything cleared up for her. It took her a while to find the energy to get dressed and cleaned up to make herself presentable. A light smile of pleasure rose when she reached for one of her sweatshirts and found none in her closet. All had been replaced with feminine blouses and silken creations—every last one with long sleeves. For her. She didn't doubt who had done it. The effort wasn't lost on her either.

Her head snapped around when a loud racket snaked its way up to the rooms from the first floor. Dressed enough to face people, she opened her door, able to hear more. Turning to search out the window she saw the sky was streaking purple and orange. Sunset was coming. It helped her ignore the chill slicing over her calm at the sound from downstairs.

David was home.

"Where is she?" He was screaming frantically. "Where's Tani?" Lily heard him clearly as she approached the top of the steps to join them.

"Calm down, David. She's asleep." Houston had a hand on his shoulder, trying to snap him out of his wild state. David was jerking to throw his hand off, but wasn't able to, too weak to be effective against Houston's stronger hold. Sweat and grime coated David's face. His eyes were swollen with large blue bruises discoloring most of his face. Lily wouldn't have been the least surprised if there was internal and deep bone damage. Shakes rolled down his body with every breath.

"Come sit down, David." Laney motioned him to a chair and Houston all but pushed him into it whether he wanted to sit or not. He whimpered on a gasped breath, fighting to not slump.

"How did you get home?" Houston asked.

Laney shared a worried and concerned look with Houston and Lily. He was there alone. He'd walked right in the front door, as if he'd never been missing. It gave Lily another shiver of unease.

Amy approached with a large bowl and a washcloth to tend to David's face. Dried blood was caked into his hair and anywhere there had been free space.

"He made me walk in." He was shaking and, beneath all the blood and bruising, every visible inch was pale. Gasps rocked his body, and each deep one made his frame roll with shudders of pain. "He couldn't—couldn't come any closer. He tried all day. Shoved me out."

Amy cautiously dabbed at his face, but he winced with every touch regardless. "I'm sorry," she murmured, blatantly apologetic for causing him any discomfort.

David shook his head. "Doesn't matter. I'm already dead." Wild eyes looked up and searched everyone. "Tani. I have to find Tani. She has to get out of here."

"She's fine, David," Houston repeated calmly, facing David. "Why Tani?"

"Because he's coming. For all of them," he croaked, his eyes growing wider. Then, David lifted his T-shirt.

Lily covered her mouth to not scream. Amy dropped the bowl of water she held and toppled backward in horror, her face draining of blood as the gnarled mess that was David's midsection became exposed. Sutured and taped to a shallow hole in his abdomen was a small device the size of a lemon. It was ticking off time.

"You have to lower the gates, whatever...they are. He—He's going to blow me up." Tears were forming in his eyes. He tried to breathe, but shuddered again. "Hurts," he hissed, his focus wavering, then he sat up straight again. Reaching, he fisted Houston's shirt in desperation. "Where is she?" He bit out the words through a pain-clenched jaw.

"We have to remove it." Houston's face was pale, fighting to think coherently.

David shook his head. "You can't. It's wired...part of my body. Removing...blows up."

"Fuck!"

David's laugh wasn't unkind. "Yeah." Then, his lids closed and he blacked out, falling into Houston's arms.

"How long before they get here?" Lily asked Houston. He lifted David with no trouble and laid him on the kitchen table. His wan face was streaked with dirt, sweat and blood. She doubted the rest was anything nearing peaceful.

Laney dashed to the window, then said over her shoulder, "Less than fifteen minutes. How long..." She stopped and swallowed, sending David a teary-eyed look. "On that?"

Houston carefully lifted the T-shirt. "Less than thirty minutes. If he walked from as far out as I think he did..." Houston raked a hand through his hair. "He walked for well over an hour, bleeding and in agony with every step. The bastard didn't give him much time to get here." Houston put a kinder hand on David's shoulder, watching the shuddering rise and fall of his chest. The immense pain he suffered for his friend sliced into every part of his face and body.

"You have to remove the ward." Lily knew none of this was David's fault, but he didn't deserve to die either. She clenched her hands at her sides to not allow the queasiness she felt to become real.

Houston's expression said it all. "I can't. Diego is the only one with absolute control over them."

Amy's head was ricocheting between the two of them, horror widening her eyes. "What wards?"

"Diego has strong magic," Lily explained.

"Well, go wake him up!" She was almost screeching.

"He's not here, Amy," Houston bit out, his head bowed to think.

Kathy came barreling down the stairs, skidding to a stop in the kitchen. "Oh my God! What happened to him?"

Houston blocked David's body with a stilted movement. "He's been badly hurt. He just got home."

Towel dried hair explained with little doubt that she had been in the shower and had missed David's entrance into the house.

"What can we do for him?" Amy neared, silent tears leaving tracks down her face. "When will Diego be home to remove the wards?"

"In a few more minutes." Laney put a supporting touch on Houston's arm, the same one that was resting on David's shoulder. Houston inched the shirt down to cover the ticking death sentence. Lily saw it as well as he did.

They weren't going to have enough time.

Numerous sets of eyes rose to search, looking for answers, a miracle. All they saw was each other.

Lily's hands fisted again. Anger fueled her words, but she kept her calm in a way she couldn't remember ever finding within herself, the whole seething, boiling mass giving her strength even when she knew she was losing energy with every minute. She did the only thing she could.

"Amy, Kathy, get Claire and go to Tabitha's room and keep everyone calm. You know what Tab can do if she gets agitated. She's awake now and not secure yet. Keep her calm," she stressed again. "Lock the door. Stay inside. You too, Laney. The more with her, the safer she'll feel."

"But—"

"Just do it!" She turned to Houston, not waiting to see if they would do it or not. "I'm not letting this happen again. He's not going to die."

When Kathy turned, Lily followed Kathy and Amy with her eyes until they were out of sight. She prayed they went to Tabitha's room. Laney picked up the bowl and washcloth, then followed the two girls upstairs with a final worried glance at David. Resignation was as apparent on her pained features. Houston stayed beside a comatose David.

"We only have to wait for them to get here," Lily said, feeling exhaustion creep up on her like a stalking tiger. Ready to pounce the moment her head was turned.

"David doesn't have the time." Houston ran a shaky hand over his jaw. "If this thing is real..." His voice caught. "Damn! Why did they have to do this?"

"Don't give up yet," Lily said, knowing she had no other option. With no warning to Houston, she opened herself up, doing the only thing she could think of to find out what they needed to know, diving into David's psyche to find out what they had done to trigger the time bomb. To find any information about Hawthorne, or Tenorio, any plans. She collapsed to her knees with a low cry, her eyes blurring as all the suffering and pain he'd lived through slammed into her like a relentless tide. Horrors not unlike the life she'd been forced to endure had been dealt to David to make him cooperate. He'd fought them, but had paid for it. The bomb was their answer to controlling him. Their answer to get what they wanted.

The girls who had been rescued. All of them. Whether they knew they had Claire or not, or were assuming it, the intent was crystal clear.

"Lily!"

She barely heard Joaquin's anxious shout, oblivious to how long she searched, walking through David's mind, his thoughts, his memories, seeking the threats floating through his subconscious. She couldn't acknowledge Joaquin regardless. Her strength was leaving her fast for trying to find the secret to David's only chance to live.

Strong arms encircled her at some point. Strength poured into her body. Slowly, her lashes fluttered, but there was little she could see. She could only stare through unseeing eyes that refused to focus properly. Joaquin was kneeling behind her, holding her tightly in his arms. She would know him, his touch, anywhere. She felt almost weightless in his arms.

"It's triggered to his heart. You disconnect it and the loss of the current of his heartbeat will detonate it." The words tumbled from her lips, feeling herself almost as a separate, disembodied being in the room.

She thought she explained it. Didn't just think it. Her brow wrinkled. *Tired. So very tired.* Her lashes felt so heavy. She wanted to rest. Hopefully, it was enough information for them to find a way to do something about it. She hoped she told them. Concept of time was lost to her as her gray world went black, completely drained.

chapter twenty

"TANI?"

Joaquin held Lily's limp shape in his arms, terrified for the brave woman. Exhaustion was a thick cloud surrounding her body.

"I'm here, David." Tani stepped forward and he tried to sit up on the hard table, struggling to breathe, searching desperately for her.

Houston was quick to put out a hand to halt him. "Don't, David," he insisted, deliberately calm.

"We have to go. He's coming." His voice cracked. "Don't let him get you." Harsh gasps for air tore through his lungs, sounding like bellows on each exhalation. "I won't let him get you."

Joaquin stood, stepping away a few feet, cradling Lily tenderly in his arms like a child. He needed to care for Lily, but the threat outside was imminent.

"We're safest right here, David," Tani said, trying to keep him calm, to stop him from jerking himself off the table and around Houston.

"There's no time!" He shoved everyone back and lifted his shirt. "What does it say?" Tears streaked down his face. Sunken eyes. Hollow eyes. Defeated.

A shouted order ricocheted from outside. The danger outside was getting closer. Somehow, they had breached the wards.

David laughed, bordering on insane, pushed past his endurance. "Too late. God, Tani. Why? Why did you have to be gone? With him. He's going to get you. I could've saved you." His voice wavered. "Could have lo…" He stopped as though he realized what he was saying.

Joaquin saw the pain in the young man's eyes when he pinned that hurt on Titania. Pain that went deeper than the pain of his body. All the love he'd never shown Tani was exposed in that one moment. Sorrow colored her face when she looked up over her shoulder to Diego.

David fought to lurch to his feet, shoving past a stunned Houston. "No!" he snarled. Weaving, he marched to the front door, whipping it open, then leaning on it. Taking one staggering, pain-filled breath, he looked at the tableau of people who had followed him.

"Put me down."

"I don't think I will."

"He's going to do something stupid!" Lily clenched at Joaquin's shirt.

"And you think I'm going to let you do something equally stupid? Again?" He trembled with the rush of emotion at having awakened, yet

again, to feel her in pain. It hadn't mattered it hadn't been her own pain he felt ravaging his body. If he was feeling it, then she was feeling it on some higher level, too deeply.

"They won't get you, Tani." Shakily, he ran a hand over his face, oblivious to anymore pain or the streaks he left behind. "They're coming. He won't stop." Another shout and a fired shot. Closer. They weren't exactly going for the covert sneak attack from the sounds of their entrance.

Joaquin held Lily tighter into his chest. Bright beams sliced the night beyond the front door, breaking apart the thick night with their search lights.

"How'd they get through?" Houston stood, glaring daggers toward the roar of vehicles.

"Drugs," Lily managed, barely loud enough for Joaquin to hear. The truth had been found in the bowels of David's nightmare. "They're counteracting the fears instilled in the wards. Forcing their own sense of preservation to ignore the sensation of the threat embedded in the ward. Hawthorne knows where Tenorio is."

"Stop it! Close your mind right now!"

"But it's what I do. What I can do." She burrowed tighter into his body.

"You're not strong enough. You can't even hold your eyes open."

She didn't argue that one with him.

"How long do I have?" David demanded, ripping the T-shirt away from his body with a rending sound.

Tani approached him, the weight of the pending moments so heavy on her shoulders, she was bent under the pressure. Diego let her go, but still followed to stand only a foot or two away. "I'm sorry, David. I never knew." Her lips trembled, regret and sadness battling on her face for the man before her. For feelings she'd never had a clue about. For a friendship that was at an end.

Joaquin saw her steal a glance over the blinking numbers on the front panel. One second at a time to reach zero. He couldn't miss the desperation in David's eyes. He knew what the young man planned to do, and he didn't need Lily's gift to make that conclusion.

For a moment, David's gaze cleared and he lifted a hand to her face. "I know. Don't let them get you. They'll destroy you," he said, emotions making his voice thick, along with all the ravaging pain and regret he felt. "How long?"

Her voice broke. She blinked, fighting a losing battle to stem the tears. "Minutes."

The first vehicle skidded to a stop, spraying dirt and forest debris for several feet, followed by two more. They were all easy to see through the front door. They had made it through and their intent was clear as men spilled out of the vehicles and gathered, all carrying weapons meant to kill, not capture. "Tell me when I have less than thirty seconds."

"You don't have to do this! There has to be a way to save you!"

A short laugh broke the brittle tension with unconcern. Joaquin could see his mind was made up. Shouts began to drift into the house from outside. "Just get away. Go far away." Resolute, his voice never wavered. Joaquin let Lily slide to her feet, watching her carefully for more signs of her physical self withering. She was tired, but was holding on as long as she could before succumbing to the fatigue her latest effort had placed on her.

David drew an aching breath. "Time?"

"Twenty-eight seconds."

He nodded with grim determination, and acceptance. "I always loved you." Then, he turned, closed the door and stumbled out to meet the caravan of vehicles.

"Stop him!" Tani's heart-wrenching cry echoed through the house, whirling to find someone to help. No one moved.

Diego shook his head. "I am not fast enough to do what needs to be done, even with all the knowledge, which I do not have. He is a brave man to do the only thing he can. They gave him no option." He cut a meaningful look to Joaquin. "Let us rid ourselves of these animals once and for all."

"Where is Nathan?" Joaquin looked to Houston, almost forgetting he was in the room when Diego answered.

"He went to feed. He is returning now to join us."

"Bastards!" Anger flared as deeply as the sadness in Titania's gaze.

Silver eyes found her, staring at the raven-haired woman raging inside at the injustice dealt to her friend, sharing the weight of a friend's loss. "Do you want his sacrifice to be wasted? Do you want his affection to go unavenged?"

"No." She swept her hand beneath her eyes. A sudden roaring explosion rocked the front of the house, rattling dishes in the kitchen. Tani stuffed her knuckles into her mouth to stifle her scream, reaching out for the door in reflex. Diamond bright tears fell in streams while hard, racking sobs shook her shoulders and body like a dry stalk in a fierce wind. Lily pressed her face into Joaquin's chest, muffling her own hard sobs from the rest.

Diego approached his wife, tenderly lifting a thumb to stroke the tears away. He drew Titania into his arms, engulfing her within his large frame. "I am sorry, *cara*. Do not doubt that." He turned to Houston. His entire demeanor had frozen to stone. "Take the women upstairs. We will dispatch the remaining attackers and remove the vehicles. Do not worry if you do not see us before dawn."

"Go with him," Joaquin urged the woman in his arms. "Rest." He needed time, even a few minutes, to do the next exchange to boost Lily's waning strength. A little privacy would also be nice. She didn't have any reserves to keep her going; she had no choice but to stay still. She nodded into his chest where he held her. He wound his hand through her hair, offering his understanding. He'd seen death many times over his life, but few had been anyone he could call friend.

Diego faded out of sight, leaving Tani standing by the door only a moment later, moving outside to begin the decimation of the last of the forces trying to reach those inside. Joaquin pressed a kiss to Lily's lips, then releasing her, he also faded out of the room.

"HAWTHORNE is out there." She knew it with certainty.

Houston shook his head, worry rising rapidly. "You are pale, Lily. Don't do it."

She walked to the door and leaned against the frame, not looking at the door, but through it. She laid a hand of comfort on Tani's shoulder. The other woman was too stunned to acknowledge it. "We can't let him die in vain," she whispered.

Looking at the woman before her Lily knew Tani was a devastated wreck. Her face was blank. Lily doubted she had a coherent thought to make under the circumstances. She wouldn't blame her if she didn't. David had been a part of Tani's band for years, a friend for as long. And now he was gone.

"Take Tani upstairs, Houston," she said. "She needs your help more than I do right now. I'll follow in a minute when I get my strength back." She was still feeling woozy from what she'd done to reach David, but she'd do it again in a nanosecond.

Houston didn't have to know she had no intention whatsoever of following him up those upstairs.

"Don't go outside," he warned suspiciously, but already moving to Tani's side. The other woman was reacting like an automaton, on autopilot, nodding to whatever Houston said. "I'll be right back for you."

"Sure," Lily replied with a wan smile, leaning on her shoulder to hold some of her weight. She lingered until he was well up the stairs with a thunderstruck Tani before slipping through the door to the dark world outside. All the lights had been extinguished, leaving the world in a shadowy, raucous pocket of time. Gunfire and screams rolled over her from her right, bodies and shapes outlined in the dark night. She stayed flush to the house, moving quickly within the wavering shadows. Dark, tumbling clouds obscured much of the starlight and the waning moon. Lightning flashed with angry bursts and crashing thunder made the ground shake beneath her feet. Crouching on the porch in the corner behind a post, she flexed her fingers and pressed them to the wood beneath her to steady her fatigue-wracked body and reached outward, seeking Hawthorne's mind. Pain splintered her control with a bombardment of needle sharp daggers, each voice erupting over her as though she sat in the center of an enclosed box and thousands of voices were screaming within. She pushed herself through it, her weight sagging against the wood of the porch in the deepest shadows of the house.

It took several seconds to lock onto the man she knew had to be there, vile and repulsive with evil motivations stirring his desires. She didn't care if the man felt any presence of her intrusion. She knew it wouldn't hurt him, but some could sense the invasion by a build-up of pressure, if they knew what to equate that pressure to.

He didn't.

Without a shred of remorse, she began to, bit by bit, pick the man's brain apart.

JOAQUIN met the first attack with a roar of rage, sending the men before him in a careening arc into the night. Blue light lit the sky as Diego hurled an energy bolt right into one of the vehicles. Screams soaked the air a beat before the large, lumbering machine ground to a halt and exploded.

"They are showing no fear." Diego's frustration was only a momentary observation as he turned to land behind another soldier. Death was swift as the man slumped to the ground in a heap.

"It has to be the drugs they took to surpass the deterrent of the ward."

Joaquin felt Diego's agreement as he cleared a swath of yet more uniformed soldiers. *"We need to know what they used. The ward will have to be modified."*

Joaquin agreed. He knew the intricacies of the wards and realized any modification would have to be applied immediately to prevent this from happening again.

Thick clouds surged in towering piles in the sky, lightning and thunder coming to his call to blanket the world in a black abyss. The three were at no disadvantage at all without light. It only added to the humans' confusion. Nathan was across the clearing in front of the house, releasing months of anguish and energy on their attackers with single-minded attention. Joaquin dove into the fight with an equal zest and determination to avenge Lily's pain, striving to obliterate any man who dared to be one of the unlucky to intrude tonight.

There were more vehicles and soldiers than any of them had anticipated. Once a way to be able to get inside the barrier had been found, Hawthorne must have been prepared with more reinforcements. Joaquin's gaze spotted a single vehicle separated in the trees and knew David had done as much as he could to stop their progress. Three were dead. One was critically injured. Silently, he wished the brave man who had lost so much a fast journey to peace.

Speed was of the essence as they blocked and removed the encroaching line of men, fighting them with swift retribution. Gunfire and bullet flashes streaked through the night. Their weapons meant little to Joaquin. Diego was creating a definite line of death, each blast purposeful, every attack sure against those that cared nothing for the people inside, only their orders.

Spotting a trio crouched low, skulking through the trees and heading for the house, Joaquin lifted his hands. Lightning arced and snapped overhead with deadly intent. The flash was blinding as it crashed into the earth, shaking the ground with its power, leaving hissing, sizzled sounds in the air and burnt scorches behind. All three men lay twitching on the ground as the sheer power of natural electricity stole their last moments.

A nearly indiscernible wave touched his mind. He closed his mind, knowing Lily did not need to see or know the details about the bloody battle being waged. Sending her sweet comfort and love, he continued. Decimation littered the ground as bodies fell one by one, or as the remaining vehicles stalled or exploded before Diego. Joaquin commanded the night sky as he methodically counterattacked the invasion, one strike at a time. Gradually, the proof of their determination showed in the lessening ranks facing the three.

Nathan's face was snarled in a ruthless mask when Joaquin looked his way again. Another body fell like a boneless rag, horror his victim's last expression, and not just the horror of the death surrounding him. Something was off with the younger man's actions as he dove for another soldier with a flying leap. Nathan's demeanor had changed completely from methodical to something much darker, much crueler.

Joaquin immediately relayed his concern to Diego, who leaped up from the ground in a rush, seeking his young friend.

"Stop him!" Diego sent a final killing shot into a group, the explosion tossing the four men like sticks into the air.

Joaquin didn't hesitate, making the connection himself to realize what was happening. Lunging for the young blond, he literally tore him away just before his teeth sank into the jugular of one of the soldiers. Joaquin locked his arms around his bucking, snarling body. Diego landed before them and efficiently ended the soldier's life.

"Nathan!" Diego didn't raise his voice, but in the next instant, it was as if a roar had silenced the clearing. Blue eyes challenged Diego, talon length nails ripping and raking at Joaquin to be freed. No one and nothing moved. Again, Joaquin felt Lily's light worry. He did the only thing he could, offering his reassurance, hiding their latest battle from her.

"Nathan, resist." Diego stood before the younger vampire, his gaze unblinking, locked on angry blue eyes. Irises that were too large glared at him with a risen rage. Fangs glinting stark white showing he'd attacked more than one. Blood still stained his lips.

With no show of emotion, Diego lifted his hands and wrapped them around Nathan's head.

The young man fought harder, yanking like a wild creature against Joaquin's implacable strength where he remained locked around his frame.

"Nathan, you are not this creature. Resist." Deep, understanding, calm. The tone of his voice was a balm. Gazes locked, battled, but Diego would not let him go without a fight. Joaquin waited for the moment that would define the rest of their lives. He knew there was no return from the insanity of bloodlust. It was the deciding line between their humanity, and the loss of the Brethren's.

"Resist, my friend. You are not lost." Diego didn't move, didn't release him, simply held him still, his eyes trained on him as if boring into his soul. Silence stretched as the three stood, one fighting himself and everything around him, one bringing him back from the brink, and Joaquin refusing to let the beast have the freedom to tear through Nathan as he knew it could.

With hard twitched jerks, Nathan calmed as if drained, his body growing pliant in Joaquin's clutched hold. His clawed hands fell, leaving behind welts and thin scratches on Joaquin's arms.

"You must learn to control the lust in you, Nathan," Diego cautioned, but without reproach. "Killing is not your life. Blood will not give you what you have lost." Wise words. Joaquin silently agreed.

A shudder shook the thinner frame in his hold and his head lolled forward. Diego released his hold on Nathan and stepped back. "Go to ground tonight and regain yourself. It is not a punishment. You were not made to kill. Do not let this"—he waved a hand behind him absently to the mangle of bodies—"drive you to kill for the wrong reasons. Never to feed,

Nathan, never for the blood. Never give in to the bloodlust when you are killing. The two can never meet. It will destroy you."

"I know," he choked out, shame radiating off of him. "Just so angry. So much, gone." He lifted his head and inched forward out of Joaquin's hold, turning to face them. His eyes had returned to normal and, except for the distraught strain on his face, he looked like he always did. "I'm sorry." The bleakness Joaquin had thought Nathan hid with his arrogance was no longer below the surface. His loss lay across his features like newsprint.

Joaquin didn't know Nathan's history or the loss he'd suffered when his life had been stolen from him, but he knew the life they now all shared was far from easy. That was one fact he knew irrevocably. Nathan was young in many ways, and the strength to combat the lure of bloodlust wasn't always easy to find. There wasn't a night since his conversion that he hadn't waged some level of the battle with himself.

"Thank you for..." Bitter self-disgust drew Nathan's gaze away, unable to look at the patient understanding standing before him.

Diego curved a hand over his shoulder. "I would save any brother, any friend."

Swallowing, Nathan blinked, then met their gazes. "I will rise when I'm ready. If you need me, call out to me. I will hear you."

"I know. You are, and will always be, our friend."

Nathan formed a hand over Diego's forearm, then laid a hand on Joaquin's shoulder. "My brothers." With a grim, final nod at each, he shifted, lifting slowly skyward with large, gray wings.

"Will he be all right?"

Both watched the owl disappear over the treetops. Concern lowered Diego's voice between the men. "As much as he can be after coming so close to the edge. He has a long battle ahead of him. You know as well as any how difficult that lure can be to resist. He will return when he is ready. Nathan is young, but determined. He will need guidance. Sending him to ground was the only option for now." Diego turned and stared out into the mess of the woods, a sea of bodies and mangled metal that had been Hawthorne's force. "Let us clear this and return."

Joaquin understood Diego was anxious to return for Tani. In just the same way he needed to be with Lily. Reaching out unconsciously, he wanted to connect with her, needing to feel her warmth, her laughter.

And found a deathly quiet that rooted his feet to the ground.

"Lily!"

His body froze. There was only a lonely echo of his own mind as he reached out and found...nothing.

A chill swelled and crashed over his soul and thunder answered, booming overhead. *"Lily, answer me!"* he commanded.

Stretching his senses, he caught a faint whisper of her, only a breath. Cinnamon.

She was outside? He knew it as surely as he was standing on his own two feet. She was weak, even weaker than she had been before he'd been forced to leave her inside with the others to deal with Hawthorne's men. She was supposed to be with the others in the house. What was she doing outside? "*Talk to me, Lily.*" He was having a hard time finding her as he opened his mind completely and scanned. She had been on the porch. Her scent still lingered.

He was standing in the exact same spot she had been in less than a heartbeat. Drawing a breath, her scent enveloped his senses. Reaching out, he sought even a trace of her. Nothing but a void opened before him.

"Is Hawthorne among those dead?" Had he been part of the invasion after all? Had he managed to follow David through the wards? Joaquin shot into the air, anger and fear stretching him to his limits. What was she doing outside? What had she been thinking? He couldn't take another episode like the escape from Hawthorne's compound. The wounds on her fair skin had dug deep into him, as deep as they had sliced into her skin. It killed him a little at a time to see her being hurt, abused, wounded in such ways.

"No. I do not see any sign of him."

"Something has happened to Lily. She isn't answering me."

He leaped over the porch rail with a weightless grace, landing silently on the balls of his feet. He could hear Diego destroying the last signs of the troops, and would soon be taking care of the vehicles. By morning, not a sign of their attack would be apparent, or left to be found.

Tension knotted his body. There was an empty feeling in his soul without her touch there, without the sound of her voice. She was too weak for anymore abuse, and she still wasn't answering his searching. Shadows crept along the forest floor, filling the spaces between the trees, offering no answers.

Diego's reply wasn't anywhere close to what he needed to hear. "*She is not in the house with the others.*" Joaquin had already been aware, but the confirmation sent a shiver up his spine with the implication.

"Open yourself to her, completely. She is your soul, even as human as she still is."

Joaquin listened to the voice in his head. *"How? I can feel her if I'm close, but she's not responding. I can't hear her."*

He sensed Diego's correction, knowing he was too busy to come. "*This is deeper. You are half of a whole. Even apart you know where the other lies, what the other is feeling, thinking. It is the gift they are to us that makes us complete.*"

Joaquin closed his eyes and, instead of seeking outward, sought inward. Searching for the beat of Lily's heart, for her warmth, for the light of her soul. Frozen in time, he listened to what he couldn't hear outside with even his keen hearing.

Crickets chirped on the low breeze, branches bending and shaking against one another, creating a timeless music in the darkness. Then, unbelievably, he felt her, heard her.

His eyes snapped open. There was no hesitation as he leaped upward, soaring over the trees.

chapter twenty-one

LILY'S head ached. Her mouth felt dry. Blinking sent shards of agony into her brain. The whole process made her dizzy so she left her eyes closed. Slumping against the porch where she must've lost her balance and fallen, she drew a breath, then another. Screams were fewer, the mangled crash of metal louder. Thuds and crunches were echoed in the silence only by the thunder overhead. She knew the storm was Joaquin's doing. Dark clouds and lightning. She recognized when he was pissed. She heard a few try to retreat, calling to one another to be heard over the screams of the dying. Try was as much as they could do. There would be no escape, not tonight, for anyone.

Her limbs felt leaden, the dead weight of her exhaustion keeping her immobile for precious seconds. Drawing her waning strength inward, she forced herself to straighten, then gain her feet. Clutching the railing in bloodless grips, she hefted herself up to roll over the top one leg at a time, sliding down to the ground only a foot or two beneath where she hung. Exhaustion made the process excruciating. An aching mechanical movement. Shadows lay deeper on that side of the house. There were no soldiers. There was only Lily.

And one other.

The bastard had escaped David's planned suicide attack. She had seen every bloody second of David's death in Hawthorne's depraved mind. The only one in the Jeep to know how David suffered, he'd leaped clear right before...

She swallowed, and closed her eyes, saving her strength where she stood, propped up like a loose cotton-stuffed doll against the porch base. She would only have one chance to do this. She was weak with the coming change and exhaustion, and weaponless. Like a coward, the commander of the trained force dying for his mission stood in the shadows watching, waiting, calculating as he witnessed the vengeance wreaked on those before him by three men unlike any he could envision.

She saw them through his eyes. Merciless, cunning, bold and fearless. Killing machines. Each gift or skill Hawthorne discovered, he quickly catalogued in his brain. The very discovery she knew Tani and the others feared was standing in the thickest shadows watching every moment, enraptured with a new greed undetected by any of the men fighting to keep those inside safe.

Hawthorne would find a way to harness those abilities, the same as he had been doing to the girls.

He had been one of the guinea pigs for Tenerio's DNA mutation cloning. And he had enjoyed the power. She felt it on him now, like sheep's wool over the wolf. It wasn't his power, only a fake skin, and he needed constant infusions to maintain it. His overpowering, twisted hunger to find the girls became apparent with this discovery. With them no longer available, his stolen gifted powers were reversing, his own body destroying what he so hungrily wanted to be. If he was the kind of success Tenorio had envisioned, then the DNA experiments had been more successful than any of them had imagined. Resilience seemed to be the only failing with the current experiments, which made their success all too real, and too dangerous to ignore.

Lily found the truth in the corrupted pathways of his mind, discovered his pleasure at being chosen, the thrill he'd enjoyed with the stolen ability he'd been chosen for. It only made him crave it more now that he'd tasted the power ripped from the girls with any means available. Hawthorne, while powerful in his own mind, was only a cog. And the man didn't even know it.

She would be doing him a favor, provided she could do it. Killing the man was impossible. Lily would never be able to kill, but her fury, her bitterness at the world stolen from her because of this man and Tenorio, fueled her even when her body wanted to lie down and sleep for weeks. She had found another way to strike back. Not just by rescuing Claire, but by reading the man she detested with every bone in her body simply because he had been one of the abusers under Tenorio's control.

Lily sent Joaquin a wealth of her love, and prayed he would understand. His tender touch was a gentle stroke on her thoughts, warming her and letting her know she wasn't alone anymore. She pressed on, patiently stumbling as best as she could toward what would most likely be her last stand.

EMPTY space mocked Joaquin. Each stretch of his mind returned to him with nothing, no answer, no sense of her, but he knew she wasn't dead. He knew it with a certainty. He felt it in a way he found to be completely unexplainable and new. At first, he hadn't understood Diego's meaning, but now it lay like the broad horizon on his conscience. There was a presence only his soul recognized. A light, a touch.

It could only be Lily. She was not dead. A snarl curled from his chest when he broke through the canopy hiding her from his sight and saw why she could not answer. Two soldiers held her arms locked behind her. She was immobile and deeply buried under the weight of the man's sick mind standing in front of her.

"Lily!" A flicker of an answer responded, but it was weak. The unknown man facing her staggered, rearing unsteadily and clutching his head as she bored into his eyes with her own.

"Kill her!" the gasping man groaned, desperate to look away, trying to move, but it was too late. He would not escape. Joaquin's attack was quick, ending his life with a rage-induced spike of lightning perfectly aimed as he launched for one of the men where they held her trapped between them. He tore her free, twisting one neck, then reaching for the other before the first found the ground.

Lily collapsed into his arms. Harsh, ragged breaths rattled from her body when she was free. With a rippled shudder sweeping over her, her sweet eyes closed and didn't open again.

Lifting her into his arms, he braced her fragile body against his and soared upward again. Racing for the mountains, he dipped and turned, spiraling downward through a thermal vent, escaping the world behind. There wasn't time to waste, sharing his predicament with Diego as he fled into the mountains, his only concern being the woman in his arms.

Tucking her protectively against his body, he traversed the cracks until he found what he needed. A hidden cavern deep in the mountain. Slivers of starlight bounced off the crystals embedded in the walls, reaching the depths of the cavern with a flickering, faint hint of a silvery glow. A single spring fed pool lapped against the farthest wall. It wasn't as secure as he usually would have wanted, but there wasn't time to find that perfect place. It would have to do.

Her body was shutting down, exhausted beyond endurance. She was running out of time. He had to give her strength. Praying became a litany in his mind that he wasn't already too late as he found a shelf to rest against, to sit down on and cradle her within the steel of his embrace. Her sleek body was limp with fatigue. "Please Lily, don't give up," he whispered anxiously into her ear. "Don't give up on us."

Ripping the collar of her blouse from the pale creaminess of her neck, he bit, foregoing the tenderness that had always made their time such a loving delight. Drawing deeply, he felt the hard shudder of her body, the reaction of her senses awakening to his invasion even if she wasn't physically participating. With every dragging beat of her heart, he reached out for her, called to her, to bring her back to him. There was only silence. Terror was slicing through him even as he licked at her throat to seal the pinprick wounds.

Tearing his shirt away, he sliced his chest. "Take what you need, lovely. Don't leave me. Not now, not ever," he quietly pleaded with a wrenched sound in his throat. He raised her until her lips rested at the break in his skin where drops flowed between her lips.

With firm control, he coerced her to take a few sips at a time until she was willingly obeying the command to swallow. He gave until he couldn't spare any more, easing her to lay cradled in his arms. Warmth suffused her cheeks first, giving the pale cast of her skin a new glow. Her chest rose and fell with less strain, her breathing becoming less haggard as the moments passed.

He had no idea how long he had before the final exchange would need to be completed. It took time for the fear of losing her to subside enough for him to become perturbed with her for being outside. He sat for endless moments doing nothing but watching her, studying her, enjoying the beauty of the woman, of her heart and her strengths as he held her in his hands. All the time envisioning as she had once done to him—his hands around her neck in frustration.

"What were you doing? Haven't you suffered enough by these imbeciles?" He wasn't expecting an answer, not yet, but he would get one. "You have got to be the most headstrong, determined woman I have ever met." It was a muttered complaint, albeit, a mild one, too happy she was strengthening in his arms while he held her. "You have got to quit scaring me like this. I can't take it," he rebuked her tenderly.

"I knew I could find Tenorio through him." Her voice was a gentle whisper, flowing over his ears like the sweetest music with renewed strength filling her.

"You went after Hawthorne?" Stunned, he was washed in at least a dozen different emotions. He hadn't paid much attention. They'd all been dressed in green fatigues and army wear. Until then, he hadn't even been positive he'd been among those in the attack. "Alone? Defenseless?"

She attempted a shrug, but all it did was push her deeper into his hold. "It was my fight."

Joaquin froze, realizing without a doubt why she had done it. He should have known, given the chance, she would, but it didn't take away the urge to keep her at his side for the rest of their nights together, by force or not, if she kept up with this kind of headstrong behavior. She had been reclaiming herself from them, finding that part of her they'd never had a right to have. Her spirit and soul. Curling around her, he brushed a tender kiss to her forehead.

"He is dead." His words were flat. She didn't acknowledge them, but he felt her relief. "Why, lovely?" Pressing against her, the cinnamon hint in her hair rose into his senses and he inhaled, needing to have her close, under his skin, to feel her light and know she was all right. He wanted to hear it in her words.

"Because if he got away again, he would return. He knew about you." She shivered once, snuggling into his body like a feline in the sun. "I had no choice."

"What were you trying to do to him?"

This time, a sense of satisfaction rose from her. "I didn't try. I did. I stripped his thoughts. Anything that had to do with Tenerio, every plan, every location. There are more like us, but he had his own trials and experiments he was in charge of. If there are more, they are not a part of his experimental system. Unfortunately, he didn't know as much as I would've hoped. We'll have to look deeper." Disappointment caved her shoulders in.

"Not right now. I'm not letting you anywhere near them, or anyone else for that matter."

Lashes fluttered and exposed sparkling buckskin eyes. "There is more, but if he's dead, most of what he knew died with him. Tenorio will be left in the dark about us." A deriding smirk lifted one side of her lush mouth. "He honestly thought he could capture and then report, brag to prove what a leader and irreplaceable part of the cloning operation he was. Tenorio knows nothing about the loss of the compound or us. He feared the repercussion for losing me again. Tenorio didn't take losing us well, apparently. Hawthorne was his kicking dog." She sighed, curling and pressing more to his body. "At least Tabitha will be free. Hawthorne was her guinea pig. That's why they held her for so long. They have to infuse regularly for the DNA mutations to hold, or their bodies reverse the mutation. None of the subjects have kept a permanent mutation."

"Really?"

She nodded, a worried crease appearing over her unfocused eyes. "The mutations were working, though. They found a way to merge the DNA strains. That is something the others need to know."

"They won't quit," he surmised.

"No, they won't."

Shifting, he moved her body up higher, leaning back to let her weight press into his chest. The taste of her skin drew him closer and he licked at her, teasing the fragrant spot behind her ear. She shivered in wakening desire. She relaxed more in his hold as the blood he'd given her began to heal her.

"It's not pitch black dark in here." Surprise in her discovery made him lift from his foray, enjoying the wonder in her expression as she absorbed the beauty of the cavern.

"There are vents and cracks allowing the stars to shine through. I know you didn't enjoy being left in the dark before."

Pleasure at his thoughtfulness warmed her eyes more. "I am feeling better," she told him with a saucy, teasing laugh, running a finger over the naked expanse of his chest, putting the thought of where they were for the moment far out of mind. A whisper of unease rose then disappeared in her thoughts when she realized why she did feel stronger, but she didn't hesitate, didn't cease the motions of her fingers on his body, weaving a fiery trail in the wake of her touch. He worried over the coming minutes, but the delicate ramble of her fingers over his skin was making it difficult to concentrate. Luscious and pink, her lips parted with a seductive curve. Golden lashes lowered, sending another shot of desire through his bloodstream. She was an enchantress.

The wealth of red and cinnamon hair flowing over his arm swayed with slow motions as she breathed, dipped, touched. The delicate silk of her stroke on his skin was drawing fires to blaze beneath the skin. Resistance was pointless.

The taste of her lips against his was heaven. Sweet, succulent and ripe, he picked ambrosia kisses from their softness. Her hand wound upward, encircling his neck, holding him closer as she opened up for him. The swell of her breast lay like an inviting gift inches from his own fingertips. Holding her close, he slid his hand up her ribs, letting her fullness fit into his palm with a gentle seduction of his own. A slow, shivering moan slipped from between her lips and she arched, craving.

"Perfect," he whispered before he stole another kiss.

The playful seduction faded away when one of her hands clutched at her stomach. "I don't feel good," she murmured. Frightened worry extinguished the budding passion from her gaze.

Joaquin's body tightened. He knew what was happening. Cramping, muscle shakes, heated, stabbing aches. Sadly, it wasn't anywhere near the pain of the transition to come.

"Relax, lovely. Let me help you. Rest." Her lashes fell under the compulsion, helping to distance her from the coming sensations.

As her body twisted and tightened in his hold, he felt her heart race, pumping fiercely, feeling it between them with her almost skin to skin in his cradled hold. After several minutes, she gradually relaxed into a deeper sleep. Knowing what she would face, keeping her asleep was the best thing he could do for her, knowing the pain. It went deep, into the bones, into the blood. He had suffered it without a single second of surcease or aid.

Lily would have anything she needed, the best he could give to help her through the coming change.

Tipping his head back, he sniffed, studying the night with a calculated stare. There was time to finish it all tonight. The next time he rose, he would be holding her, where she was meant to be. Next to him. For eternity. Running his fingers through the hair framing her face, he pushed it clear, exposing the delicate shape of her face, the clean paleness of cream glistening from the sparkled refracted light. Faint pink warmed her features, like the blush of a spring flower. With reverent care, he bent and kissed every mark along her jaw, stealing away her pain, destroying it for the both of them.

The rippled shocks of the first change were fading away, leaving only the beat of her heart, the slow rise and fall of her chest as she rested, gathering strength. With every touch of his lips to her skin, he sent her wave after wave of his love. She would know no other pain, know no other abuse after the change. She would be cherished in ways she had yet to be introduced to.

Burying his nose into her hair, he held her like the precious treasure she was to him.

Sending his voice out into the night, he asked his friend, *"All is well? Everyone is safe again?"*

"It is done. David's death has been a shock to Titania and the others."

Joaquin understood. The magnitude of his loss to them all was in the hollow replies. Joaquin had seen the shock of loss and devastation on Tani's face before he'd left with Diego to face the attack.

"We will both return tomorrow night. Together. I know Lily holds no blame against him. Neither do I." He said those words, then realized he meant them truthfully. If Lily could forgive David, so could he.

"Your words are a comfort to us. Hopefully his sacrifice and Lily's has bought us time to ensure our security. She is a strong woman, brave. It is good she has found someone who will protect and cherish her spirit. It gives us all hope."

A blessing of friendship faded as the last well wish for the discussion from Diego, leaving Joaquin once again in the calming silence of the night. Together, they would share the information Lily had risked herself for. She had risked everything to learn what she had about the mutation DNA cloning, and the revelations were chilling, to say the least. The girls in the house were in even more danger than any of them had originally suspected if there had been success in the experimental efforts. It was Lily's won battle that had garnered the information. It was hers to share.

Rising from the rock shelf with her still embraced tightly in his arms, he carried her to a flat area in the cavern. Directly beneath his feet stretched several yards of rich soil, soothing and cool for resting. It would be a perfect healing spot after the next exchange for her.

Lowering to his knees, he envisioned a thick blanket to touch her skin rather than the bite and chill of the dry earth. He had only his faith in his love, in her strength, and in Tani's existence as proof she could survive what he was about to attempt.

Like the others, until Lily, until finding this group of oddly mismatched, yet perfectly melded, friends, he'd had no idea bringing a female into the

Brethren was possible. What he was attempting with her was an act he had never once thought to do on his own. He was also prepared to join her if she could not survive it. Living for another eternity a second time without his love was an insanity he did not want to face. He locked his fear and doubt away when he laid her on the blanket. He could only have one focus now.

Ensuring she was comfortable, he laid down next to her and brushed a kiss to her eyes, drawing her awake with a tenderness that shook him to his core. A love so deep, he burned as it poured through him.

She moaned, a purring sound of pleasure and wonder. Like the heated crest of the morning sun, her eyes opened with a slow rise of her lashes. A single deep breath made her chest rise. "Is it over? Did I die?"

He chuckled. "No, lovely." He ran a hand through her hair, brushing its thick weight with a pleasure he would always desire. "It isn't over, but soon. And I won't let you die. You should know that. You are too precious to me to let this little thing steal you away from me."

She gave him an exasperated look. "Little? Did someone give you a different set of lines? Because this isn't exactly a little thing to me."

He smiled, knowing her anger wasn't deep. "I know, *corazón*." He pressed his lips to hers, a gentle, loving kiss that said what he was feeling so much better than words could have, wanting to strip her fears completely away.

When he released her, her eyes were clear. The only sign of her worry was the tautness in her body. "It's time, isn't it?"

He brushed a final kiss to her lips. "Yes, lovely."

She swallowed, then nodded. Looking upward to focus on the ceiling, she said, "Okay. I'm ready."

He could only shake his head at her bravery, to face the unknown head on. "I'm not going to let you face this alone, Lily. I'll be here with you."

She lifted a hand between them. "I'm not going to go insane with some kind of blood sickness, am I? Tani said you either do or you don't when you first change."

Joaquin hadn't been aware of the consequences of when he'd first risen, but realized it was absolutely true. When he smiled, he felt her relax again. "No, lovely. I'm here. As you ground me every night since we've met, I will hold you when you first awaken and every night thereafter. There will be no chance of you falling to the hunger."

"That sounds wonderful," she breathed, her eyes seeking his with their glistening warmth. And trust. Her lashes fell, and she licked her lips. "I still love you, Joaquin. No matter what happens. Thank you for loving me."

"I do love you, Lily. And I will love you for many, many long years from now." He lowered to whisper, a slight sound that was an enchantment. "Relax. I am here." Sliding an arm beneath her to cradle her into his shoulder, he brought her closer, then swept the fall of her hair away. Caresses carried him up and down the column of her throat, enticing her, pleasuring her with his tongue and lips as he adored her. When she had fallen completely under the languid spell, he broke her skin once more, taking deliberate patience to not rush, to ensure nothing could go wrong. This was either the beginning, or the end.

The honeyed sweetness of her heartbeat was a miracle, so unlike anything he'd ever experienced. Knowing she would soon be like him made him almost drunk on the richness of her life. All the things he could show her, teach her, share with her. Someone who would spend her life with him, with whom he could spend his joys, his fears and dreams with. He reined in his giddiness. Soon, first he had to ensure she survived to see the other side of the night with him.

Cradling her closer, he used the utmost patience and tenderness with every draw to not make a mistake. Listening to her breathing, the pulse of her heartbeat against his lips, he released her, roaming his tongue along the silky heat of her throat like a fiery confection to be enjoyed. Devoured. He almost grinned at his own mind's wanderings. He loved the way she tasted, in many ways.

This time, when he split his own skin, he rose above her until he hovered over her. Cradling her head in his palm, he positioned her mouth beneath his neck with his body stretched along hers, close enough to feel the swelling and ebbing warmth of her skin.

"Drink," he ordered, a hoarse command, swept up into a maelstrom of emotion. "*Take my life, my heart, the way it is meant to be.*" A sheer sensuality exploded over his skin when her lips feathered over him. He groaned, his entire length tightening with a blazing hunger that stole every thought out of his mind other than the feeling of her suckling mouth on tender tissue. Her arms encircled him to fit him into her embrace as perfectly as two pieces of a puzzle. His fangs actually ached with the sensation, never having experienced anything so heady, so overpowering, as her against him, taking what he offered selflessly. He arched against her, lost to the all-consuming bliss of feeling her mouth on his vein, drawing steady pulls, accepting his life's blood for her own. Growls of blistering ecstasy walked up from his chest. He was unable to stop their sound, their deep rumbles echoing through the cavern. Energy crackled around him and, for a split second, he couldn't see as his entire body ignited.

"Enough," he ground out. He shuddered as she withdrew with a final lingering kiss over the wound.

Madre de Diós. He practically collapsed at her side, flat on his back staring up, feeling awash in the wonder. If that was what it felt like to... He swallowed. The intensity rocked him. He would live a thousand lifetimes if letting her draw from him felt that good. And she wasn't even changed yet. How intense would it be when he no longer needed to help her get through it, when she came to him of her own free will? Would she crave him the same way he craved her every touch? The roof of the cavern spun for a second as his imagination took flight, envisioning the future, the true redemption he'd been granted.

A shiver rocked his body, his hardened length at an aching stand within his jeans, screaming to feel her, to find completion within her luscious body. Was this what Diego had meant, calling these women 'gifts' to them?

Even as he made the connection to their bond, their need for each other growing to be inseparable, the first signs of hell were sending shockwaves through Lily.

Curving around her to hold her close, he gathered her into his arms, pushing his discoveries away to examine later. Shivers stole up and down her body and heat sent a wild flush outward until her body burned. Unseeing, her eyes snapped wide open and sweat broke out on her skin.

"Joaquin." The single whimper was croaked as her throat convulsed, her body curling up on itself like a tight ball of yarn.

He ran a caressing hand down her hair, sweeping over her. "Shh, lovely. It won't last." She twitched, then arched painfully, whipping almost out of his hold with the force of the first shock. Her agony grew with each moment, cutting across her pale features as her body twisted and bucked. Wrenching hard, she screamed once, a hollow, tortured sound that reverberated through the cavern. He pressed his forehead to hers to absorb as much of the pain and heat as he could. Another silent thrash tore over her body, encompassing her, pulling and bunching muscles beneath skin that continued to burn.

Rolling to his knees, he lifted her sweat-drenched body, hurriedly clawing away clothes that hampered her until exposed skin flamed brightly against the open air. He crooned patiently as the ripples grew, then faded, one after another as they traveled up and down her body, destroying the remnants of its living humanity. Heaves racked her frame, expelling everything but her bones until she lay propped against him, limp and helpless. He knew the feeling, and knew the pain. Thankfully, the pain of the full conversion wasn't something she would ever know. He would die himself before he would allow her to feel that much pain.

Brushing soaked hair from her face, he stood, holding her close, cherishing her. Carrying her to the pool, his clothes vanished with hardly a thought as he stepped down into the pool. The earth warmed water was much cooler as it swallowed her overheated form and sent her into a convulsed shake. "Easy, lovely," he breathed against her temple. There wasn't an answer, only the dying sound of her heart as it struggled with the changes taking over. It would beat in memory for a few hours until the dawn, then like the rest of her, and him, would fall into the null sense of daylight sleep. It would never beat again unless she purposely made it do so.

Breath rattled in and out of her lungs, existing in the last moments of life her body would ever know. Lowering her to rest against his chest, he settled her on his lap in the water where he tenderly washed her clean, removing any signs of the strain of her change. The conversion was complete. She was only one sleep away from waking like him.

It was hard not to doubt, but he knew Diego wouldn't purposely mislead him. It could be done. Something about this woman made it possible. Something about Tani had made it possible for Diego. They were more than any other; they were meant to be.

Failure—her death—was simply not a possibility he wanted to dwell on. Steady in his hands, he ran his fingers through the wealth of red flowing out over the water, watching as it darkened in the water to a shimmering russet, so deep and lustrous, it was nearly blood red. Water lapped at her body, caressing her with a gentle motion as he cleansed her from her shoulders to her toes. It was hard to not linger, to enjoy her curves and the silken feeling beneath his fingers. Lifting her once more, he knew he would have many more nights to savor and cherish her by his side. Tonight, she needed to heal. Rest was the only cure.

With a sweep of his hand, he removed the signs of her conversion, opening the earth several feet deep once it was gone. Running his hand down her body, he removed water droplets until she was dry. "Lovely," he purred against her lips, giving her a final kiss before dropping them both weightlessly to the bottom of the earthen pit. With a contented sigh, he sent her into a deep sleep to not feel the earth around them, then with a final thought, he sealed them both in. To rest in each other's arms until the coming night beckoned to them once more.

LILY wasn't sure how it happened, but there was a sense of not being awake, then she was. Just like a flip of a switch. No awareness, then total awareness. It was unnerving. She didn't remember falling asleep. There *was* a memory of pain. She frowned, trying to make sense of it all when a thumb brushed over her brow, soothing the worried marks.

"What is the matter, lovely?" he purred close to her ear.

She was lying on her back in a long shirt, feeling the end of the sleeves where stiff cuffs lay over her knuckles. She relaxed as soon as she heard his voice. Beneath her there were...pillows. She stifled the chuckle. Joaquin had a thing for sultan pillows. Lily actually liked them. There was a low mellow sound of lapping water to her right.

"Am I dead?" she asked with a hesitant catch, the words barely a whisper of sound.

Warm laughter rumbled in his chest. "No, Lily. Not dead."

"I survived?"

Lily felt his breath on her cheek, then her lips. "You feel me, don't you?" Her body almost turned to him, entranced with the seductive feel of his mouth. Her skin definitely sparked in the wake of his lips.

"I remember some," she breathed, trailing off when his lips moved from her cheek to her temple, then down to her ear and further.

"I am sorry. It was impossible to block everything. You only suffered what I had no power to take away."

She rolled to see him where he lay beside her. Warm and molten, his gaze caressed her, wandering with definite hunger over her face and beyond. She blinked. "I can see!" A short gasp erupted as she focused, arching upward to take in the beauty of the cavern. "This is exquisite."

"I'm glad you approve," he murmured, dropping those honeyed kisses on her shoulder and throat. She was beginning to suspect he had something other than conversation on his mind.

Her fingers dug through the rich layers of his hair. "I slept the day away?"

"I know. It makes you such a slacker," Joaquin teased, nibbling wherever he could find skin.

Laughter shook her body, and she tweaked his hair to make him stop with the heavenly kisses. "I can't think when you're doing that."

A devilish grin appeared on his lips. "Why do you have to think? I know of several things we could do instead."

She smiled in answer to the grinning impetuousness on his features. Then, reality hit. Freezing, she slowly, cautiously ran the tip of her tongue over her teeth. They still felt the same...sort of. There was an unevenness that hadn't been there before. Thinking about it seemed to make them tingle, but nothing happened, and they certainly didn't drop the way she'd seen Tani's teeth appear. "Where are they?"

He rose on an elbow to look into her eyes. He didn't play down her question. "They are there. When you feed, they will lengthen automatically. It doesn't hurt," he added, watching the play of expressions on her face.

"Have you..." She licked her lips, trying to take it all in, trying to put her tumbled thoughts to words.

He ran light fingers along her chin, soothing her. "We have all night, as long as you need or want to adjust."

Dazed, she simply looked up, unfocused, to the ceiling where stones seemed to gather whatever light there was and sparkle back at her. "I survived, but I don't feel different. Not really."

"There are differences."

"Do I look different?" she asked a little breathlessly, feeling a faint spike of hopefulness.

He shook his head with compassionate understanding lightening his eyes. "No, they are there." She sighed, gazing upward again. "I've told you, they mean next to nothing to me. The only reason they have meaning to me is because they have meaning to you. They are your past. They will never again be your present or your future."

"How am I different?" Not that it mattered. She still felt like herself.

"How do you think you're different? What do you feel?"

"Well," she slowly began, studying herself. "I'm not hurting anywhere. I don't feel weak like I did." Her gaze roamed the roof of the cavern, picking out individual stones with ease, even as far over their heads as the ceiling ranged. "I can see really well, and I think my hearing has gotten better."

"Yes," he agreed. "What else?" He neared her and dragged his tongue over exposed skin peeking from beneath the collar of her shirt. Joaquin, on the other hand, appeared to be gloriously naked.

She shivered beneath the sensual path he left behind. "That feels really good." Breathless for a different reason, she arched her neck to give him more to play with.

"Trust me, lovely. There will be plenty of time to learn. I will guide you, teach you. I'm finding it increasingly difficult to leave you alone."

She let her fingers ply through his hair again, feeling the strands burn her skin as they flowed over her. "We have time?" she whispered, searching his face.

"We have eternity," he replied, then he lowered to tenderly caress her lips in a kiss that wrapped her in his heart as his hands wrapped her into his body.

About the Author

With more than half a dozen ebooks currently to her credit and her first print book released in 2008 to rave reviews, Diana Castilleja has kept busy since she started writing professionally in late 2004.

Diana currently resides in central Texas with her husband and son. When not focusing her energy on her family and her writing, she loves to travel and haunt bookstores. She's lived in several states across the south and Midwest, as well as traveling to Mexico. With moving every year or changing schools since the fourth grade to her sophomore year, she learned reading was a fast escape. The freedom to read about anything and everything has fueled her adult imagination. She is most likely currently sitting at her desk, having it out with her keyboard writing her next book.

http://www.dianacastilleja.com

She can be reached at:
Diana.Castilleja@gmail.com

Diana Castilleja also writes under the pen name
Diana DeRicci.
Feel free to learn about these stories at her website.
http://www.dianadericci.com

PURPLE SWORD PUBLICATIONS
Publisher of romantic speculative fiction
www.PurpleSword.com

www.ingramcontent.com/pod-product-compliance
Lightning Source LLC
LaVergne TN
LVHW010051110826
845155LV00028B/282

* 9 7 8 1 9 3 6 1 6 5 4 5 2 *